Dallas Blood

First Edition

Christopher P. Nichols

Dallas Blood

First Edition

Published by The Nazca Plains Corporation
Las Vegas, Nevada
2007

ISBN: 978-1-934625-04-0

Published by

The Nazca Plains Corporation ®
4640 Paradise Rd, Suite 141
Las Vegas NV 89109-8000

PUBLISHER'S NOTE
Dallas Blood is a work of fiction created wholly by *Christopher P. Nichols'* imagination. All characters are fictional and any resemblance to any persons living or deceased is purely by accident. No portion of this book reflects any real person or events.

Cover Art, Perry Brooks Nichols
Art Director, Blake Stephens

Dedication

I dedicate this novel to my family of artistic folks, my father Perry, a true renaissance man and my mother, Mary Nell, a fine painter. My brothers, David Trelawney, a renowned Production Designer in films, Peter Boyd, a fine musician; and Carlos Hamon, a terrific mechanical designer, my son, Perry Brooks, another painter in the family.

Acknowledgements

My wife, Libby, who inspired the title and ending of <u>Dallas Blood</u>, Joe Rice, a constant supporter of the work and major contributor to the back cover notes, Earl Bentley, who also contributed to the back cover notes and has been a writing companion on two plays, *Death Wind* and *Lamia*. Word Smith did the first proofing. Becky and Sam Godfrey did the final proofing. Perry Brooks Nichols, my son who did the cover painting. Special thanks to all of the professional and student actors, designers, and technicians I've had the pleasure to work with over the years. A toast to the folks of the New Arts' years and beautiful ladies.

Dallas Blood

Christopher P. Nichols

Contents

Prologue

Two o'clock in the morning. I had just finished a third reading of *Blood Wedding* and was suddenly scared that I had picked the wrong play to direct. It is a simple enough story: beautiful country girl in Spain is betrothed to a hard working young man who would give her a good life. But the wrinkle is that she still may feel a desire for someone in her past who perhaps lingers outside her window at night occasionally. This man is the only character in the play who has a name, Leonardo. He is married, has a child, and his wife is pregnant with another child. He is irresponsible, neglects his wife, and rides his horse , a rare possession for these folks, constantly off into the night. After the wedding ceremony at the celebration dance the bride runs away with Leonardo. The bridegroom goes after them. In the woods, the bride tells Leonardo to leave her, He hears the bridegroom coming, they meet and fight to the death. The mother of the bride, the bride, and Leonardo's wife meet at what may be a church. The mother possibly cuts the bride's throat. It is a constant rage of passion, filled with poetry, a large cast, and mysterious characters in the woods and I loved it. But it is so powerful that I wondered, even doubted that I could give it the full production it deserved. I supposed that almost every director has doubts while preparing for a play and I have certainly experienced it, but this was different. There were no precedents for the play because our production at the Civic Theatre may be the first in the States. The playwright, Federico Garcia Lorca, was known here primarily as a poet, but his plays were important in Spain. After the first couple of readings, I thought I saw the whole piece in my mind, and began to block it on paper, but it didn't feel right. In the past, I had been able to block out a play in several late night sessions, go to rehearsal, and put it up on stage. This play needed music, dance, several sets, and terrific lighting and costumes...so my collaborators must be more special than I had ever worked with before. No more thoughts about it tonight, perhaps the next two days away from it will help.

I turned off my reading lamp. I couldn't sleep. Suddenly all of the loneliness of the past months came back in dark thoughts. The relationship with a terribly possessive actress had separated me from all of the people I considered to be my friends. She didn't want to share me with anyone. It was even difficult to have conferences with actresses in my casts. Our sexual encounters, though rare, were difficult because of her constant demands for commitments of love and faithfulness. Finally after six months of being together, we went through three weeks of almost violent arguments with short make-up periods, I decided I had to end the relationship. She threw a screaming tantrum, saying she would never see or speak to me again. She had done what she said she would do, to my great relief. I had fears of her showing up at my door in the middle of the night, but she disappeared. The whole affair had changed my feelings about getting involved in any close relationship with a woman or even making new friends at the theatre. I believed the people at the theatre and at work thought I had become a shy and distant loner, which I had not been before. Perhaps the weekend and the final auditions leading to production will bring a new outlook. I had directed two shows since the difficult break-up and both were fairly successful, but without any real flair. I knew I had been directing by the numbers. I wasn't missing that hard relationship; I had lost a passion I had felt before. Well, *Blood Wedding* had better bring that back or I was in for a big failure.

Chapter 1
La Feria del Artes

Friday, and no more auditions for three nights. They were postponed so I could attend the Dallas Arts Festival, which was part of my job at the theatre. The event was held twice a year, in the spring and fall, at Scott Hall, and was a great excuse for much of Dallas' arts community to get together. Things actually got started around noon, but my 2:30 arrival wasn't bad considering the past two busy weeks at the Dallas Civic Theatre, or Little Theatre as it was known locally even though it wasn't so little. I guess it was little compared to Broadway theatres, but how the hell would I know about Broadway? Even visiting New York was beyond my present resources.

I was lucky to also have the weekend off from my bookstore job, which supplemented my income from my work at the theatre. An old friend of my father's, Carlton Franklin, owned it; I had flexible hours and all the books I could read. When I had started working for him five years ago, he had said to think of it as a scholarship as long as I was working at the theatre. The academic scholarships available after high school weren't enough to cover what I needed to live and study theatre and chip in at home. For awhile, I had moped quietly about the loss of my Carnegie-Mellon dreams, but the moping had abated as the Little Theatre work got more intense and after I built, with my father's help, the apartment behind my parents' house. It had been an old double garage and storage area turned into a shop. When Dad had moved his small furniture building and design business to an old warehouse closer to downtown in Deep Ellum, I had grabbed it. Over six months of weekends, I learned more than I had ever wanted to know about building and scrounging materials. The plumbing ditches were the hardest part, and the wiring was the scariest, but having a sanctuary was worth all the effort. I even had an alley entrance so rowdy theatre folks coming over late after rehearsal didn't bother the family.

The Sart family…well that's a whole other story, which I'll get to later, except to say that mother and older brother Daniel were painters and younger brother Jeordie was a kind of teenage mechanical genius. Not a very practical lot.

The whole family group was involved in the Festival. Paintings by mother and Dan, furniture by Dad, and some strange sculpture by Jeordie made from old machine parts. Seeing Dan would be good because we hadn't talked in a couple of weeks. He designed theatre sets for me about twice a year, but he hadn't been able to this year. His "scholarship" was being taken in and supported by Marilee Grant, a beautiful young widowed arts patron in Highland Park. It evidently was true love with them. It certainly worked for Daniel, his art got better with every showing. I was the only family member with nothing tangible to show for my efforts except for the posters with my name as director for shows at the theatre.

Alone was not the happiest way to attend the Festival on the one day I wouldn't be working the theatre booth, but I had been alone for several months. The last relationship was such a burn that starting in any sort of new one was far from my mind. However, being alone was getting to be a bore, so maybe I was healing. The Festival crowd was always fun, and I hoped for some interesting encounters. Maybe I would at least recruit some new theatre patrons. Everyone at the theatre was an unofficial fundraiser or finder of volunteers. My position as an artistic staff member, at thirty-five dollars a week, put me pretty high up on the salary level for the difficult economic times, and recruiting was a job requirement. I had worked my way up to directing several shows a year and reading plays and, of course, selling tickets at the box office and building sets. My boss, Barney, was the executive director. His esteemed title meant he kept the books, raised money, and served as lobby charmer. He had long ago accepted that his crush on me would remain unrequited, and that the closest he would get to me was to be a mentor.

Finding a parking place was harder than usual, but I took finding a vacant lot in an alley off Routh Street as a good harbinger for the Festival. I was enjoying the new luxury of driving. My "new" car was a '34 Ford V8 Coupe my Uncle Willy had found for me. It's a great car, with no back seat. Only four years old, it had been submerged in a flood in East Texas. Uncle Willy had salvaged it and rebuilt the motor and all of the running gear, and had even added a dark burgundy paint job.

Walking out of the alley, I joined a group of potters I knew who were on their way to set up a booth. I knew from the State Fair Arts Combine, which was more of a social group than anything else. I had done a small show in a tent at the Texas Centennial that was very successful and a nice boost to artistic credibility.

Among the potters was Gwen, an extraordinarily cute girl I had dated in the past. "Well hello there, Tim Sart," she smiled.

Gwen was carrying two pots and accepted my offer to help. We had shared a delightfully rare non-possessive sexual encounter off and on for two years, but not recently. I had found her to be on the edge of being too beautiful, too Bohemian, and too clever, but being with her had been a great learning experience. I hadn't realized how sexually innocent I was before her. She teased me about my reclusive theatre life, which I interpreted as her reason for why I hadn't called her. I didn't mention my late, lamented romantic tragedy, but she immediately saw through what I had hoped was an enigmatic smile.

"Oh, Tim, did another actress attempt to burn up your soul?!"

I remembered that her ability to read my mind, sometimes right in the middle of making love, had slightly intimidated me. I followed Gwen to her booth, where we parted with a vague promise to see each other again over the next two days. She did reach out and squeeze my hand, which I took as encouragement.

The Festival was primarily being held outdoors, set up on the grounds surrounding Scott Hall, extending on to the large grass parking lot adjoining the arts facility and concert hall. It was early, so it wasn't really crowded yet, but that would change by late afternoon. It was easy to forget how large the arts community was in Dallas. The Festival made me feel much less alone in a perhaps unwisely chosen career. My parents defined the force that drove us into creative endeavors as a curse.

Everywhere were people I knew so the greetings were constant as I made my way to check on the Little Theatre booth.

The first thing I saw was a banner above the booth announcing our next play as "F. G. Lorca's *Blood Wedding,* directed by Timothy Sart." My first feelings of embarrassment were quickly stifled as Barney greeted me with a hug and cheek kiss. His inquiry about how auditions were going was unnecessary, since as executive director, he was in and out of the theatre every night. A couple who lived in Lakewood was helping to sign up volunteers and sell tickets. They had moved here from the East and were desperate for culture, especially theatre, and the Civic was the only show in town. They were nice folks and terrific supporters of my work. I had been to a couple of board of sponsors meetings at their elegant home, where the husband had pulled me aside urging me to go to New York. He might as well have said China! Perhaps I was afraid that with little solid experience under my belt, I would fail in the big city.

Lakewood was a prime area of support for the theatre, as were the Park Cities, both Highland and University, Swiss Avenue, and even Kessler Park in Oak Cliff across the Trinity River. Oak Cliff had always been sort of a mystery for me. I had been to parties at Kidd Springs but my only real contact with the area was a girl I met at a minor gymnastic meet, I believe at the Sokol Club. Her name was Karina Smalley, we had never been more than friends, but she was a great girl and a real beauty. I don't think we ever even kissed. She was a cheerleader at Sunset High School and a good tumbler. She was a cheerleader who actually did flips and things up and down the field. Finding her house the first time was a real challenge for someone from across the river

Two girls who worked backstage joined us at the booth and offered to help this afternoon. Barney said the evening crew was set, the head of the sponsor board and a Highland Park group, but tomorrow night was mine because of the big Saturday night crowd. He said the director of the current show was always a good sell at the booth, but I had my doubts.

So this night was mine to roam. After crossing almost halfway to the hall entrance, I suddenly stopped as a sort of hot flash of fear or doubt raged through me, probably brought about by seeing that banner with my name on it as director. As I looked around at the decorations strung between the light poles and the people, I became almost dizzy with the activity and colors. It all became a blur for a few seconds. Everything slowed down and I felt fearful of dying, of something happening to me. I started thinking of where I was in my life, that shock of realizing that I'm alive here and now, and not something of the past or future. What was I doing here at the Festival playing the role of an interesting artistic fellow striding around searching for approval? Was I a deluded fool attempting to appear important in a ridiculous art form? Did coming from a family of "artistes" justify my reach? Is it even possible to make a living? Daniel sells paintings, as does Mother, and Dad's furniture is in constant demand. And who could tell maybe Jeordie would break out into some sort of respectable financial success. As for me, I didn't draw, paint, or sculpt. I certainly didn't dance or sing. But theatre? And to direct? A shiver ran up and down my spine just thinking about the play I was working on: Spanish blood, love, and passion. Did I know enough about passion to ask people to pay money to watch my innocent version of actors playing Spaniards writhing about the stage screaming "Love, blood, death?"

I have no idea what set off this fit of delving into self, but fear of failure must be the constant companion of every young director. I wasn't usually haunted by doubts. Although my future was not of the secure sort, every new show was more exciting and much more demanding and scary than the last, especially *Blood Wedding*.

These thoughts lasted no more than a few seconds, and when I looked up, the Dallas sky was beautiful and big. It helped to answer the question I asked myself of why I should stay in Dallas. Not that the sky was the reason, but it was a sky that I knew. I've been to the woods of East Texas and it's different there, as it is above West Texas. I liked this one. A bit of a different hue that gives me some sense of knowing where I am.

"Tim! Hey! Over here!"

I emerged from my reverie to see Dick Ayers, who had been my best friend all through school. He had left Dallas a couple of years ago to study at the National University in Madrid. Now, I was surprised to see him waving from a booth that sported a FREE SPAIN banner. I was surprised because politics never had been a part of the Festival before, but the Bohemian and liberal nature of the arts folks and their belief in this cause seemed to overpower the more conservative supporters. The civil war in Spain was a cause celebre in our community. In a spirited discussion one night last year, even my father said he wished he were young enough to go, but my mother had told him, in no uncertain terms, not to even consider it. Politics were mixed in with every conversation about the war, but my sympathies towards Russia and Socialism were limited to the theatre.

Dick had written me to tell me about *Blood Wedding* He had seen it in Madrid and raved about how passionate it was and how he had cried. That was a good enough recommendation for me, but finding an English translation had been almost impossible, not to mention the royalty situation, which was complicated by the war. But my boss at the bookstore had solved all my problems through a contact in Argentina.

I hadn't known Dick was back from Spain, so I walked towards him, curious and eager to renew our friendship. As he came out from behind the booth, I noticed he looked gaunt and that he walked with a cane and was wearing, of all things, a beret, not a typical look for the ex-football hero of Woodrow Wilson High.

The booth was colorfully decorated with the flags of Republican Spain and the Abraham Lincoln Brigade and was occupied by several people, most whom of looked familiar, except for an extravagantly attractive European-looking woman standing next to Dick. He hugged me and patted my back. Very European. He said he had only been back a couple of weeks after spending several weeks in the American Hospital in Madrid. It turned out he had been wounded in some sort of battle at the barricades in Madrid. He was different, not the old hail-fellow-well-met boy of the past; now he was obviously mature and had acquired a knowing worldliness. He introduced me to the woman next to him as his new wife, Camila, who had been his nurse in Madrid. He said he had returned to Dallas to continue school and recruit for the International Brigades and, he added, not for the Socialist cause, which was a mess over there.

"Aren't they one and the same?" I asked.

"Most of the Americans and Canadians over there were pure liberals in the democratic sense," Dick replied.

"Well, I'm glad you're back and alive. Big step, my friend."

"I was there, and it was happening all around me...so...well, I knew I was going to get involved, long before I did, but I decided discretion was the order of the day. I saw some good theatre in Madrid, Tim," Dick said, switching topics. "The best was *Blood Wedding*. I saw the poster this morning. Very daring, my man, I hope I didn't lead you astray."

"Come see ours and try not to compare them, please."

"Your shows were always interesting, at the very least. Latin passions now, huh?"

Looking at his new wife, I said "And you too, my friend?"

Dick laughed heartily, then turned and hugged Camila. She blushed and laughed along with him.

"Oh, Tim, if you but knew!" Dick exclaimed.

"Good to see you Dick, let's get together soon." It seemed a good time to leave him because about ten people had gathered to talk to him. We hugged again, promising to talk soon. I walked away then turned to look at him again. "Damn! Spain," I thought. "And I'm in Dallas. Perhaps this will be a good Dallas year, not Madrid in the spring, but good work and, hopefully, new people. Its ridiculous being as lonely as I am and it's not just love lonely or friend lonely...Shit! I don't know what I feel, just change coming. I hope it's good."

Walking toward the exhibit hall, I heard my name being called again; I turned and saw no one. I then realized it was Jeordie, hiding, pulling one of his constant practical jokes, so I called him. He walked out from behind a confused group of folks and gave me a silly wave, as did the girl with him, whom I recognized as Jill. About three years ago, she had walked up to Jeordie and me sitting on the porch and said she knew all about girls and boys. Jeordie and looked at each other and then at her in question.

"Boys have penees and girls have ginas," she said, than walked off.

I thought, at the time, that was a cute way of saying it, and certainly less clinical, but I leaned toward the 'Latin'.

"Where you goin', big brother?"

"I was looking for Daniel, but you'll do. I haven't seen your new piece, either."

"Well, it's in there, Tim. But I don't think I've really finished it."

"Jeordie, with your sculpture, how will anyone ever know if they're finished?"

"Is that good or bad? I thought it was kind of a joke to even bring it here, but Mom kept after me until I gave in. She likes my stuff, but I'm not sure I want my friends to see it. They already think me and our family are strange, but that's okay because it's half true...the family, that is."

Conversations with my younger brother were always challenging. Our mother said he got his wild curly red hair from her grandmother, and that it fit him to a tee.

"Speaking of family, where is Daniel?"

"He's in the exhibit hall, worrying, as always, about how his stuff is hung."

"Tim, we're gonna meet some friends over at the pop stand. I'll see you later if you're home for dinner."

"Probably not...," I answered.

Jeordie and Jill were off, disappearing like a couple of woods sprites.

As I walked into the exhibit hall, which was off the concert hall lobby, I saw Daniel. He was having trouble rehanging a painting. I stepped in and grabbed one side of it painting to give him a better balance. He was surprised but turned and smiled. "Just in time, Tim."

The painting was one his new large canvasses, a six-foot-square view of the Trinity River at an almost flood stage at dawn in colors different from any I had ever seen. It was so damn powerful, it was scary. With me helping, he was able to reach behind and place the wire on two picture hangers. He straightened it, and we stepped back to view his new installation.

"I was afraid one hanger wasn't going to hold it," Daniel explained. "I had hung it last night, but had second thoughts this morning. Not exactly the proper procedure after a show is already open, but I had nightmares about it falling. Not a big enough crowd yet, so...Hey, brother, thanks. You guaranteed yourself a free beer later."

"Are you sure only two hangers will do the job? This thing is more like a mural. Is it upside-down?"

He gave me a squelching look, then faked a punch to my stomach.

"No, I thinks it's terrific, Dan. Did you have to wear some kind of funny glasses to see those colors?"

"Well, actually, yes. Marilee had them mailed to her from France. They combine dawn and twilight with rainbows and lightning flashes."

"Would you design me a set using them? Perhaps 'A Midsummer Night's Dream'"?

"Sorry, had to send them back, it was a short rental plan. Moreover, they were rather addictive, I didn't want to take them off, and Marilee wouldn't pose in a Polynesian sarong. So this is a one-of-a-kind piece."

"If it's as good as I think it is, you may have to get them back."

"Perhaps I can...remember that phrase from the Russian stuff you were reading?"

"Emotional memory?"

"Yes, won't be the same...but is it ever?"

Our word games had started when we were little and were still one of the great joys of our relationship.

"Is Marilee coming this afternoon?"

"She was here awhile ago, but decided we needed some barbecue sandwiches to get through the day. So a quick trip over to Oak Lawn was in order. I told her to get an extra one since I figured we would see you."

"Thanks, I've never turned down Oak Lawn barbecue. How does she like that new roadster?"

"She thought a Packard could be a bit too ostentatious, but after I drove it I said forget it. Damn, it's smooth...And how's your 'Uncle Willy Special' doing?"

"Great. Hell, I feel ostentatious just having a car."

"Yeah, well, forget about those feelings and enjoy it.

A group of people was trying to get a better look at his painting, so we ambled of toward the entrance.

"Let's walk out to the patron's parking, meet Marilee, and have a fender picnic. She will remember to bring a couple of bottles of wine. It's a man's job to open the wine. Very continental, no?"

"Yes, very. I'm intimidated. But I'll try to conceal my innocence. Do I have to use a French word occasionally?"

"I hope not. North Dallas High was no prep school...But I did read some 'Lost Generation' books."

"Is it possible to be a 'Lost Generation' if you're still where you're from? I think I got lost crossing the Festival grounds...or maybe Gwen confused me for a few moments."

"Are you seeing Gwen again? As I remember, you said she spooked you...?!"

"Well yes, and she still does, but at times, spooky is good," I said with a laughing shiver. "Perhaps I'm ready for some more spooking. She seemed ready to try again."

"Damn, brother. What's the holdup? If she were sitting around in a coffee house in Soho, there would be about six bearded poets and painters hanging around her like puppy dogs. But don't you do it that way."

"That would be a sure way for her to decide she's not ready to try again. I don't puppy dog too well. Well, maybe I was headed in that direction before the last situation fell apart. Self-flagellation with a small 'cat-o'-nine tails' would have been more appropriate there."

Daniel laughed. "These girl experiences are supposed to make you happier. It's not all, 'When in disgrace with fortune and men's eyes'. But then, perhaps I'm luckier than most. At times, I look at Marilee and can't believe she loves me. Then she'll turn and just nod with a smile that says she's as happy as I am."

Almost on cue, Marilee pulled into the parking lot with top down and her hair blowing, obviously delighted to see us. The new bright yellow Packard was spectacular. She also had a terrific Chrysler woody station wagon, but this new beauty was more in her style. I walked around the Packard and admired it. Uncle Willy long ago had turned me into an admirer of automobile design and engineering, and this car was top of the line. Chrome letters on the side of the hood proclaimed "Straight 8."

Marilee opened the trunk, and I helped her unload and unfold a table with three camp chairs. Daniel opened the wine, a very good, as he said, French Pinot Noir. We proceeded to devour the barbecue sandwiches. Being with Daniel and Marilee, I was reminded of what an inspiration they were to me that it was possible to achieve real happiness in love.

Marilee was always impressed with the size of the arts community in Dallas, even though she and her cotton-baron family were long-time arts supporters. Although Marilee was a few of years older than Daniel, he looked older because he was graying prematurely. She had come back to Texas from her eastern schooling, Bryn Mawr, I think, and met the man who became her first husband. Grant was a flamboyant young oilman who specialized in foreign drilling and wildcatting. They had led an adventurous life overseas and a great life here in Dallas. She had inherited from her family an Italianate villa that backed up on Turtle Creek, and Marilee and Grant had added a spectacular swimming pool and a canoe dock. Grant had been one of the founding members of the Brook Hollow Golf Club, where he and Marilee held an annual costume party if they were in the country. Grant had died in an oil field accident in Java four years ago, and Marilee had taken over the drilling operation, drowning her grief in work. Two years ago, she and Daniel had met here at the Arts Festival. At the time, she didn't know he was a painter, and he didn't know who she was. Because her major had been art history, they struck a spirited discussion about the exhibit. Daniel and I had spent a whole night talking a couple of months after they met. He had been in a kind of a shock about having met her and fallen so completely in love. Of course, by this time, he knew she was wealthy, but she also was totally in love with him and adored his painting. She convinced him he wasn't a rebound for her after Grant's death but a completely new, unexpected love. He said their love was a sweet surprise for both of them. He had eventually moved into her home in Highland Park, and she had built a wonderful studio for him with northern light, and a patio off the swimming pool. Even though living together was not done, especially in Highland Park, Marilee had always been considered artsy so there hadn't been any scandal attached to them. Not that they would have cared because their social life didn't go much further than occasional dinners out and the traditional costume parties she still hosted. Their life was pretty much each other.

Marilee brought to mind a yachting picture from Town and Country, with her long curly light brown hair. Her figure was spectacular, just beyond petite, and she had an uninhibited laugh to which Daniel had the key. Sometimes in the strangest places, they would hold each other, putting their heads together as if they shared some private communication. Daniel had tried to describe their feeling by saying they had crossed an "enlightening threshold" together. Well, I didn't know about that, but I did realize that Daniel was beyond lucky to have found Marilee.

Marilee wanted to know how *Blood Wedding* was going, but since I only had two days of auditions under my belt, I didn't have much to say. I almost wished they hadn't printed up the posters so far ahead of opening, because for the first time, I was worried about the outcome. I guessed that all directors, especially young innocents, are anxious and excited about each new show, but this Spanish thing was scaring the hell out of me. Wanting to do Lorca and doing Lorca are two different things. I must have read the script about twenty times and couldn't believe how good it was...but now it seemed that all of my study and preparation had nothing to do with putting it up on stage with any sort of validity. I guess the added pressure of so many real artists in the family could be good for art, but....

I didn't tell Marilee all of those thoughts but more about how my planned blocking didn't look interesting, just flat.

She saw right through me, though, and cut to the chase. "Are you bored with your first ideas?" she asked.

I had been so excited about how I saw the play being done, but perhaps she was right. I was beginning to understand that odd feeling I had had earlier as I crossed the Festival grounds.

Daniel started laughing and said, "She does that to me occasionally."

I sat up, suddenly alert. How, I wondered, does one describe a sudden alteration of perception as if a voice from above is screaming a truth in your ear? I wasn't sure "epiphany" quite fit. I started thinking of all the times when, after reading a play, I saw it all in my head and stuck with those ideas. Even though I was usually well received as a director I had always felt something was missing...and now, well. I looked at Marilee blankly for a moment. Yes, that was, of course, it. Since starting to direct, I had wanted more than anything not to be considered arrogant, but just a fellow struggler in the creative collaboration. But I now realized I had been arrogant, my arrogance being that I thought my first ideas were special. In these few seconds, I began to feel that everything I had done before this was shallow to the point of embarrassing.

Marilee must have thought she had upset me. "Timmy!"

She was the only person who called me that except, occasionally, for Mom, whom I always scolded for it. But from Marilee, it seemed gently endearing.

"Daniel's way of working is what made me think of that – he starts over almost all the time. I don't mean totally but he steps back and rethinks, sometimes for days. Isn't creating a painting like directing a play, a sort of stacking ideas to get to the end? I'm not implying that you're not inspired, maybe just a bit frustrated. I remember how excited you were when you found this play, and I certainly don't see in you great self-doubt, just some questions about what next."

"At the very least now...some questions...but thank you, Marilee, wonderful girl."

"Why thanks?"

"Well, you may have changed me...or helped me solve some problems or maybe even the problem."

Daniel said, "I think I know exactly what you're feeling. I thought for years that the things that would change me as a painter would be to come in the studio and stare at the canvas. Of course, it does sometimes, but quite often it happens in one of those talks around the table with Mom and Dad.

"Now, and I don't always know how, but Marilee challenges me constantly. It's not even intentional on her part, it just happens. I wasn't floundering before her, but my ideas seem to be more exciting, at least to me. Do you feel good about how it's going, or is it, as Marilee said, a bit frustrating?"

"I thought my study was going pretty well for a real hard play, but I haven't been feeling the usual confidence about my work, as if I've been missing something. I mean, I know the play, but I know it's more powerful than what I'm coming up with. What I at first thought was a strong concept now seems rather vapid. Yes, I'm not sure where to start, but I think I'm excited. It's amazing what barbecue does for the arts!

"I think it's the Pinot Noir more than anything I said." laughed Marilee.

"Tim, Dad always calls it his second look, and Mom, her turnaround, that is she literally spins until she's almost dizzy and then starts again."

"It's probably time to start spinning."

"Well, Timmy dear, don't do it in front of your cast, it may scare them," Marilee commented dryly.

"I think the best thing to do is try not to think about it for couple of days."
"Why don't you start by coming over tonight after the festivities here?" Marilee suggested. "I have something special for you, Timmy. Perhaps it will serve as an inspiration. And please bring someone, if you wish."

Daniel gave a sly look, "Maybe Gwen, brother?"

Marilee started packing up the picnic basket up, "Let's do the Festival, Sart men. I want to see how Daniel's 'Flood Zone' painting looks. Have you seen it, Timmy?"

"Yes, Dan was rehanging it before you got back."

"Do you like it?" she asked eagerly.

"I think it's absolutely terrific, more than I expected, yes…and I more than like it."

I wandered back through the growing crowds talked to Dick again and made plans to get together the following evening, then built myself up for seeing Gwen. She teased me about my shyness and whispered that I should pick her up at nine-thirty, from which I inferred that this invitation deserved a shower and the rare use of cologne.

Chapter 2
Viva Villalobos

I shared some of my mother's always-terrific meatloaf with my parents. They had both had a long day at the Festival, although I hadn't run into them. They both loved Daniel's paintings, especially "Flood Zone." Dad had received a couple of furniture commissions and Mom a possible portrait job. As expected, Jeordie's machine piece had been a mystery to all. Dick Ayers' return was a welcome event; he had always been Dad's favorite of my friends. They both had been surprised at my seeing Gwen but glad at my retreat from solitude. Mom even had ironed a shirt for me, a rare event.

I hardly ever shaved twice in one day, but this seemed like a good idea. Gwen literally bounced into my car. Unknown to me, she had not dated anyone else since our last time together.

"An artistic choice," she said, "No distractions!"

She leaned over and kissed me saying, "This is nice, Tim, it's good to be with you tonight."

It's amazing how a few words can be so arousing, even if I were misinterpreting them.

Driving into Marilee's is like going to a secret place, a one-lane winding street that turns into an almost hidden gateway that suddenly reveals the facade of the Italianate villa. Not terribly large, it is strikingly otherworldly and elegant.

There were no other cars, and I was glad it would be just the four of us. Marilee's door is rarely locked, and if you're expected, the protocol is to go in and find her and Dan. They were on the patio just off the sunroom/sleeping porch, Dan in camp shorts and Marilee in one of her muu muus. My dungarees and Gwen's multicolored shift were a match for their apparel. Marilee hugged and kissed Gwen like a long-lost friend, she owned a couple of Gwen's pots.

Dan just pointed at her, saying, "Hey there, fine potter girl."

They were having Martinis. Marilee excused herself to get the surprise she had mentioned earlier. She returned shortly with an exotic bottle and four brandy snifters on a tray.

"This, dear Timmy, is the next step in your encounter with Spanish passion."

She handed me the bottle. It had a fanciful crest and said 'Viejo Villalobos Gran Especial.'

"Have you ever had Spanish brandy?" Marilee asked.

"No, I didn't know they were known for brandy. Is it different from the French?"

Marilee laughed and said, "It's so different and if to your taste...Well, we'll see what you think."

Gwen seemed to be as excited as I was about it. "I love Cognac, but have seldom been where it was available, or around anyone who had some, but...."

"Then this is a celebration of Timmy's delving into the Iberian ways," she said pouring snifters for Gwen and me.

The aroma shocked me, but didn't quite prepare me for its smoothness. I loved it. Brandy had always kind of burned, but not this, and the taste was different from any I had tasted before. I drank the first glass too quickly, as did Gwen, who didn't say anything except for making "Oohs" and "aahs.

"Slow down, brother, the night is young," Daniel cautioned.

Marilee reached over to stroke Dan and said to me, "I take it my surprise is a success?"

"Well, in a day of surprises, seeing Dick, our parking lot talk, and..." I looked at Gwen, "and this delightfully new brandy, yes, Marilee, you've done well!" I held up my glass in a toast to Marilee and Daniel.

Daniel raised his glass and finished his Martini, then said, "I'll have some of the Villalobos and tell you my good news." Marilee beamed at him, "We didn't know about this when we asked you over...but Dan, go ahead..."

"Jerry from the Fine Arts Museum said this afternoon that he wanted to add `Flood Zone' to the permanent collection with a Purchase Prize."

"Wow!" was all I could say at first..."Uh, have you told Mom and Dad?"

"Not yet...until I'm sure of it."

Gwen went over and hugged Daniel, "Two Sarts in the museum! You've arrived!" She was referring to the large pastoral of Mom's that had won the Texas Annual Exhibit at the Centennial.

When the evening ended, Marilee gave me an unopened bottle of the Spanish brandy in a box with two snifters.

Plans were made to eat Mexican food together after the Festival tomorrow, with assurances that Dick Ayers and his wife would join us. Dan had already invited our parents.

On leaving Marilee's, I asked Gwen if she wanted to stay over.

"Please, if I may?"

Gwen held on to me going to my apartment. My reading lamp provided the only light. She moved close and started undressing me slowly, kissing my lips and then my chest. Undoing my belt, she reached down and took me in her hand, squeezing gently. "Oh! Dear Lord, Gwen...Gwen, I want to touch you...!"

"Yes, Timothy, I want you to...but just a moment."

She pulled down my dungarees and put me in her mouth, but for just a moment, then lay me down and began to undress, standing at the end of the bed. Gwen was petite, slim, and swaybacked with a cute bottom, with radiant long curly light-blonde hair. She then jumped up on the bed standing over me. My, God, she was beautiful in the low light. Her pubic hair glistened from her wetness. She lowered herself down onto me and I thought that was it for me, it was just too good. Gwen then rose up and off me, lying down beside me. We held each other, kissing and touching. I gently rubbed her to a gentle orgasm. I kissed her breasts and moved down to her soft tummy. She asked me if I would keep moving down and kiss her down there.

"I...uh...yes. Will you tell me what...or how to...?" I had never made love like that, but the brandy had certainly quelled any inhibitions, and I wanted to be as close with her as possible. I started to rise and she stopped me. She sat up and straddled my chest and, moving closer until her cunny was at my chin. The sweetness of her overwhelmed me as I pushed my mouth into her, kissing what must have been the right place because she took my head in her hands, pulled me even closer to her, and laughed and cried out softly.

"Yes, Timothy, touch me there with your tongue...!"

I did, and she shuddered, pulled away, and rolled over beside me.

"Do you have anything?"

I reached into the drawer and found a prophylactic that I had thought would never be used. She took it, put in on me, and pulled me softly on top of her. As I entered her, she seemed to squeeze me and we made wonderful love several times without leaving each other. It's not that I felt powerful, but the new intimacies seemed to bring out something in me that I didn't know existed. It had always been good between us, but tonight had been special.

She lay beside me. "How sweet, Timothy, I knew it would be nice being with you after so long, but that was wonderful."

I held her, feeling very tired but as if all tensions had left me, more than relaxed, with kind of a new feeling of completeness.

"May I stay with you all night?" she asked.

Of course, I didn't want to get up and drive her home, but most of all I wanted to stay close to her.

"Yes, please do, I don't even want to sleep...but...," I whispered.

More quiet, then, "Timothy, was something bothering you earlier this evening? I don't mean us being together again after so long, but something else...your new play maybe? I saw the poster. Is it going well?"

I hadn't mentioned anything, but this was more of a sweet concern than her usual omnipotent awareness.

"I thought it was until the last few days. I mean, I love the play; it's just a lot harder than I imagined. Almost everything else I've done had been done before and they were very American. *Blood Wedding* has been done, too, but not in this country. In addition, the whole Spanish Civil War thing, and a completely different approach to an expression of passion...and love. This afternoon, Marilee turned me sort of topsy-turvy with an almost too simple question about my perhaps being tired of my first ideas. That was it, of course. I was so sure of the way I saw the play being done that I wasn't letting loose or being open to rethinking. Now I know I can approach it anew. Just while I was holding you, I've come to a decision not to have a strict blocking rehearsal....uh...it was just a flash," I said, embarrassed. "...I mean I wasn't thinking of it when we were...uh..."

"Don't worry...I understand 'crazy artists' and how their minds work."

"'Crazy artist,' huh? Well, thanks for understanding. Yes" I kissed her and drifted into sleep.

In the morning, I slipped into the house to get us some coffee. Mom saw me get two cups and said, "Wait!" She got me a small pot, smiling. There are sometimes special benefits to being in a family of rather progressive artists.

"Is it Gwen?" she asked, as if she hoped it was.

I nodded and barefooted it back through the yard to my apartment.

Being Saturday, neither of us had to be anywhere early. We sat in bed with our coffee and talked. Gwen had no inhibitions about being bare-breasted in front of me, but it made it difficult for me to concentrate on our conversation. She was, at the very least beautiful, her breasts just above small and seeming to point upward.

"Timothy, I'm leaving Dallas..."

"What...?" I sat up quickly, not believing what I had just heard. I knew that she wasn't the type to make any sort of commitment, but to hear she was leaving after the previous evening...

"Why? Where?"

"I'm joining an artist's combine in the Hill Country near Austin. It's partly sponsored by the University and I've saved up enough to stay there for a year. I think I've done some good work here, but Sanger's during the day and the studio at night needs to change...Timothy, I had no idea we would be together or that I would feel the way I do. There was a look in your eyes that made me want to hold you and...well. The evening with Daniel and Marilee was special and so were we together...I..."

"When are you leaving?

"This next week, the bus, Tuesday."

"Gwen! Damn! I thought perhaps we...well, I..."

I couldn't think of anything to say, certainly not please don't go. She seemed so sure about what she wanted to do.

We took a shower together, and I got ready for the day at the Arts Festival, took her home, and waited while she changed.

As we pulled into the parking lot, I asked, "Are you up for some Mexican Food tonight? It will be quite a collection of people."

"Yes, I would love to do that. I'm glad you're not so upset about my leaving that you don't want to spend any more time with me".

"I'm more disappointed than upset. I don't like it, but I do understand why you are leaving. I would do the same if the opportunity came up. Last night I thought how good it would be for you to be with me during the next weeks of rehearsal and the opening. You would certainly have been an inspiration. But what the hell...we're together right now."

"Yes we are, and I'll try to be an inspiration from afar. I know that if you weren't also a 'crazy artist,' you wouldn't be so understanding."

"Well, *carpe diem,* as the Romans said."

"Yes!" she agreed. Let's seize both the day and the night," she agreed eagerly. "High school Latin does come in handy sometimes. Will you share some of that Spanish elixir later?"

"Indeed I will." And we joined the Festival.

Chapter 3
La Comida con La familia y unos Amigos

The Festival is usually packed on Saturday afternoons, and this one was no exception. It was a beautiful spring day in Dallas. The springs here are what make it a wonderful place to live, with beautiful skies and almost perfect weather. Twice I've seen the Festival almost rained out, but not this one. It's hard to beat middle '70s temperatures and a gentle breeze. Because I was manning the Dallas Civic Theatre booth all day, I was wearing a tie, one Gwen had given me. After last night, I would have worn a cape and hood if she had asked me to. We parted with a hand squeeze and I watched her walk away, both sad for me and thrilled for her. She had decided on classy bohemian attire that, even if it didn't help sell a bunch of her elegant pots, it would surely bring about some lengthy admiring conversations.

Barney was already at the booth talking to some people who were new to Dallas. He greeted me in his usual effusive manner and introduced me as if I were an up-and-coming genius in the art world. Very embarrassing, but the new people seemed impressed. They asked about *Blood Wedding*. They had never heard of it but had seen an earlier Lorca play at an avant-garde theatre in New York. I told them I thought it would be the first American production, although one was being mounted at Yale that could possibly beat ours, I certainly wasn't going to hurry our process just to beat them to it. They asked if I was related to the Sart whose painting, "Flood Zone," was in the art exhibit.

"Yes, my older brother, Daniel."

"While we were looking at it, a ribbon was hung beside it that said 'DMFA Purchase Prize.'"

They couldn't have delivered better news, and it would certainly add a high note to tonight's dinner gathering. I told the new folks a little bit about our family, and introduced them to one of the possible actresses in *Blood Wedding*, Carolyn Caruthers, who had just arrived to help at the booth. After more talk about the Civic Theatre and the play, they decided to join the Benefactors Guild and bought half-season tickets to boot. All afternoon, a constant flow of people visited our booth, mostly our usual patrons and theatergoers, but a surprising number of new potential audience did stop by to talk and take season ticket flyers and other printed handouts that Barney had prepared especially for the Festival. Carolyn spent most of the afternoon trying to get me to talk about the play, which I resisted, much to her dismay. She was an experienced actress with years of solid work behind her at the theatre. I had worked with her twice before, both good experiences. She was up to play a very difficult mature role, and seemed to be as troubled as I was about the complexity of this new play.

Later in the afternoon, Gwen dropped by to bring me a chicken salad sandwich and a Dr Pepper. I managed to eat the sandwich, all the while keeping up the theatre chatter. While Gwen was there, Mom and Dad dropped by to tell me about Dan's Purchase Prize. I pretended not to know about it, but I certainly didn't have to pretend to be happy for Dan. Mom told Gwen how much she liked her pots that she had seen earlier.

Gwen said, "Choose one! It's yours."

Mom was truly shocked at the offer, knowing they would probably sell, and that Gwen could certainly use the money. Gwen continued to insist and Mom accepted, hugging her. I think she may have realized that perhaps Gwen was saying something more than please accept a gift. Mom walked back with Gwen to her booth, while Dad stayed behind for a few minutes to share a father-and-son rehash of the day. He was proud of Daniel's inclusion at the museum, and he considered me as having been accepted there because of an intimate Commedia Del Arte piece I had done in the big room at last year's State Fair. Dad had furnished two of the lounges there several years ago. Of course, Daniel was already quite successful with private collectors, so I guess it was a Dallas thing, establishment approval.

As it turned dark, the lights came on. Strings of colored lights hung around the perimeter of the outside booths area and across to poles in the middle. The crowd had grown, and the evening had become very festive. Groups of musicians roamed the crowd as loudspeakers announced the start of several events inside the hall: chamber music, a dance program, and the awarding of the arts prizes. There were many more people than could comfortably fit in the auditorium, and more were coming. A Mariachi band had set up in the parking lot, where an area had been roped off for dancing. Later, a country swing group would perform.

A surprise visitor to my booth was my younger brother, Jeordie. This year Dad had bought him a recorder, for which he had a startling talent. Tonight, he had been playing and skipping around like a wood sprite. He had even put some leaves and ivy in his hair. I thought that if I ever got the opportunity to direct *A Mid Summer Night's Dream*, he would be my Puck. He leaned on our counter just able to look over and asked if I had heard about Daniel's award. He said Mom wasn't letting him come to dinner tonight because it would be too late, but that it was alright because he wanted to listen to his radio. Saturday-night radio programs were his favorites, but I sensed he was disappointed. Making a faun-like face, he skipped off into the crowd.

Several more actors came by to help. I was about talked out from selling the theatre and *Blood Wedding* so I took a break and went to the exhibit hall to check with Daniel and Marilee. Dan was surrounded by folks asking about "Flood Zone" and his other two paintings on exhibit. Mom was off to the side, ever the proud parent, but also stood by her painting, next to Dan's. And wonderfully enough there is a red sticker by the title denoting it had sold. Definitely a good weekend for the Sart painters. Dan saw me and came over to tell about the plans for tonight. On Festival weekends, a Mexican restaurant on Harry Hines Boulevard stays open late, and our reservations were for 10 at 10. Marilee had gone shopping for ice and wine to bring to dinner since the restaurant was licensed to sell only beer. Mom talked with me about Gwen, unaware of her plans to leave Dallas.

"What a nice, creative and attractive young woman, Timothy, and she seems to really like you," she said, raising an eyebrow slightly.

I agreed and left to find Dick Ayers to tell him the evening's plans. At the "Free Spain" booth, I was told that he and Camila were at the Mexican music dancing area. Even though the dancing area was crowded, Dick and Camila stood out because he was dancing with a cane, which worked surprisingly well. I waved to get their attention and they gracefully spun over to me.

"What are the plans, Tim, old man?"

I gave the time with no need to give directions because Dick and I had been there many times in the past. This evening was going to be Camila's introduction to Mexican food. She said it was what Dick had missed most when he was in the hospital in Madrid. She said he had kept asking for his doctor—or so she had thought. When he was past the point of delirium, he had finally explained to her that the Dr Pepper he was asking for was a soft drink. Of course, there was none to be had in Spain.

I had another hour and a half to kill before the gathering, so on my way back to the booth, I dropped by to see Gwen. She saw me coming and waved. A rush of sadness hit me as I thought of her leaving, but I admitted to myself that there was no real future for a long-lasting relationship even if she stayed in Dallas. It wasn't that she didn't care about me, or I about her, but her drive as an artist allowed no constant distractions. She was grabbing at the moment, as I was, because she probably saw this time as our last time together. And she was a delight that surely must be a rarity, or so I thought in my limited experience.

Gwen asked if we would have time to freshen up before joining the other folks. She said she could leave in about 45 minutes and could easily do everything at my place. I quickly agreed, thinking of our quick shower together. She squeezed my hand and said she would come to the theatre booth when she was ready to leave.

The next three quarters of an hour was spent selling season tickets. My happiness seemed to make me persuasive. I sold 10 tickets and signed up 15 new volunteers. I worried about boring people to death talking about the challenges of mounting *Blood Wedding* and the excitement of directing new material, but it seemed to work.

I was truly excited about the evening, Gwen, Daniel's award, and spending time with Dick and Camila. It wasn't difficult talking Barney into letting me leave early after my successful ticket-selling.

Gwen walked up carrying two beautiful ceramic pieces, a vase and a large bowl.

"These are for you and your minimal apartment, my dear Timothy Sart. I can't take anything with me and these are two of my best so...you won't ever forget me."

We scooted off to my car, got to my house very quickly, and literally jumped into the shower, making love in a way that was new to me. It was an extremely pleasant way to start what could turn into a long evening.

Gwen loved my car, not because it was a bit of luxury for someone of my ilk, but because it was more sporty than the usual. Uncle Willy was into dirt track racing and built cars at his shop as a sideline to his machine work. The car had a rumble to it that came from the special exhaust system he had built into it. She made an "ooh" sound when I started it up, as if it excited her. I liked it, too, but I was used to it. My driving was usually of the most conservative sort, but her excitement made me more of a daredevil, not reckless, but I had more fun than I usually did with the built-in "zoomy" qualities of the car. Gwen had never met Dick Ayers, so I briefed her on his last couple of years. She said he was lucky to be alive, but that sometimes tragedy can bring about new happiness, referring to his new wife. I agreed that getting shot could certainly be classified as a tragedy. We both hoped he would reveal more details of his Spanish adventure tonight.

There was a fiesta-like quality in the air in Little Mexico across the street from the restaurant, and within, strolling guitar players added to the feeling. Bustamante's had the best Mexican food in town and during the Arts Festival, it was a real gathering place. The patrón, Sr. Bustamante, greeted us at the door and took us back to the patio. I think we knew someone at every table. Although we were not late, Gwen and I were the last to arrive. My father, at the head of the table, stood up and greeted us with hugs. More hugs and kisses as I introduced Gwen to Dick and Camila.

My mother and Gwen spent a couple minutes in intimate conversation. Gwen must have revealed her new plans to my mother because there was more embracing, and I got a motherly "Oh, well" look.

Marilee and Daniel had brought a tub filled with ice and large bottles of wine, which started flowing immediately as if our arrival had turned on the spigot. Once everyone had a full glass, Dad stood up and offered a toast to Daniel for his Purchase Prize from the museum. Everyone else on the patio also stood up and applauded, and Marilee, looking very proud, hugged and kissed him, happy tears streaming down her face. Daniel beamed and raised his glass to everyone on the patio. I took the opportunity to stand and toast the safe return of Dick and his new wife from Spain and the civil war there. Camila seemed a bit overwhelmed by the attention and the celebration not with shyness but in a desire to get to know all of us, her second new big family group in a short amount of time.

After the toasts, we were served with plates of Mexican treats of all kinds – empanadas, shrimp, tostadas, and little skewers of broiled meats. Marilee had told El Patrón to go all out, so we were swarming with waiters and Sr. Bustamante checked with Marilee every few minutes. Marilee introduced him to Camila, and he was thrilled to meet a new arrival from Spain. They embarked on a spirited discussion in Spanish, evidently about the war and the difficulties of the Republican cause. "No necesitan Los Russos...!" he repeated several times, and Camila agreed.

I thought this would be good time to ask Dick about his experiences that had led up to his being shot. Dick knew it was coming, but he was hesitant to speak.

"Are you sure this is the right time, Tim? This is Daniel's and Mrs. Sart's night, not mine."

"It's your night, too, Dick. You're safely back with us, and that's cause for celebration, too," said Daniel.

"The night is still young, and being an incurable romantic, I want to hear about you and Camila," insisted Marilee.

"Yes, yes…please Dick." My mother urged.

"Well…I never was a member of any military group but remained a graduate student at the National University in Madrid. Of course, my sympathies were with the Republican side, being a rather progressive-minded American, family tradition, and all that. The whole thing started not long after I arrived in '36. The educational situation remained rather isolated in the beginning but there were factions building up at the school that caused only a certain amount of confusion at first and then became full-scale demonstrations and rallies. The majority of the students seemed to side with the Republicans, and Madrid was the Democratic government's capital while the Royalist-Franco faction seemed to be headquarted in Granada. Classes went on, although in a rather chaotic fashion at times. Some teachers left to follow their own regional loyalties and the various military factions…."

At the head of the table, my father asked, "What was it like in the city, were people scared? Were there shortages?"

Camila chimed in her charmingly accented English, "I think the first changes were noticed in the hospital where I worked. Trucks started arriving in with the wounded, and I saw things beyond my worst bad dreams. I was unprepared for what war could do to people…and the hours spent there were never less than twelve or thirteen a day. Sometimes we couldn't even leave. All of a sudden, we had half the doctors to do ten times the work because some were called to the front and others joined the Franco factions. In the beginning, though, everyone I knew thought it would be over quickly and the Republican National Army would put a stop to it, but the German and Italian intervention changed that."

"How about the Russians?" asked Daniel.

"Well, we don't know yet," said Dick. "Before they got involved, people had hoped the USA would help, but because of the Russians I don't think there's any chance."

"Why?" asked Gwen. "I thought Spain was a Democracy, elected leaders and all that."

"It is, but of a different sort, and with a strong Socialist Party with ties to the Communist parties in France and, I guess, elsewhere." answered Dick.

"Yes, international politics are a real mess; I'm very happy Mrs. Sart here decided for me…that is to not even consider volunteering. I would probably be in a mud hole with a bunch of Lincoln Brigade crazies eating old mutton, and not here celebrating Daniel and Mrs. Sart's successes at the Festival. Right, Mother o' the family?"

"Yes, almost man o' the world and international set," laughed Mother, "Please, carry on, Dick."

I hadn't expect my mother to be this interested in war stories, but I knew she liked Dick. She had always asked about him when she knew I had received a letter.

There was also that scare about Dad wanting to get involved. If ever there was an earth mother type, she was a classic example. Our house had always been open to her sons' friends. Sleepovers were common, and her meat loaf, lamb curry, and peach cobbler had always been Dick's favorites. She would let me know they were coming up so I could call Dick to invite him over. I don't remember him ever turning down an invitation.

Dick and I had been fast friends since meeting one summer at Camp Tejano when we were about ten. The East Texas camp was a rare extravagance, but that summer they had offered a Spanish language workshop, which my parents thought was a good idea for me. And it was great; I loved the Spanish studies, swam in a lake, rode horses, and met Dick. Going to different high schools didn't separate us. I would go watch him play football at Woodrow Wilson, and he would come to see my feeble attempts at acting at North Dallas. Though it was quite a bit grander than ours, I was just as welcome at his house in Lakewood. With its big houses, and even some swimming pools — Lakewood was a sort of Dallas version of Highland Park. The Park Cities, Highland and University, where Southern Methodist University was, were incorporated cities in the middle of Dallas. Dick looked at me, smiled and nodded in a good-to-be-here fashion and continued his story.

"Madrid was actually very exciting during the first year, even more international. The clubs and tapas bars were filled with writers and volunteers from all over the world. It was a kind of desperate celebration because most were on their way to the various fronts. The Russians were a dour lot who spoke none of our languages. English and French were the linguas francas, but you heard everything. I met some great New Zealanders who, for some reason, felt a kinship with a real Texan. There were also a lot of women who weren't exactly camp followers but seemed to chase the excitement wherever it was in the world. As a student, I wasn't really a part of the war. I hoped it would all be over soon and I could finish my studies, come back to the University at Austin, and go to law school. But if you were there, you couldn't help getting involved. There were constant parades of troops passing through Madrid on their way to the front. The Lincoln and George Washington Brigades were the most interesting to watch. They were less military in their marching and waved flags from almost everywhere. They yelled and sang with their fists in the air as if on to victory, but as I know now, it was off to the slaughter. They were a sort of semi-disciplined Foreign Legion with men from all corners of the earth – Americans both white and black, Arabs, French, Greeks, Orientals, and Latin Americans. Yes, there was a romantic quality to it, but it was also sad, because after this if there was no victory, there was no home."

"Were you scared of the outcome and thinking it was time to get out?" Daniel asked.

"No, well obviously later, but no, not at first. The cause seemed so right, and it was a vivid experience to have all of this happening around you. As things progressed, we could hear the battles in the distance and eventually I wanted to see it. I had been awarded my diploma in a rush as the University became more chaotic.

There were ramparts not far outside of Madrid manned by students and townspeople, along with a city militia. I went with a group of mixed nationality students. As we got closer, the noise increased…and there it was. The wide road into Madrid was blocked at the southern end of a small village that had been an exclusive retreat outside of the capital. Cars were turned over, and buses were situated sideways to form the fighting positions. The Republican cannons were to the East and West away from the village. As we arrived, their barrage ceased, but not the other side's. Their shells were dropping on the gun positions and not the town. There was a lot of screaming and barking of orders. Hundreds of people were running around, frantic, and the wounded were being carried to the rear ranks. There didn't appear to be much of an organized military group, just lots of people carrying rifles. Someone up at the barricade started yelling for us to get down because an enemy barrage was coming. And it did. Shells began to come down in back of us and we had no choice but to run towards the people up front. It went from curious excitement to overwhelming horror. I think I had visions of watching the war from afar, like those stories of people taking picnic baskets and riding out from Washington and watching Gettysburg. That changed real quickly as the sun went down and there was no real darkness because of the explosions. It lasted all night, and there was an attack in the morning. I had spent hours under an overturned truck but crawled out when everybody came out of hiding running to the barricades. Two of my companions pulled me along with them, and the attack was on. I didn't have any sort of weapon so all I could do was watch it happening in front and in back of me. That went on almost all day until a man ran up to me with two rifles and gave me one. I had no desire to shoot anyone, but an attack was on, so I climbed up the barricade and fired into the advancing troops. I don't know if I killed anyone, and I don't want to know. Our artillery started up again and the advance was stopped. I was there for one week. By then I decided that I had better go back to Madrid and not get further involved. I gave my rifle to the member of an arriving militia. But before I could get out, another bombardment started, and I was hit in the leg by a piece of shrapnel. Tim, do you remember when I broke a couple of ribs during the last game of my junior season?"

"Yes, I spent about fours a day at your house listening to you moan."

"Yes, well, I thought I knew what pain was…I didn't. Shocking and immobilizing pain…and blood. Luckily, there was an ambulance unit close by and heading into Madrid. There was almost not enough room for me, but the English driver heard me screaming in English and piled me into the front seat where an Irish attendant put a tourniquet on my leg and gave me some morphine pills. I woke a day and a half later in the hospital where Camila worked. My leg had been operated on. I had a strange hallucination that was a half dream when I first awoke. Some kind of large animal, like an elephant or hippo was standing on my leg, so I awakened screaming. That was my first sight of Camila, her trying to hold me down. I didn't fight her because I was sure she was an angel catching me in midair…falling into heaven, that is…! I eventually calmed down, realizing I was still alive and that my leg was still there. And Camila spoke to me in English, though she said I had been babbling in Spanglish, so she knew I spoke Spanish. I had lost a lot of blood and the pain was raging, so the first week, needless to say, was the worst I had ever experienced except for..."

Dick put his arm around Camila and kissed her cheek. She shyly returned the kiss as tears pored down her face.

"And...and then?" Gwen prompted.

"Then...well. There was no then for awhile. Just being in the hospital talking for hours with Camila and falling very much in love."

"I neglected almost all my other nursing duties and stayed as much as I could with Dick. Yes, me too, I also fell so much in love that the war disappeared from my mind."

"That sounds like me and Daniel, without the war...well, you know what I mean. These Dallas boys." Marilee said, and then laughed slightly.

"With a Sartian spell, they entrapped us, Marilee," my mother added.

Gwen had to say, "Bless the spell...?!"

"Perhaps it was your lamb curry that gave me a bit of Sartian magic, Mrs. Sart," Dick added.

"Stop...! It was the other way around, we were enchanted, not you all, ladies." I said.

"My middle son speaks the truth."

"Thanks, Dad. More...Dick?" I prompted eager to hear the rest of his story.

"Camila, took me to her family's house to recuperate, and they quickly accepted me as almost a family member. Her father is the surgeon who fixed my leg, so I couldn't have asked for better care. They realized immediately how we felt about each other but felt very strongly about me getting out of Spain in case things got worse. But I had no intention of leaving without Camila. After several weeks, we decided to get married. Living together but apart was becoming intolerable. We would talk all day and into each night, and I was learning to walk again. Neither of us was getting any sleep, and she wasn't going to the hospital in any sort of regular fashion. One night, we fell asleep in each other's arms. It wasn't a real intimate situation, just exhaustion. Her parents woke us up the next day. They were very upset, but when we revealed our desire to get married, they accepted it with genuine joy and arranged everything. We were married a week later in the garden in back of their house. We got her a new passport at the American Consulate. My papers said I was a student and I had my diploma, but the wound could have been a problem. Camila's father got a statement from a police commissioner friend saying I was an innocent victim and not a combatant. We crossed the border into France through Barcelona and worked our way up through the country by train to Le Havre, where we caught an American ship to Baltimore. We stayed there for several days to acclimate Camila to the U.S. and then spent a week in New York, where I saw a doctor about my leg. We just got here three days ago. We're living with my parents, who adore my beautiful wife. I would've called you, Tim, but I knew I would see you at the Festival. That's the story in brief, with many more tales to tell.

"Bravo...bravo!" cheered my mother and Marilee offered up another toast as the food arrived.

Gwen asked Daniel how much the Purchase Prize was. He said it was a whopping seven hundred dollars, which was quite large since Mom's prize for the Texas Annual had been only five hundred.

Daniel and I talked about *Blood Wedding* and the problems I was having with a concept for the set design. I was considering a complete rethinking after my conversation with Marilee the day before.

In Camila's honor, Marilee had ordered a special paella, prepared Texas-style, with beef, pork, and chicken. What a feast! The conversation never stopped, and Gwen leaned over to me a couple of times to say how great the gathering was, not mentioning that it was probably our last night together.

Many compliments passed around the table on Marilee's Texas paella. Even Camila, after her first encounter with enchiladas, applauded with mouth full. I wanted to know more about Dick's injury, but he didn't have much to say except that it wasn't as bad as he thought it was in Spain and it would get better.

Daniel asked, "Where to now, Dick? Are y'all going to stay here in Dallas?"

Dick first laughed that it was good to hear someone say, "y'all" again. "I've applied to law school at Austin, and hopefully Camila can finish up medical school after taking whatever is needed at the university to be accepted. We didn't mention that she was in medical school in London before the war started."

"I decided to go back home and help in any way I could," Camila explained, "even though I had just finished my third year. My father tried to talk me into staying in London and finishing, but I'm sure now that I did the right thing." She put her hand over Dick's and smiled. Mother came over and sat behind Camila to get to know her and welcome her to the family. I gave up my seat and let Gwen join them in girl talk. Daniel had moved to sit beside Dad, so I accepted Marilee's gesture for me to join her.

She asked how things were with Gwen. She didn't seem surprised that Gwen was leaving but was disappointed for me. She then leaned in closer and told me, "Tim, part of Gwen's persona is her will o' the wisp duality…not that she doesn't care about you because she obviously does, but she is out of place in Dallas and needs to be a full-time artist. She can't do that here. You know that, don't you? You're trying to do the same thing, but you need to be where there's a theatre. In a way, yours is the best of all possible worlds, but hers isn't."

"I know you're right, and actually I didn't expect us to be together again, so these last couple of days have been a real treat and, I think, an inspiration. I've been more or less alone for several months, and these last couple of weeks have not been a great success artistically…not a failure, as we talked about yesterday afternoon. Oh! And by the way, you gave me the impetus to possibly try a whole new approach to my direction. The ideas aren't solid yet, but they're coming. If Gwen were staying here, I wouldn't have really expected it to be a consistent relationship. But, wow, what a goodbye."

"Yes, 'such sweet sorrow.' Forgive the reference, but it seems to apply. Do you have to work tomorrow and when is she leaving?"

"No I don't, and I think Monday."

"Well, if you don't think it will be too late, why don't you two join me and Daniel for the season's first night swim? The dark will be our suits. Daniel would love it, and dinner doesn't have to be the end of our celebration."

"I'll ask Gwen, but I don't think she'll say no, so, let's plan on it."

I moved around back beside Gwen and whispered the invitation without mentioning the swimming part. She turned and nodded yes with a smile.

The dinner party lasted another half-hour. There were many hugs goodbye, and I made tentative plans to get together with Dick for drinks after rehearsal in the coming week.

We arrived at Marilee's close to 11. As Dan pulled into the garage, Marilee joined us at the front door. They went upstairs, telling us to join them at the pool cabana and have a drink while we waited. There is a complete bar by the pool, and ice in a small refrigerator. I had bourbon and mixed Gwen a shaker of martinis. Daniel came out first, wearing a robe, and carrying two for us. He lighted several candles on a table and one on the bar and then turned out the lights. "It takes a bit of the shyness away!" he explained.

It was then that Gwen realized the potential for swimming in the nude. "Did you think I wouldn't come if you had told me, Timothy?" She took one of the robes and went into the dressing area at the back of the cabana.

"You weren't trying to pull a fast one, were you, brother?"

"No, she agreed to come before I could tell her of the plans. She's not exactly the shy type, anyway. It's my first time, also, or here anyway. Obviously, it's not a problem. I think she wants to get right to it."

Marilee joined us in her robe just as Gwen was coming out of the dressing room.

"Timmy, what's the hesitation? Gwen, I'm glad you came because it seems we may not be seeing much of you any more. Good for you, but a loss for us," Marilee said.

"It's an opportunity that I've been waiting for but never really thought would come. It's great to possibly be able to work all the time at pottery design and finally be able to pursue ceramics with other artists. I'll also have the best studio in the state, of course shared with others. Too bad there's not a theatre...eh Timothy?"

"I'm not sure about theatre all day, every day, especially without a public audience. I think that's what makes theatre creative, a constant awareness of a critical audience looking at your artistic product, not your process."

"Tim, you're getting too philosophical, too late in the evening. Marilee, what would you like?" Tim made Gwen one of your special 'New York' martinis. Share those?"

"No, some of the Spanish brandy, please. I brought a bottle down. Would you open it please, dear heart?"

"A sus ordenes, mi amorcita. I'll have some myself."

"Timothy, I believe your play, Dick's return, and the brandy are affecting everyone," giggled Gwen.

"Yes...well. I wish I had known there was brandy out here. This bourbon, though wonderful, is changing my evening. It's making Gwen glow in the dark."

"Thank you...I think, Timothy. Why don't you grab that robe and go change?" Gwen said. "I need the shock of the pool."

"Well said, Gwen. We may not wait for you, Tim. Take a candle, it won't break the spell."

I went into the cabana and undressed, and heard Gwen squeal as she went into the water. When I came out, all I saw were three heads bobbing. Marilee and Daniel were in the deep end holding on to the side and to each other. Gwen was waiting for me close to the cabana. I dropped my robe next to hers and eased into the water. It was as cold as a lake.

There wasn't anything exhibitionistic about it, no parading around, just uninhibited people enjoying themselves in a safe place. Marilee was right about the dark being our bathing suits. And at this moment, Gwen and I did love each other as if grabbing a beautiful moment in time. She moved in close as if to warm me, and put her arms around me. The shiver from the cold went away as we kissed. The feel of her wet breasts on my chest was very different and immediately arousing, which she noticed. She reached down to squeeze me gently, and turned me around putting her legs around me, and slipped me inside her. My hands on the side of the pool held us up, and the water gently rocked us. We kissed and tried not make any noise as the new sensations increased. Very quickly, we both shuddered as we came together. Gwen moaned and cooed, gently putting her chin on my shoulder, keeping me inside her.

"Timothy...Timothy, how delicious."

I couldn't think of anything to say, except to kiss her ear and whisper, "yes...!"

Across the pool, Daniel and Marilee were laughing in an intimate way, unaware of us and our lovemaking. Their happiness together was an ongoing wonder, and at that moment I envied them deeply. "Timothy, I am going to miss you and us," Gwen said. "Will you write me about your play because I know I won't be coming back to Dallas for a long time? My ties here are not like yours. I think our future is good memories."

I knew what she was saying was a true. I didn't want her to go, but I had always known she would leave sometime. The next thing I knew, we were making love again, and we must have made a bit more noise than before, though we tried not to, because Daniel and Marilee climbed out of the pool and put on their robes.

Marilee went over to the bar, filled two snifters with the Spanish brandy and brought them to us. "Your goodbyes have rather overtly affected us. We're going upstairs to finish our celebrating. Anyway, I think we'll make it to the bedroom if we rush! Goodbye, dear Gwen. Do good work." She kissed her palm then placed it on Gwen's cheek.

Gwen said, "I will…Goodbye, Marilee, and thank you." She waved at Daniel across the pool, and they left us.

Back at my apartment, we slept in each other's arms. No more lovemaking, just being close. I woke up before Gwen late the next morning. The sheets had been pushed off during the night. I looked at her for half an hour realizing again how striking she was. She woke up, smiled at me, pulled me to her and kissed my tears; we made love for the last time with a desperate intensity. Then she was up and in the shower. She emerged, dressed, and sat down on the bed beside me. "Goodbye, Timothy," she said. And was gone.

Chapter 4
Ensayo

I realized later that Gwen hadn't asked for a ride to her apartment. I think she wanted to walk the five blocks and avoid another emotional parting. I sat up for a few moments, facing the shock that she was really gone. I hadn't thought about her in months in any tangible way, just wavering fantasies occasionally, and then...Wham!... She was back for this brief vivid and passionate collection of moments. It was if, before leaving, she wanted to teach me not to be a selfish lover as a goodbye gift. Well, whatever her reason, it had worked. She had broken through my shyness about intimacies I hadn't really imagined. I smiled thinking of her slim beauty lying beside me and said a silent thank you, Gwen.

I decided to read before getting up, eating, and working on *Blood Wedding*. I had been working my way through Somerset Maugham for several months and was about to finish <u>Cakes and Ale</u>. It seemed that I paused after each few paragraphs to think of Gwen and the last two days. It had been a total immersion into the Festival, old friends, family, and new sensual experiences. I was a delightful blur of all kinds of feelings. One of the lasting images of the weekend was of Daniel's painting of the Trinity River floods. Gwen had commented that it looked like Daniel was changing. I guess all of the people around the table last night at Bustemante's were changing. Even my parents, but I hadn't figured that one out yet, just something good and different. Perhaps they were more at peace with each other. They had just seemed happier and more affectionate. I just then realized what had been going on around the house for the last few weeks. I had been so self-absorbed that it had passed by me. Dad's new shop, commissions, and a design competition he was entering in New York with a folding chair he created, and Mom's new larger paintings that were taking on a realistic still life quality. It had been a long time since I had heard them praise each other's work so much It surely hadn't been like that seven years ago.

Then, Mom and Dad, were headed towards divorce. It had scared the hell out of Daniel and me; Jeordie was too young to tolerate the fights and screaming, but he didn't understand much and just cried a lot. I didn't know until later what had been going on. Dad had been engaged in an affair with an attractive divorcee for whom he had designed and built some furniture. When Mom found out, she had retaliated with a painter she had met at an East Texas art retreat, and she told Dad about her dalliance. They had stormed and screamed for a week, and then Dad had left the house for several days. Mom called the woman Dad had been seeing and told her to stay away from her man, and it seemed to work. Dad had returned and they went off together for a week while Daniel and I took care of Jeordie and wondered what was going to happen. They came back and everything slowly returned to normal. A year later I asked Mom what had happened and she evidently felt I was old enough to know the truth. I was shocked, which she eased by saying artists do crazy things sometimes and that she and Dad had decided that what they had together was better than they had realized. Several months later, I told Daniel and we went to Dad's shop out back and asked him to tell us his version. He said he wished we hadn't found out about it, but said it had been his fault. He said the hard part was finding out what Mom had done, but when Mom had called the other woman, he realized how much Mom really loved him. And if she could forgive him, he could damn sure forgive her, so they had decided to work it out. That week they went off together turned out to be better than a honeymoon they had never had. He said that as bad as it had been for six months, it had sure helped their marriage, but he wouldn't recommend it as a way to rediscover lost romance. Dan and I left him with hugs and an appreciation for his candidness with us. It left us, as we discussed later, with the awareness of how lucky we were to have parents who could go through something like that and come out stronger and more in love than before.

It was actually good to be alone, not to evaluate, but to get ready for the coming weeks and new ways of thinking about directing. After awhile I put away the Maugham and reread *Blood Wedding*. In the middle of the afternoon, I showered, went into the house, made a sandwich, and called Marilee. They had just gotten back from a late lunch at the club. She was starting to go over some business papers but said it could wait until tomorrow. Daniel was in his studio stretching some canvases. When I got to her house, she met me at door. We went into the library. She had several books laid out on the big table, one by a Cornell professor entitled Art Logic.

"I've been thinking about our conversation at the parking lot picnic and trying to remember where I had heard or read what inspired me to make those comments about rethinking your approach to the play. It came to me late this morning, and I mean late. I remembered that in an art class in college, my teacher had talked about secondary and tertiary visualization, which means second and third look, and referred it to all art, not just painting. He didn't relate it to theatre but he did recommend this book. I read it and was amazed at its simple explanation as to how all art is created... general to specific and all that, but in the chapter on visualization, the writer describes good art as being made only after your first thoughts are discarded as the obvious, no matter how interesting they may seem. Only in that way is the viewer stimulated. Otherwise, it's within the bounds of his own imagination; he may admire the technique but not the concept of something new, or unthought-of before."

"Last Friday when we talked, you remember me saying that when I read plays, I visualized it in my mind I saw the whole production, the end product. But *Blood Wedding* has needed new wheels to turn in my head, but I didn't know it. I thought it was just hard. Trying to discard your first thoughts is difficult, but perhaps they shouldn't be so carved in stone. I don't think it's study then forget, but read, read, then study, then rethink...uh...maybe. I think of all the different sketches that Mom makes before she put oil on the canvas. Dad does the same thing, first just general shapes, and then he gets more specific with each design drawing. For some strange reason I thought theatre was different because it's living art.

"Timmy," Marilee said, warming to the subject, "I just remembered an exercise we did in class. My teacher said it was to train us get different perspectives or go from one art form to another. He would play a piece of music or show us a painting and we had to express our feeling about it in a different art form. For a painting, we had to find some music, dance, or dramatic speech that affected us in the same way as the painting. Everyone would have to do something different. At first, I thought it was an arbitrary exercise, but very quickly, I began to realize how it helped or even opened new windows in my head. Does that make sense to you?"

"Yes, it's beginning to. Strangely enough, I remember something Dad did with Daniel and me when we were little. He would lay out big pieces of drawing paper and pour out a stack of pastel crayons, then he said for us to draw what he played. Daniel and I would draw furiously as he played the piano. It was obvious early on that Daniel was much more adaptive to the exercise. As I remember, he filled several sheets with flowing colors while I was still struggling with detail on one or two, but it was great fun."

"Daniel has told me a lot about when you two were growing up, but never about that. Sometimes when he's painting, he plays classical music, so maybe he's using the exercise still without realizing it. Timmy, this the first time we've ever really talked, not counting last Friday, about your directing. I've seen almost all your shows and they were all good. I haven't read *Blood Wedding*. Is it that hard or just a different sort of theatre?"

"It's both, and it's more passionate than anything I've ever attempted. My original concept would work, but now I'm not satisfied with it and I go into audition callbacks tomorrow night. Auditions are always dangerous. I've made several mistakes that I was so sure of before rehearsals. Most of the works on directing are pretty skimpy except to match your cast to the show and think about ensemble. Well, that's not very close to real life process. Most directors hear rehearsed auditions pieces with some possible ad-lib situations and make decisions from that, and mostly with people they've worked with before. However, a lot of new people are auditioning for this show, and I've been fooled in the past by auditions where the actor never goes beyond his rehearsed presentation. I can't take a chance like that now, but I'm going to reread Stanislavsky. I haven't done that in a long time."

"I haven't read him, but then I never studied theatre. I do remember my theatre friends saying he was the basis of modern drama. The Drama Club at Bryn Mawr was too bohemian for me. Their shows were fun, though, and quite often very Russian."

"There is all kinds of new stuff happening in New York, new groups and new political theatre. I don't think it would go over here in Dallas, but I sure would like to watch their rehearsals."

"Timmy, you don't have to stay in Dallas forever. There's theatre all over the country."

"I've got a pretty good situation here, my own place, a car, a supportive boss at the bookstore, and the theatre job. But yes, I do need to go to New York and take as many workshops as possible. I'll get there, perhaps next year for a few weeks."

"My offer still holds for you to stay at my apartment," Marilee reminded me.

"When are you and Daniel going up?"

"After our stay in Taos, but we're not sure yet. Daniel wants to have paintings ready. I think it's time for him to have a gallery show up there."

Daniel walked in, "Are you two plotting and using my name in vain? Tim, we don't see you for weeks and then three days in a row. Good company. I've just got the grill going with an extra steak out. You'll stay?"

"I'm right at the point of imposition, but yes, thank you."

"Timmy, you're doing no such thing," Marilee protested. "Besides, we haven't finished our talk. Time for cocktails, Sart men."

The steaks were excellent and the conversation spirited. No theatre talk for awhile, just the Festival and the dinner at Bustamente's. Marilee wanted to include Dick and Camila in future gatherings at her house, and I heartily agreed. Both Daniel and Marilee asked about Gwen and my feelings on her leaving. I said it had been a special surprise to spend time with her at all. Of course, I didn't want her to leave, but it couldn't have gone on with the intensity of the past three days…but it would have been nice to try to spread it out over several months.

"My coming rehearsal schedule is going to dominate my life in the coming weeks, plus there's the bookstore. Perhaps I'll have some time to study and prepare during the day. My boss is very supportive when I'm in rehearsal. I think I'll find a new way of approaching this piece. The frustrations I'd mentioned before are slowly turning into what I think is a new excitement. Marilee, our discussion is beginning to make new sense to me. May, I borrow that book Art Logic for a few days?"

"Timmy, it's yours."

"How's the design for the show coming?" asked Daniel.

"It's not, yet. I have a concept meeting with the designer before rehearsal tomorrow. We've only had a couple of very general talks. I like her…thanks for the recommendation."

"Well, I knew I couldn't do it, and she actually studied stage design. She called me last week saying she was excited about the show."

"That's good to hear. I hope she stays excited."

"Timmy, you're already a good director and have a great feeling for stage pictures; Daniel explained that to me after we saw your last production. I think this new challenge is going to be a terrific experience. I just wish I could help more."

"More? It's up to me now, Marilee. You have given me the confidence to change. Whichever direction I go is certainly going to be better than where I was headed," I assured her. "I genuinely fell in love with this play. Remember, Dick Ayers started this whole thing and you said the right thing at the right time: Go back to my imagination, not just rely on technique. The technique has to be there, I'm not worried about that. And I must get home and do some reading. Another great evening to end a whirlwind of a weekend"

"For us also, brother. I'll try to drop by rehearsal this week."

"Do you mind if I come some evening?" Marilee asked, "I'm getting excited about *Blood Wedding*. Watching it develop could be more fun than waiting for it to open." When I got home, I remembered a book I had about a Russian director named Vachtangov and some strange things he did with a production of Turandot. I ended up reading much more than about that production. His wild imagination evidently set him apart from the Moscow Arts Theatre where he started. I also went back and read the appendix of Stanislavsky's second book On the steps of production.

That evening I stayed up way too late reading, but it turned out to be worth it. Stanislavsky had always rejuvenated me, even if in the abstract, and the Vaktangov book gave me an idea for a set.

I arrived at the bookstore early and talked to my boss about doing some studying during the workday. He said it was fine as long as I stopped when customers came in. My desk was near the front of the store, so I could work on the play and see anyone who came in. Luckily for me, it was a quiet morning and I was able to read the play in a new light. I decided not to spend hours moving Jeordie's little lead soldiers around on a tentative ground plan looking for a blocking scheme, but to give the actors much more freedom in developing the movement for their characters. I would set up zones rather than strict blocking patterns and shape the piece as it developed in rehearsal.

After working with about five customers, I ate the lunch that my mother had prepared, a meat loaf sandwich and a Dr Pepper. Just as I was wrapping up, Marilee came in. She apologized for the interruption but she had some news. She had gotten a letter from friends in New York who were moving to Los Angeles. Their daughter had accepted Marilee's invitation to visit Dallas awhile before joining the family in L.A. The father was a petroleum design engineer who had worked on several projects for her company. The family was originally from France, where Marilee had met them, but had moved to London and then to New York. The daughter and Marilee had become close during her visits with them, and what had started out as business became a friendship. Marilee assured me I would enjoy meeting her.

"Timmy, I know this comes up right after Gwen's leaving and you're starting in rehearsal, but she is charming and sophisticated. Her name is Claire Levant. She's twenty-two, petite, and rather striking. She should be in later this week. I'll take a couple of days to show her around Dallas and get acclimated. No pressure, but please plan to come over next weekend," she urged. "I'll call you later this week."

"Marilee, of course. But of all the eligible men you know in Dallas, why me? Compared to a sophisticated girl from Europe, I'll be an uneducated innocent. Are you sure you don't want to introduce her to someone else?"

"Well...I told her there was someone special I wanted her to meet. And that's you, Timmy. Sophisticated does not mean pretentious in Claire's case. She is very down-to-earth and enjoys the arts. She studied art history and just finished her master's. I'm glad her family moved to the States. I had advised them to get out of Europe last year. Her father can work anywhere and will, I hope, eventually work for me because he's the very best in his field. Fifteen years ago, he got his engineering doctorate at

A&M, so he's no stranger to the U.S., but he's always worked internationally out of Paris. Very few men in the world can go into a difficult field and set up drilling rigs as well as he can. He solved some problems for Grant in Java that saved at least a year of set-up time for drilling. And don't have doubts like that about yourself! You are a special man and a fine artist," Marilee scolded me.

"Thanks, Marilee. How long is she going to be here?"

"As long as she wishes. No date is set for her going to L.A., so it really depends on her. She's very good company and welcome to stay as long as she likes. Daniel met her in New York and feels the same way."

"I feel like the chosen one, and that's alright, besides I surely need to meet someone new. Next weekend is fine for me. Just let me know."

"Great, Timmy. I'll call you here or at home." She hugged me and dashed off.

It was good to look forward to weekends again. After Gwen left, I had thought several times of the lonely days ahead, especially after the excitement we had shared. It was also good to be spending more time with Daniel and Marilee.

I went back to Vaktangov and his production of Turandot. He had actors come out in special costumes and change the set. They became a part of the production and he called them "Zanies." There were several different locations in the play and scene transitions were going to be difficult. Perhaps with Spanish music and Gypsy Zanies...?! I would see what my set designer had to say later today. Five weeks is long for rehearsals, but not for set design and building, especially with all-volunteer help. The designer was being paid but certainly not at professional rates. The Civic was really all there was here and as close to professional as anything in Texas, or even the Southwest. Nowhere in the country would I have had the opportunity to direct like I had here. But then, I had been at the theatre for ten years. I had started working backstage when I was fourteen and was directing children's plays at sixteen.

It turned out to be a busy afternoon at the bookstore, but I felt good about the preparation and study I had done in the morning.

At dinner, I found out that Jeordie had sold one of his sculptures at the Festival. Everyone had lots of questions about *Blood Wedding*. Both parents and Jeordie volunteered to help, Dad to build, and Mom to paint sets. I got to the theatre an hour and a half before the callbacks were to start. I asked my volunteer stage manager, Ginger, who had come in early also, to gather as many scripts of the play as possible. My ideas about trying new things included a new way for me to cast the show. Ginger seemed excited about the coming rehearsals and would take notes for me in my conference with the designer.

As Ginger left to get the scripts, the set and costume designer arrived I had known her for a year because she occasionally worked as a carpenter for my father at his shop. He had been doubtful about a female carpenter but had given her a chance on a couple of commissions and had liked her work. She had mentioned to me that she had studied theatre but hadn't said in what area. It was Daniel's suggestion to seek her out. We went to my little office in the back of the storage room. It held only a small desk and a couple of chairs, but it was nice to have it. Our main problem, I explained, were the many set needs of the play. I told her about my idea of the Vaktangov "Zanies." We brainstormed about the idea of flying the sets, but I remembered an idea I had this morning that wasn't quite complete yet. I asked if she could design a pop-up set that would be like a children's book. They could be on roller platforms that went into the wings as they became no longer a part of the play and a painted backdrop could end the play in the woods. The upper part of the backdrop would be sky and mountains with the forest below. The Zanies could move the platforms around in half-light with Spanish music playing and raise up the settings for the Bridegroom house, Leonardo's house, the Bride's house, and the church with bridal dance area. She and I agreed that the different sets should be not realistic but more suggestive or abstract with bright colors growing darker as the play got darker, with red undertones of light for the last scene. I wanted to stage the fight to the death, an offstage part of Lorca's concept.

"How about something like Javanese shadow puppets?" She said with the excitement of a new idea

I wasn't quite sure what that was, but after she described how they worked, the idea sounded interesting.

"With the actors being the puppets," she added, "Perhaps we could work it out with some sort of projection device, even a fresnel lamp mounted on the floor, and having their shadows appear on the scrim?"

"My word, that takes my original thoughts to a new level," I said in admiration of her brainstorming a possible solution.

She thought we had the time to figure it out, and then we talked some about costumes, which I wanted to be in the simple Spanish peasant style, but with a romantic flair. She immediately resolved that by showing me some drawings she done. Scarves, shawls, boots, and hats were her answer, and they looked terrific. Hopefully, I said, we weren't going way beyond our production possibilities.

"Tim, I love this play so much that I've been dreaming about it every night. It's passionate, happy, sad, mysterious, and almost shocking. I've moved back in with my parents so I can work full-time on it. Let's go all the way with it!"

"Good! I feel the same way about it. I'll talk to Barney again about the budget, and if we need more, I guess we can talk to some of the patrons. I've never done that before, but as you said, let's go all the way with it! She laughed and clapped her hands in delighted anticipation. We talked a few more minutes about schedules and deadlines. I told her that if possible I would like a definitive floor plan by the end of the week. We agreed to meet in the middle of the week, and she left.

Ginger came in and said the scripts were on stage at my table and that the actors were here and ready.

I walked into the theatre from backstage, which came off more dramatically than intended. The actors were sitting in theatre seats all over the room. I asked them to come up on stage and take chairs that were stacked off right backstage, then form a large crescent or semi-circle upstage. Ginger brought out two chairs and a small worktable for us. I got a stool from backstage that I liked to use when giving notes after rehearsals. I set myself up in the center of their crescent and began to describe the process I was planning to use for final casting and starting rehearsals.

"Since the last time we were together, I hope most of you have had the chance to come in and read the play if you hadn't read it before the first round of casting.

This started an enthusiastic discussion of the play. All of them had read most of the play, either here at the theatre or at the bookstore, where two copies had been set aside for actors and potential audience to study.

"That's a good start for any casting, much less the beginning of rehearsals. Obviously, I love the play and see directing it as an extremely challenging process, and that's why we have five weeks rather than the usual four weeks. Already you can see that things are different. Everything changes now. I'm not going to look at new audition pieces, we're going to do the play tonight with you moving in and out of the process, and we will walk through it. Now you know why I asked that anyone called back be willing to spend the whole evening here."

As Ginger handed out scripts, I took the time to look at the group. They were different from any group of actors I had called back before. I wanted a European-Spanish look for the cast. I knew several blond ingénues and dashing leading men who were disappointed by the call, but there was a new group of Mexican and Latin American actors who rarely felt there was a part for them here. I had put a special ad in both the Morning News and the Times Herald about the auditions for new actors for a new English translation of a famous Spanish play. The entire group had been impressive in the first auditions. From the original sixty or seventy, I had selected twenty-five, all strong-looking, from older characters, to characters, to younger-looking actresses, to the leading players for the Bride, the Groom, and Leonardo. I decided then and there that I wanted them all in the cast. They all had scripts and were looking at me intently, ready to start.

"I want all of you in the play. I wasn't sure of that until I saw you together. There are, as you know, three scenes that can have a large group of people on stage. I hope you are interested enough to consider that. There will be leads cast, of course, but I think we need to develop a real ensemble for this show that is a part of the play almost all the time in production. The cast will change the set as we progress through the show. The set will be very different from anything I've worked with before. A backstage crew could do it, but I think it would be much more exciting if the ensemble does it in costume as if we're creating a total vision of the community portraying a passionate and tragic folk tale they have actually lived through; not done as a pageant but as a collective dream that haunts them. At times, the play will be very loud, even raucous, and then soft with a constant musical underplay that will be almost cinematic. The set changing will be like a dance that will enhance the continuity. The costumes will be from rough peasant garb to a just short of elegant gypsy flamenco performing group. All the colors will progress through the show, lighting, set, and costumes… sun-bleached and washed out to bright with reds raging through its complete spectrum… deep blues with heavy grays and browns. I'm adding some special effects in the last scene…nothing too strange or elaborate, just some sort of projection from behind for the fight to the death scene between Armando and the husband. Of course, as you know this isn't a part of the written script, but I think it will add to the desperate passion of the ending."

Immediately everyone had questions.

"When will you do the final casting?" was the first asked almost simultaneously by three actors.

"After tonight's work. How do you all feel about including everyone in the ensemble…first, before you answer…yes, it does expand the play in a different way with a kind of epic quality that will make it more exciting. Remember, this is the first American production with no precedents. This will be like a laboratory-workshop from the first rehearsal on. Every time I read or study the piece, new ideas form in a way that seems to demand a new style of acting; almost presentational in some scenes, not quite what Brecht describes as epic, but something new for all of us."

Carolyn Carothers responded to the question about the large ensemble, "Yes, I want to do the play…just being involved sounds like something much more exciting than the usual production. Can you tell us more about your vision, which is terrific so far?"

No, not really. That will happen in rehearsal. I think the passion of the play is the guide. In the past week, my directing plans have changed drastically. There won't be any blocking rehearsals in the first couple of weeks or maybe not at all. I want to shape the play giving you more freedom to explore the characters working in zones rather than specific marks."

Carlos Allende, an older Hispanic actor who was new to the theatre and came in with a terrific audition asked, "That doesn't mean you're going to leave us confused about blocking up to the end, does it?"

"No, no…everything will be set well before the last couple of weeks, just more exploration in the beginning weeks. You're playing the characters and I want your imaginations not to be limited."

Liza Farquar stood up to ask a question. "Tim, I don't really understand. I'm used to learning my lines, that is if I have any, when I get my blocking. I'm not sure I can do this."

"Liza, I know it's unusual, but I hope you will go along with it. I truly believe this play needs a new approach. I guess it's just a matter of trusting me."

"Well, I certainly haven't regretted trusting you in the past, so I'll try…but I do have my doubts… not about you Tim, just about your approach."

"To try is all I can ask."

Two other actors who I had hoped would be solid members of the ensemble stood and said they weren't sure enough of my ideas and were leaving the cast. I hoped this wouldn't be the beginning of an exodus of more of the cast.

"Will ensemble actors without major parts have to attend all of the rehearsals?" was the next question by a young actor whom I had called back because he was also a dancer.

"In the beginning, yes, to get the overall feeling and sound, but the second week will concentrate on major characters and scenes. Is there anyone who wants to not be considered for a major role but as a member of the ensemble?"

Several of the actors starting laughing. "Carry on and let's see what happens," one of them said, and one of the really strong young actresses stood up and said, "I want to do this show, no matter how you cast it." Then, to my relief, the rest of those who had stayed stood and agreed to join the effort.

I thought that maybe I had sold the production, after all, with my spur-of-the-moment idea of the large ensemble.

"Well, let's start. I want to read the play all the way through moving people in and out. I have my ideas about the parts, but who would like to read for what parts?"

Ginger took notes as I chose the first group. Then we proceeded through the scenes. The older actors caught on rather quickly. The potential leads started experimenting from the beginning. I wanted the Wife and the Bride to both be beautiful, striking presences but different from each other. Both needed to be capable of extreme passion but in distinct manners. The husband needed a romantic gentleness and a self-assured quality that would make him attractive to the bride whatever her doubts…the promise of a good life and all that, but her overwhelming desire for Leonardo has to overrule her good intentions. Leonardo needed to be charismatic and dangerous. His betrayal of a good Wife is driven by his restless desire to possess the bride, no matter what the cost, which doesn't appear to frighten or deter him.

As the rehearsal progressed, I became excited and stopped frequently to shape a scene and go over it with different actors. The actors appeared to be as excited as I was, sitting on the edge of their chairs as they waited to step into the scenes. At times, I was almost frightened by the play's passion. Even in the innocence of this first broad staging, I felt an emotional surge from almost tears to an anger about what the characters were experiencing in their rage towards tragedy.

I staged the last two scenes several times as a self-inspiring action for new scenic ideas and casting. We had taken two short breaks, and I had never seen a group return from breaks so quickly, nor had I ever seen such active conversations at an audition. As I went to my stool, they scurried to their chairs ready to continue. After the fourth time on the final scene, I stopped and asked Ginger what time it was. It was almost midnight! We were all exhausted, but the past five hours had flown by.

"I will see you all here tomorrow and announce the cast and we'll discuss more concept and characterization. I am very excited, I hope you are," I closed.

A mature Mexican actor laughed and said, "Por seguro, jefe!"

They begin to leave, but all approached me with handshakes and hugs, or just back-pats and nods. I had never had a rehearsal end so emotionally. Ginger had taken over ten pages of notes about my directing and stagings. She assured me they would all be typed up several hours before tomorrow's rehearsal for my perusal.

When I finally got home, I went into the house and had a sandwich, glad none of the family was up. In my room, I sat in my soft chair after pouring a glass of the gifted Spanish brandy, knowing I was too wound up to sleep. After a few a moments, I realized I was shaking and crying. Finally, sleep came.

I woke up the next morning later than I should have, confused about the emotions I had experienced last night. I remembered my reactions to my first reading of the play. The theatrical passions in it had amazed me, and I wondered now if it would be too much for a Dallas audience. At this point, though, it didn't make any difference if it was a bit much for Dallas because it was part of the season. I had already dived into the challenge, and it was changing my entire approach to directing and commitment to a new way of thinking. Perhaps last night's tears had been a result of the fear and excitement I was feeling about *Blood Wedding*. I knew it hadn't been because of Gwen's departure, or at least that hadn't been a big part of it. I think my last days with her had prepared me for *Blood Wedding* as much as Marilee's inspiration.

I was at the bookstore by ten, which was late, but Mr. Franklin was more interested in how the auditions had gone. I explained that it became a rehearsal with everyone called back a part of the show.

"Tim, are those Russian books changing your style?" he probed.

"Yes, to some extent, but I think it's more the play, and wonderfully enough, conversations I've had with Marilee. I'm not sure if it's a catharsis yet, but it's sure something."

He laughed and said, "Maybe Daniel is experiencing something similar because his painting at the Festival certainly shows new approach. I liked it a lot. I've known Marilee for years, but I didn't know she was a muse."

"Yes, she could be. She sure spurred me towards some new ways of thinking. I was beginning to feel doubtful about the way I had directed in the past and wanted to head in new directions with *Blood Wedding*. She hasn't read the play so her comments weren't subject-specific, just kind of a way to get new ideas. It worked, and she has also given me some new books to read. There's no doubt she's a special lady. Daniel is a lucky man."

"You know I believe in your work, both at the theatre and here at the store. Tim, don't downplay the influence of your family. They're a special group of artists. Hey, I heard that Jeordie sold a piece of sculpture…that completes the circle. Maybe you should consider keeping a journal about your new ideas as the rehearsals progress."

"I may have already started," I said, remembering Ginger's notes last night and the pages I wrote before I had drifted off to sleep.

A customer came in, which ended our talk and started my workday. It was busy all morning and slow in the afternoon, which gave me the time to write at my desk. I started to write out a cast list that I thought became fairly obvious for the leads as the rehearsal had progressed, but the smaller roles were still in doubt. I decided not to rush that casting.

Chapter 5
El Audazito

My stage manager, Ginger, and I met an hour and a half early at the theatre. I first went to see Barney in his office to let him know what was happening with the auditions so far.

He said, "Spain is in the news every day; why not shake up Dallas with something this new? It's certainly not a political play. We haven't really lost money on any show this season, so why not take a chance. Tim, you convinced me several months ago that it's an important new play, and we will be the first U.S. production for a community theatre. I don't think a college show counts," he said referring to the production being mounted at Yale.

"Good, Barney. I didn't doubt your support, but I'm concerned that my ideas about the set and costumes may push the budget some. My designer will give me her shop estimates later this week. And I really do want to use live music during the show. Would it be possible to pay a guitarist a nominal fee for the run?"

"Perhaps, but only a small nominal," he cautioned. Any chance of getting a volunteer player?"

"Possibly, but the person recommended is very special and would have to sacrifice working on the weekends. You know I wouldn't ask if I didn't think it was an important element," I explained.

"Okay, Tim, but try for low nominal. I don't want to set any precedents that will upset the volunteer spirit here."

"Of course. I agree with you. Oh! By the way, my whole family has volunteered to help. And I'll be glad do to some fundraising if you need me to.

"The program will look like Sart family promotion. But that's good."

At that point, his phone rang so I waved myself out of his office and read Ginger's notes from last night while she posted the major's cast list. Her notes were excellent, more than a good record, but a basis or back-up for my journal. Ginger wasn't surprised about my casting, thinking also that the choices were rather obvious. Her notes gave me confidence about my idea of shaping the piece through rehearsal. I knew it wasn't a truly original idea, but inspired, perhaps, by the reading I had done in the past days, and especially by the book Marilee had given me about art logic. In the past shows I had directed, I had changed blocking several times when either actors or I had come up with a better idea on movement and or interpretation. Perhaps starting like this from the beginning would create better collaboration between the cast and me, even though I was sure it would be frustrating for them at times.

At the beginning of rehearsal I announced my decision on the leading roles which was accepted quickly as if they already knew from the work in the first evening. Everything went even better than the previous night's session. I started out with a discussion about the characters and the beginnings of interpretation and a bit more on show concept, which I told them would grow as the rehearsals progressed. Part of the concept was that I wanted to work in complete run-throughs of the play for the first couple of weeks so we could get a solid feeling of continuity; then go to act and scene work. This surprised the actors, but they seemed ready for almost anything.

The work-through went well, and a couple of the minor parts fell into place. I didn't force the four-and a-half-hour marathon of the night before, and we ended in applause for the night.

I didn't cry or shake when I got home, just had a sandwich and a little brandy, and then fell asleep rereading the play again.

The next morning at the bookstore, Eddie Flournoy, the guitarist I had talked to, came to see me. He was an American who had studied in Spain with the best Gypsy flamenco troupes. He had even done some bullfighting. He left Spain when the civil war started, returned to Dallas, and was now teaching at SMU. Being a great fan of Lorca's work, he was interested in being a part of the first U.S. production. I liked him from the moment we met.

My concept of a constant underscoring of music excited him. He had heard of *Blood Wedding*, but had not seen it in Madrid. To my delight, he said he would like to do the show, and asked if he could be a part of rehearsals to get a feeling for the production and the way I worked. I explained that I was trying a new approach in my directing style so things would be different from the usual rehearsal process. He said he had never worked in the theatre before, so he wouldn't know the difference. We talked for about an hour, and I gave him a tentative rehearsal schedule and two scripts, both English and Spanish. His last words were for us not to even talk about money and he would arrange his schedule so he could be available for rehearsals and the production dates. We shook hands and he was gone.

I couldn't wait to call Barney at the theatre to tell him the good news. Not having to pay even a nominal fee for the guitarist would give us a pinch more in the budget. I called Ginger to tell her about this new layer that had been added to the concept. I had told her before that getting live music was a longshot, so we both felt this was a real coup.

Marilee had asked me to let her know how the auditions went, so I called her, too. She and Daniel were having a late breakfast, or an early lunch.

She laughed at my excitement, "Timmy, that's great. Now I really want to sneak into your rehearsals…Oh! The friend I mentioned has arrived, so don't forget about this weekend."

"I'll be there, Marilee. By the end of the week, I'll be so stirred up by *Blood Wedding* that I'll have to try not to be a 'theatre babble' bore."

"I don't think that's possible, Timmy. I'll tell Daniel about the guitarist. This weekend or 'sooner" she signed off.

That night, in reaction to the night before, I started the practice of notes before rehearsal. Eddie Flournoy joined us, and I explained to the cast his part in the show.

He introduced himself individually to the cast, speaking Spanish to some. He planned to watch and listen primarily, but occasionally would play softly if I gave the okay.

The actors were now wearing rehearsal clothes; the women in long skirts, the men in boots and hats. There was a surprising amount of line work for such an early phase, which was a good omen for commitment. I told them not to get too set with line readings, but to keep trying new things all the time unless I put a momentary set on a scene. Putting a play up on its feet this soon was confusing at first, but I started working with them pointing out zones and stepping back to see the stage picture. I had never been up on stage with the actors all the time before; usually, I was out in the house giving directions and critique, a directorial voice out of the darkness. But there was nothing passive about this production, and I liked it.

About three quarters through the first two acts, I noticed that two women were sitting close to the back of the house watching. This wasn't unusual, because I didn't generally close rehearsals until the last two weeks. Then I realized it was Marilee and, I assumed, her visitor, Claire Levant. I waved, signaling we would be having a break soon.

We finished the second act and Ginger called the break. I walked back to greet Marilee and Claire. In the half dark, all I could tell about Claire as we shook hands was that she had very pale skin, long, almost curly, reddish hair, spoke softly in a charming accent, was petite, and was beautiful. I could tell nothing about her figure except that she wasn't thin.

They had been there long enough to hear Eddie play during a scene we had run through for the third time. Marilee loved it. Claire agreed, nodding. I went back onstage to talk to Ginger, almost ready to start again and work a bit before with Eddie and several actors. I turned as the actors gathered and saw that our viewers had left.

The rehearsals progressed slowly. I had never worked so hard. Each evening late and part of the afternoons, I spent studying the play, reviewing Ginger's notes, and writing my journal. The journal turned out to be much more valuable than I had expected. It seemed to stimulate new ideas about possible blocking, scene transitions, and character interpretations. Some of the actors were more used to learning lines as they were blocked, so this freer way of working was a new challenge for them. It was a collaboration they hadn't expected, but they found themselves with the freedom to use their own imaginations, and found they liked it. Some actors could not quite adapt all the way, so I gave them more specific direction. It was turning into a good collaborative balance. I sometimes felt as if I were a cast member rather than the director, because I spent almost all of my time with them on stage shaping and giving individual directions. Sometimes I would walk beside them guiding to new positions. Other times, I directed movement and interpretation speaking softly beside them as they moved, telling them not to stop but to act as if I was in their heads giving ideas. At moments where the lines needed more truth or character contact, I stopped everything and had the actors face off and speak the lines to each other. Though all of this was disorienting at first, it felt like it was working.

On Friday, I met with the designer and approved the floor plans, the set rendering, and costume sketches. They were better than I had hoped for. She had taken my concept and gone even further and, in the process, better. She promised to spike the stage and finish the elevations over the weekend. I met with Ginger for an hour to plan the evening's work and headed into a rough run-through with the cast. Eddy improvised and played through every scene except the marriage celebration. Most of the cast held scripts, but some were off book on the shorter scenes. It was beginning to look like a play, but I knew the hardest work still lay ahead. My notes and critique were fairly short, and I told them we would work on the first half Monday and Tuesday, the second Thursday and Friday, and the choreographer would work on the wedding party Wednesday, when we would also try to set the staging for it.

The old Hispanic character hugged me and said, "Gracias, El Audazito."

It was a Spanish word I didn't know, but I took it as a compliment. Ginger brought me a note from Marilee asking me to come by for drinks if it wasn't much later than 10:30. She, Daniel, and Claire would be sitting around the pool. It was 10:15.

Chapter 6
La Aparicion

I pulled up to their house at 10:25. I wished that I had had time to go home, shower, and change clothes; but I was in fairly good shape. I went through the unlocked front door and walked through the house to the back. Daniel, Marilee, and Claire were sitting around a table almost in complete darkness. I greeted them and Marilee brought me a glass of brandy.

"Ginger said you were almost finished so I hoped you would be here. I'll light some candles."

Daniel and I shook hands and hugged, and I turned to Claire Levant. Marilee had lighted about ten candles very quickly. As each one added one more light, Claire became more visible. As she stood to greet me, I was speechless, only able to stammer "Hi...!"

She gave me a sideways European handshake and said, "Hallo, Ti-mo-thy," making three distinct syllables of my name in the most beautiful accent. All I could offer in return was a silly grin. I had never seen anyone like her. She seemed to glow in the candlelight. Her hair was a true auburn, long and curly. Her skin was also auburn shaded and so light that I thought a touch would bruise her. Her face reminded me of my Dad's favorite movie star, Louise Brooks, but Claire was more pixyish with her shy smile. She was tiny but full-figured. She was a true apparition like a cherubic fairy.

When I was finally coherent, we spent the evening discussing *Blood Wedding* and Claire's trip to Dallas by train. Marilee brought out some snacks, which I attacked with an embarrassing hunger. Claire laughed at my trying to eat and talk at the same time. Her laugh was almost as uninhibited as Marilee's. She seemed interested in my new approach to my directing style, and I told her of Marilee's contribution to my new way of thinking.

Both of them had studied art history and had read some of the same books. She knew Art Logic well and said it had been an important influence on her writings at school. Claire loved Daniel's paintings and wanted to see the new one at the Fine Arts Museum. I quickly volunteered to take her. As midnight approached, I began to fade but wanted to talk with her all night. Daniel and Marilee watched us with an amused attitude, pulling back to listen to Claire and I talking and laughing. I gave in at 12:30 and rose to leave. Mr. Franklin had given me weekends off during rehearsal, so I invited Claire to the museum tomorrow afternoon. She literally clapped her hands in delight as she accepted. Marilee suggested we make it a foursome, and Claire shyly said that would be wonderful. Daniel even agreed, quickly saying he would like to get out of the studio for a couple of days. Marilee told me to be here around noon for a light lunch and reminded me about tomorrow evening's dinner and swimming.

Dick Ayers and Camila were joining us. Before I left, I asked Claire what "audazito" meant.

"It means little brave one," she said. "Why?"

"One of my cast members called me that"

"Oh, my word!" she laughed softly.

That night, in a night of filmy visions, I dreamed of her face and laughter. Claire became a part of my dreams of *Blood Wedding*, not as a character but just there, perhaps watching me. I woke up and slowly tried to reach back into my dreams for something to hang on to, but I couldn't.

I ate breakfast quickly but had time to tell Mom and Dad about the week of rehearsals and the evening at Daniel and Marilee's. They were surprised about my new enthusiasm for the play. They both said they had never seen me this excited and committed. I said that I was also scared, hoping *Blood* Wedding didn't turn out to be more of a challenge than I had bargained for.

They both laughed, and Dad said, "Well, now you're into it. Every project that's worthwhile is frightening. I almost didn't send my new chair to the contest in New York last month. Don't start having doubts about your play. Maybe your talent for directing has made all of your other productions too easy."

Thinking back, I didn't think any of them were easy, but they were nothing like this production. I had done all of them like the directing texts said to, and now I was stepping into a whole new realm of process with no real precedents, just tidbits of ideas and examples, almost all in the abstract. Mom hugged me and went into her studio room, and Dad headed off to his Deep Ellum shop.

I had close to three and a half hours before I was due at Marilee's, and I needed to work. All of the actors knew I wanted them to sing or chant several parts of the play where the writing was in expansive poetry, lullabies, and descriptive lyrical passages. One of the hardest, I thought, would be the awakening of the Bride. It includes individual actors and small choruses, some of them off stage. Most of the actors said it wouldn't be a problem for them, and Eddy said he could help with it. He was proving to be a valuable collaborator, not interpreting the text, just as a part of the artistic process. He watched and listened carefully, especially to my notes. He said he trusted the concept and knew it would develop and change as rehearsal progressed.

I spent a full hour on my journal, and began to write out Monday's opening notes and critique.

I tried to dress as sharply as I could without overdoing it. It had never seemed that important before, but there was no doubt why. I had no visions of anything special happening with Claire, but I had never met anyone like her. Her sophistication and worldliness was intimidating, but that didn't seem to come from her, just me.

Chapter 7
El Museo y Despues

I drove up to Daniel and Marilee's door and went in for the light lunch Marilee had prepared. Daniel, already sitting at the table, gestured for me to join him.

Marilee came in with a pitcher of iced tea. "Welcome, Timmy, have a seat. Claire's on her way down."

"I am here," Claire said as she entered the dining room. She took both of my hands and again said, "Hallo, Ti-mo-thee!"

I laughed, charmed by her greeting, and said, "Hi, Miss Claire." She was so beautiful in the daylight I was shocked. I realized I was staring at her unable to say anything more. She smiled and turned to sit.

The sandwiches were excellent, a selection of Salmon and Lamb, plus a sweet Greek salad.

After we finished eating Marilee pulled the new Packard around front and put the top down. Claire and I jumped into the back seat, Daniel got behind the wheel as Marilee moved over beside him, and we were off.

On the way, Daniel drove up Swiss Avenue to show Claire the beautiful houses. Marilee told Claire this was just one of the parts of Dallas with magnificent homes, and that Lakewood was nice, as was Kessler Park in Oak Cliff across the river.

"I pictured Dallas having just one enclave of big homes, like where you live, Marilee. This is certainly more than I expected. I hope I have enough time to see everything. Perhaps I was too much influenced by visions of the wild West."

Daniel laughed saying, "The wild west really begins at the next town to the West, Fort Worth."

Daniel circled around back to Haskell Avenue and on to Fair Park.

I told Claire a little the history of the fairgrounds. I described the big Centennial Exposition two years ago and how Mother and Daniel had helped paint the murals, Dad had designed the furniture for the Art Museum and the Hall of State, and about the show I had done in a tent behind the Hall Of State. Daniel drove all around Fair Park to show Claire what it looked like. She liked the Hall of State best, especially the Indian statue. She asked if there were any Indians around Dallas.

"I don't know of any, but Marilee says there are a lot in Oklahoma."

"My company has offices in Tulsa and Bartlesville, and both are close to reservations. It would be fun to drive up there some time, or even take the train. There are parts of Oklahoma that are beautiful, and the Ozarks of Arkansas are close."

Claire quickly asked, "What are Ozarks?"

Marilee laughed, "That is a kind of funny word. They're mountains, not quite like the Alps or even the Rockies, but they are beautiful."

Claire loved the murals on the Centennial Building. We pulled around to the lagoon in front of the Fine Arts Museum. We passed through the ornate doors through the foyer and into the large room. I had always loved the heavy wooden beams and high ceiling. Around a center area was the furniture Dad had designed. Daniel's painting of "Flood Zone" from the Arts Fair purchase, and prize was hanging. Our Mother's painting that had won the Texas Annual last year was right beside it.

"It seems as if they're honoring the Sart family." Marilee said with pride.

"Well, Dad's furniture is always here, but I didn't expect to be up front like this and have Mom's right beside it," said Daniel. "This is great. Eh? Tim?"

"Yes, I love it. I like the "Flood Zone" even better than before."

Claire seemed somewhat taken aback back by Daniel's piece, "Oh, My. This is something special. It is wonderful, Daniel. I don't think I've seen anything like it."

Marilee was thrilled by her reaction, "Now you understand why I'm trying to get him to exhibit in New York."

"I do, Marilee. Do you want to Daniel?"

"Well, of course, but I don't have enough paintings ready yet."

"The way you're going, you will soon, Dear heart."

"Perhaps, I hope so."

"We're going up there later this year, to talk to galleries."

"I'm trying very hard to talk Marilee into not giving up the oil business and becoming my agent," Daniel kidded.

"No problem about that, Daniel, I just believe in you so much."

"Igualmente, sweetheart." They kissed and hugged in front of his painting. Claire and I laughed and smiled at their obvious love for each other, and looked around to see the other museum visitors watching and smiling, too. A couple came over to Daniel, saying how much they admired his work.

Claire turned to look at Mom's painting saying it was lovely, "You must be very proud of your family, Ti-mo-thee."

"Yes, very much so. It makes what I do seem rather trivial."

"Oh, No, Ti-mo-thee! Theatre is one of the grandest arts because it is so ephemeral. I know it must feel like there is nothing lasting about it, but I remember many plays that have moved me deeply and I can always bring back the emotions I felt. Marilee tells me you are a fine theatre artist, so you must not think it is not as important."

The director of the museum, Jerry, joined us, having heard we were there. He hugged Marilee and shook hands with Daniel saying how much he liked "Flood Zone." Marilee was on the museum board, so her presence was always welcome. Her family had been major contributors for years. He turned to me, to shake hands and mentioned how anxious he was to see *Blood Wedding*. I had no idea word about the play had gotten around that much, but he couldn't have said anything nicer, especially after the exchange Claire and I had just had. I introduced him to Claire, and he actually spoke French with her. Jerry was a well-know Texas painter, as well a museum director, and had studied in Paris in the early thirties. He had been a close family friend for as long as I could remember.

Claire and I walked around the other exhibition rooms. Even though I had grown up in the museum, there was always something from the permanent collection I hadn't seen in awhile, along with new acquisitions. Claire loved the extensive collection of Texas Regional Art. She had studied art history, but had never seen a real collection of Southwestern art. After a good two hours, we met Marilee and Daniel at the museum store. Claire bought several books about Texas artists, and Marilee gifted her with a special hard cover book about the museum's history and the collection. We drove back, taking short tour of downtown. Marilee had already taken Claire to Neiman-Marcus, but they hadn't driven around. Marilee suggested I take Claire to the Palace for a film and to hear the organist while she was here, to which agreed

Claire smiled and asked, "Can we see a Cowboy movie, Ti-mo-thee?"

I wondered what Marilee was up to. What ever it was I liked it. Maybe she must know something I didn't know...yet, I thought.

Daniel decided to include a drive around White Rock Lake in Claire's tour. Claire seemed fascinated with everything, which I thought funny since she had lived almost all of her life in Europe. I asked her how Dallas could possibly compare to all she had seen.

"It doesn't compare in any way, or I don't compare it. It's all so new to me and so different. Europe is an old world; this Texas is like being on a different planet, a very sweet one. I like it. It's so spread out. On my train trip here, there was what seemed like unlimited space for hours. In France or England there is nothing like the openness I've seen traveling across America."

Marilee joined in, "Just wait until your go across the west to California. It takes almost a whole day just to get out of Texas with two more big states before California. I think Dallas, Houston, and San Antonio have more people than all of New Mexico and Arizona."

"Oh my, the movies and books didn't really prepare me. I like it very much. Ti-mo-thee, have you traveled much in America?"

"No, just in Texas. I've been to the woods in East Texas and out West with my mother when she studied with Peter Hurd. We took a family trip to San Antonio several years ago. We did go down to Galveston for a week on the beach, which was great. Traveling by car in Texas is a serious business. I don't mean old wagon train stuff, but lots of hours in a car. Of course, I want to see Europe, especially London and Paris. And being in the theatre means I've got to make it to New York someday soon."

"Timmy, my offer always stands, about you using my apartment in New York," Marilee reminded me.

"He is going, even if I have to drag him there. Right brother?"

Claire was surprised at what Daniel had said, "To drag you there?"

Marilee laughed out loud, "Explain that, Timmy," She challenged me.

" He just means that one day he will come to me and say, 'we're going to New York," and I will say that I can't, and he will say, 'No excuses this time,' and we will go to New York." I mimed being pulled by the arm.

Claire thought that was one of the funniest things she had ever heard. I thought she was going to start bouncing she laughed so hard.

Daniel turned off of Gaston Road onto Lakewood Drive to show Claire one of the most beautiful parts of Dallas. Then to Lawther Drive around White Rock Lake. I pointed out the Bath House and swimming area as the closest thing to a beach in Dallas. She thought the lake was wonderful and I hoped we would be back to it alone. We drove back on Mockingbird Lane by S.M.U though University Park to the secluded villa on the creek.

We got there about 4:30 and Marilee suggested I stay and have a swim. The Ayers were not due until around 7:30. I thought this a fine idea, and perhaps I could do some work. Claire said she was going to take a short nap and join me later. Daniel also opted for a nap. I had never been able to take naps, but Daniel could doze off anywhere. He said it was a 'gift.' Marilee attacked the kitchen to set up for the coming evening so she would be free later for a swim while Daniel got the grill going before the guests arrived.

I went out to my car and got my satchel filled with play notes, journal, and two books, Stanislavski's and Marilee's Art Logic. *Blood Wedding* had gotten me in the habit of taking my satchel everywhere. I grabbed at every opportunity to prepare. I now kept my bathing trunks at the cabana. The water was cool but not cold and very refreshing. I swam back and forth in the pool then just floated and thought about the day and evening before.

 I had never before so quickly had feelings about a woman, I didn't know what the feelings really were, but I sensed, and hoped, they were mutual. Perhaps Claire was this way with every man she had just met and kind of liked. Well, who knows? But whatever it was, it was nice. I knew she wouldn't be here very long and I only had the weekends, so some possibly very pleasant hours spent with a beautiful, smart, funny, and sophisticated lady is just what I needed, a good respite from the pressures of the play and my job at the bookstore. I got out of the pool and shook like a dog to dry off. I took a quick shower in the pool-house, dressed, and laid out on one the lounge chairs. I started reading but I dozed off, only to be awakened and hour and a half later by Claire standing beside me.

"Hi, there, special lady."

"Hallo, Ti-mo-thee."

"How long have you been out here?"

"For just a few moments, I was watching you sleep. You were so peaceful. Do you feel rested?"

"I didn't even know I was tired. I never take naps in the afternoon. It has been a good day. And how about you?"

"I feel fine, my little sleep was the right thing to do, and yes the day was special. Did you get any work done? I picked up your book. It had fallen beside you."

"No, not really, maybe half a chapter."

She pulled a chair over beside me. Her dress was filmy and loose-flowing showing more of her figure. There was a softness about her that I had not seen before. Her waist was small, and her ankles and calves were pretty and shapely. Yet she was full-figured in a hidden manner, almost as a protection, as if that part of her would remain a mystery.

"I must be careful in the sun because my skin is so pale."

Pale was not quite the right word, I think luminescent is a better description. There must be few women in the world like her, I had seen pictures of girls in Ireland but with hair that was red rather than Claire's beautiful auburn.

"I know of Stanislavski, but I have not read him. He founded the Moscow Arts Theatre, true?"

"Yes, and his writings are a constant source for me. This is his last book, different from the first two, more a primer of experiences."

"Oh. You're so serious about the theatre, I mean in your preparation. Painters don't usually read about art when they're out of the studio. Is it the literature that is a part of it, I know that sounds like an innocent question, but I've never really known a theatre artist before, I mean not to talk with about their work, especially a director."

"I thought I was serious before, but this play and the whole production are more difficult than all of my previous shows. They've all been important, to me at least, and they did fairly well at the box office, but this is something completely new. It's not quite a world premiere, but one of the first in English. My friend, Dick Ayers, who's coming tonight, is one who told me about the play. He saw it in Spain, loved it, and thought of me. He sent me a copy in Spanish, which I struggled through. My boss at my job got the new translation for me, strangely enough from South America."

"Did you like it from the first time you read it in English? Was it different from your Spanish reading?"

"I liked it in Spanish, but I certainly couldn't have translated it and didn't have the rights, or permission to do it anyway. It was a lucky break the translation became available. It's still a problem with the war going on there. I think my boss had as much fun finding the play as I did when I started trying to convince the manager of the theatre to let me do it. The passion of it scared him at first, but the poetry won him over."

"Yes, Lorca is a wonderful and passionate writer. I only really know his poetry well, but I did see a reading of a drama in Paris, in French, of course. I wish I could see your play. Experiencing a writer I like in three languages will be fun."

"Will you be here that long? You said, 'will be fun'."

"Did I? When will you start performances?"

"In five weeks."

"Oh my. I don't think I will be here that much time. My parents will be expecting me in Los Angeles."

"That's disappointing; I would have really liked you to be able to see it. Hmm...Would you want to come to rehearsals? It would be a rough vision of the play; as a matter of fact, I would be glad to have you watch it happen."

"Yes, I would like that. Perhaps I could stay a bit longer, two weeks or so more. Do you think Marilee will mind? I don't want to impose on her. I don't want to do anything that would harm our friendship."

"I guarantee she wouldn't mind. I think she's thrilled you're here. I've invited her many times to my rehearsals, and she's come. She says the process is as exciting as the product."

"I'll tell her then."

"Good, then come any time. Claire, tell me more about you. Marilee has told me only that you're from France but have lived in England for the last year or so and have studied in both countries, Art history, right?"

"Yes, not to teach, but to work in a museum. Well, I think you know my father is a petroleum engineer, and has worked for Marilee's company in Java. He thought we needed to leave France for all kinds of reasons, and he had good opportunities in Great Britain. This last year she talked him into moving us to America. I had finished my studies at the University of London and even had a chance to work at the Victoria and Albert museum, but my father insisted that I come here with the family. I have a younger brother, Jean Paul, who is fourteen. He's quite a character who's decided he wants to be in Hollywood movies."

"My younger brother, Jeordie, is also fourteen and a character of the first order. I think he's also cursed with this artistic thing. He sold a piece of sculpture at the arts fair last week."

"Ti-mo-thee, I'm sure it's a blessing, not a curse."

"I hope you're right. What else did you study?"

"French literature was, of course, required and I also majored in languages. That is what you say here isn't it? To major in a subject."

"Yes."

"Spanish because we quite often vacationed in Spain and England. I didn't know that I would eventually live in England and now America, so it was an especially good decision. English because I wanted to read novels and plays in English, I love the literature especially Shakespeare, Kipling, and the romantics. I've been reading modern novels lately. I like Somerset Maugham most of all."

"That's great. He's my favorite. I'm just finishing Cakes and Ale. I wish his short stories and novellas would go on forever. Have you read Rain?"

She replied by laughing and clapping then said, "I read it twice. Did you see the film with Joan Crawford?"

"About three times. I thought it was terrific. Since you know Spain, have you read Hemingway's The Sun Also Rises?"

"I read it first in French, but liked it so much better in English. I thought Lady Brett was an even sadder character than Sadie Thompson was. Oh! My family and I went to the Festival de San Firmin in Pamplona, though it was long before I read the novel, and I was too young to really appreciate it. My brother and I watched the nighttime festivities from our hotel window while our parents enjoyed the evening parties. The daytime was fun. My father wanted to run with the bulls, but my mother put a stop to that. Jean Paul and I did get to wear white shirts, red neckerchiefs, and berets. I still have that beret.

"It sounds like a great adventure. How long were you there?"

"Four days I think. There was so much celebration going on at night that I do remember we almost never got to sleep until morning when things settled down."

"A beret, I always have wanted to wear one, but in Dallas it would just be strange."

"Oh, Ti-mo-thee, you would look great in a beret."

"Thanks, but I think I'll wait until I have more of an arts status."

"Well, perhaps you need a beret just in case that status happens suddenly."

"Maybe I could go the beret store...finding a beret in Dallas would be as big of a challenge as directing *Blood Wedding*. That's funny we have so many reading habits in common, well, not funny but a pleasant surprise. I wonder if..."

"For some reason, I don't know what, I'm not surprised. I don't think we will have any trouble finding something to talk about."

"Neither do I."

"What do you wonder?"

"If there's more..."

"Me too."

"My friends will be arriving shortly. Would you like to walk down to the creek before they get here?"

"Yes, that would be nice."

As I stood up, she took my hand and turned to walk with me. It was a sweet surprise.

"Ti-mo-thee, please don't think I'm being forward. It just seemed natural to hold your hand."

"No, Claire, I probably would have reached for your hand if you hadn't taken the lead. Yes, it does seem natural."

"I've not met many people with whom I immediately felt a special kinship, especially not young men. Most men look at me and make a face that looks like they're thinking, 'what a strange girl.'"

"They sound like strange men to me. You're certainly not strange in any way."

"No, you didn't look at me like that. And thank you. At first, today, I thought you were very shy, and then when we started talking, well, I didn't think that any more. When I met you that first night at the theatre, you looked very romantic. The handsome young director walking down from the stage in the dark. I think I remember a word from Jane Austin's, or someone's books, I was "smitten" by you. Is that a good word?"

"Yes, it is. Thank you, for putting words in my mouth."

"You are welcome, Ti-mo-thee. I was a little embarrassed to say it fearing you would think me silly and laugh at me. I'm glad I was brave enough to say it."

"So am I, Claire. I was having trouble trying to describe my feelings about you, but yes, I'm "smitten" by you."

I suggested we try the rowboat. Claire liked the idea, not showing any fear at the prospect. I rowed us down stream about 25 yards. As a little boy I would wander the shores of the creek hunting frogs with a group of friends, but I had seen this area only once before from a boat. This is one of the most beautiful places in Dallas. The houses backed up on the creek like nowhere else. Willows and old Oaks hung out over the water even though it's fairly wide here. All of the houses are secluded and separated by trees and stonewalls. Several are classic old south looking, but most are very European. Marilee's is almost hidden by trees, but looks like a romantic vision of Italy.

"This is a lovely place, Ti-mo-thee. It doesn't look like what I thought Texas would be. It's almost like a secret place."

"To most of Dallas it is a secret."

We didn't talk anymore but looked at each other smiling. I stopped and relaxed for a few seconds then in an unconscious impulse leaned forward and kissed her. She gently kissed me back and I pulled away. She made a little sound, taking a big breath."

"Ti-mo-thee, what is...?"

She didn't finish but just slightly leaned towards me and I kissed her again, longer this time as she responded. Just then we heard Marilee calling us from the dock and we realized she had seen us kissing. As we arrived at the dock, Marilee was standing with her hands on her hips, "Well, that was quite a sight. I think you must thank me immediately for introducing you two."

Claire climbed up on the dock, hugged Marilee, and said, "Yes, thank you, dear Marilee. We are 'smitten.'"

Marilee laughed and put her arm around me, kissing my cheek. I smiled, not quite embarrassed, more shyly happy.

"The guests have arrived 'smitten' ones."

We walked up to the patio with Marilee's arms around both of us.

"I told you she was a special lady, didn't I Timmy? I really had a feeling you two would like each other. But I thought it would take a couple days to happen."

"Some things are just a mystery, Marilee. Right, Claire?"

"Yes, Mr. Ti-mo-thee Sart, I'm happy it's not a scary mystery, well, it isn't yet."

We all laughed at that.

Everyone had gathered close to the pool. Daniel was preparing the barbeque grill, and Dick and Camila were watching him trying to get it lighted. They turned as we walked onto the patio. Dick hugged me, and Camila kissed my cheek. I introduced them to Claire. Camila and Claire immediately started speaking Spanish to each other. Dick joined them and tried his French, which turned out to be very fluent. Dick turned to me and said forgive their delving into their European selves. Marilee said it was good to hear something beside English.

"The Spanish will get Timmy in the right frame of mind for his Lorca experience. Dick, Camila, let me show you Daniels studio."

Dick said, "After seeing 'Flood Zone' I definitely want to see more. Do you mind, Dan?"

"No, not at all. It's a mess with my recent work scattered around the room. I'd like to know what you think of it."

As Marilee took them to the studio, Daniel offered us drinks.

"Tim, there's a pitcher of Martinis and beer iced down. Claire, what would you like?"

"I love Martinis, or more like Martini. I don't think I've ever had more than one."

Well, you're among friends. It will be our secret if you have two. Tim, I know you want some Spanish brandy, but that's later."

"Yes, it may have been a mistake to introduce me to that, but a Martini sounds great. Do you need something, Dan?"

"No, actually, I'm having Bourbon. Which you can have if you please."

"No, thank you."

I poured drinks for Claire and me. Claire had her's over ice.

"What are we having from the grill tonight, brother?"

"I'm trying something new tonight, lamb ribs. Marilee found them at Simon David, also some chicken and some very good Italian sausage."

"Lamb is my favorite, but I've never had the ribs," said Claire.

"They're a bit greasy, but they should be great. Tim, did you get any work done this afternoon, during nap time?"

"Well, brother, a surprise, I fell asleep."

"That is a rarity. Claire, he's never been able to take naps, even when we were kids. This play is changing you, maybe for the better."

"It's certainly changing me, I hope for the better. Perhaps it's just tiring me more. Too much thinking, I even dream about it."

"You need the weekends then. I needed to get out of the studio, too. I started a new big canvas this week and I think I dreamed about it, not sure though. Perhaps it was Marilee dancing in my head."

"Ah! Sweet dreams."

"Indeed, awake and in my dreams."

Claire laughed at our brother talk and said, "It sounds like love to me. I woke Ti-mo-thee up when I came down and I'm glad I did. We went for a boat ride."

"Is that why Marilee was calling out for you? I thought you might have been hiding."

"Claire didn't really wake me up, she was just there, and I awoke. I almost wish we had been hiding, but the boat ride was great."

"Its so beautiful here, Daniel. Seeing the house from the water gives a different view of how secluded it is, and this is in the middle of the city. Isn't it?"

"Well almost. Sometimes I feel like my studio is out in a secret place in the country."

"My word! These Martinis are great. Did Marilee find a new recipe?" I asked.

"I think she did, but it's her secret."

"Yes, I like it more than any I've had before," chimed in Claire.

Dick, Camila, and Marilee returned from the studio. Dick said, "Daniel, your new work is terrific. It looks like its time for an exhibition."

"Can we buy one? I like them all." asked Camila.

"You're right about the exhibition. We're going to New York soon to find him a gallery." Responded Marilee.

"Even better still, why don't you choose one and consider it a wedding gift?" said Daniel.

"Thank you, Dan. That's more special than you can imagine. Camila, it's your choice."

"Oh, Daniel, we certainly didn't expect that. How wonderful! I already know which one I want. The scene of the snow and farm. Is that in the western part of Texas?"

"Great choice. He did it earlier this year in near west Texas," said Marilee," He went off by himself and came back with several great pieces. I wanted to go, but business kept me here. I sometimes can sit for hours and watch him work, I think it distracts him but he won't say."

"No, sweetheart, you are in no way a distraction but an inspiration. To change the subject away from 'my art', Dick, how are you doing? Is the cane a permanent thing?"

"I don't think so, thanks to Camila's father. If it had been an actual battlefield injury, I could have lost the leg, but being just outside of Madrid made the difference. They got me to the hospital quickly and her father is a masterful surgeon. The muscles were torn up and I lost a little bit of bone, but my new doctor here says it looks like everything's going to grow back together and perhaps in a year, no cane. Not even much pain anymore, just a couple of aspirin occasionally. And, of course, you know I had the best nurse in the world."

"And I had the best patient," laughed Camila.

I asked, "How is it going now over there? Have you heard from you parents, Camila?"

"I think it's very bad. My father won't say much except that it's worse in the hospital. I want them to leave Spain, but I don't know if they will. I hope my mother will be the determining factor. Daniel says a surgeon of his skills will have no trouble working here. My father is republican and a patriot, so...well."

"I love Spain." Claire said, "For a while we even had a house on the southern coast. I hate the idea of a civil war there."

"And how about you, Claire? Do you miss France?" asked Camila. "Marilee said you had been living in England for a couple of years."

"I don't expect I'll see France for some time. I liked living and studying in Britain, but I like you, Camila, I am a new American. I have resident papers and plan eventually to work here, I don't know where yet. I guess it depends on where my parents live."

"I hope it's going to be here. I'm still trying to get your father to consider Dallas," said Marilee.

"Well, I think it would be alright with me. I like Dallas so far.

What are you going to do, Camila? You were a nurse?"

"I hope to go back to medical school. I finished my third year in London, but I went back to help in Spain."

"Where were you studying there? I finished my studies at the University of London."

"I studied there, too. I hope I can finish my degree; it depends where Dick goes to law school. Dios mio, meeting a schoolmate in Dallas. If you're here long enough let's have lunch together. There were so many things I liked about London, especially the museums and parks."

"Oh, Camila, I would like that very much. I don't know how long I'll be staying. I don't want to wear out my welcome at Daniel and Marilee's. I hope to see some of Ti-mo-thee's rehearsals."

Marilee responded quickly, "Claire, don't be silly, you can move in here if you like. I told you that in New York last winter. Timmy's rehearsals? Well, that's a good sign. Folks, Timmy and Claire are 'smitten'!"

Everyone thought that was the funny, much to the embarrassment of Claire and me.

"Oh, Marilee, I didn't know you would tell everyone. It was a secret."

"I'm sorry Claire, but it was so cute when you told me. Besides, we're all smitten here. Right?"

Daniel from the grill, "At the very least 'smitten', my dearest heart."

"When I first met Camila, I was certainly 'smitten'," said Dick.

Camila seemed confused, "What is 'smitten'? I don't know the word."

Marilee answered, "It's sort of like, almost, love at first sight."

"Yes, I think it was like that when I first saw Dick." Camila smiled at Dick.

I said, "It's sure something at first sight, but then..."

"But then nothing, Timmy. I knew it would happen. Just a rare intuition."

Claire flushed, then looked at me and smiled.

"Just a little bit more at the grill, how about a new round of drinks and a toast to being smitten."

"Some more of your Bourbon would be great. Camila dear, another Martini?"

"Not just yet, but soon, perhaps."

"Do you mind if I have another, Ti-mo-thee?"

"Of course not, I'll serve and join you."

The lamb ribs turned out to be tasty. Marilee told about finding them. She had had them in Java and wanted Daniel to try them on the grill. She toasted him throwing a kiss. We spent the evening in great conversation. I discussed my week with the play again thanking Dick for sending it to me; Claire and Camila discussed their reactions to Texas and America. The most serious discussion was Marilee telling us the worries about keeping her drilling operations going in the east, saying a pull out was in the plans. We talked so much that we almost forgot about swimming.

Both Marilee and Daniel decided it was time for an evening swim. Dick and Camila had brought their bathing suits and mine was in the cabana. All went to change and Claire looked at me almost in fear.

"Do you want to swim, Ti-mo-thee? I'm hesitant, but Marilee took me to that store downtown this week to buy a suit."

"Why are you hesitant? If you want to, I think it would be fun and a nice topper to the evening."

"I've always been very sensitive about my figure and shy about swimming."

"Claire, there's no reason for you to feel that way with me, I think you're beautiful."

"You've only seen me in clothes. I look like a pear, or actually more like an overblown hourglass."

"Did you notice that Marilee turned out most of the lights and you're with friends, not on a public beach?"

"I like you, Ti-mo-thee. I don't want you to see me as some little grotesque girl creature."

"Do you want to swim?"

"Yes, very much."

"Well, then there now, let's do."

I went to change after Dick and Camila came out of the changing room. Daniel was out and pouring snifters of Spanish brandy, which I though would be the drink of the season, or at least during my Lorca experience. We were all in the water when Claire came out of the house. She had wrapped a large towel around herself. She came close to where I was in the water by the pool's edge, dropped the towel and joined me in the water. She had stood for a few seconds before coming in, and I was shocked at how truly beautiful she was. Yes, full-figured as I had never seen before, round with a small waist and secret seemingly large breasts hidden under a frilly top. Her suit had a little skirt that didn't really hide her derrière.

"Claire, don't you ever be shy with me. I think you have the cutest figure I've ever seen."

"Do you really mean that? I've always thought of myself as ugly, I mean my body. I stick out too much every where."

"Don't think 'too much.'"

"Have you seen photographs of that ancient little figurine of an earth mother called the Virgin of Willendorf?"

"I think so, in one of the art books at my house or the bookstore."

"Well, that's what I've always thought I looked like."

I laughed and hugged her. "No, you don't. I'm a man who finds you to be an extraordinary woman; that is everything I know so far."

"Oh, Timmy, I don't know what all of this means, but I feel very lucky. It all seems too fast but not the thing wrong to do. Do you feel the same way?"

"Yes, it seems as if we met weeks ago."

"I feel that, too. I wasn't thinking of meeting someone or even hoping to. I hope you don't tire of me during our weeks together. I did talk for a few minutes with Marilee about my staying for a couple of weeks longer. I must call my parents tomorrow, though."

"You know I'll be busy at work every day and in rehearsals at night."

"Then perhaps you won't tire of me, but I do want to come and watch rehearsals when you will permit me to."

"How about Monday and the other days of the weeks? I'll even come and get you and bring you back here."

"That sounds very exciting, but I do know Marilee has some evenings planned for me."

"She's not going to be introducing you to many more eligible young men, is she?"

She knew I was kidding, but not completely.

"No, she is not. She's very pleased about our being 'smitten.'"

We kissed shyly and joined the others at the shallow end.

They were talking about coming plans for the year. Dick was going to recuperate during the summer and wait for his reply from the law school at the University of Texas. Camila had already talked to Parkland about nursing. Marilee and Daniel planned to go to Taos where Daniel could paint, before their New York gallery search. Marilee said they surely weren't leaving before my show opened. Claire took my hand under the water and gave me a sad smile, which I knew meant she was leaving before my play opened.

The evening didn't last much longer. There was no real water frolicking as there would have been during the day, just relaxed conversation enjoying the calming nature of the water in near darkness. I could tell that Daniel and Marilee considered Dick and Camila to be new friends whom they would enjoy spending many good times with. Claire mentioned coming to my rehearsals which immediately interested Camila. I was pleased Spanish lady could possibly help me with some of the things I didn't quite understand about the culture. I gave her an open invitation, and Dick said he would bring her but not stay because he wanted to know nothing about how I was directing before it opened, just the surprise of the play in English. Spending this time with Dick reminded me of how much I had missed him. He had been my only best friend. I felt an envy of the two other couples, because of their permanence and love. My caring for Claire had been a wonderful surprise, but I was well aware she would be leaving soon. This was very different from my experience with Gwen, because I had known there was no future, but with Claire, so soon, there was a different feeling of a strange kinship. I didn't expect a sexual relationship; I didn't think it was possible because I couldn't imagine Claire rushing into that no matter what our feelings were for each other.

Dick, Camila, and I dressed. Marilee handed out the robes she always kept in the cabaña for her, Daniel and Claire. Dick and Camila proposed an evening at their house; they were staying in the rather large guesthouse behind Dick's parents in Lakewood. Dick assured me it wouldn't be during my rehearsal workweeks. They left with hugs and laughter. Marilee proposed the four of us sit together for one last brandy. We talked about the evening, Taos, and Claire's liking Daniel's paintings. I was glad *Blood Wedding* didn't come up. When they went upstairs, Claire and I walked out to my car.

"What a nice evening, Ti-mo-thee."

"Indeed it was, Claire."

"I like your friends very much. You made feel very much at ease, I've been so shy about myself that..."

"Claire, you don't ever, ever need to feel that with me. I think you are a glorious woman."

She just sighed and stepped into my arms. Her softness was wondrous. She didn't have on her little heeled shoes so her petite height fit me, I could still sense her reticence and pulled her away a bit to look at her face, which revealed a new openness. I cupped her face in my hands; even in the almost darkness she glowed, her luminescent complexion magical. She came into a kiss with me without the innocence of before in the boat."

We held each other for a moment. I told her I would be studying and writing in the morning and then to the theatre in the afternoon for technical work watching the spiking of the stage, but asked if she would like to go out for dinner in the evening. I suggested Mexican food. She said Marilee and Daniel had a previously arranged engagement so it would be fine and that it would be fun to try this new taste. I promised to pick her up between six and six-thirty. I took her hand she had placed on my cheek kissed her forehead and was off in the night towards home. I slept deeply with reoccurring dreams of her kiss and for the first time since she had left, no thoughts of Gwen.

Chapter 8
Domingo con Technicas de Theatre y El Vaquero

I slept late but not so late that I couldn't join my family for a big breakfast. I told them about the last two evenings with Marilee and Daniel, and about Claire. They wanted to know everything about Claire, I guess only because I kind of drifted off when I mentioned her. They weren't nosy, just curious about someone who affected me so quickly. I acknowledged she was a special new friend but for them not to expect a new big romance because she wasn't going to be here for long. My father said it sounded good to him, Mom wanted to meet her, and Jeordie asked if she was as cute as Gwen. I gave him a look that ended that avenue quickly. Jeordie talked about school being out soon and said that he planned to spend as much time as possible at Uncle Willy's shop learning how to be a better welder and try some more metal sculpture. I realized I hadn't seen Uncle Willy in a while and suddenly thought I wanted him to meet Claire. If anyone would understand my feelings for her, it would be him though I wasn't sure what my feelings were except something new. A whirlwind of emotions-*Blood Wedding* and Claire. She wasn't going to be in any way a distraction and I looked forward to her being at rehearsals occasionally. Both parents reaffirmed their commitment to work on the production. I was constantly amazed at their support for my theatre choice. We got into a short conversation about the fragility of choosing the arts as a way of life. Dad said he was more of a craftsman than an artist, which Mom disagreed with immediately, saying his designs were art. Jeordie said for us not to worry about him because he was going to be either a "shaman" or an engineer. That ended the meal with laughter.

I spent two hours studying my new floor plans and writing in my journal. I took a long shower and found myself missing Claire. Nothing had ever happened this fast before; I had known and spent time with Gwen for weeks before I kissed her, long before our recent encounter. There was something so different about this even knowing there was no future. Claire was an apparition with a most solid form.

I went in through the back door of the theatre and found my designer and Ginger hard at work on stage, spiking with different colors for each scene. I walked the stage and suggested several changes, which weren't big enough to change her design. They facilitated the movements and potential blocking changes that I knew would happen. I realized the show was becoming more of a visual happening in my mind. I had written in my journal about working from general ideas to specific ones. Purely specific was dress rehearsal and I was glad I had four more weeks. I hoped these thoughts weren't a rationalization for chaos, but I was excited, not feeling the trepidation that occasionally crept in. My mother had given me a soft lecture last year about how fear of failure cannot be a part of the creative process except as an inspiration. I knew she was right, but of course, it still appeared as a rush of reality, like those moments I experienced last week at the arts Festival.

We laid out the rolls of colored cloth, which were one-half-inch in width, in the out-line of each major set piece. They were smoothed out and tacked down. Each scene had a different color-the first act single colors, second act, two overlapping colors, and the third act three colors. Ginger made a large legend poster and mounted it near the stage manager's station backstage. I got a smaller copy she had done in watercolor. When we finished spiking, the stage was a colorful grid, which I walked several times to see if there would be too many confusing overlaps; there weren't. The designer and I set up a table in the wing with the most light and studied the models she had made on Saturday. It looked like the pop-up idea would work but the scene paint colors didn't seem to fit what I had in mind. She acknowledged that was the main problem she was having in finalizing the design before elevations were drawn. I told her to carry on with the elevations and asked if she minded if my brother looked at the models. She knew Daniel's work and especially loved his colors from 'Flood Zone,' I hadn't talked to Daniel about any collaboration on this show, but I thought he would agree to help. I went to the office and called him. He was actually excited about helping. I told him I was taking Claire out to dinner tonight and would set up the models on the table in the library with the sequence of left to right, first scene to last scene. We talked a few minutes about my concept of exploiting the natural passion of the piece. He thought bright earth tones using reds to increase in strength as show progressed. I liked what he said, and he would try to have something by the end of the week. I had approved the set so the colors were not the most urgent except for costume harmonizing. Once Daniel worked on some colors, the costumes could be finalized.

I spent some more time with Ginger going over her notes from Friday, and rounded things up just before six.

I arrived at Marilee's at 6:20. Claire met me at the door and helped me carry in the models of the set. We set them up in the library. Claire thought the idea of pop-up units was intriguing as I explained it to her. She asked questions about the set up and who would do it. I told of my idea of the "Zanies" moving in and out and how it would be the cast as stage crew doing it to music.

"Is that your idea?"

I described what Vachtangov had done with Turandot, but that he used people who weren't in the cast and they were in black outfits.

"That's funny, Lorca being influenced by Russian theatre, but I love it. I want to see it happen..." Well, perhaps I'll see the beginning of it happen. Oh, Ti-mo-thee, this so exciting. I wish I could help."

"Have you ever helped build sets?"

"No, but I could learn. I could help paint. Would that be good?"

"Yes, that would be great! Consider yourself hired. We won't start that for a couple of weeks...so...you may have to stay longer than you planned."

"I called my parents today and said how much I liked it here. They said I could stay as long as I liked but that they missed me."

"I hope you didn't tell them about us yet."

"Oh, no, that would scare them to death. They are very protective and forget that I'm a grown woman. I was almost on my own in London for two years, so they trust me being with Marilee. What is there to tell yet? This is awfully fast between us, isn't it, Ti-mo-thee? I was so excited about us going out tonight. This something very new for me. Did you think about me at all? Oh, how silly of me to ask that..."

"Very silly, I'm shocked that you would ask it...why we barely know each other. Let me think...Did I think of you? Humm...! Well, before I went to sleep, in my dreams, the moment I woke, and, oh, yes, all during the day. But that's all."

Claire laughed, hugged me, and kissed my cheek. And said, "What a strange coincidence! Me too, about you."

"Shall we go and have some Mexican cuisine, Mademoiselle Claire Levant?"

"Oui, Monsieur Ti-mo-thee Sart."

This was the first time Claire had been in my car, and she liked it. I told her the whole Uncle Willy story and even how much I wanted her to meet him. I told her about Uncle Willy's adventures in the Navy on a gunboat in China and about his business at his machine shop and how he built cars for a racetrack here. She also was excited about my family wanting to meet her and said that a dinner was in order before she left.

"I've never learned to drive, Ti-mo-thee. Could you teach me?"

This was a surprise, but she explained that if she was going to live in America, someday she would have a car, and why not learn now. I told her to watch what I did in shifting the gears, and how to use the clutch and the accelerator. I assured her when I did give her lessons we would go somewhere where there was no traffic. She thought that would be a great adventure. I laughed about how learning to drive could indeed be considered a "great adventure."

"Well, it will be for me. We didn't have a car in England. My father knew his Renault wouldn't work there because of the side of the road they drive on."

"What kind of Renault was it?"

"I believe it was called an Avant Traction. My father loved it, but he sold it when we left France. The autobuses and the underground were so efficient in London that he just never got another one. But he does have one in Los Angeles, though I don't what kind it is."

"Would he mind if I taught you to drive?"

"Yes, he probably would, but only because he would consider it his duty to teach me. I don't think he would have the time because he is already traveling quite a bit; besides it would be more fun with you. Don't you think so, Ti-mo-thee?"

"It's fun just talking about it."

"Good. Where are we going to eat? Is it the same place where Marilee had that big dinner?"

"No, I called and they're closed tonight. I thought we would try the El Vaquero in Lakewood. It's been one of my family's favorites for years; and I think you will like it. Dick Ayers said that while he was in Spain the two things he missed the most were Mexican food and Dr Peppers."

"Oh, I had a Dr Pepper today."

"How was that?"

"I'm not sure, it must be an acquired taste. In England, I think the equivalent to Mexican food is Indian, as in East India."

"I truly didn't believe you meant Navajo or Cherokee cuisine. What about in France?

"Do American Indians have a cuisine?"

"I'm sure they must have something, but I've never heard of it."

"In France it's North African food, like in Algeria; and sometimes I miss it. Paris does have everything though, but I never saw a Mexican Restaurant."

We arrived at El Vaquero and got a good booth, which was a new form of seating to her. She loved the way the restaurant was decorated in the Mexican style. We started off with a Mexican beer and I suggested cheese Enchiladas or a Chile Relleno. She chose the enchiladas.

She asked what my favorite style of art was. I explained that I had been exposed to art all of my life and that my tastes were rather eclectic. She was surprised that I liked the Pre-Raphaelites and that she reminded me of Rosietti's paintings. She blushed saying she considered that a great compliment because she had written a paper on them and had also fallen in love with their romantic vision, even though she didn't consider it the greatest of art. Diego Rivera and Picasso, two of my favorites turned out to be hers too. We talked and talked, and she liked the food. We found even more things in common, architecture, the history of republican Rome, and the renaissance. She told me about plays she had seen in London and asked what other plays I wanted to direct.

"For sure Berthold Brecht's *Three Penny* Opera and one of Somerset Maugham's plays. Everything we choose has to be measured by commercial potential, but every season I can sneak in something like Lorca. I think Maugham would work just fine; I don't know which one yet, perhaps *The Constant Wife*."

The evening ended too soon. We sat in my car in front of Marilee's and talked more, then we kissed with more passion than we had experienced so far.

"We are going too fast, perhaps Ti-mo-thee, but it still seems to be the right thing. I'm a little scared. Not of you, but of what I am feeling. It is a new experience for me. I've always been careful about any relationships, but I think that was because I hadn't met someone like you."

"What's so special about me? An uneducated Texas boy?"

"You're not uneducated. You are very smart and well-read. You're an artist who knows more about everything than most well educated people I've met. You're a wonderful Texas boy. And what's so special about me? No, no, I'm not asking for compliments, it's a kind of rhetorical question. I feel like an out of place little French girl starting a whole new life and I didn't expect to meet a you, anytime, anywhere."

"I've been trying to figure this out, too. Everything about you is good, but I think we shouldn't try any more to understand what's happening, just enjoy it for the time we have. This is hard to say because I don't want to think of an end."

"You're saying what I was thinking. We have some time and I can't think of end either...Can I go to your rehearsal with you tomorrow?"

I laughed out loud and hugged her.

"Yes, you may, Claire. I was going to almost insist that you come. I'll be by to get you at six. It will be a long evening. Is that alright?"

"Of course! I think it will be exciting and I'll try not to be a distraction; I'll sit way back in the dark."

"You don't have to sit way back, but I'll be real busy for the whole evening."

"That's fine, I expected you to be busy because I know how important it is to you for this to be good."

We kissed again and I walked her to the door.

I sat in my room and had a snifter of brandy. I thought of Claire and how different it was from Gwen and the heartbreaker before her. Nothing but good thoughts. I was changing as if new windows were opening in my mind. Before I slept, Claire's beautiful face appeared in the dark... "And made the black night beauteous."

Chapter 9
La Semana Segunda del Ensayo

Monday at work was good; just enough customers for the store to do well, and not so many that I couldn't work on my script and journal. I found myself wanting to write about Claire, so I wrote in notes on the bottom of each page. I didn't write about how attractive she is but what is most interesting about her as a person; her laugh, her interests, what I knew about her life experience. Then I tried to describe her. Her face was different in that her resemblance to Louise Brooks without the flirty pout was a constant element of curiosity. Her face was more round than Brooks' and her eyes green, of course I'd never seen a color picture of Brooks. Her accent was a combination of French and British English, just listening to her talk a joy. And no more writing about things I knew or even the mystery of her appearance while I was directing Lorca.

Thinking about Claire seemed to give me new ideas for rehearsal. It seemed to clear my thoughts and I was able to come back to questions with a new spirit. Never had a person affected me in this manner; yes, Marilee helped me to think in a different way, but that was through conversation and recommended reading. Perhaps it was that Claire made me want to be a better artist. Of course, that's true because I wanted her to be impressed by my work, or I enjoyed her presence and our hopefully mutual attraction. Yes I'm sexually attracted, but not like Gwen where it was the dominant force. I didn't have sexual fantasies about Claire like I had had women in the past; with us, a kiss has been a high point and a thrill. My journal took on a new duality; the play rehearsal, and the mystery of Claire.

I left work a little early so I could run home grab a bite to eat, shower, and shave again. I dressed more spiffily than I usually would for rehearsal and I was off to pick up Claire. She answered the door ready to go, dressed more casually than I had seen before; slacks with a light long jacket both in earth tones of brown and purple. She looked great. Over her shoulder was a satchel similar to mine.

"I've brought my drawing pad. Do you mind if I sketch, Ti-mo-thee? I'm not really much of an artist, but I can draw and I like to record experiences that way, like a camera."

"No, I don't mind in the least. This is something new about you."

"I've been doing it for years. When I was young, I thought I wanted to be a painter; but I realized I liked studying art more than making it. In France I took life drawing, and then just started making scrapbooks of places I went. I haven't had a chance to draw since I've been here and I'm excited about watching your rehearsal. I haven't shared this part of me with many people, Marilee doesn't even know."

"My word, I hope you find it interesting enough to draw. From out front in the house it will probably look pretty chaotic."

"I'm sure it looks better than you know now."

"You know, this could be a great help to me. Stage pictures have been important to me, but the way I'm working now doesn't give the usual freedom to constantly step back and repeat everything. I'm trying not to stop the flow. Claire, every time we're together there's a new surprise."

"I wasn't sure I should ask you or bring my pad, but I wanted a record of you working. It would be wonderful if I could help you this way. Oh, Ti-mo-thee, I'll try not to be a bother."

"Now that's silly and impossible."

"Good, Monsieur Sart. Oh! I forgot to tell you; Daniel spent part of the day working on colors. I think he's excited about helping. He likes the design and says it's innovative."

"I'm getting more family collaboration than I expected, and now you. Yes, this is good; I'm happy, yes, this is good."

"I'm happy, too." She squeezed my hand.

When we entered the theatre Ginger was in the office waiting with the elevations from the designer. I told her that Daniel was working on the colors for the set and that he thought it was an innovative design. I introduced her to Claire and said that she would be doing sketches during rehearsal and how it could possibly help develop the stage pictures. We went over Ginger's notes from Friday again, looking for any new thoughts for the evening. The three of us had a cup of coffee that Ginger had made in the theatre kitchen. She and Claire struck up a quick friendship.

The cast started arriving at seven and we met on the stage. I introduced Claire to each member individually; she spoke Spanish with the Latin actors, which impressed them, a good start for Claire's involvement. Claire found her place in the house. I gave notes, critique, and what I wanted to achieve during the evening. Ginger pointed out the legend for the stage spiking. They walked the stage for a few minutes finding the taped first act layout. We worked the first act going through and repeating each scene. Eddy Flournoy arrived a little late and started working the music into the act. The actors had evidently worked very hard on getting off-book; even though they carried their scripts, they rarely used them. I walked through each movement and constantly gave character notes. In an hour and a half, we had a beginning set for the act, it was still rough but a good flow. I decided we had the time for a work-through of the second act after a break. I went down into the house to see Claire, taking Eddy with me for an introduction. They talked about Spain and Flamenco music; it turned out she was a real aficionado. I hadn't told her about the live music in the play.

The rehearsal went even better than expected. It was a great experience having Claire in the house. Friends had watched before, but her being there became a soaring inspiration. I didn't perform for her; I just worked more clearly with a stronger feeling of confidence. I decided right at the last moment to have short warm up sessions before each evening started. The idea I had was to use a Shakespearean sonnet memorized with physical exercise. I thought perhaps it would help to create concentration at a higher level.

After the practice, the older Mexican came up me and said, "Ella es mucha mujer, Audazito. Creo que tienes buena suerte por esa projecto."

He was right. I was having good luck. Claire in her gentle manner, was making everything better.

I met with Ginger for a few minutes before taking Claire back to Marilee's. She met us at the door demanding that I come in for a nightcap. I readily agreed. We sat in the library and Daniel showed some of his beginning ideas on colors. They were brilliant, much better than I had imagined they would be. He said he would do colored drawings of each set piece. Claire told me how much she had enjoyed being there and then she opened her sketchpad for me. Her work was beautiful. She had several drawings for each scene, even including me in the ensemble. Daniel was impressed by her ability to capture the feeling of a rehearsal. I asked if I could take them to study for the next session of act one. She was thrilled that I liked them and wanted her to continue.

I just smiled at her and said, "Indeed, dear lady. It looks you've become a part of *Blood Wedding*, and a most welcome one."

After our brandy, she walked me to the door. I told her about my idea of trying warm-ups before rehearsal starts. She asked why I wanted to do that and I said that even though it was going well, it took the actors a while to get into the process.

"Perhaps reciting a poem would free them up for starting, to concentrate on something completely different from the play, to free them of any distractions or anticipation. It could also be a vocal warm-up for the poetry in the piece. What do you think?"

"If you believe it could help in any way, why not try it? I don't know much about this, but I trust your ideas."

"I thought possibly a Shakespearean sonnet would be good. Do you have a favorite?"

"There are so many I like but twenty-nine has always been a favorite. Do you know it? 'Fortune and men's eyes...'"

Yes, I remember the line. Daniel even used it last week. I'll read it tonight."

We just held each other for a few moments. Finally she said, "Thank you, Ti-mo-thee."

"You thanking me, I'm the one who needs to be thanking."

We kissed long and nice, and then I was on my way home. Before going to sleep, I read the sonnet, the perfect choice. Good peaceful sleep.

The next day at work, Claire, Marilee, and Camila dropped in. I was glad Camila had made the connection. She asked when she could watch rehearsal and I mentioned that the choreographer was coming Wednesday. Camila liked that idea, saying that Dick would bring her. We talked for a few minutes and Claire bought a couple of books about Southwestern Art. As they left, Claire turned to me with a smile that was almost as good as a kiss.

I had the chance to spend some time with my boss. He was interested in how rehearsals were going and seemed enthusiastic about the new things I was trying.

He also said he was postponing inventory until after my show opened. This was of enormous help to me because taking inventory totally dominates your time during the workday.

When I left for the day, he shook my hand and said, "Do good work, Tim."

I nodded thinking how valuable his support was. It was the second time somebody had said that.

When I picked Claire up for the evening, she was dressed in a completely different manner. Marilee had taken her shopping at Sanger's and a ranch store on the Fort Worth highway. She was wearing a pair of Levi dungarees and a tan jacket with pockets; she called it a light barn coat.

"It was difficult finding something to fit me, but everything I brought with me seemed wrong. Do you like it?"

"I think it's great. Did they have jackets like that for me?"

"I think so. I was constantly reaching into my bag for different pencils though I do feel like I'm going on a hunting trip in Africa. Look at my boots."

They were some short suede women's riding boots.

"You're starting to look like a Texas girl."

"Well, thank you sir. I hope that's good. Is it?"

"Without any doubt, Mademoiselle."

At the theatre, we met Ginger in the lobby and were joined by Barney. Claire charmed him immediately and I told him about the sketches she was making of rehearsals and how much it was helping me. Within a few minutes, Camila and Dick joined us; he checked on the time to pick her up still refusing to watch the rehearsal which knowing Dick I understood completely. He said Saturday night was good for them at their house. Claire and I agreed quickly. We went into the theatre where the girls found their place to watch. In my meeting onstage with Ginger, I revealed my idea on warm-ups and she liked it. The choreographer, Aurora, arrived and I introduced her to Claire and Camila. She was a recent immigrant from Mexico who had studied in Spain before the Civil War. She also had read my call in the paper for cast, crew, and dancers. Camila was thrilled to meet someone who had spent that much time in Spain. They exchanged reminiscences about Madrid in Spanish. Eddy soon arrived and he and Aurora went on stage to set some music for the marriage party in act two.

At seven the cast set up in their crescent on stage. In the beginning of my notes and critique, I described the concept of the warm-ups. They all were pleased by it, and I dictated Sonnet Twenty-nine. I asked them to have it memorized by Thursday spending the time on it that they would on lines from the script. They had gotten used to taking notes in the pads I had asked them to use. Carolyn Carothers, who was playing the mother; she was almost too glamorous for the role; already knew the sonnet. She stood up and recited it very dramatically. The cast applauded and several commented on how appropriate a choice it was. Carolyn said her husband had used it when wooing her. I quickly thought to myself that perhaps I should learn a couple.

Aurora and Eddy explained how they would work for the evening, and Aurora demonstrated some basic steps to Eddy's music. We did a speed through of the beginning scene of act two as Aurora and Eddy prepared further then it was their rehearsal. Aurora had read the play in Spanish and loved my idea of expanding the wedding party into a dance celebration. I set up the stage picture for the opening of the wedding gathering and stayed on stage with them through out the evening.

After rehearsal, we adjourned to the lobby where Barney surprised us with several bottles of wine. He had never done anything like this for any of my shows in rehearsal. It was a terrific gesture of support. Dick made it for one glass, equally surprised by the small celebration. Camila introduced him to Aurora and Eddy; they were both curious about his experiences during the war wanting to know about any new development over there.

On the way to Marilee's, we talked about the success of the collaboration of Aurora and Eddy. In the library Claire showed me her drawings of the evening and as before they gave me a new perspective.

When I was leaving Claire whispered closely, "It is wonderful watching you work, Ti-mo-thee." Then, a sweet goodnight kiss.

The next morning at breakfast my parents asked if I would like to bring Claire over for dinner on Sunday night.

"I'll ask her tonight, but I think she would like it very much. She's mentioned she would like to meet the rest of my family."

"Hey, big brother, do you mind if try out my new Brownie camera?" asked Jeordie.

"I don't think so, but try not to be obnoxious about it. Be sure to ask Claire if she minds."

"Okie dokie. That money from my selling a sculpture also got me a new little radio."

"I've already had to show him how to turn down the sound twice," laughed Dad. "Terry and the Pirates is not my favorite at that level."

Jeordie was off to school and I had a few moments alone with them.

"Timmy, I don't believe I remember you spending this much time with a lady friend. This seems awfully quick; she must be a special girl. How do you feel about her?" asked Mom.

"I don't think 'special' quite describes Claire. She's more than that. We're both a bit confused about how it feels to spend time together. Not bad confused, maybe just amazed. I know she's a sophisticated, well-educated, European girl, which is part of my amazement. How could she care for...?"

"Timmy, there are very few men who are as special as you. She must see in you what I always knew was there. You're already a success in your work. How many young men can say that?"

"Well, whatever it is between us, I like it, even though I know she will go to California to be with her parents."

"Are you sure she will? I hope this isn't going to be like Gwen."

"It's nothing like me and Gwen. I've already spent more time with Claire than I ever did with Gwen. That was mostly a physical attraction. I don't know if I truly understand what love is, but I think I'm learning a bit about the concept. You'll understand when you meet her."

Dad finally said, "A concept? Don't be too analytical. Just enjoy these new feelings. It's about time for you anyway. You've been too much of a loner. Maybe it's just good luck for you to have met her."

"One of my cast members said the same thing the other night...hummm. Marilee had a good feeling about us before we even met. Yes, could be, but I believe it's more than just good luck."

"Tim, there's nothing more than good luck." chided Dad.

"True, Timmy, and quite often some happiness comes with it," added Mom.

In rehearsal we tried out my idea for warm-ups. The cast recited the sonnet as I led them in simple physical exercises, then they did it in a staggered chorus with groups of two saying the same line. It worked and we started with much more energy and concentration.

Rehearsal went very well, with new discoveries happening constantly, but some places were extremely difficult, especially the chanting of the poetry. The ending of act one was a scenic problem I couldn't quite see yet. Some group singing offstage or upstage? Or could I get a balance from working from both sides? I tried both ways several times deciding on using the whole stage both on and off. The bridesmaids and friends are awakening the Bride and preparing her emotionally for the wedding and the aftermath. The actor playing Leonardo had grown enormously. He was getting the idea of a romantic villain. There had to be a reason the Bride would give up everything for him. His seductive wooing needed from the beginning to be obviously dangerous, but his charisma must almost scare the audience. In an old melodrama, they would be screaming, "Don't listen to him." The actor playing the part was not Latin but a Highland Park cotton broker who had played several parts in the past two seasons. He was tall, dark, and moved with dancer-like fluidity. The actress playing the Bride was a beautiful South American woman with an earthy Gypsy look whose husband had met her in an oil well drilling sojourn in Colombia. I had met them as theatre patrons and didn't know of her dramatic aspirations until she auditioned. The "Bride" and the "Bridegroom" were a striking couple except that she seemed almost too good-looking for him. He was a student at SMU who acted with the Arden Club there. The four of them had the most difficult task in the production. If the passion and chemistry between them didn't work, the show wouldn't work; and they knew it. I started in Thursday's rehearsal to spend extra time with them. I would let the other actors run lines or practice the dance while I worked their scenes. "Leonardo" at first had a hard time being rough with the "Wife," then saw the contrast he needed with the "Bride," the sacrificing of everything for an obsession from a past rejection. The Bride accepts her betrothal to a potentially successful husband, but her lustful passion for Leonardo drives her to betrayal. They are doomed, which still must be a surprise. The Bridegroom and the Wife are the tragedy, all of this happening as a dance of death. The third act is almost a fantasy epic, first in a forest then a church-like scene, totally white. I was sure it would take a full week to stage. We still hadn't solved the problem of the fight to the death and I didn't want to give up on it. I had thought several times about Ginger's comment on the shadow puppets. A scrim with Leonardo and the Bridegroom behind it with a soft light projecting their shadows and using gobos projected on the front for the forest could possibly work, but the segue into the last scene, still keeping their bodies in view, was still a challenge.

Eddy's guitar was already adding continuity, especially between the scenes, even with no sets to change yet. He and Aurora had agreed to full dance and movement rehearsals every Wednesday. In all of a director's work, an ensemble is hopefully a part of the process, but I didn't think I really had ever achieved it to the extent I was now. The cast was working harder than any I had worked with in the past. They seemed more excited about the play in every rehearsal and accepted completely what I was trying to do.

Claire's drawings were beginning to help me more each day, and she was enjoying being a part of the production. After rehearsal, we would sit in Marilee's library as I studied the drawings. After Friday's run-through, we worked for awhile, then joined Daniel and Marilee for a swim. Daniel had finished his color renderings for Ginger. Claire and I both thought they were perfect for the play. Daniel had read the play in the middle of the week and had started completely. He said the passion of the piece had rather knocked him for a loop, so he needed to re-think his approach. Marilee and I both laughed about his reaction, reminding him of our discussion in the parking lot at the art Festival.

The swim cleared away my exhaustion. Claire and I stayed outside alone by the pool lying close together on a lounge chair. We kissed and looked at the stars not talking about the play or us. For the first time I pulled her close to me stirring up new feelings in both of us. She only said my name softly and held me closely. When I knew it was time to leave, she walked me to the car.

"Tomorrow I need to work all day on my journal and go over Ginger's notes. There are some problems coming up I have to solve before Monday. I'll pick you up at six for dinner at Dick and Camila's."

We were both looking forward to seeing Dick and Camila.

I had mentioned to her earlier dinner with my parents on Sunday and she was anxious but excited.

"I am, of course, nervous about meeting them, Ti-mo-thee. Are they always so welcoming to your lady friends?"

"There haven't been that many lady friends. Actually this is the first time for this sort of invitation."

"What have you told them about us?"

"Not much, except that you are a special friend. They've never seen me spend so much time with someone and just want to meet you. I believe you will feel completely at ease with them. My brother, Jeordie, will also join us."

"After getting to know Daniel and you, of course, I'm looking forward to meeting them. Do you think they'll like me?"

"Yes, I do. It's going to be very different from Marilee's. A kind of humble family of struggling artists."

"I know that, and I know I will like them."

"Would it be too much if we spent Sunday afternoon together? We could do some driving lessons and maybe drop by Uncle Willy's."

"Ti-mo-thee, I know I'm going to miss you tomorrow. No it's not too much. I was hoping you would ask me to do something or just be together. I've wanted to meet all the Sart family after knowing you. My goodness, I'm feeling so happy, I never thought of myself as being unhappy, but...oh, Timmy, you make me so happy."

"You called me Timmy, did you know? I like it."

"Did I? Do you mind?"

"No I don't."

She hugged me laughing kissing my ear then my lips. I just seemed to pull her up to me in a caring rush

"Claire, Claire, When I think of you, I smile and...I'm so happy too. When we're apart I want to be with you, I mean just be. And I love it when you're at the theatre with me, I've never been so happy when I was directing before. You make me want to do very good work. I want you to be proud of me."

"It meant so much to me when you liked my drawings. And you're making me feel a part of something very special. And I am proud of you."

"Good night, dear heart."

Saturday was the best workday so far during the two-week rehearsal period. I wrote ten pages in my journal and set up Daniel's color renderings next to the models. On a second look the colors worked even better. I read through Ginger's notes and laid out Claire's drawings. Her sketches gave me several ideas on adjusting my stage pictures though still early in the scenic positioning. What they did was save me about five or six hours of stepping back to view a scene then repeating it.

After four or five hours of work, I went to the theatre to see the designer and show her Daniel's renderings. She had her volunteer group lay out the lumber for the wagons that would carry the set pieces. We went into a conference with the completed elevations of the set and the color renderings. She felt the colors were better than anything she could have come up with; her only doubts were about mixing them. Did we have the right hues at the theatre shop to achieve it? At this point I volunteered my mother to help. The designer knew she would be working full time just to get the set built so any help was welcome, especially a color expert. Her ensemble spirit matched the cast. At this point Ginger joined us with more notes for me from Friday and a concept for the show program. Three hours later, I was back at my place resting, reading Ginger's notes, and reading the play another time. I actually took a short nap then showered, dressed, and was on my way to pick up Claire.

At Daniel and Marilee's, everyone was in the living room. I joined them and told Daniel about the reaction to his colors. He said he would be glad to help mixing the colors, too, and how much fun it would be to work with Mom. Claire brought me a package wrapped like a present.

"Open it now, Timmy, please."

"It's good to hear someone else call him Timmy," Laughed Marilee.

"Don't expect me to, Tim. And Marilee don't you start calling me Danny."

"Well, sometimes you are a Danny, but Timmy fits your brother more for me all the time."

"Y'all stop this. The right ladies are calling me Timmy. No one else may."

"Y'all? I haven't heard you use that before. That's real Texas. It does mean you-all, doesn't it?" asked Claire.

"Yes, second person plural" added Marilee with a finger in the air in a funny professorial accent.

"I tried to get out of that habit, using 'y'all' that is. Perhaps to sound more cultured," I said.

"I like it. I like you to sound Texan," said Claire.

We all laughed at that and I opened my present. It was a light barn jacket in dark blue, and it fit perfectly. I smiled at Claire and squeezed her hand. She knew I liked it. I wore it that night.

The guesthouse that Dick and Camila lived in was not in any way diminutive, as guest houses go. It was beautiful with three rooms and a patio overlooking the pool behind Dick's parents house. When we arrived his parents came out to greet us, I had not seen them for several years. They immediately took to Claire, commenting that their favorite Dallas men were being charmed by these wonderful European ladies. They obviously loved Camila because they both kissed her as they wished us a good evening.

We had drinks on the patio and Dick and Camila told us more about their escape from Spain. It had been no easy trip from Madrid to Barcelona. They had been stopped several times with Dick's papers being questioned as to their authenticity. In one small town they had to wait for two days waiting for a telegram to get to and from the authorities in Madrid. They stayed in Barcelona for a week so Dick could rest. The crossing into France was also difficult, but Dick was able to convince the authorities of his student status and that their marriage was legitimate. After that, France was a pleasant trip but you could feel that the uneasiness about the Germans. Getting on the American ship was almost like reaching home, and they were grateful for an uneventful crossing.

Camila and Claire reminisced about London, the university, their favorite restaurants, and museums. I asked Dick about his trip to Pamplona for the running of the bulls. He had mentioned it in a letter.

"What an adventure that was! I got almost drunk on wine and ran with them. I got knocked down but luckily wasn't gored, though several other people were. The fights were the best I had seen up to that point and the party was unending. Two weeks later, I saw Manolete fight and you knew very quickly why he is called the best. His control in the ring is magical. I think I saw all the other great matadors but no one, and I mean no one, was like Manolete. Oh! Tim, I brought you something."

Dick left the room and brought back a bag and handed it to me. A night of presents. I reached in and pulled out a leather bag with a spout and a shoulder strap.

"What's this?"

"Oh! Timmy, it's a bota!" cried Claire "You fill it with wine and push it together."

"What?"

"It's the traditional wine-carrying thing in Pamplona. You hold it above you head and, as Claire said, you squeeze it and the wine squirts into your mouth. I don't expect you to carry it around. It's more for hanging on your wall."

"It's great, and it will go up on my wall."

"Tim, reach into the sack again," Dick said.

I did and pulled out a beret.

Claire laughed and hugged me and almost cried saying, "See, maybe you have reached that artistic status already. Oh, Timmy, put it on."

I did and Claire started crying and kissed me.

"See, I was right. You do look great in it."

Dick and Camila were opened mouthed at what had happened between Claire and me. "I hoped you would like it but what was that all about?" Dick inquired.

"Well several days ago" I replied, "we had a conversation about berets. Dick, I love it, I'll try to get my nerve up to wear it."

"No rush, I just wanted you to have one. You're a true artist now, Tim. Anyone who has the nerve to put on Lorca's *Blood Wedding* here, and in a new way is a true artist. Camila couldn't stop talking about your cast and what you were doing."

Camila had cooked a classic Spanish Paella, seafood and all. We ate to the fill, drank Bourbon, and laughed. Old and new dear friends. Sometimes Claire and Camila would go into the kitchen, I think to talk away from Dick and me.

"Tim, you and Claire seem to be getting along rather well. True?"

"Yes, I believe it's much more than getting along, but neither of us is sure what. I don't think I've ever been happier."

"I believe one could also say she's happy, too. This is first time I've ever seen you like this."

"You're certainly right about that. It's very easy and sweet, with no pressure, primarily because I know she's leaving to go to her parents in Los Angeles. I think they're probably trying to persuade her to go there as soon as possible. I don't know this for sure, but I kind of suspect it."

"Maybe they're not. Perhaps she just feels the pressure from them. Well, enjoy every moment. This is a rare experience for you, and about time. Try not to see the end coming, even if it's inevitable. I wish I could give you some comforting advice, but that's it."

"Marilee has talked to her father about working full time for her company, but that's fairly far in the future. He will probably go to the Far East if it remains stable there. But you're right, 'Carpe Diem,' and each one has been good."

"Well, my friend be strong. She appears to feel the same way you do; who knows what will happen?"

The girls came back from the kitchen laughing as if sharing a secret, a recipe

I hoped.

We left Dick and Camila's, having strengthened already strong bonds.

It was early enough that I thought a drive around White Rock Lake would be pleasant. It was. I drove up to Winfrey Point and parked the car overlooking the lake. It was a beautiful clear night and too early in the season for any serious mosquito attacks. We talked about everything, the evening, Dick and Camila's Spanish adventure, the play, my presents, and her parents wanting her to come home. She said she would be talking to them in the morning and had no idea what would happen but she was sure they wanted her to leave soon. Then we folded into each other's arms. Claire started crying very softly saying she didn't know why, except that she was very happy and it just kind of overwhelmed her.

"Timmy, I've never had something come over me like this before. Do you remember us talking about the mystery of being smitten and that I hoped it didn't get scary? I've been scared several times you would forget to come get me to go to the theatre, or that you would call and say you needed to work alone. I've always been so independent and never bothered by postponements or cancelled plans."

"I know exactly what you're feeling. I sometimes fear that you might call and say that you can't come, or that I would come for you and you would be gone, you know, just gone. Once I even wondered if you were real, that I would go to Marilee's door and she would say, 'Who'?"

There wasn't anything more to say. We pulled each other close and came as close to petting as we ever had. Her softness was beautiful and I wanted to touch her but was hesitant to rush or offend her in any way. She sensed this and took my hand and placed it on her breasts. We kissed with a new passion.

"Timmy, I've never wanted anyone to touch me so much before. I've been frightened of letting anyone close to me like this, but not with you. I was afraid you wouldn't like touching me, that..."

"I do, you're as beautiful to touch as to see and to be with. I've never, well, I..."

"You don't need to say it, I know it...just hold me, Ti-mo-thee."

And I did. I kissed her face and her neck. She whimpered and kissed me back. And I also knew we could go no further, not here, not now, not yet, perhaps not ever.

As we drove back, Claire sat next to me, her head on my shoulder. At the door she reached up and put her arms around my neck and said, "Goodnight, my dear Ti-mo-thee."

I told her I would pick her up at noon tomorrow. She just smiled and nodded. I slept dreaming she was in my arms with her head on my shoulder.

Chapter 10
Tio Willy y La Comida con La Familia

I had called Uncle Willy to find where he would be on Sunday afternoon. He said he would be at his shop, which was good. I wanted Claire to meet him in his real environment.

Claire ran out to meet me, "I can stay until your play opens, Timmy."

"What? How did that happen? Great!"

Marilee came out, "It was mostly my doing. I couldn't stand the thought of her working with you on *Blood Wedding* and not getting to see it. I kind of created some travel plans that can always be postponed. So, I put on some strong persuasion and it worked. I hope it doesn't mess up my relationship with her father, but it's worth the chance. Besides you two are the happiest folks I know, well, next to me and Daniel. And the trips are almost legitimate because I had thought of them, but that was before the 'smittening' happened"

I laughed and hugged Claire and Marilee at the same time. Claire and I just stood and looked at each other smiling, holding hands.

Dan came out greeting us. "Great news, brother, we're as happy about it as you two seem to be. Claire is more like family than a guest."

As we were pulling out of the driveway, Claire turned to make sure Marilee and Dan had gone back in the house.

"Stop Timmy for a minute."

I did and she moved over and kissed me, then said, "You can go now, Monsieur Sart."

On the way to Uncle Willy's I told her how close I had always been with him and how he had gotten me interested in cars and machinery. I had liked working with metal and Daniel liked working with wood so I had spent untold hours at Uncle Willy's while Daniel had spent time with Dad building furniture. When we drove up, there were several people getting their race cars ready for the evening races and asking Uncle Willy questions He waved and joined us, opening Claire's door for her. He is a bit shorter than I am and stockier with the same unruly shock of black hair as mine. He had always sported a thin movie-star-like mustache. I introduced them. He was immediately taken by her. He showed us around his shop describing his new projects. Most of his business was for his machine shop, but the building of cars was beginning to take over most of his space. The shop was a big brick building with a high ceiling and big garage like doors in the front. He had placed big fans hanging from the rafters, so it was almost breezy. He showed us his new special project, an open wheeled roadster with a big Cadillac engine in it and exhausts coming out the sides with long round mufflers showing. He said his lady, Rosie, wanted an open car and this was it.

"This may be more than she wanted, but we'll both be driving it so I made it more of a sportster. I am having second thoughts, and may try to find something else for her."

I asked him if he had seen Marilee's Packard.

"She brought it by the second day she had it," he nodded, "Now, that's a classy piece of machinery. I drove it in the neighborhood and didn't even scare her, of course, Marilee is quite a classy lady, so I wouldn't expect anything less than the Packard, although I did try to talk her into buying a Lincoln."

He had heard that Claire was staying with Marilee and that that was how we met. He talked about how much he loved Daniel and Marilee and how they seemed to be the perfect couple. We agreed with that and Claire said staying with them couldn't be more comfortable. Uncle Willy teased me about theatre saying I sure would have made a good machinist and mechanic.

"Now, that's a real profession, Miss Claire, maybe you could be an influence on him. Even Jeordie's making art from old metal parts. You know, that boy has read every engineering book I have here in the shop. He's one of the best I've ever seen with the mathematics of it."

"I'm looking forward to meeting the family tonight especially Jeordie since I have a brother the same age."

"Tim's mother called and told me y'all were gathering tonight for one of her special dinners. They're just as eager to meet you."

"Goodness, I hope they're not disappointed," Claire said, frowning slightly.

"There's no chance of that, I guarantee you of that. I knew you must be rather special to get this character here to spend time with you. And by the way, Tim boy, it's time for you to bring that '34 of yours in so I can make it even better. I think it's time I put in some more modern brakes and I've got a bigger engine I'd like to install. I think you would really feel the difference."

About this time, his wife, Rosie, drove up. She had heard I was coming by and wanted to meet Claire. Mom must have been spreading the word. Rosie was almost tiny and bubbly cute with curly blond hair. She and Uncle Willy had never had children and considered me almost a son, and I thought that Jeordie was now stepping in since theatre had taken over my life. Rosie hugged me and surprised Claire with one too.

"Sister had invited us over tonight but nothing interrupts Will's race night. Besides we hoped you would come by today, and here you are. Well, no wonder everyone wants to meet you. Tim's dad said you're from France, but you're looking like a Texas girl."

"I'm from France, but I've lived in London for the last two years. My family moved there and I went to school at the university. And I can thank Marilee for my new look."

"That Marilee is an influence on everybody, in a good way I mean. We sure miss her and Daniel. Will said he saw her a couple of weeks ago when she came over in her new convertible. Have they opened the pool yet? That's always a highlight of the summer and they insist we use it. Oh, Claire, has Will shown you my new car? I can hardly wait till he finishes it."

"Yes, the first thing. It looks almost more European than American."

We all went into Uncle Willy's office and had a Dr Pepper from his iced down cooler that always seemed to be filled.

"I think I'm beginning to like the Dr Pepper, Timmy."

We laughed and I told the story Dick had told about his calling for Dr Pepper when he was in the Madrid hospital. Rosie said they had heard he was back and had brought home a beautiful Spanish wife. Uncle Willy said he was just glad he got back in one piece and what a mess it was in Spain and a whole bunch of other places, and how it looked like China was in real trouble with Japan. He told us of having seen the beginning of that in Manchuria.

"Has Marilee talked about her business in Java? Now may a good time to get out and cut the losses."

"She mentioned something about it last week, but I don't think she will take any losses. Evidently, it has been good for her, Grant made sure of that before he died."

"Well, she'll still have Oklahoma and Burkburnnet."

Rosie stepped in, "How long are you going to be here, Claire? Dallas could be a good place for a new home."

"My father has set up his business in Los Angeles and they expect me to come there after Timmy's show opens. I just found out today I could stay until then."

"Well, that's good news, nephew.

"Yes, at the very least, good news. Claire's helping me with the production and her being able to be at the opening is going to make it more of a celebration."

Rosie chimed in, "That means we'll see you again. We insist!"

"No matter what, we never miss one of his openings. He's turned us into theatre fans and it sounds like this one could be real good," said Uncle Willy.

"I think real different is a better way to describe it."

"That's alright, too, Tim. I'm used to that around here."

We left Uncle Willy and Rosie with hugs and waves and went looking for some good semi-deserted roads. I thought maybe Fair Park, with little traffic and its wide streets and a large parking lot behind the livestock barns would be good. I found a completely open area, stopped the car and got out so Claire could get behind the wheel. I adjusted the seat with a pillow from the trunk and gave her instructions.

"What if I hurt your car, Timmy?"

"You won't, I'm right here."

With several rough starts, she was able to go in first gear and with instructions got into second with a bit of grinding. She steered around the lot, stopped, and started again. As she gained more confidence, she loved it. Everything went slowly, but she was driving. She laughed, giggled, and squealed with every success and mistake.

"I think I would be too scared to drive on real streets with other cars around. Am I doing alright, Timmy?"

"Fine, perfectly fine, I assured her, "There's no rush to get out in traffic yet. With several more lessons you'll be on the streets. It's alright to be scared at first, that makes you more careful."

On one of our stops a Texas Ranger from the station there pulled up and asked us what all the stop-start was about.

"Teaching this lady from France how to drive in America."

He introduced himself, and Claire was thrilled to meet a real Texas Ranger. He said he guessed the fair grounds was about as good as anywhere to learn when there's not many people here, but we should probably cut it short since people would be coming soon to picnic around the lagoon and go to the bandshell. Claire and I traded places and drove to the parking in front of the art museum and walked around the lagoon. We sat in the grass, watched the ducks and talked about the visit with Uncle Willy and Rosie.

"They are some of the sweetest people I've ever met. They really love you, Timmy. This is a real Sart family day for me. I hope the evening goes as well, I so hope your parents like me. What have you told them about me and us?"

"Well, that I care for you and that you're helping me at the theatre. They're just surprised I'm spending so much time with one person and they want to meet you."

"A good surprise for me too. I don't know what..."

"I think I know what you're trying to say. I feel the same about it being so right. It's as if we've found some kind of magical place in time. I hope that doesn't sound too strange, but I don't know how else to describe it."

"No, not strange at all. Whatever it is, I'm changing, I mean I'm different, or I mean I'm experiencing something different."

"Yes, me too. I want to tell you everything I'm thinking or ever thought. I want to tell you what I feel about theatre and why I want to do it."

"Why do you believe you decided to go into theatre?"

"I hadn't thought about it that much before except that I like it and can do it, but since meeting you, it has become more clear. I was in a lot of theatre in high school, and I like to work with people. The other "artistes" in the family work in a solitary fashion. There's a chapter in the first Stanislavsky book, "communion." It's more or less about connecting with others, more to the actors viewpoint, but this production has changed that. And it's a French word that makes it different, ensemble. I couldn't work in a studio alone all day, not that I have the talent for it."

"Who cares if you have the talent for the studio? I know you're talented in theatre. I see you every evening working with your cast and it's wonderful. I wish it were that clear for me. Well, I guess it is. I know someday I'll work in a museum. But I also want to tell you everything I'm thinking and about places I've seen, and my dreams...can I tell you enough how happy I am when I'm with you?"

"No, but sometimes you don't need too, your smile tells me. And, of course, your kiss."

"May I kiss you now, Monsieur Sart?"

"Oui, Mademoiselle Levant."

We lingered awhile by the lagoon.

"Is the museum still open?"

"Yes, I believe so."

"Could we go in for a minute? I want to see Daniel's painting again and your mother's, and your father's furniture before tonight."

On the way to my parents' house Claire asked, "You've never told me your parents names ?

"Dad's name is Charles, no diminutive; and Mom's is Eleanor but she prefers Elly."

"Don't worry, I won't walk in and say, hallo Charles, hallo Elly."

We laughed, "I think they would love hearing you saying their names the way you do... Shar-lez...Ell-ee!"

I drove up the alley to my parking place and went through the back gate as I pointed out my little apartment.

"May I see it tonight?"

"Without almost any qualms."

She giggled and, "Almost...?"

"This morning I thought you might see it, so I cleaned it up, and if I know Mom, she also put her touch on it."

"My goodness, you make me feel very special."

We went in the back door and to the kitchen.

"Timmy, sometimes the front door is the proper entrance. Claire, I'm so glad you're here, I'm Elly. Please."

She shook Claire's hand then said, "Oh, that's not enough, my dear..."

And she hugged Claire, "Welcome to our little house."

"Thank you, misszuz Sart"

"Now, now, Elly!"

"Ell`ee...I love your house. Art is everywhere."

Dad came in and did a double-take when he saw Claire, "My word! So this is the lovely French girl who has made Tim so happy...Hello, Claire. Welcome. Please call me Charles."

"Thank you... 'Sharlez'."

"Elly, from now on I want you to say my name like that."

Mom laughed out loud at that and gestured for us go into the living room.

"Meestuer...I mean Charles, Did you make this furniture? It's lovely?

"I have a hard time with anyone else's design, so yes, my stuff is all over. I'm glad you like it."

And the paintings, they are yours, Ell`ee?"

"Most of the canvases are mine, but some are Daniel's early work."

"We went in the museum for a few minutes today. I wanted to see Daniel's Flood painting and your large still life again. I like them both very much."

"Tim said you studied art history, so that's a real compliment, and he showed me your sketches from the theatre. You're quite talented yourself."

"I can sketch but when I started trying to use oils, I knew it was time to stop. What do you think of Daniel's new painting? His colors are extraordinary."

"They sure are. He's found a whole new way of approaching his work. He's left me behind on that."

"No, no you both work so differently and these portraits! They're wonderful."

"Thank you, dear."

Dad stepped in, "Let's have a cocktail. Marilee taught me her special recipe for Martinis. How's that?"

"I think I'll have Bourbon, Claire?"

"Marilee's Martinis have become a favorite of mine, too. Thank you."

Mom sat down and pulled Claire down beside her, "Will called us and told about your visit this afternoon. They both fell in love with you."

"Oh, they are the sweetest people. He is funny and Rosie is the perfect match. They made me feel like...well, part of the family. Is that alright to say?"

"Yes, it is, and I hope we can make you feel the same way here," called Dad from the kitchen.

We heard some skipping footsteps coming down the hall, and Jeordie burst into the room. He stopped in place and stared at Claire, then said, "Wow, you're beautiful, you look like a movie star! Hi, I'm Jeordie."

Claire blushed in her auburn red way and laughed, "I thought you might be. Timmy tells me you are fourteen. My brother, Jean-Paul, is, too."

"Timmy?! He must like you to let you call him that."

I gave Jeordie a strong look and, "Enough little brother!"

"Hey, Claire, can I take your picture? I just got a new camera and Tim told me to ask you first."

"I suppose so."

"Little brother, don't overdo it. Of course, I would like a whole roll."

"Jeordie, if you must and Claire doesn't mind, but don't be obnoxious," Mom said.

"Yes, ma'amm." and he was off to get his new camera.

Mom wanted to know all about Claire's life in France and England and how she liked Dallas so far. Claire responded softly and told an abbreviated version of her life. She also described how Marilee had made her feel so much at ease here. Dad asked about her parents and how soon would she have to join them.

"I thought I would be going to be with them very soon but this morning they gave me permission to stay until Timmy's play opens. Marilee also had a talk with them and so I will be staying. I would have been most unhappy if they had refused. I so want to be here to watch rehearsals and do what I can to help. Timmy told me you both would be helping to paint and to build his settings."

Dad smiled and said, "We've gotten involved on several of this shows. Most everything is done by volunteers, so why not us?"

"But also, you will bring a special expertise. It has become quite a family endeavor. The colors Daniel has created are so perfect for what I think Timmy's vision is. Perhaps Jeordie could take photographs."

Jeordie entered as Claire was finishing, "Great idea, Claire. What do you say big brother?"

"Not a bad idea at all, but you'll have to wait until the last week when there are lights on the stage. Could you do it and make no noise or be a distraction?"

"Of course, I want to help, not be a problem. Thank you, Claire. I've always wanted to help but didn't know how before. I'd better get a lot of practice, uh...starting now."

Mom laughed and said, "Well, that completes the circle."

We talked and laughed as Jeordie moved around taking pictures. Finally Mom said it was time to eat.

"I've fixed one of Timmy's favorites, lamb curry. I hope you like it, Claire?"

"Curry is one of my favorites, too. If you live in London for any time, you get used to it as a cultural cuisine, and in France, North African, or Algerian dishes are a national favorite. It's also very spicy."

Dinner was a big success and my family insisted that Claire come back any time and that she didn't need an invitation.

We left through the back door and went to my apartment. Mom really had put her touch on it because I had never seen it this clean. I turned on my reading lamp and started to turn out the overhead but Claire asked me to wait. She wanted to see all the paintings and posters I had on the walls. The portrait Mom had done of me when I was a little boy caught her immediate attention.

"You look just like that now, well, I mean you look like that grown up. These are Daniel's aren't they?"

"I've liked everything Dan has painted and he gives me a painting a year almost. Not this year yet, but he told me to choose one and I haven't been able to make up my mind on which one. I hope to get one with his new colors but it really depends on what he needs for his potential New York show. I don't believe there's any doubt he'll get one, especially if Marilee has anything to do with it."

"If I know anything about the New York art world all Marilee has to do is just be with him and get introductions. He is genuinely unique."

"This is a nice flat. I wish I had had one like this in London."

"Did your parents let you live alone there?"

"No, but our house was big enough that I had a separate entrance. It was a... is basement the right word?"

"If it was underneath, yes."

"Then a basement flat that connected to the rest of the house with a little door under the steps up to the front door."

"It wasn't quite like living on my own, but if I had had the opportunity, I would have done," she continued, "My parents would never have allowed that though. I don't know if they ever will. They are very protective. If they didn't know Marilee so well, I wouldn't be here now. Thank goodness for her, yes?"

"Indeed, thank goodness for Marilee for many things."

Claire sat down on the bed and I sat beside her.

"I don't believe I'll ever forget this day, Timmy. I've never felt this close to a different family before. Are they like this with everyone?"

"No, not usually. It's that they truly liked you, from the moment they met you. They're pretty good at judging people at first sight. It's always taken a while for them to accept my friends, but you were a 'hit'"

"A hit?"

"Like a 'hit' show, a big success."

"Oh. Well all of your family is a 'hit' with me, too. You are a 'hit'"

I laughed and hugged her and we lay back together on my bed. I snuggled in close with her. She whispered something in French in my ear. I didn't ask what it meant. I whispered to her, "Pienso en ti, Claire."

"Timmy, hold me. It feels so nice."

"I moved my hand down to the small of her back and she moved even closer. I ran my hands over her thighs, so soft. I moved up to her derriere, round and full, but equally soft like she was made in a way I never imagined."

"I'm so big back there, Timmy. I'm a bit embarrassed for you to know me like this."

"No, don't be. You're a beautiful woman to touch and hold."

"Oh, Timmy."

And we kissed and I caressed her breasts and she kissed me, opening her mouth and our tongues touched, like a sudden burst of electricity.

"I'm not scared of us, but I feel a little out of breath. Let me look at you."

Her eyes were misty. I kissed them. She cried a little, not shaking but tearing with a smile."

"To cry because I'm happy is wonderful, Monsieur Sart. I've never laughed or cried this much in my life."

"You smile pretty good, too."

"You're being a silly boy, but don't stop it."

I glanced at my alarm clock. It was midnight and time to go. We parted sweetly at Marilee's door just holding each other."

Chapter 11
Mitad del Ensayo

Breakfast Monday morning was an interesting rehash of the night before. Both of my parents understood why I had been so involved with Claire for the last couple of weeks. Their only worry was how it would affect me when she left. I told them I was reconciled to it.

"Timmy, remember I said that sometimes with good luck comes happiness but at its end a sadness may come. Please be ready for that knowing you had a special time and that it can make you stronger," Mom said "I know that's not much of a solution but I just don't want your heart broken. Claire may experience the same thing. I saw her happiness and how at ease she is with you. I can tell she truly cares for you."

"Enough of this sad talk," my father declared "I think she's a wonderful young lady. We both liked her immensely. Enjoy your time together. You never know what will happen so it's really now that counts; and please bring her to see us more."

Jeordie came into the kitchen ready for school, "Tim, I sure liked Claire. I can't wait until I get this roll developed. Her brother sounds like a guy I'd like to know. She's not really going to leave, is she?"

"Yes, after my play opens."

"I'll have my photos by the end of the week. I hope they're good. I want one of her to put up in my room and show my friends what good-looking girls my brother knows."

And he was gone. My folks and I talked a bit more about when they would be needed to help at the theatre. I didn't let the conversation bother me, I knew I would see Claire in the evening. Moment by moment. All of this talk is taking a too serious a turn. I must accept that Claire and I are having fun and enjoying each other's company and...well, it's a good time at the right time. I sense and feel it's more, but then so does she.

Monday at work I had a surprise visitor, Uncle Willy.

"I had to go to the bank downtown so I thought I would drop in and see if I could take you to lunch."

My boss and Uncle Willy had known each other for years. He had found rare auto repair books for him and even some auto racing prints, which hung all over his office. They talked for a few minutes and Uncle Willy asked about a shop manual for an Auburn Roadster. He had found a wrecked Auburn in Tulsa and wanted to restore it. Wow, an Auburn! The boss gave me a lunch break, and we left for some Oaklawn Barbecue.

Over sandwiches and iced tea, Uncle Willy told me his main reason for stopping by.

"I didn't want say anything yesterday, especially in front of Rosie, but I was kind of shocked when I saw Claire. When I was in Shanghai I met a girl. She was a white Russian whose family had escaped the revolution and civil war there. They had lived for a while in Vladivostok, Port Arthur, and finally settled in Shanghai, China, where there was a fairly large White Russian community. She looked so much like Claire I couldn't believe it. Her name was Adriana and she was a looker. Claire is more beautiful, but their figures, skin, and hair are almost the same. I was there on a long shore leave and once we met, we spent every minute together. I fell head over heels in love with her, but her family would have none of it. Up to that point, I had never been happier and it was a sad parting. We wrote for a while but that ended when she got married to another Russian. Of course, I don't know how I would have gotten her into this country, much less how she would have liked it here, but it was a great life experience. Yesterday I saw you kind of going through what I did. When Claire said she had to go back to her family, it all came back to me. I guess all I wanted to say was enjoy every second you're with her. There's always been a special kinship between us, Tim, and I guess even more now. That was the long time past, and I was lucky to find Rosie, but it sure welled up when I saw Claire."

I was touched deeply by his story and all of a sudden missed Claire. I wouldn't tell her about this because I feared it would hit her even harder. It wasn't a sad story, just a shock that his past would become my present. I assured him that I would remember his advice, as if I wasn't already.

In between customers, I worked on my journal and planned the rehearsal for the week generally and for tonight specifically.

Claire jumped into my car and we were off to the theatre. Every time I saw her now, she seemed more beautiful than I remembered from the day before. She was excited about the week, looking forward to watching the play grow. When she got home last night, Marilee was still up and they'd had a long conversation.

"Marilee understands how much being with you for rehearsals has been and is a good experience. I told her of all the different things I've done, but working on this is the most intriguing. I studied hard in London, wrote papers, traveled for research, interviewed artists, and got my diploma early; but they were done by me alone for me, but this is like you described, a group involvement...an en-sam'-'blay. I believe what you're doing is important and my being a part of it is the first time I've felt important. Oh, and I think all of your family is wonderful and so does Marilee. I thanked her several times for bringing me here and bringing us together, Timmy."

I couldn't say anything, I didn't know if I could speak without choking up. No one had ever said things like that to me. When we arrived at the theatre, we walked to the door holding hands.

The rehearsal started in high spirits. My note session cleared up most questions from the cast, and they understood where we would be going with the work this week. I laid out the zones tighter for the first act but still giving them the freedom to develop their characters' blocking. I talked about technique using something I had worked on, on Sunday morning. I tried to describe it as 'scenic positioning,' or where on stage they would be most effective in relationship to their characters, the other actors, the audience, and that they go together all the time.

If that became a part of their thinking and growth, I explained, the whole play would be more effective in touching the audience. One actor asked what if it didn't feel natural. I replied that nothing on stage is natural and that all is for the audience's visual viewpoint. They must be able to see each gesture and expressive nuance. If they miss anything it's our mistake. I want them to hear every word, and see every thought on your faces. I want them to be shocked by your expressive power, by your reactions to the moment, everything a surprise. If you anticipate, so will they and the moment is lost. We lose them for a few seconds and it's hard to get them back. I had no idea when I started my notes that I would be saying all of the things I did, but it worked. They were leaning into my words, some taking notes, some in just high concentration. No rehearsal ever had started for me with such a feeling of ensemble; we were together. No questions. They all stood up for warm-ups. I turned to Ginger, who was just looking at me smiling.

"I feel like I just took a course in advanced theatre. That was great. Tim," she said.

We proceeded into the first act after warm-ups with the sonnet. I roamed the stage adjusting the groupings and stage pictures that I had seen was needed after studying Claire's drawings. I was on stage with them every minute, beside them, side directing for individual actors as they moved or went through a short movement and interpretation of scene breakdowns. Eddy's playing was a more involving part of each scene. He was improvising for the moment and finding new ideas, as were the actors. It was all working as I had hoped. I was improvising with them and I felt a surge of excitement when the ideas we were having together jelled into strong creative steps. They all knew I had a concept from a knowledge of Lorca's play and was trying for more than just a presentation of the script and to take the passion of the characters to a level beyond the audience's expectations. Beyond all of our expectations.

When I called for a break, the cast yelled out and applauded each other as if they had taken some steps that were new to them. Then most of them just sat down on the stage, while others ran for a drink of water. The older Mexican actor passed by me. "El Audazito!" he said.

I walked out into the house to spend a few minutes with Claire. She stepped into my arms. "My goodness, 'El Audazito', that was thrilling to watch. I couldn't draw fast enough. Sometimes I stopped just to watch you."

We went out to the lobby for a drink of water and to sit down. Suddenly I was out breath, as I realized how well the rehearsal was going. Things continued to go well for the second part of the evening. I felt we had built a beginning for the first act.

After rehearsals that night and the next night, Claire and I talked nonstop about everything. We laughed and stopped to look at each other and smile, then started up again.

We left each with tender goodbyes, almost as if it would be a week before we would see each other instead of the next day. On Wednesday, Camila joined us again for the dance practice with Eddy, Aurora, and the cast. She asked if I would mind if she watched the run-through on Friday, and afterwards Dick would join us for drinks somewhere. Of course, I agreed to both suggestions.

The wedding party was starting to look like a Flamenco celebration with couples dancing to Eddy's playing and individuals stepping out to hold the floor. It was still an innocent staging but headed toward something even more vivid than I had hoped for. Eddy, Aurora, and I held intense conferences of ideas as the evening progressed. During one of these talks, I had the idea of asking Aurora if she would join the cast and perform a solo sequence during the wedding party. Eddy immediately said it was a great idea, and we both looked at her.

She reached out and took my hand saying, "Claro que si, el Audaz." She had heard about the old actor's name for me. I took it as a sign of respect that she didn't use the 'ito' on the end. I turned and told the cast, and they applauded.

It was hard to believe that it was going so well but it was. I was still going into an unknown territory. I wondered if I could pull all of this together into a powerful show. The process can't be better than the product. "The show didn't work but the rehearsals were great wasn't what I was after."

At the store, I worked and planned, studied, and wrote in my journal. I set goals for each evening and how it related to the total production. I started visualizing generally the next three weeks to set up for the final week of run-throughs and two night of dress and tech rehearsals to set the lights. Claire's drawings were a revelation. I could lay out each scene seeing the progression and how I needed to adjust for segues between the scenes and enhance the stage groupings. I knew they would be even more valuable when the cast started changing the sets.

With Claire's help, my being on stage all the time turned out to be no drawback at all. I had never thought of myself as being part of the cast before and didn't seem to be inhibiting the actors. I was close but I don't think, intrusive. I knew I would pull back gradually as we headed toward dress rehearsal.

After Friday night's work, Dick met us in the lobby. He suggested we go in his car, a new Buick sedan, leaving my car at the theatre. We went to a private club downtown. His dad was a member, it stayed open late on the weekends. We ordered drinks and Camila talked about the run-through.

"I saw the whole show, Tim. I know it's early but it's there, she raved, "If it keeps growing like this it's really going to be something."

Dick told us more about having seen it in Madrid, "It was in a much smaller theatre and very intimate and close. I loved it but I can't wait to see yours. The audience went crazy in Madrid, applauding and jumping up and down. I don't expect that to happen here just because that was Spain."

"Once in London I saw a standing ovation. Would that be good here?" Claire asked innocently.

We all laughed and I said, "At the very least, that would be good. One can hope."

I hadn't realized how hungry I was until dinner arrived, but had I never felt so energized. Claire and Camila strengthened their friendship, and Dick and I were glad to renew ours. We laughed and talked going back to the theatre. I drove Claire home with her head on my shoulder. Claire had dozed off.

The next day was to be a busy one at the theatre. I was going in at 10:30 and Marilee was bringing Claire over in the early afternoon.

At breakfast on Saturday morning, Dad joined me. Since Mom had gone to the art supply store, he and I had a chance to talk for the first time in weeks without anyone else there.

"Tim, does your meeting Claire so soon after Gwen's leaving have anything to do with your feelings for her. I mean, like 'on the rebound?'"

"No, I don't believe so. I know Gwen had some feelings for me, but not in a way that would have given any sort of permanence to our relationship. I think she was just saying goodbye. It was a terrific weekend, and I learned a lot about love, or about making love. She's a good lady who needed to leave Dallas. I doubt very seriously if I will ever see her again, and she said as much. She's gone, and I feel no great sadness about it. Now Claire is a different matter. Our having met is more like a 'quirk of fate.' We could have met anytime; it just so happens it was shortly after Gwen left."

"That's good to hear; I guess 'quirk of fate' is the best way to describe it. Your mother was concerned about your being hurt. I told her my God, you're a twenty-four year old man not some fragile teenager. She still feels you're vulnerable because of Gwen. And after meeting Claire, we understand why you've been so happy. It's not distracting you from your work on the show, is it?"

"No, not at all. As a matter of fact, she's an inspiration and her sketches have been a great help in helping me delve into my new directing approach. I doubt that I would do every play as I'm doing this one, but it will certainly be a big influence if it works, and it does seem to be."

"I know it's kind of frightening when you turn creative corners," Dad agreed. "I've gone through it several times, and so has your mother; and it looks like Daniel has changed the way he uses color in a big way. Yes, a couple of times it hasn't worked for me, but as you said it influences everything afterwards. Don't have any doubts about it."

"I don't, really. It's been so all enveloping that I haven't had any time for them. I love the play, my cast is terrific and hard working, there's a whole lot of collaboration going on, and there's Claire. One of the best things I've done is to keep a journal. Every day when I write, I have new ideas, all of which have been useful. You know, Dad, I never knew how important it could be to have a lady you care about who is so supportive of your work. I've always been so solitary in it, and I thought that was the way to do it."

"Well, that in itself is a revelation. I guess you've noticed how much closer your mother and I have been lately; it mostly has to do with being supportive of each other's work. Of course, we started out that way, but as we later became dominated by the need to support the family and still do what we felt we had to do, we drifted apart emotionally and physically. Well, you know all about that; but something happened this last year. We just started looking at what each other was doing. She truly liked my chair design for the New York contest and my ideas for some commissions, and I fell in love again with her paintings. It has helped everything around here, and I mean everything, if you know what I mean, son."

I laughed and said, "Yes, I understand what you mean, Dad; that's great. "

I got up to go to my room. Dad came over and put his arm around me, which was rare, and said, "We're all excited about your work on this show, and Claire is a rarity, a special rarity. Don't even think about her leaving. It's good now, and perhaps that's enough. Maybe she's going through some big changes, too."

"I think she is, but I don't know how it's going to affect us. Well, I know how it's affecting us now but...well...I"

"You don't need to say anything more, I understand; more than you know."

We seldom had heart-to-hearts like this, but when they did happen they were always good. This one had been especially good. I had only thirty minutes to write before getting ready for the afternoon, but they were some of the best minutes yet.

When I arrived at the theatre, the designer and I worked a bit on the plans, then started gathering the right lumber for the day. We had decided to not use any flats, but instead to use thin plywood braced with frames. It wouldn't be as light as flats, but less likely to tear or break during the many set changes. The lighting designer, who did all of the shows at the theatre, came in with his design for just general lighting, and we had a good conference on what I wanted for the production. He like my ideas for the colors and scene separations. He agreed to finalize once he had studied Dan's colors for the set. His two volunteer assistants came in, one from SMU and the other from Highland Park High School. They started bringing out the lighting instruments and prepared to hang them. It was a beehive of activity by the time Mom and Dad arrived at around noon. Mom had studied Dan's renderings and wanted to start gathering the right colors for the eventual mixing. Dad worked with the designer in solving some of the problems on the pop-up scenery. I went to the office for a budget conference with Barney. By the time I got back on stage some of the cast members had arrived to help. At two, Claire, Marilee, and Dan came in. Claire was in her dungarees and had gotten some canvas tennis shoes to work in. She greeted me with a hug and a shy kiss. A good day got better all of a sudden.

I squeezed her hand and said, "Hi, there, Super Girl."

"Hallo, el Audazito."

Dad and Mom both greeted Claire with a hug. Marilee kissed both of them. Dan hugged Mom and slapped Dad on the shoulder. I had felt family before but not like this and Claire was a part of us.

Marilee brought a big basket of sandwiches and a bucket of pop she had gotten at an Ice House. Everyone took a break to enjoy Marilee's treat. After eating, we all went back to work. Marilee had a conference with Barney and offered help for the budget needs. It was an unexpected surprise, her reason being that she had no building or painting skills but she could help this way. I didn't know what to say except thanks. It was enough for her. She just laughed and hugged me and said she wanted to help more than giving me a couple of books.

Dan and Mom collected most of the paint needed but said they had to get some more for the most difficult mixes. Claire stepped right in carrying wood and learning to use a hand saw and drill. She had never used a hammer before and got a sore thumb as a result but was enjoying every moment of the afternoon. Jeordie walked in after a bicycle ride to the theatre and had his photos from the last weekend. They were very good. The family groupings were something we didn't have, and Mom wanted some more prints made. The ones of Claire and me together brought her to tears.

"I like this photography thing," Jeordie enthused, "If I ever sell another sculpture I'll get a better camera. I don't think Uncle Willy will be disappointed if I agree to take pictures of his cars. Maybe I'll try to put together a darkroom during the summer if Mom will let me use that empty closet in back of the kitchen."

Dad said, "Slow down, son. One roll does not a photographer make."

"One roll? I've taken almost six rolls this week at school and everybody liked them. I've decided I'm going to try to get on the newspaper staff at North Dallas next year."

Mom looked at him seriously and asked, "And what about engineering school?"

"I can do both, can't I?"

"Yes you can, son. What about being a 'Shaman?'"

"Aw Dad, I just said that to shake up Mom."

Mom got a half-serious laugh out of that, knowing what a trickster Jeordie was. Dan and Marilee left after a couple more hours letting Claire and me know that we were expected for dinner and a swim. Dad realized he had some hinges that would work better than those the theatre had and that there wasn't much more he could do. The designer was exhausted, ready to call it a day. Mom had totally reorganized the paint cabinet and needed to get home to fix dinner for Dad and Jeordie. Most of the crew had left, and I had only to have quick conference with Ginger and get her typed notes from Friday's rehearsal. Claire ended up sweeping the stage and helping to put away the tools. I wanted to change clothes before going to Marilee's, perhaps even take a quick shower, and Claire said she could visit with my parents while I got ready.

We both went in through the back door at my house. Mom insisted Claire sit in the kitchen with her while she prepared dinner, and Dad joined them. I rushed out to get ready and was back in the house in less than thirty minutes. Dad was having bourbon while Claire and Mom enjoyed a glass of wine. Dad insisted I join them for one drink before leaving. They had been having a spirited conversation about modern art. Claire told the story of having seen Picasso in Paris several times and even going to his studio with a group of students and their professor, who was a friend of his. Mom commented that it proved Picasso was a real person. Claire laughed and squeezed Mom's hand in response.

Claire asked if they had seen Daniel's latest work in his studio. Neither she nor Dad had, and both were anxious to see it. Claire remarked that a couple were even more powerful than "Flood Zone"; one was larger, almost abstract, and another was a brilliant triptych.

Jeordie came just before we left and almost shouted out, "Hi, Claire. Did you have fun at the theatre today?"

"Yes I did, and I like your photographs very much."

"Thanks, I'll get some more prints of those two you liked."

"Remember, not the one of me but of Timmy and also the family group."

"I'm putting one of you up on my wall."

"You had better be careful, it will give you nightmares."

"Well then on Tim's wall. No, I'll take the chance."

"Timmy, you didn't tell me your brother was so brave."

"He's not, he still has to sleep with a light on."

"Claire, don't you believe a thing my big brother says, I mean about anything."

"Oh, my! That's a frightening thought. Timmy?"

Dad stepped in, "Claire I think you're safe with Tim. Right Elly?"

"Well, Claire, he is a man, but one of the more trustworthy ones."

"Ah, my parents to the rescue. Jeordie we need to have a serious talk someday if I ever have the time, say later this summer."

"Gee, Tim, I better go put that on my calendar. No, Claire, Tim's alright. He even likes my sculpture."

On the way to Marilee's, Claire noticed I hadn't brought my satchel. "This, dear heart, is a real night off. Tomorrow I work."

"Good, Timmy. I was thinking the same thing. I won't insist on talking about the play. Today was fun, though. It seemed like a good amount was done. Did you think so?"

"Yes, but it's only a beginning. This is actually a pretty big show with lots of complications ahead, but it was a good day. You were great. How's your thumb?"

"It doesn't hurt anymore. It was just like in the cartoon movies. I actually hit my thumb like Donald Duck would."

"And you were a big girl. You didn't even cry. Funny girl, cries when happy, laughs at smashed thumb."

"The answer to that is I've never been this happy before and everyone has had bumps before. There's a difference in happy crying and I did get better with the hammer, didn't I?"

"Yes, you did. You built a whole frame for a plywood flat."

"I am now an experienced theatre craftsman or girl. But I must admit I almost cried when I hit my thumb. When I cried out, I thought you were going to come over and make a scene."

"I almost did. I could imagine your parents' reaction to your hand being smashed while being forced to work backstage in a little theatre."

"I'll try to hide from them that I've become a theatre slave. No, Timmy, when you asked across the stage, 'Are you alright, Sweetheart?' all the pain went away."

She giggled and put her head on my shoulder, and I put my arm around her.

At Marilee's, Claire went up to her room to take a bath and I joined Daniel in his studio. He said he wanted to do a bit more work on this new canvas before starting up the grill. This new one was kind of a skyline view of Dallas with an exaggerated Trinity River behind it. It was separated into three or four different color spectrums as if each section had a different filter in front of it. The spectrums were both vertical and horizontal.

"Boy, wait until Mom sees this one. She's very excited about your new approach to colors, but this one is absolutely...I don't know what to say, other than it's brave. You had better hide this one after it's finished or it will be gone before you ever get that New York show."

"I hope that means you like it. I thought I may have gone too far with it, but as I work on it, I'm not sure I've gone far enough. There are a couple of other ones I'm working on at the same time. I don't think I've ever gone back and forth so much before. They're over there."

He pointed across the room. I went over and held one up. This one was of White Rock Lake with the city behind it, also extraordinary. The other was a vertical painting about two feet wide and six feet high. He evidently had painted it in his backyard, it was of Turtle Creek going from their dock to the north; shore line, trees, boats, kids fishing, and the houses all Italianate. It was Dallas but it wasn't. Horizontal color bands progressed narrow to wide from the bottom to the top; and a sort of diagonal filter effect running from a corner on top to the opposite one below. They were breathtaking.

"These are perhaps my last paintings of Dallas. I'm looking forward to Taos and the mountains. What do you think, brother?"

"I like. What's in between now and Taos"

"I'm doing some figurative drawings. I want to do one of the family. All of us."

"You're not going to require a sitting, are you?"

"Nope, just how I see us."

He put down his brushes to clean, turned, and said, "It was great working with Mom at the theatre today. Claire has sure become a part of the whole production. Her sketches are quite good, I can see how they're helping. How are things with you two? I only get the girls' viewpoint."

"And what is their viewpoint?"

"Well, it seems that Claire is having the time of her life. Marilee said that when she knew Claire in the past, there was a kind of sadness about her. She had always seen glimpses of her sense of humor but there was a holding-back quality about her. It's as if she has flowered or come alive. Marilee did say that Claire said she never expected to meet someone like you."

"My word, we've become a major gossip topic. I don't really know what to say about us, except that we're having a good time together."

"Please don't think I'm trying to dig into your personal life, but...well, I guess

I am. You've usually seemed to be sort of a loner, not including Gwen, but I did understand that situation. Remember that I had known Gwen for years and she was a real will o' the wisp. I knew as well as you did that there was no chance for any sort of permanence, just those occasional rages of passion; and rest assured that I'm not speaking from personal knowledge. But very quickly, you and Claire have gone way beyond smitten. Am I correct?"

"Yes you're correct, we're beyond smitten. I believe that was a cute, and it was, word from Jane Austen that described our instant reaction to each other. We've tried to figure it out but have given up and decided to enjoy what's happening. Dad and I had a talk this morning about the same subject. Everyone seems to be concerned about us, and what's going to happen when she leaves. Well, I don't know what's going to happen. It's true I'm having feelings I've never experienced before. She is a wonderful woman, and I certainly didn't expect to meet anyone like her, either."

"Are you falling in love with her, or should I say have you?"

"Yes, I have, if falling in love means I think of her every minute and feel most alive when I'm with her; and she not a distraction from my work but a true inspiration; and she tells me she feels the same way. I didn't believe I could say that. I don't know much about love as an experience. I read about it and I direct it in plays, but...and what's even more interesting is that I understand *Blood Wedding* with a new depth every day. Is that love? You certainly know more about it than I do."

"It sure sounds like love."

"Too quickly? I don't know what that means. I believe if we had met each other in a situation where we couldn't be together all the time, it would have taken longer perhaps, but it would have happened. I have no doubts about it, nor does she, I believe. Please don't say anything about this conversation. We haven't told each other we're in love with each other. And we may never get the chance, but I feel extremely lucky to have met her. I know Marilee is glad we're so happy together, but this has got to be between us."

"I'll truly honor that request, but it wasn't even needed; this has been between brothers."

"Good. Please don't think I'm upset with you, because I'm not. Actually I was able to express something I didn't think I could. Love...yes...saying it certainly puts all my questions about what's going on into perspective. You know if Dad had asked me if I was in love with Claire, I probably would have said something like, 'Gee, whiz, Dad...I don't know.'"

"There's something you should...Well, on second thought nothing."

"What?"

"Oh, just love advice. I decided you don't need it."

Marilee's entrance into the studio ended our brother-to-brother talk.

"Would the fabulous Sart brother like to have a swim before lighting up the grill? I think I will. Timmy, Claire will be down in a few minutes. She told me about the visit with the family, and how much they made her at ease. I assured her that wasn't always the case, so they must really like her. Her answer to that was she hoped so because she really liked them."

"There's no doubt about them liking her. I wasn't surprised, she's not just a regular girl as I think you are well aware of."

"No she's not just a regular girl, and right now she's a ridiculously happy girl. And I sense it's more than the usual Sart men's charm."

"Well, I don't know about that, but right now I'm a ridiculously happy fellow."

"Yes, I can see that, Timmy. Good for both of you."

We went out on to the patio and pool deck and I changed into my trunks in the cabana. The cool water was a delightful release. I was glad we had agreed not to get into any play talk. I needed the separation. Daniel and Marilee joined me in the pool, all of us 'frolicking' and splashing each other. In a few minutes Claire came out jumped into the water laughing and swam to me, trying a dunk. I was able to quickly dunk her. She came up sputtering and giggling and put her arms around me. There didn't seem to be any reason to be inhibited around Dan and Marilee any more. They came over to us and put their arms around us. Marilee kissed Daniel and me in a playful sweet way. We all worked our way to the side of the pool and held on.

I talked about how much I liked Daniel's new paintings and was eager to see what happens with his figurative subjects. Claire had been impressed with the filtered color effect varied in layers .She had been to all the major museums in Europe and New York, but had never seen anything like it. Marilee said she wasn't going into the studio as much while Dan was painting because she was enjoying the surprise as he finished each new piece. Daniel seemed rather humbled by the praise, but he was obviously excited by what had happened in his work.

"I don't know if what I'm doing is good or just different and strange."

"I feel the same way about my play."

Breaking a pledge to mention the play went by the wayside as I realized I had said the same thing as Dan just did. I didn't believe either one of us had doubts about where we were going. For me it was as if I had been caught up in a whirlwind that had taken hold of me and I was going where it carried me.

Claire commented immediately, "I'm sure your paintings are good Daniel and Timmy; theatre is the most ephemeral of the arts but if the production is as exciting as what's happening in rehearsals it's going to be wonderful. Of course, I am biased, but I still have a pretty good critical eye. If I'm moved and touched by what's happening this soon, well...I think you're both brilliant artists."

"Hear, hear! I couldn't agree more, bien dicho, Claire." Cheered Marilee.

We got out of the pool and instead of getting dressed we wrapped towels around us. Dan attacked the grill, announcing that steaks were the offering tonight. Marilee mixed up some of her special Martinis, and Dan and I chose bourbon. We sat around the patio table, not talking as much but enjoying each other's company. Claire sat close and held my hand. Marilee mentioned how beautiful Taos was in the summer and how glad she would be to get there next month. Claire was curious about New Mexico, not knowing there were mountains and forest there. The steaks were as good as they get and the Spanish Brandy followed dinner.

Marilee and Dan took one more quick dip in the pool and then went inside and up to bed. Claire took care of clearing the dishes and then joined me on the poolside lounge chair. Our bathing suits were almost dry by then.

"Did you notice my bruises? If I bump into anything I get bruised, they don't hurt, but it's so unattractive."

"No it's not, it's just you. Claire is Claire, is Claire, and I like Claire."

"Thank you, Monsieur Sart."

She leaned into my arms, and I kissed her long and softly. We had never been this close before without being fully dressed and it was a physical encounter that changed our whole reaction to each other. Our touching aroused a newer passion, not a frantic lust, but awareness of our caring.

"Timmy, you make me feel like an attractive woman when you hold me close. I can't get enough of you...I mean I don't want this to stop; this just being close."

I stroked her thighs and back, still amazed that she could be so soft and appear so firm. I touched her covered breasts and she made little sounds that drew me closer. I kissed her face and eyes and shoulders feeling that incredible little electrical shock of being with a woman who returned all of my feelings in her own passionate way. I didn't think of anything but the present, especially not any sexual advancement; I wanted to feel every moment of this gentle awareness of each other.

We whispered about the goodness of our happiness and time together. We practiced saying our names and new endearments, where one word seemed to recite long romantic poems. We were both on the edge of a new level of our relationship. If this was love, it was a reason for existence.

We both started dozing a bit and knew it was time to go home.

"Timmy, will I see you tomorrow?"

"Let's have dinner together. I've got to write and plan for the big week coming up."

"I will miss you, but I know how important this week will be."

"Don't you dare think I won't miss you too."

"I know, sweetheart. I need to spend some time with Marilee. She has mentioned lunch at the club. Do you mind if I write you a letter?"

"No, but don't mail it."

"I don't know if I could be with you when you read it."

"Well, mailing it may be good. I've already written to you but haven't put it all together in a letter. Let's do that."

"Maybe I can say things that are hard to say out loud."

She walked me to my car, kissing me long and with an almost writhing passion. I wanted to tell her something that I wasn't sure she was ready to hear or that I had the nerve to say yet.

Chapter 12
La Carrera al Final

Sunday morning breakfast was pleasant with little talk about Claire or the play. Both parents thought the time I was spending with Claire at Daniel and Marilee's was good for me. They felt Daniel and I needed to get as close as possible before our careers took us away from each other. Jeordie showed me his photos from school and I told him he just might have talent as photographer. He seemed all consumed by it, which was new for Jeordie. Even his dabbling at sculpture hadn't interested him anywhere near as much as using his camera.

My late morning and the afternoon were dominated by writing in my journal and writing out plans for the week. Building a play in rehearsal through improvisation with the script was much more demanding than the usual process. Improvising created a more collaborative approach to imagination, but to work it must get closer to setting a scene or I would be improving ad nauseam. Each day of rehearsal I had to see where the next step needed to be. The major parts of each scene were now blocked into tighter zones of about three feet of freedom for the actors to find new but slight changes. The response so far from the cast was that they appreciated the opportunity use their imaginations and not be locked into a tight blocking pattern. And they trusted me; when something wasn't working in their movement or interpretation, they knew I would see it and head them in a better direction more often than not. The most difficult part about what I was trying to do was the intense concentration it demanded from all of us. Each step had to be layered on the last in a productive manner, or there was a danger of wallowing into a process of indecision. We didn't have the time for let's go back and try what we did before. My being with them on stage all the time made the difference; I got no farther from them than the lip of the stage, and gave directions as they worked. I would talk to them but they wouldn't stop, it was as if I was whispering ideas and they would adjust physically or advance interpretation. Every day I gained more confidence but I was teaching myself and using every bit of technique I could garner from the best writers on theatre.

Claire's drawings had made the difference for me in setting better stage pictures and she was getting better as she understood more how her drawings worked for me. Her work was getting faster and more broad without all of the detail but of grouping as we progressed through the scenes. At this point, I wasn't sure that what I was doing would work with a more traditional play such as a Somerset Maugham that I wanted to direct. *Blood Wedding* is so open for new ideas for the many scenes with difficult segues and fantastical settings that I believe it demands new ways of thinking. Sometimes when I write in my journal, I got scared to death, hoping my ideas made the creative leap to production; but it was so damned exciting. The writing about it seemed to give the improvisation more discipline. I got more facile in advancing the script with an outline of the process. Part of the outline was written out and another was of arrows drawn toward listings of emotional desires for the scenes and individual and group interpretations; it looked like a scientific formula for an experiment. I understood it, but I'm not sure anyone else would, well, except for Claire. I showed her my diagrams and she had some ideas about how to make them clearer.

Claire enters my mind every time I stop writing for a minute. I wonder what she's thinking and doing, and then I think of a question I want to ask her: What do you think of this idea? Should Eddy come in stronger here? Should I spread the dancing out more? Why are you more beautiful ever time I see you? Never have I had someone close to talk to during rehearsal, especially someone as close to the show as she has become.

In the middle of the afternoon Jeordie came to tell me I had a telephone call.

"Hallo, Timmy." It was Claire.

"Hi there, wonderful girl. How's your afternoon going?"

"It is fine, but I miss you."

"And I you."

"Marilee just talked to your parents about us all getting together tonight. I wanted to tell you and see if you agree. She says the club is having a nice Sunday night buffet and we're all invited. What do you think? Do you want to go?"

"It sounds good to me. Do you want to?"

"If you do. We were going to be together anyway weren't we?"

"Of course. You couldn't possibly think I would change my mind?"

"I hope not, Timmy. Let's go then, I enjoy being with your family. Could you be here at six for a little time together before we leave?"

"How about earlier? I can be there at five. Is that too early for you?"

"No, all I have to do is dress. I had a delightful bubble bath an hour ago. I'm glad you're coming earlier I'll be at the door. Bye mi 'audazito'."

"Bye, super girl."

I worked on my journal for another hour and made out diagrams and notes for the week in general knowing I would have a chance to be more specific at the store during the day. I read the play again and went back to my notes several more times. I read Ginger's notes from the past week. My concentration was getting better everyday and my thoughts of Claire helped. Having someone believe in your work was a great advantage. I finished, got ready, even wearing a tie for the club, and put on a jacket that Uncle Willy had given me last year. He had gotten it in Hong Kong years ago, but it was still stylish and made of a beautiful dark blue silk. I went into the house and told the family I would see them at Marilee's.

When I drove up to the door Claire came out. As I got out of the car, she stepped into my arms, "Hallo, Timmy. You look so handsome," she whispered.

I stepped back from her and looked at the absolutely breathtaking outfit she had on. It was a deep rich burgundy that made her auburn hair and glowing skin even more striking.

"Do you like my dress?"

"I don't think 'like' quite says how beautiful it is."

"I got it at that store downtown. Is it Neiman's?"

"It looks like a Neiman-Marcus dress."

"I was saving it for your opening, but I couldn't wait."

"Don't give it a thought. Now is right."

We went into the living room and sank down in the cushy leather sofa. She wanted to know how my work had gone today, and I told her in detail about the diagrams and journal writing. She was interested in everything. She told me about her day, and that it had changed because they didn't go to lunch at the club. Marilee talked her into a swim early in the afternoon and they sat around the pool and discussed Marilee helping me and the family. The Sart family had given Marilee a whole new feeling of completeness and she expressed it in loving terms of trust and support. She had been worried at first that she wouldn't be accepted, but there had been nothing of the sort. Her relationship with Daniel from the beginning had been so good, and our family had became a part of it. She had described how close she had felt with Uncle Willy and Rosie.

"Marilee surprised me with something she said; that she thinks she wants to be a Sart...that she wants to marry Daniel, but she hasn't told him. We have become very close since I've been here but I didn't expect her to become that open and trusting. She said it was alright to tell you but for it to go no further."

"My word, that is something! Of course, I won't say anything. My impression has been that what they have now is too good to change."

"Yes, but she feels because her of money that Daniel may resist. I think she's wrong about that. They would have fallen in love if he had had money and she didn't, or if neither one had any money. They are as happy couple as I've ever seen. Don't you think so?"

"I believe what they have is amazing. And, you know, I believe Daniel would say marriage is just fine with him. It could make their life easier in a way."

"Evidently, she has no doubts about their relationship at all and wants to be a real member of the family."

"Well, she already is, but I understand, I think, what she wants is to be named Sart; not just be accepted as Daniel's lady friend. Hmmm..., Maybe she wants to have children with Dan?"

"You are a smart man, Monsieur Ti-mo-thee Sart. I'm sure she does too. She didn't say as much, but I could just tell by the look in her eyes. She loves and adores Daniel so much that I believe she's ready for the natural progression of it."

"It's good that she is talking about it, and to you. You know, I don't think she's had anybody to talk with before you came. Most of the people she works with are men, and I haven't noticed that she has any close women friends. But then I haven't been around that much until lately. I mean, I usually see them about once a month. Well, anyway it is an interesting turn of events. Did she say she was going to approach Dan about this, or just wait and see what happens between them?"

"I don't think she's sure about what to do. It doesn't seem to be urgent, and perhaps she was just seeking some advice or support. That's kind of funny considering I'm probably the most innocent woman she knows,, in these sorts of matters anyway."

"Well, I know she respects your intelligence and for sure she knows you're not a scatterbrain."

"A scatterbrain?!" Claire laughed, "What a funny word. What does it mean? Wait...Scatter means to spread out, but with brain?"

"Yes, your senses spread out in all different directions...uh? Not logical. Silly? Well, I think you're very logical and only silly at times."

"Timmy, you're being silly right now. Do you think I'm a silly girl?"

"No, I don't. You are the most un-silly girl I've ever met. I swear on a stack of funny papers to the moon that's a true statement."

"Oh, Timmy. I don't want you to ever think I'm a scatterbrain."

"I think that's the least of your worries. As a matter of fact, you're the smartest lady I've ever known."

She leaned over into my arms. I kissed the top of her head. Her hair's beautiful scent held me for a moment, and I then turned her head toward me.

"Claire, at times I have a whole new rush of feelings for you."

"Me too, Timmy."

I kissed her gently.

"You want to know what I told Marilee?" she asked.

"If you want to tell me."

"I said that on their travels to New Mexico and New York, away from Dallas would be a good time to bring it up slowly with Daniel. You know, not all at once like 'let's get married, Dan!' What do you think?"

"I believe that's the best thing you could have said. Very good advice, Mademoiselle. What was her reaction?"

"She agreed. I believe she was thinking the same thing and just needed someone else to say it."

"They would sure have beautiful children."

"Yes..."

Claire stopped there, went very quiet and looked at me. Suddenly tears started down her cheeks. I kissed her forehead and pulled her into my arms.

"Are you alright, Claire? Did I say something to upset you?"

"No, no, Timmy. I just had one of those; what did you call them? Rushes of new feelings?"

Luckily I had brought a handkerchief. I handed it to her. She took it and wiped away the tears.

"Have I 'messed' up my face, Timmy?"

"Impossible, sweetheart."

We sat quietly, her head on my shoulders. I leaned back and looked up at the ceiling, knowing I was feeling new emotions I had had no experience with. It was very good but bittersweet.

"Claire...?"

"Yes, Ti-mo-thee?"

"Nothing, I just wanted to say your name."

Marilee walked into the living room, "Forgive the interruption, smitten ones, but Daniel and I are going to have a cocktail. Would you like to join us?"

Claire and I smiled at each other and said together, "The smitten ones!" We laughed at her teasing.

"What do you say, Mademoiselle? Shall we join the older smittens?"

"Oui, monsieur Sart. It would be a pleasure."

We followed Marilee into the den where Daniel was mixing martinis for the ladies; I opted for Bourbon. About this time we heard the parents drive up. Marilee went to the door to greet them.

They entered in high sprits, happy to be with all of us. Hugs and kisses all around. Claire was included as if she was a family member, which made her obviously happy and at ease. Dad was a man who enjoyed dressing for a dinner outing. He wore a new suit from Titches and a tie that mom had painted for him. Mom was elegant in a flowing green dress she had made from a pattern from Paris. Standing together the familial likeness between Daniel and Dad was striking. Their light brown curly hair and Roman noses were so different from mom and me. We both had almost pug noses and her hair had been black like mine before it grayed into a platinum blonde silver. We all sat and the parents brought us up on family business news. They both had gotten new commissions for furniture and portraits. Considering the way the economy was, they were doing quite well. Daniel talked about going to Taos, and Marilee mentioned her worry about conditions in Java and a possible pull out soon. Everyone assured me they would be there to help at the theatre for the next two weekends. Marilee promised food, treats, and to do any errands that were needed. Mother asked the question I didn't want to hear. When was Claire leaving after the show opened. Claire didn't want really to discuss it, but sweetly said she would arrange it with her parents, who expected shortly here after the date. She didn't mention they weren't aware of the production or her friendship with me. Marilee seized the moment to free Claire from any more questions and said it was time to go. She said she would pull the Chrysler around front. There wasn't any tension because of the questions asked of Claire; there was too much love in the room for that. We climbed into the big woody station wagon; which easily sat the six of us and we were off to the club. I had noticed that on the way to the car Mom was holding Claire's hand. Two wonderful women.

The drive out to the club on Harry Hines Blvd. was enjoyable. Marilee turned to us in back and told stories about past parties at the club and her costume extravaganzas. I had gone to the last one in a lion tamer's outfit. Marilee had fixed me up with the cute daughter of a club member who was more fun than I had expected. She had been in town from college. I never saw her again; which was alright. There was a table waiting for us and we got seated and ordered cocktails. The buffet line was incredible, leg of lamb, huge shrimp, roast beef, and roasted chicken. The conversation at the table was easy and Claire seemed to feel good about being in this almost complete family gathering. Uncle Willy and Rosie weren't able to join us because of the races at Diablo's Hollow, a dirt track venue that they never missed when he had cars entered, but they were toasted. Claire talked about how much she had liked meeting Uncle Willy at his shop and hoped she could see him again before she left. I promised her I would do my best to make it happen, but she realized *Blood Wedding* would take precedence over almost everything for the next two weeks.

After dinner we all went out on to the terrace for brandy. Two board members of the theatre were at a table on the way, and I stopped to chat for a minute. They seemed enthusiastic about the play asking how rehearsals were going. They knew two people in the cast who had told them how an exciting a process it had been so far. I turned to join my family, took a few steps and stopped in my tracks. Claire was standing at the stonework railing of the patio lighted by candles and the lanterns set for the evening. She was talking to my mother. The lights around her set her off in a gentle red glow; she turned slowly toward me with no expression, saw me and smiled. Her deep burgundy dress, auburn hair, and glowing skin gave her a new beauty I had not seen before. I remembered my comment about Rosetti's Pre-Raphaelite paintings and for a brief moment she took on the countenance of one of those women. I knew she was beautiful, but now I saw her as the most striking woman I had ever seen, much less known. She saw that I had stopped and tilted her head in a question. I smiled and waved to her. When I reached her she held out both of her hands. We stood looking at each other for a few seconds.

"Well, you two." My mother said, "You act as if you haven't seen each other for days." She laughed and hugged us both.

Claire leaned toward me, "What were you thinking when you stopped, Timmy?"

"Just how beautiful you are."

"You look wonderfully handsome yourself, Monsieur Sart."

Dad brought out his package of Camels and offered them around. Claire, Dan, and I joined him. I rarely smoked but always enjoyed the taste, and I was surprised to see Claire join us but she said she also enjoyed the taste occasionally. The evening was a huge success.

At Marilee's we saw Dad and Mom off with hugs and promises that Claire would visit them again before she left. Mom felt that seeing her at the theatre was not enough visiting time because everyone would be so busy. Dan and Marilee went off to bed and Claire and I went out back to the pool patio and laid out on the recliner.

Claire snuggled into my arms and held on to me with an urgency and feeling of sadness. She whispered about not wanting to leave in two weeks. There was nothing I could say in response, except my own regrets and how I wanted to slow down time and make our days together like a short lifetime. She agreed and promised not to talk about it, as did I. We kissed and grew closer. She pulled away a bit so I could touch her. Her dress was cut low enough that I could kiss and stroke the tops of her breasts. Their softness was like a down pillow. As I kissed her there, she whispered my name, kissed my neck, and rubbed my chest. I moved my hand down to her waist and over her thighs. She took my hand and moved it to the inside of her thighs.

"I want to be so close with you, Timmy. Touch me there."

I slowly moved my hand down to her, and she opened her legs a bit and pulled her dress up to her knees. I reached up under to her bare skin. She reached down and touched me. I hadn't realized how aroused I was.

"Oh, Timmy...I truly do wish that..."

She didn't finish the sentence, but I knew what she meant.

"So do I, Claire."

She was as aroused as I was because I could feel her wetness. She pulled me close to her again and we wrapped our arms around each other.

"We mustn't go any further, Timmy. You know that don't you?"

"Yes, if you don't want us to, but I don't think I could ever be too close with you. My feelings are...well, I don't know if I can even express it; this is something new for me. It's as if all of a sudden, I mean sudden like in the last few weeks, You and I, it's a lot more than just smitten, which I hope Marilee never says again."

She laughed softly then whispered, "I was smitten the first week we were together and now, yes, it is a lot more. This is new for me too, Timmy. And it's wonderful and a little scary because I am...I'm not going to say it. But, yes, let's do savor every minute. The next weeks are very important for you in your work, and I hope I can help because it's become very important for me, too. I want your play to be a great success, just like us. Do you think we're a great success, Timmy?"

"If success means am I happy, am I literally thrilled every time I see you and hold you close; yes, I'm a success already; and the show hasn't even opened yet."

"My word, as you say, if we are more of a success than now I may pop like a balloon. I already hurt from smiling so much."

"Me too. I think I smile in my sleep, especially when you dance in my head."

"You know, I've never dreamed of anyone else before you. You don't really mean I dance around in your dreams? Do you?"

"Well, not like Fred Astaire and Ginger Rogers, but more like you're here, then there, and we're together. Once I was watching you comb your hair and you turned around and looked at me, then we were in the boat again for our first kiss."

"I dreamed of that, too, but it was in a different place, France I think."

"France? I've dreamed several times that I wake up and you're beside me. Do you remember when I fell asleep right here and I woke up and you were watching me? Kind of like that, but more so."

"More so? Oh, you mean I was lying beside you."

"Yes. It was so real it did actually wake me up."

"Well, I will dream of you tonight, Timmy. And I'm sure they will be 'sweet dreams,' I remember a woman in an English novel saying that to her child when she was putting him to bed. I think we are living a sweet dream, but it's real."

"Yes, Claire, it is sweet. It's like being able to taste life."

"When you kiss me I can surely taste life. Oh, Timmy, I...Hmmm, I will miss you tomorrow. Did you look at my drawings today? Were they a help?"

"I studied them for almost an hour. They will probably be even more important for the next two weeks. Hey, I have an idea; could you watercolor some of them? I think it would be great to hang them in the lobby as a kind of exhibit for the run of the play. It will be almost as if you're still here."

"I could do that if you think they're good enough. I am better at watercolors than the other mediums. That's very exciting; thank you. I'll go tomorrow and get some paints. Marilee and I had planned to go shopping anyway. Timmy, I will still be here in spirit. Your play and your work are special to me. Perhaps with my drawings here you won't forget about me too quickly."

"Oh, Claire, there is absolutely no chance of me forgetting about you."

"Nor I you, sweet man."

At this point I wanted to hold her all night and talk about a million things.

"It's getting late. I don't want to but I've got to go home and get at least some sleep."

We got up and walked to my car.

"Claire, I forgot to give you something."

I reached behind the front seat and brought out a large envelope. She opened it and pulled out two of Jeordie's photos, one of us together and a portrait photo he did of me this week.

She squealed with joy and held them out, "These are the best gifts I could have. They are very good. I think Jeordie does have talent. They are going to go on the table beside my bed."

"That's where mine are going, except one of them is a picture of you."

She reached up, put her arms around me and kissed me gently, "Good night, sweet, good man."

I drove off thinking I was beginning to understand even more that conversation Dan and I had had about love.

I dreamed of Claire that night. She danced in my head as the vision of her at the club returned in many variations.

At breakfast, Mom asked about Claire and me, "Is this getting more serious between you than you bargained for or expected?"

"Yes, it is.

"Timmy, she is a glorious young woman and I can see that what has happened between you is something so good that it must be very confusing. Of course love is glorious and...confusing. When I saw you two looking at each other last night, I knew you're in love."

"We are in love I believe, though we haven't said so to each other, and I don't know that we will, perhaps because if we do it changes everything. Her leaving after we had said we were in love with each other would be...I...I refuse to get into those thoughts. Mom, directing *Blood Wedding* is the most difficult and exciting theatre experience I've had and meeting and being with Claire is the most exhilarating emotional experience of my life, and they have mixed together to make each better. As you well know, Claire has become an important part of my work life too. Her belief in and support of my work has been a revelation. I just didn't know it could be like this. I mean love, I guess. And something really strange, everybody wants to talk with me about us; you, Dad, Uncle Willy, Dan. Not in any critical manner but kind of to give support in a way."

"I believe one of the reasons for that is everyone likes Claire from the very first minute they meet her, and the change in you. You have been rather a loner most of time with brief whirls...like Gwen, but nothing like you and Claire, never even close."

"That's certainly true, never even close. Well, Mom, to be continued, I'm off to work...I probably won't see you until tomorrow morning. Perhaps it would be better if it's not continued. We can discuss colors for the set or what a nice day it is."

"You're right. Too much talk about a life abstract can muddy the waters."

"You're getting too philosophical, dear old painter lady"

"Get yourself to work, young director man. I love you, Timmy."

"I know, Mom. Thanks for caring."

I hugged her and was off to the bookstore.

Mr. Franklin, brought me a new book he had found. It was about a Russian director named Meyerhold who had broken away from the Moscow Arts Theatre to try out new ideas. It was a light customer day so I was able to review my plans for the evening, study Claire's drawings, read the play again and make notes, and read Meyerhold. It seems he went through similar thoughts, as I had been having, on a completely different scale and of an almost distant time, but his work came out as a new approach to the stage. Everything seemed to inspire me now, even if it was only his trying to change the way he worked.

Claire called me in the early afternoon to say she had gotten some watercolors at the art supply store. She asked if I had had time to get lots of work done and to tell me she missed me and was fixing us some sandwiches. I told her I would pick her up at 5:30 and that I missed her, too. Just hearing her voice lifted me up for the next three hours. My diagrams for each scene were getting clearer and more precise. I knew that tonight I could set the blocking for the first act without any doubts especially with the help of Claire's drawings. I spent the last hour on my journal and wrote a short note to Claire, more a note of thanks for her inspiration.

At Marilee's, we sat in the kitchen eating and discussing the rehearsal. She showed me a preliminary watercolor, which was more than I expected.

"I told you I could watercolor, Timmy."

"I didn't doubt you, but this is really fine stuff."

"Fine stuff?" she laughed, "Your play is fine stuff, too."

"I'm much obliged for those words, these sandwiches are fine stuff, too, Ma'am."

"Merci, Monsieur Texas talking theatre man."

At the theatre almost everyone had arrived early and was warming up, going over lines in groups, trying new music, practicing dance steps, and finding rehearsal outfits. I went into a conference with Ginger and read over her notes. Claire set herself up in the house. The choreographer came in to give some new combination instructions. The stage crew had done an amazing amount of work over the weekend so we had the beginnings of a set to work and practice set-up with. Eddy and I talked about where he would be during the play. I had decided I didn't want him hidden from the audience so we set a platform on the far-down-left of the stage. From that viewpoint, he could watch the play as it happened as well as be a part of it. I wanted him to walk into the wedding part scene as if he were a guest. I started having individual conferences with the actors, giving notes and blocking advances. The costumer builder also was working at getting final measurements, and we discussed and agreed on the color mixes changing as the show progressed from scene to scene. Everything was coming together successfully. At seven, I called everyone together for the pre-rehearsal session.

"Tonight is the beginning of the final thrust toward production, I began, "I know it seems like we have three weeks, but we don't. We open on Thursday of the third week. So, let's say it's two weeks, then full run-throughs starting a week from Friday. I personally think we're way ahead. I know everyone is-off book, and every scene is ready for the final shaping, and the blocking will be set by the end of the week. Wednesday will be a complete dancing rehearsal for the wedding. Aurora will be here every night to work with you. Eddy feels he has the music for every scene and the segues. The technical rehearsals will be more difficult than the usual process because you will change the set to music and the lighting will enhance every transition. I've been assured that all of the costumes will be ready by the middle of next week and, of course, there are always changes to be made in fittings and color combination. Tonight we will try to use what we have of the set, actually to see if it works, and I'm pretty sure it will...well, it did on paper."

Several of the cast laughed, and some held up their hands for questions.

"Tim, since the set folds up and out, will it stand the wear and tear?"

"Well, that concerns me too, but my father has had some good ideas about how to solve that problem. He is using some double folding hinges that are also double strength. The extra bracing will be on the side that doesn't have an entrance. They will clip at top and bottom, which you will do. It's actually going to be a lot easier than it sounds. I think the technical rehearsals will solve any of those problems. One thing that could help would be for you to spend as much time as possible here on the weekends and try them out as they are built. The set wagons should be very easy to maneuver on and off stage. It doesn't mean the whole two days, just some of the time. I know we all have another life; work, families, and all the other things that interfere with theatre. Your commitment and patience to this rather overwhelming process has been terrific. I have no doubts that the concept is working towards creating an interesting and exciting piece. I'm excited, and your work and extraordinary growth in this process gives me the impression that you are excited also."

"Tim?" a cast member named Liza Farquar, who was playing the Wife, said, "This is my fourth show here, and what I've really liked about this experience is that it has been different from anything I've done before. I think I've grown as an actress and I love the play more than I thought I would and I liked it before rehearsals started. But since we're not doing as much intensive scene work, do you believe we will find the passion and intensity the script demands?"

"Yes, and the main reason I believe that is because most of the work you've done before has been tightly blocked very close to the beginning of rehearsal with very specific character directions so there's been a kind of security. But what I'm trying to do, as I said in the opening concept discussions, is for you to reach for your own creative perspective starting from general ideas to more specific as we progress, and you have done that. Please believe me when I say I like what's happening. I'm not going to be hesitant in my critique, as I think you have noticed. One of major fears a director has is the casting of a play. I think I have won in that category; all of you, with no exceptions, have gone way beyond what I had hoped for."

"El Audazito?" The old actor insisted on still calling me that, "For the first two weeks, I did feel that insecurity, but last week it came together for me. I started to understand why you were trying it this way. What I especially like is the run-through at the end of each week. I believe you justified it by saying it was for continuity, but I had no idea what you were talking about until the second week. And, I think you mean understanding the play from beginning to end and knowing more each week. Last Friday we had a complete play without the...Como se dice? Especificades? Si?"

"Claro que si, mi amigo viejocito."

"No tengo preguntas, maestro," he laughed.

Alina Gutierrez, one cast dancer-crew, said "Tim, changing the set is going to be rather complicated. How is that going to be coordinated?"

"Ginger will give assignments for set-ups. Some of you will work from stage right, the others, stage left. It's going to be a traffic direction situation," I explained, "As you know, it will be done to music and half lights, so I want it to be closely timed and semi-blocked; but things will happen. I don't want you to worry about bumping into each other. We will take the time for it to be worked out. That will be a part of the tech rehearsals. Is that enough of an answer, Alina?"

"I think so, but when you say music, do you want us to dance around in the process?"

"Well, in a way. One of the reasons we're having so many dance rehearsals is that I hope we can move as if you were a Flamenco troupe. Not so much dance steps, but an attitude of movement. Aurora, could you give a demonstration?"

Aurora stepped between the cast and me, and began to walk and circle the stage in beautiful swirls, in almost prancing movements. She made several on and off-stage entrances and exits and gestured for the crew-cast to join her. In five minutes, they all were moving in the beginning of exactly what I wanted. Her practices with them had really paid off.

The cast members applauded, and we bowed towards her.

The actor playing Leonardo asked about the fight scene between the Bridegroom and himself, "You mentioned something about an Eastern puppet show. How will that work?"

"There will be a painted drop up-stage, the forest, a platform, and the scrim. You two will be on the platform entering from opposite sides. The backdrop will be low-lighted from above and high on the sides. You will be visible through the scrim, but hopefully almost shadow like, as there will be some red lighting from the front on the scrim. Aurora and I have discussed the fight as almost a dance, not the usual stage combat."

"Could we get that as soon as possible?"

"Yes, Aurora, can you do that Wednesday?"

"I can start some of it tonight, Tim; during the break and tomorrow evening."

"Great. The platform between the drop and scrim will be a hold-over from the wedding scene. The Wife will run on-stage from the right, up on the platform and stop the dance to tell us of Leonardo's escape with the Bride."

"Tim, I love that. I knew I would be upstage but I wasn't sure how I could use my voice to make up for being so far upstage." Liza Farguar said, "How wide will the platform be?"

"Three feet. The platform is really a rather long ramp so your entrance can be more dramatic. The men will enter it in the black, before the drop is lighted. The ramp wasn't on the drawing of the floor plan because it was a late idea. There won't be any more major changes. That was just something I hadn't solved until this week. I liked your coming into the dancing party from upstage, but I realized it wasn't enough for the moment. The ramp will be a foot and a half high so you will command the stage."

"Thank you, Tim, That was a great late idea. Don't hold back."

"I won't. But don't worry, folks, I'm not going to change the play to another one at the last minute. To a Noel Coward or something. I think I like *Blood Wedding*. Are we ready to start? No more questions, which were all good, by the way."

Everyone was ready to go, and we did. The rehearsal was difficult and long, but we set the first act and repeated it in a run without stopping and starting.

This week was the most important yet as my concept began to jell into a process. There were problems that I had to rethink and two of the cast-crew had to drop out. A couple of romances had started up, as they always do in a large cast, but that turned out to help because it added an intimate flair to the dancing. Aurora and Eddy even started seeing each other away from rehearsals, but at this point there wasn't much time away.

Each evening after the theatre, Claire and I drew closer, though I was too exhausted to spend long late evenings together. We explored each other more, both intellectually and physically. We were as close to being lovers as we could be without actually making love. One night, we fell asleep together on our lounge chair by the pool. At dawn, we kissed each other awake.

Claire giggled and whispered, "Timmy, you're the first man I've slept with and all we did was sleep, well almost."

"Almost was beautiful."

We walked to my car and kissed through the window. Then I started to drive off, stopped, turned to her and mouthed, "Love you."

She suddenly had a surprised look, smiled and nodded, turned and ran to the door, and mouthed, "Me too." And waved me off.

That moment sent wonderful chills up and down my spine. Driving home, I laughed with tears pouring down my face.

Mom had breakfast waiting for me after I showered, shaved, and dressed. She didn't say anything but just smiled and winked at me several times, knowing I hadn't slept at home.

Work was busy all week, but I had the chance to write in my journal. I also wrote a letter to Claire that I knew I couldn't give to her, at least not yet. I probably would have to send it to her someday. Claire's drawings and my diagrams were finalizing my process.

Each day before rehearsal Claire and I ate together at Marilee's and I told her of my plans for the evening. I asked what she thought about some of the new ideas, and she knew the play so well by now, that she was adding to my plans. Practically everything she added was a new step added onto mine. When we got to the run-through on Friday the cast was taking big steps in characterization and movement. With only a few problems everything worked. After the run-through and notes, Marilee walked in and announced she had beer, wine, and pop for everyone in the lobby. It was our first real cast and crew party. You can read and write about ensemble, but until you really experience it, it's a mystery.

Dan, Marilee, Claire, and I went swimming late in to the evening. Claire was becoming less self-conscious, and had removed the little skirt from her bathing suit. She was magnificent. In the water, her skin was luminescent in its pale glow. We laughed, played, and drank Spanish Brandy. Alone, we held each-other and I kissed and touched her breasts. She shuddered as I gently suckled her nipples. I felt and caressed her wetness as she held me. We stopped and embraced just before we both reached a climax to our passion.

Claire nuzzled my neck and whispered, "What we are feeling is very difficult at times. Isn't it, Timmy?"

"Do you mean our stopping and holding back? I don't want you to ever feel that I'm rushing you into something you may not be ready for, Claire."

"I know that. You are as gentle and tender as a man can be. We've done nothing that I didn't want to happen. But that's not what I meant. To be this intimate and know that...well, I do want to make love with you so very much, Ti-mo-thee, but I...am so frightened...that you will hate me when I leave. Remember what you said about having a little lifetime together? It is, isn't it? Our own little lifetime together?"

"Yes, of course, I remember, I think I said it like that. If it's all...I don't mean it that way, but all has been and is, well here we are right now...Oh, Claire, I..."

She put her hand gently up to cover my mouth, "The other morning when you stopped and told me that you...well, I think you told me that you felt...love for me, my heart stopped and I was so happy that I went upstairs and cried for a long time. Marilee heard me and came in and asked what happened. I told her, and she hugged me so hard I lost my breath. Then she cried..."

"I don't know why you believe I will hate you when you leave...I couldn't ever. Sad, and lonely for you but never..."

I pulled her into my arms, and we just held on to each other.

On my way home I thought about my present life and theatre. One of the ideas a director constantly talks to his casts about is staying in "the here and now" and not anticipating the coming moments, as if everything was happening for the first time in existence. "Our little lifetime together."

I slept late, had breakfast, and got to the theatre by 10:30. It was a beehive of activity. Everything technical was in the process of being built, hung, or painted. I immediately went into conference, first with Ginger and her notes from the week. Eddy and Aurora were practicing in the lobby, and Camila had come to help. She was working on the dancing and set-changing movements. The costumer showed me her first set of costumes for the leads. She had completed all of their scenes and had the skirts for the rest of the actresses. Dad and Mom arrived with the supplies they needed. Dad even brought in some special new lumber pieces, plywood that he could bend and shape. Mom had ordered several gallons of custom-mixed hues for the set pieces and the backdrop that she and Daniel were going to paint. Yes, Daniel had decided to get involved., he said because that's where everyone was. He arrived with drawings he had done for the backdrop for the third act, and they were terrific. Mom had designed the drop for the first two acts. I had hoped that Claire would be with Dan, but she and Marilee had gone shopping fairly early.

The set pieces that folded up and down were beginning to work. The new hinges that Dad had used were the answer. For awhile, I thought my idea for a pop-up set was going to be changed because it wouldn't work, but Dad had designed a way for the floor of each new scene to be added as it was changed. They would clip on as the wall was brought up. Each new set wall also had a brace that folded out as it was brought to vertical and each one had a crown that was added to the top so they wouldn't be square across the top. It seemed complicated, but the cast-crew worked with each as it was completed; slowly at first but the problems were solved. The wagons were simple and much more quiet than I thought they would be. Dad had found some hard rubber wheels instead of metal ones, and they did the trick. He had gotten so excited about my idea that he had spent several nights at his shop drawing up the plans and devising ways to make it work.

Daniel and Mom were up on ladders drawing out the backdrop for the first two acts with charcoal attached to long sticks.

At 1:30 Marilee and Claire arrived with food and drinks. Claire and I went out to the lobby and found a secluded place near the office and kissed our greetings. She said she had some surprises for the evening. Our social whirl of family gatherings had become rather overwhelming but delightful. I felt like it had been one long celebration since I had met Claire and rehearsals had started. Tonight we were going to my house and then with my parents to Uncle Willy and Rosie's house for dinner.

The afternoon's work went well, and I felt we were way ahead of the tentative schedule I had set up. With the cast that was there, we rehearsed the scene changes with all of the completed set and it worked. Dan and Mom finished the backdrop for the first two acts and mixed the paint for all of the set and backdrops. I had three final conferences and made plans for the stage work the next day. Dan took Claire back to their house, and I went home to get ready for the evening. An hour later, Marilee brought Claire to my house and came in for a visit. She and Dan had been invited but were unable to join us because of a long-planned dinner with business associates, but she never missed a chance to visit my parents at the house. Dad mixed us pre-dinner Martinis, and we gathered in the living room. Claire had carried in several bags with her saying they were her surprise for the evening. Jeordie joined us and sat as close to Claire as he could without getting in her lap, camera in hand trying to get close ups of her. Claire proceeded to open her bags and handed a package to Jeordie. He was a bit taken aback to be receiving a gift since it wasn't Christmas or his birthday. He looked at Claire in a combination of shock and adoration. He unwrapped the gift and found a box containing a new camera.

"Claire, this is a Leica!" he cried out. "It's the best camera made in the world! I don't believe it!"

Included in the box were ten rolls of film and two more lenses.

"I think a young man of your talent should have the best, and a family of artists should always have a good camera in the house," Claire told him as she hugged him and kissed his cheek.

Jeordie turned red and laughed. He immediately pulled out the instructions and got to work, he already looked like a professional on assignment.

Mom's present was a Colombian Ruana, a shawl with a split down the middle and worn over the shoulders. She loved it, especially its muted pastel colors. She paraded around the room and pulled Claire up into a tearful hug.

Dad opened his gift and found a broad-brimmed Australian hat with a leather band and a cord that hung down below the chin. It fit him perfectly.

"It's too perfect, Claire, and just in time for summer. Thank you, sweet girl."

She shyly handed me a package. I was hesitant but opened it to find a beautiful soft leather satchel. It was such an appropriate gift that I was shocked. My old canvas one was on its last legs. As I held it up and strapped it over my shoulder, she clapped her hands and hugged me asking, "Do you like it, Timmy?"

"Are you kidding? It's beautiful! "I took both of her hands and just looked at her. "Thank you." was all I could say.

She hugged me and whispered, "For my most special man ever."

Marilee stood up, "Well, I wouldn't have missed this for anything. She's been planning this for two weeks with the help of Town and Country and National Geographic." She said her good byes and left, saying she wished she and Daniel could have spent the rest of the evening with us. We were all in a kind of shock about the gifts Claire had given us. They were extravagant and beautiful; Jeordie's camera was the big surprise. He was thrilled and taken aback by the generosity. He had already loaded it with film, put on the portrait lens and was at work taking pictures. He said he didn't really need the instructions because he had been reading about using the best equipment, though he never expected to have a real Leica. I wanted to take my satchel out to my room before we left and asked Claire to join me. As soon as we were in my apartment and the door was shut, I turned and hugged her.

"How on earth were you able to get those gifts, I mean they are wonderful, but Claire...?"

"You mean because they were expensive?"

"Yes."

"Timmy, my father is very successful and I came with a letter of credit and a bank draft, which Marilee helped me with. It was for quite a lot of money, and I've spent almost none of it since I've been here. Why not share it with people I care about? Besides, it's a tradition in my family to give gifts spontaneously just from happy feelings. Never have I felt more welcome and loved than I have before coming here. I know I will never be the same because of the happiness I feel now and have felt with you and your family. I knew that my gift for Jeordie would be a surprise, but I truly think he has talent. Don't you think so, too?"

"Yes, I do and he was already seeing the limitations of his Brownie. I have no doubts about his potential, and now...you know, I was about his age when I got into theatre, and people believing in me made a real difference. You're an amazing woman, Mademoiselle Claire Levant."

"Thank you, Mister Ti-mo-thee Sart. I think you're an amazing man."

She reached up and kissed me softly and then said, "Shall we join your family before they go off and leave us, which wouldn't be bad but I do so want to see your Uncle Willy and his Rosie again."

The family was piling into Dad's station wagon as we came out.

"I thought I was going to have honk for you, son," Dad teased as we joined them.

Jeordie shared the back seat with us as he had special weekend permission to join us and stay up later. If he got bored, he knew he could listen to Uncle Willy's radio. The drive to their house was almost a sight-seeing trip for Claire because it was new part of town for her. They lived on East Grand Avenue up on a hill with a great view of the Sammuel forest area. As we pulled up the hill Aunt Rosie and Uncle Willy came out to greet us with hugs and kisses as always. Uncle Willy was especially attentive to Claire, which she loved. We went through a gate to the backyard of his house, which he had turned into a Chinese garden like one he had seen in his travels in the East. He had built a fishpond with an extensive collection of big gold fish. His large patio was made of pieces of thick slate with a large redwood table surrounded by cushioned chairs. He had set torches all around that would be lighted after dark. The environment instantly charmed Claire; she literally gasped and covered her mouth.

"My word, Uncle Willy, this is beautiful...Oh, may I call you Uncle Willy?"

"Yes, you certainly may, Claire; and thank you. We wanted to create a sanctuary that was very different from the rest of our lives, I fell in love with the gardens I saw in the Orient, but it did take me awhile to convince Rosie, and now she loves it and works hard in her gardening efforts to make it even more so...well, you saw my shop. It has a chaotic quality that demands a peaceful place away from it."

"We've been very lucky in the last couple of years," chimed in Aunt Rosie. "Will's shop has been a success with the racing and a precision parts contract from the Ford plant, and my job as a legal secretary downtown has been good. But a great deal of that is getting ready to change..."

"Rosie, what do you mean, change?" my mother interrupted.

"Is it alright if I make the announcement, Will?"

"Now's the time, sweetheart."

"We thought it would never happen, and it's on the edge of possibility, but we're going to have a baby. About time, huh?"

"Oh, Rosie, that's wonderful!" My mother almost screamed as she rushed to hug her.

My Dad bear hugged Uncle Willy and patted him on the back.

"It's a big surprise for us, too. We thought we were too old for this to happen, but we're thrilled."

Claire looked at me, tears streaming down her cheeks. Jeordie was recording every emotional moment. Uncle Willy noticed Jeordie's new camera and asked to see it.

"Lordy, Jeordie boy, where did you get this magnificent piece of machinery?"

"Claire gave it to me today."

"It looks like you believe in this boy as much as I do, Miss Claire."

"Yes, I do...Oh, I forgot..." Claire ran back out to the car and came back with a large bag. "I have some presents for you."

She brought a large tube and handed it to Uncle Willy, and a wrapped package for Rosie. The tube held several European-racing posters. He unfurled them with appreciative sounds.

"These are almost too good for my shop, but that's where they're going up, framed in my office. You sure know how to choose for folks, Claire. I've always wanted some of these, but could never find them. Thank you, dear girl." He smiled at her in a way I had never seen before. I think he was looking at the daughter he hoped to have this year.

Rosie said, "Will, look at this!" as she opened her present and held up a bright burgundy Colombian Ruana "Oh, Claire, this is beautiful. Thank you so much." She reached out and took Claire's hand.

My mother nodded in approval and looked at Claire and then at me. I knew what she was thinking; this was a very special young woman. I nodded back in agreement. My Dad still had his arm around his brother watching all this, proud to be the patriarch of this family.

Uncle Willy stepped out into the center of this gifting celebration and said, "I believe it's time for a toast to our lovely French guest."

"No, Uncle Willy, I'm on my way to becoming an American girl, but I will accept the toast. I may make one myself."

Uncle Willy turned to the bar he had set up for the evening, "Come make your choices." He had mixed up a pitcher of Martinis and also had bourbon for Dad and me. He had one of those terrific spritzer bottles for making soda. "Jeordie, there are a couple of cold Dr. Peppers for you."

After we were all equipped with drink, he proceeded, "Best of wishes and a good life to Claire and to my theatrical nephew. You are a joyful presence, Miss Levant."

Claire blushed, "The joy is mine in the acceptance you have shown me and the love I feel in your presence. May the future hold wonderful things for the extraordinary Sart family. Thank you for everything." She then turned to me, kissed her fingers and placed them on my lips.

I was startled and touched. A rush of happiness overtook me as I looked at this beautiful, good woman.

Dad and Uncle Willy proceeded to fire up the big grill on the patio; the ladies went inside to prepare salads and vegetables. Claire wanted to watch the grill set-up.

"I've had more outdoor prepared dinners in the last few weeks than I've ever had in my whole life before. It is a real Texas custom, isn't it?"

"It comes from the old west; you know, around the campfire and all that. Would you agree with that, Charles?" said Uncle Willy.

"Could be, but I think we just enjoy being outdoors. We don't do it much at all at our house, but that's really because we don't have a good grill like this one."

"Whatever the reason is, I like it. We've done it every weekend at Marilee's."

"Towards the end of March, we start and go all through the summer, Rosie and I try to cook out at least twice a week. What about in France?" Uncle Willy asked.

"Well, never in the city, and rarely in the country. We quite often eat outdoors, but the food is prepared in the kitchen. We never had the beef steaks like here. We had a lot of picnics, just like in the Impressionists' paintings. I have no idea what it will be like in Los Angeles, especially since my father travels so much. Perhaps I can take a Texas tradition there."

"Be careful. It gets in your blood real quick, Texas that is," Dad added.

"There are a lot of things about Texas that get in your blood rather quickly," Claire said as she took my hand.

"Do you have to go to California? Why don't you just stay here? You already seem like part of the family."

"I...well, my parents are very serious about me being with them. This is the first time I've been away from them for any length of time. They are extremely anxious about my being away for so long. And several interviews have been arranged at the museums there. But I don't want my time here to end...I...Oh! Timmy, I don't..."

She unabashedly came into my arms holding me tight, and started sobbing openly. I nuzzled into her neck, trying to comfort her, but feeling my own fears of her leaving rising up.

Uncle Willy immediately said, "I'm sorry, dear. I shouldn't have asked."

She turned to him, "That's alright, I over-reacted, I think because this is such a wonderful evening. Perhaps I should join the ladies inside." She squeezed my hand and went inside.

My father and uncle looked at me, saying nothing, but wearing expressions that spoke a thousand words.

We grilled the steaks and fish and the ladies brought out the other fixins'. Claire came to Uncle Willy and hugged him and then my father.

My mother asked, "Gentlemen, I don't know what you all were talking about, but we had a crying young lady in there."

"It wasn't sad things, Elle, we just don't want Claire to leave, " Dad replied.

"Nor do any of us...but evidently she must. End of story."

Claire laughed at this and, "Please let's enjoy, I am so happy to be with you."

And we did. Uncle Willy lighted the torches, which gave a truly magical touch to the evening. As the cooking finished, we all had another drink. The food was good and the conversation took on a happy flair as Uncle Willy told stories about his recent racing experiences and Rosie talked of her excitement about the baby, which she said was due sometime in December. After dinner, Claire asked about our family's history in Texas and Dallas. But before Uncle Willy could answer, a "hello" came from the side gate as Marilee and Daniel joined us. Their dinner had ended early and they knew we would be sitting on the patio. My mother immediately told them about Rosie being pregnant. Marilee squealed and hugged Rosie as Dan shook Uncle Willy's hand.

"Will, give us something to toast you all with," laughed Marilee.

"We still have some Martinis mixed. How about that? Or your choice of anything else?"

Rosie held up her hand, "Wait a minute! Today I bought two bottles of good French red wine, and I would like to try it. If I drink another glass of Iced tea I'll burst or be leaving this good gathering quite often."

"Aunt Rosie that would be perfect for me. Marilee?"

"A French wine in honor of you, Rosie, and our sweet guest from France. I would love it," Marilee said as she took Claire's hand.

Uncle Willy opened both bottles as Rosie went in to get some wine glasses.

After we toasted Rosie and Claire, Claire blushed and took my hand, then reminded Uncle Willy about her question on the family's history.

"I'll try to get it right, and what I can't remember, Charles will."

"Carry on, brother."

"I haven't heard enough of it, either." Marilee said.

"Well, both sides, Elle's and ours, are third generation Dallas folks. We go back to Tennessee, Kentucky and Virginia before that but the first here was Granddaddy

Perry Sart, who came just before the Civil War. He was pulled into the conflict and became quite a hero and was awarded the rank of Colonel. I was told by buffs that if he had been on the Union side he would have won the Medal of Honor twice. In two battles, he captured the regimental Union banner and was wounded both times. He was the youngest colonel in the whole Texas contingent. Early in the war, he assisted General Lee as a liaison because he was well-educated and he knew the west. He later came back to Texas and joined in many battles in Missouri and Mississippi. After the war, he came back to Dallas, got married to a Bowser, and started a family and He started a business; I don't remember what it was. Charles?"

"A small general store, I think." Dad added.

"After that failed, he joined the sheriff's department and quickly became the head deputy. His sad story ended when he was sent out to arrest a member of the Younger gang, John I think, at Scyene just east of Dallas. He was killed in a gun battle there, the first Dallas law officer killed in the line of duty. That was in the middle 1870's. By that time our grandmother had had three children. She had some real tough times but taught school here for almost forty years. Our Daddy tried making it as a writer of Western stories but later went into the land business with a friend of his named Lemmon. During the teens and twenties, he did quite well but was ruined by the bust in '29. I believe losing all that broke his heart and took away his will to live. At one time they owned almost all of Oaklawn. Lemmon went on to other things, and Daddy died in '32. Momma finished her novel in '36 and died shortly afterward. The manuscript has disappeared, but someday it will be found, I hope. I read most of it several years ago and thought it was a great story, though it went on for six hundred pages. That's our story except that I went into the Navy in '33 for four years as a machinist on a gun boat in China and elsewhere in the Far East."

"Claire, don't ever get Will going on his adventures over there," Dad cautioned with a twinkle in his eye. "He can go for three or four hours straight. My story is that I fell in love with making things out of wood."

"Charles, you do more than just make things. You're one of the finest furniture designers in the country." Mom said, never losing a chance to brag on Dad. "I think it's kind of funny that one brother chose metal, the other wood."

"How about your family, Ell-ee?"

"They were mostly architects and builders, and were also ruined by the bust in '29. I started drawing when I was three or four and have never stopped. Charles and I were introduced to each other by a friend of mine who had been trying to get us together for months. I think we both resisted falling in love, believing it was a distraction. Well it certainly was, and it continues to be, but a nice one."

"I wish my family had been more artistic," Marilee said. "I thought I knew a lot about art until I met this family. Daniel never fails to amaze me in his depth of knowledge. Claire, I think you have gathered this is one creative bunch of folks."

"When did your family come here, Rosie?" Claire asked.

"Actually they didn't get here until the twenties. My Daddy was a cotton trader from Louisiana. He's still a great character. I know you would like him, Claire."

"Our Daddies knew each other back in the cotton boom days. Rosie and I met each other at some ball when I was in my early teens," Marilee related, "I thought she would have been the ideal big sister, and now she kind of is, except more of an aunt. When Daniel introduced me to Will and Rosie I couldn't believe I was seeing her again, though I don't think she remembered me."

Rosie laughed, "You're right, I didn't at first, but I sure remembered your Dad. He was one of the grand old men of the cotton days."

"What wonderful stories of your families, I wish that someday I could tell you about mine." Claire said putting her hand on my arm, "but I think we're all going to be busy with *Blood Wedding* for the next week; and then...well, this has been one of the nicest evenings I've ever spent."

My Dad stood up, "I think it's about time to go. We are all thrilled to death about your news, Rosie. Elly and I sure will be happy to have a little niece or nephew."

Mom went in the house to get Jeordie who had fallen asleep on the living room sofa. He must have taken three rolls of film during the evening but had faded as we got into the family stories.

"Claire, it was so special we could have this night before you left. We think the world of you. I've never seen this boy so happy. I hope you can come back and visit some time," Rosie said as she hugged Claire.

Marilee asked Claire if she wanted a ride home, but I said I would take her. Claire agreed, saying she wanted to spend a little more time with me. On the way home Jeordie slept with his head on Claire's shoulder. When we got to my house we resisted going into my apartment knowing we would probably fall asleep and not wake up until morning.

On the way to Marilee's, Claire leaned on my shoulder and talked about how much the evening meant to her, and said she felt like she had a new family. I pulled up at the door, and she came into my arms.

"Timmy, these next days are so important for you. Let's not let any sadness into them. I'm happier than I've ever been and I'm so proud of you and what you are doing with the play. I want to share every moment I can with you and help in any way I can. I want what we feel for each other to be an inspiration and not a distraction."

What she was saying could not have been better. I knew that the next week could the most important in my theatre life so far, and she was a big part of it.

"I don't believe I could have had half of my ideas without you. Oh, I could have gotten the show up, but not like I think it can be now. You've been like a...a muse. I told you before there's never been anybody like you who really cared about how truly good my work could be. You do inspire me to be better than I thought I could be. I do want you to be proud of me. And you haven't been exactly on the sidelines. Your drawings have been and are wonderful. They've made it possible for me to stay closer to the actors on stage, and I think you could also be a pretty good stage-hand."

Claire laughed softly, "Even with all my bruises?"

"Yes, even with all your bruises, beautiful Mademoiselle."

"I love you, Ti-mo-thee."

"I love you too, Claire."

We held each other for a few minutes, kissed, and she went in.

I was too tired to read or study but lay in bed thinking of what Claire had said. She was right. Our encounter had been a whirlwind of emotions and very much tied to my directing. We had met just as rehearsals had begun, almost five weeks ago, spending every available moment together, very happily with extraordinary feelings of passion and an unbelievable ability to communicate with each other. The play and Claire were a new life experiences, and it's not over yet. I fell asleep holding Claire close to me in my dreams with the colors of the play shading filmy visions of our love.

The next morning at breakfast my mother told me she would be glad when winter got here so she could wear the ruana Claire had given her and about the excitement over Rosie's being pregnant. Jeordie was going to set up his dark room now that Mom had given permission to use the extra little storage area. He was wearing his new Leica around his neck like a foreign correspondent on an assignment. Mom said she and Dad would be at the theatre as soon as they could. They knew this was the final Sunday for finishing the set and drops and were eager to make it work and look as good as possible.

I got to the theatre at 10 and started in with the usual conferences. Barney showed me the proofs for the program. I had given him one of Claire's drawings to use for the cover. Her simple style of capturing the essence of the scenes was perfect. It was of the wedding party and beautiful, and was also our first program cover in color. I told Barney not to let Claire see the program because it was a surprise. It was my way of dedicating the show to her.

Ginger and I went down to the basement to see the costumes. To my surprise, they were almost all finished. Usually, they came in about two days before opening. The only changes I wanted were several variations of trim added to the women's blouses and a couple of the skirts. Every male actor now had boots and hats to wear. I decided to go half-costume on Tuesday and completely on Wednesday to give them enough time to get used to them and still time for any last minute adjustments. The complete set of boots would help the dancing, and the hat would give the look I needed to see. I then found the time alone in my little office to read my journal from last week's rehearsals. Just as I finished, Claire walked in.

"Hallo, Timmy."

I turned to her, "Hello, sweetheart. I didn't expect you this soon. I'm glad you're here. Good morning to you."

She was dressed in her dungarees and barn jacket with her satchel over her shoulder. Her hair was gathered in a long braid. Maybe because of my dreams or our last words the night before, she seemed even more beautiful.

"When I went inside last night I almost ran back out to stop you and not let you leave me. I missed you terribly last night."

"You danced in my head last night, dear heart. Come here, Mademoiselle," I said as   I stood and reached out to her. She put her arms around my neck and kissed me, then just leaned against my shoulder.

"Did I interrupt your work?"

"No, I just finished reading my journal and was thinking of tomorrow's rehearsal. You came in at just the right time. Did Dan and Marilee come with you?"

"I came with Dan. Marilee is coming later with food and drinks. Your parents just arrived with a lot of supplies. Dan is helping them unload. Timmy, do you mind if I work in the lobby for a while coloring some of my drawings?"

"Claire, of course I don't mind. That's as important as anything else. I hope you can choose your favorites by Wednesday so we can get them matted to hang in the lobby."

"Will you help me choose them? I want you to be pleased with the choices."

"You could choose any one of them and I would be pleased. I like them all. The complete show is there in sequence."

"Do you think that if they are in sequence, it will give the show away, I mean there won't be any surprises?"

"Well...if the fight in the next-to-last scene is shown or the death of the bride in the last...yes, it possibly could. But all of the drawings stand on their own as art."

"You're right about the last two scenes, I won't hang them."

"I hope that you will let me have those to hang in my apartment."

"Oh, Timmy, you can have them all. You inspired them, and you gave me the opportunity to try the drawings as a help for you. I just wanted to sketch because the play was so beautiful and passionate."

"Who knows what the audience will think, but they will see Lorca, or anyway my version of it."

"Well, I think it's good now, and you have a whole week left."

"Yes...and what a week it will be. I'm actually excited about the rehearsals. It's usually a desperate run to get the show up as best you can. You know, sweetheart, it's almost a miracle any piece of theatre gets to production, so many things can go wrong. If you know any little magic spells that bring good luck, bring them out."

"I do have a book of spells that I brought with me, but only you may know about it. It must be kept a secret. Although it is in French and I don't know if it will translate into an event that involves the English language. Perhaps if I first translate the spells into Spanish it will hold on to its European origins...it could be dangerous, though. Are you willing to take the chance? You could be turned into a frog or even a monkey."

"Yes, I'll take the chance. Do we have to sit around a bunch of candles go into trances and chant in strange ancient tongues?"

"Well, you're supposed to do just that, but I think we can adapt it to Martinis around the pool."

"Thank goodness! The only trance I want to experience is the one I go into when you smile at me. Do you think we could arrange this tonight?"

"Yes, I think perhaps we can."

"You're on, dear girl."

"I'm on? Yes, I'm on." Claire laughed and took my hand. "Are you ready to go upstairs?"

"Yes, on to the ramparts."

Claire went on to the lobby to color her drawings. Barney told me later that he had barely been able to hide the programs in time.

Most of the actors had come in to rehearse with the pop-up set pieces and help hang the remaining lights. Dan and Mom were painting separate drops, and Dad was finishing up new designs on the wagons and pop-up features. I worked for two hours with the lighting designer on the focusing of the special effects for the last two scenes. The scrim was flown in, and we rehearsed the fight scene on the ramp, which was a permanent set piece upstage. I blocked them coming together from opposite sides of the ramp. Fresnel lighting instruments were mounted just above the stage floor level with the top of the ramp. The scrim was just downstage of the ramp, and I had cut out gobos to project from the house lighting position onto the scrim. As the actors came closer to each other, the fresnels were dimmed up projecting their shadows on the rear of the scrim. This idea came from the designers mentioning the shadow puppet concept, and it had worked so far. Their fight to the death took about an hour to choreograph. They used prop knives that had blades which collapsed into the handles. As they died, lighting came up from above to illuminate the backdrop; and the lights below kept the bodies of the Bridegroom and Armando in shadow barely visible. I had decided to play the last scene on the same set with the women encountering in the forest for the execution of the Bride.

For the tech-through of the fight and execution everyone pulled back from the stage to watch. Though it didn't have the full effect without costumes and music, but everyone actually cheered when it was over. I couldn't believe it had worked so well. We all took a break to eat.

"Timmy, that was very exciting and I know how worried you were about it," Claire said as she met me coming up the aisle. "Camila came out to the lobby to get me. I almost missed it."

As Marilee handed me a barbecue sandwich she said, "Well Timmy, if the rest of the play is as exciting as that was, you've got a real success going."

"It is as exciting, Marilee, I promise you. And I think I'm being objective, well, maybe not completely. I've seen a lot of plays in London, but none I liked as much as this."

I knew this last scene was extremely crucial for the play and had to be received well by the audience. Yes, it seemed to work, but I saw many potential problems; the segues between the scenes were very difficult and the acting needed to be raised several levels. The passionate nature of the piece could turn it into a melodrama without a lot of intense directing reaching for those parts of the script that make it the great play I believed it to be.

Part of the afternoon was spent testing Dad's design for the rolling pop-ups. The big question was if they were sturdy enough to withstand the wear and tear of multiple use. We worked out all of the problems we could find and hoped that if any more appeared, we would be able to solve them during the week. After the testing, the set pieces were painted so they could dry by Monday night's rehearsal. Mom had to remix only one batch for the first act. When the paint had hit the smooth plywood it seemed to change to a much darker hue. She and Daniel found the right mix quickly.

Aurora, Camila, and Eddy had arrived in time to eat earlier and worked on the choreography with the actors as they finished their set changes. The two leads, Leonardo and the Bride, worked on their encounter during the wedding party.

At six, all of the actors in the wedding party arrived for a called run-through of the completed choreography. We cleared the stage while Eddy and Aurora gave some quick notes and they proceeded through the scene. They finished in thirty minutes. I gave some acting notes, and the day was done. After everyone else had left, Marilee, Daniel, Claire, and I joined Barney in the lobby for a glass of wine. Dad and Mom were so exhausted they couldn't stay. Barney was in high spirits about the play and a rather generous gift Marilee had given him for the production.

As we all walked to the parking lot, I asked Claire if she wanted to go somewhere to eat before going home. We both wanted some time alone together, though Marilee had extended her usual weekend Sunday night invitation. Claire said that would be fine except that she needed to be back at Marilee's fairly early because she was expecting her parents to call about nine Dallas time. We weren't dressed for any thing special, so we went to the open-all-the time restaurant on Lemmon at Oaklawn. We got a booth in back and relaxed into a sweet discussion about the day. Claire was happy about how her painting had gone and promised to show them to me later in the evening. I told of my concerns about the acting in the first scene and the encounter between the Bride and the Wife. The actresses were both strong, but it just wasn't working yet. The older Mexican actor was still having some trouble remembering his lines. And I felt the general lighting of the show needed much tuning up. There were still some interpretation problems that I wasn't sure how to solve yet.

I stopped and looked at Claire, realizing this was the first time in my short theatre career I had someone to really discuss my concerns with. She listened and reacted with questions or suggestions. She didn't try to be an expert on theatre, but led my thinking in a good direction. We didn't talk about us, that being a given at this point. We were happy just being together, with no need to analyze what was going on. We were in love and enjoying our time. Nothing was said about her leaving. There was nothing to say about it.

We finished our sandwiches and drove to Marilee's, arriving about 8:30. Marilee asked us to join them on the patio. There was a phone out there so Claire wouldn't miss her call. Daniel served us both a Martini and we talked about the day and the show. Dan was pleased with how the colors turned out and wanted my opinion on the drops. I said I was truly thrilled by them and that they were much more than I had hoped for.

"The artistic depth that you and Mom have contributed is immeasurable. And Dad solved problems that were inherent in my crazy idea about the pop-ups. What all of you have done to help this production has been amazing. Claire's drawings, now watercolors, are a new way for me to approach directing. I hope that in the future, that can be repeated in some way; perhaps Jeordie could photograph my rehearsals. Did I tell you that Claire's work is going to hang in the lobby during the run of the show?"

"Claire told me," said Marilee. "She was almost jumping up and down with excitement. I think it's a great idea because they are very good."

"You're darn right, they're good," said Dan. "Claire you have a real feel for watercolors. It's a difficult medium. I keep going back to them, but it's a constant learning process."

"Thank you, Daniel. Coming from you, that's a great compliment."

"Well, everybody's art is in the show. This takes family collaboration to a new level. Yes, Claire you are like a part of the family. You know everyone feels that way."

"Yes...I do know that, Timmy. I feel the same way...if I..."

Just then the phone rang. Marilee answered it and spoke for a few minutes to Claire's parents. Claire then took the phone and talked for what seemed a long time. It was private because she conversed with her father and mother in French. Afterwards she sat down and was sadly quiet.

"How was that, Claire?" asked Marilee.

"Of course, they are glad that I'm alright and have enjoyed my visit. But they said there should not be any consideration of my staying longer. I must be on the train next Sunday. Things have been arranged...They... I told them I was going to a play this week that Daniel's brother directed, but no more. They would not understand or accept what has happened here."

She then looked at me.

"They are very strict and protective, Timmy. I believe more than you can imagine."

"Evidently so," I said, but without any anger or even resentment, just accepting.

"Timmy, European traditions and family connections are so different from what we know here," Marilee said to console any bad feelings I might not be showing. "I wish Claire could stay here, and have offered it, but I wouldn't even try to convince her parents to let her stay. I care for them very much and hope that her father will eventually work for my company. Perhaps if that happens they will move to Dallas, and, well...I don't know."

"When I came here to visit, I had no idea, as you well know, that I would meet Ti-mo-thee and...you understand what has happened between us, Marilee?"

"Yes, I do Claire, and it's wonderful. Before you ever came to visit, I wanted you two to meet. I didn't know you would care for each other so much so quickly."

"Not to contradict, Marilee, but it doesn't seem that quick to me. Does it to you Claire?" I asked.

"No. These five weeks seem like a year."

"And I believe we've gone beyond caring." I looked at Claire.

"Yes, Timmy, I've cared about several people, but being in love with you is a different world all together. But...I..."

"You have to leave. I accepted that a couple of weeks ago."

There was silence for a few minutes.

"Please don't think I was belittling your feelings, but even Daniel and I have a hard time talking about love; but he knows I love him more than I ever thought I could possibly love anyone, I had a happy marriage with Grant, but as you said Claire, a different world."

Dan stood up and announced, "It's more than settled that we are folks in love. You two have another week, minus a few hours, so let's celebrate what time you have together. It's still early. Let's have another drink and then go swimming."

"Good idea, my dearest Daniel. Have I told you lately how much I do love you?" Marilee asked.

"Not enough, and I you," He answered.

"I believe a swim would be wonderful. Timmy?"

"Indeed, sweetheart. First the drinks...eh?"

"Coming up, little brother."

Claire got up and kissed me on the top of my head and took my glass to Dan.

Marilee laughed and winked at me. "Little brother? After *Blood Wedding* nobody is going to think of you as anyone's little brother."

"Thank you, Marilee, but do you have influence with John Rosienfield?"

"Even if I did, I don't think I would need to use it."

"John Rosenfield?" Claire asked.

"He's the critic at the Morning News. His words are golden to the theatre-going public," Marilee answered.

"Well, he never pans a show unless it's really bad, and he's always liked my work before. I'm not going to worry about that. I'm feeling pretty good about how it's going. My plans for this week are more solid than anything I've done before. With all the help and collaboration from everyone...well it's been great. Dan, those drops you and Mom did really are special. They're like murals that should be preserved. I want Jeordie to get some colors shots."

"I'll get him some film this week," Marilee volunteered.

"He's getting pretty good in that darkroom he set up. Claire, he loves that camera."

"I knew he would, Timmy. When you told me how much he likes machines, I had no doubts."

"I do believe your Martinis are getting better, or maybe it's the company," Dan said.

"I tried a bit more of the olive juice, Daniel. And thank you. Are you ready to go up and change, Claire?"

"I am. Timmy, I'll meet you in the water."

"I'll be awaitin'."

She laughed, "My Texas boy."

Dan and I went into the cabana to change. "Hold on tight and be strong, Tim. None of us want her to leave."

"I know, I just didn't expect anything like this to happen."

"Nor did she."

We eased into the pool, setting our glasses on the edge.

"Well, at least it's a good thing for you to know what real love is like. Before Marilee, I didn't know if I ever would."

"Yep. I now know."

The girls appeared shortly. It was almost dark except for the candles Marilee had set out, and Claire looked beautiful. This week, to my surprise, she had gotten a two-piece bathing suit. She walked around to where I was standing in the water and sat down on the edge. I put my arms around her and kissed her bare stomach. I then lifted her into the water. We laughed and kissed.

"Do you like my new suit?"

"Yes, Maam, I do."

She pulled in close to me, "My goodness, Timmy, you are so.."

"Seeing you in your new suit and kissing your tummy kind of..."

She laughed. "To use your words, 'evidently so.' I don't think you should be climbing out of the pool anytime soon."

Dan and Marilee were sitting on the steps on the other side of the pool, talking quietly and laughing softly occasionally. The cool water calmed me down a bit and we swam over to them holding our glasses above the water. Dan reached over and kissed Claire on the cheek and Marilee kissed me lightly on the lips.

"I hope you two realize how much we love you, I mean as a couple," Marilee said hugging Claire.

"I think so, I mean I've never been loved like that before, yes I do. You make me feel like I have a big sister."

"Well, you do," Marilee assured Claire.

We finished our drinks and Marilee said, "I think Daniel and I need to go upstairs. We seem to have fallen even more in love tonight, if that's possible. Should I blow out the candles?"

"Yes, please." I answered.

"Make yourselves at home in every way, dear hearts."

"Good night, brother and Claire." As they left, Dan put his arm around Marilee. She leaned into him and they were gone.

"I think they are very lucky. Don't you Timmy?"

"Yes, but then so are we, Claire."

"I know we are. Our having met and being together is the happiest thing that ever happened to me. My leaving doesn't change any of the feelings I have for you... forever."

"My word...forever?"

"Yes, I believe forever. I know our parting will be sad, but our weeks together have changed me. You have said many times that *Blood Wedding* is play of passion. I feel a passion for you that was not a part of me before. Yes, of course, it's you, but I didn't expect to ever experience what I feel for you at this very moment and all the time. When we're apart, I yearn for you. Is that the right word?"

"It is, I have the same feelings when we're apart."

"Hold me, Ti-mo-thee. Be close to me now. I don't think I can get enough of you."

We kissed with a new special passion. I felt like my tongue was making love to her and she returned the feeling with her tongue in my mouth. I kissed her neck and worked down to her breasts. I pulled the shoulder straps of her suit down her arms.

"Oh...Timmy. Kiss my breasts."

I undid her suit in back and took it off of her. We had never stood this close before. In the moonlight, she took on a new beauty for me. Her breasts seemed to start at her shoulders and fill her chest, full but as soft as a down pillow. Her nipples were a rosy color, not pink, and grew as I kissed and sucked them. I put my hands around her small waist and pulled her to me.

"Timmy, I want to make love with you so much, but I'm still afraid. I don't know why. I'm not afraid of you but because it will be so wonderful that I won't want to stop. Do you understand?"

"Yes, I do."

"Can we get out of the water? I'm getting a little cold."

I climbed out and got her a towel. She wrapped herself in it as she walked up the steps.

"Let's get robes from the cabana." I lighted a candle and walked into the changing room. I put the candle on a shelf and dried off then dried Claire. In the candlelight she was an apparition of beauty. Her full figure, small waist, and pale skin were an ideal of classic loveliness. I put the robe over her shoulders and warmed her. I reached down and felt her round bottom.

"Dear lord, you're a magnificent woman. I want to be as close to you as possible right now."

"Me too, Timmy."

"May I take off the bottom part of your bathing suit?"

"Please do. I want you to touch me, and I want to hold you."

I knelt down and pulled her suit down and was startled. In the candlelight, I could see her. I mean that she had just a soft puff of auburn pubic hair and I could see her. Every woman I had known before was hidden behind pubic hair. It was like a flower. As she stepped out of her suit, I pulled her close and kissed her there.

"What are you doing, Ti-mo-thee?

"You are so beautiful, I couldn't not kiss you."

"I never thought of myself being pretty down there. I've always been embarrassed that I had so little hair there."

"Don't ever have that feeling again because you are pretty."

I started to pull down my trunks.

"Let me do that, Timmy. May I?"

"Are you sure, sweetheart? Of course, you may."

Claire moved in closer and took my trunks by the waistband and began moving them down my legs. She knelt down as I stepped out of them. She took my erection in her hands and stood up.

"I think I am as wet as you are big and hard."

I touched her and opened her lips and rubbed her opening and little bud that was growing. She was moving her hand on me.

"That feels so good, Timmy. Can we make love a little bit?"

Suddenly she shuddered and made little sobbing sounds, then kissed me softly then hard.

"Oh my, Timmy, don't stop touching me yet. I haven't felt anything like that before, just a little bit with you, but not like that.

"Claire, you are so beautiful to touch."

"You touch me so beautifully, Timmy. Can we go lie down on the lounge outside? I've been standing on my toes so long my legs are getting sore?"

I laughed and took her hand and picked up the candle to light our way.

"Would you like some Spanish brandy? I think I would."

"That sounds good, yes, please."

I went to the bar and poured out two snifters. I opened the cabinet and got a small light blanket that Marilee kept there for cool nights, as this one was getting to be. After arranging two tables beside us, I spread out the blanket over us and we snuggled together sitting up and drank our first sips of the brandy.

"I love this brandy. Timmy...I hope you don't think I was too forward. I am very shy about being as close as we are, I never thought I could be this uninhibited, but tonight I was so attracted to you. You were so handsome today at the theatre I just wanted to watch you every minute, but I never would have finished my watercolors and I didn't want to embarrass you."

"I thought I was the one being forward tonight. I didn't want to rush you, but when you came out in that new bathing suit I was lost. And did you notice how many times I came out to the lobby today."

"You promised that you wouldn't let us distract you from your work," she laughed.

"You didn't and won't. This play has become important for both of us, I think. I mean that I feel you beside me all the time. To direct the most important production of my career and fall in love with you at the same time, has taken, how can I say this without sounding pretentious, it's taken my awareness of being alive to a new level. It seemed that before time just passed and I worked. But now every minute is special... I..."

I don't believe I could have said what you just said in English. I have thought the same emotions in French. Yes, your play is very important to me. You are... important to me...tonight is important to me. I am living with you in my heart and soul."

I kissed her forehead and just held her. We said nothing for a few minutes.

"It feels so natural to be this close with you...with no underwear on," she laughed softly. "We're almost nude."

"Do you mind if I take my robe off? The blanket and the robe together are too warm?"

"No. I will too."

I stood up. "Lean forward, Claire."

I lowered the back of the lounge more so we could almost lie down. I snuggled down beside her and for the first time felt all of her close to me.

"This feels so good, Ti-mo-thee. I love you, and I love being this close with you."

I ran my hand from her thighs up to her lower back, pulling her closer; and up to her neck and through her hair. We smothered each other with soft kisses. I whispered in her ear, "I love you, dear Claire."

Our breathing raised as we both began to have our passions rise again. She spread her legs for me a little as I touched her. I could sense her nipples harden against my chest. My erection touched her and she put her arms around me and thrust herself to me.

"Oh, Timmy, I want you inside me, but I know it's not safe."

"Yes, I want to also, but you're right, it's not safe." As much as I wanted to make love with Claire, I didn't want to frighten her or have her worry about getting pregnant. "I'm almost glad I wasn't prepared because there is an innocent sweetness about our being nude together and not making love."

"I am, too. I don't mind if we wait for the right moment. But I think I've wanted to make love with you since the first moment I saw you, though I wasn't aware of it."

"I must have felt the same way, but I wasn't aware of it either. I was such an innocent before we met, and every one of our days together has been a surprise of new feelings."

"In our way, Claire, we've been making love since not long after we met, I guess I mean, making a love, or letting a love happen as if we had no choice. I've always been reticent to let feelings of closeness happen. Maybe I've never trusted anyone."

"I know. I thought I was sort of cold-hearted. I've been courted but I resisted it. Yes...I never trusted. Being with you seems so natural and real. What you said before about every minute being different is true."

"Do you think it could be arranged for us to spend some of our last nights together?"

"I will try. I want that, too. Do you mind if I ask Marilee for help on this?"

"No, I think she is the one who could help us. We know she believes in us."

"Claire, I adore you. Do you remember us talking about Marilee and Daniel... the natural progression of things?"

"About her and Daniel getting married and having a baby?"

"Yes, but ours is different. Our almost making love is our natural progression."

"It is, isn't it?"

"And as I said, that new bathing suit of yours enhanced the progression."

"Goodness, and I just wanted to be more modern. Timmy, I adore you, too."

We dressed and she walked me to my car. I arranged to pick her up in the early afternoon after I did my show preparations. Our kisses were different now. I was in love with Claire Levant and she with me.

When I got home, I was wide awake. I wrote in my journal, working until three in the morning with new inspiration for the play. The last run-through had been good, but there were so many highs and lows yet to be realized. The technique needed to be extended. The poetry was not yet perfected. Some gestures must be broadened and others made subtler. The vocal work must have more variation and in places almost shocking for the audience. I wanted to hear sounds from the audience in reaction to the higher moments; I wanted to see them lean forward in concentration and hold on to the person next to them. I wanted to hear them say 'Oh, no!' when the bride runs away with Leonardo and cry when the mother kills the bride. I wanted more from the music, and without any doubts, Eddy wanted this too. I wanted the dance to rise to more of a crescendo with the Wife's dramatic run out on the ramp with the screaming announcement that they had left together on Leonardo's horse. I wrote how I felt each of these elements could be achieved and an introduction speech and critique list for the rehearsal tomorrow. I finished my writing and in the dark thought of Claire in my arms. As sleep came, Claire's drawings came alive in my imaginary sight.

Chapter 13
Destino

I awoke late on Monday morning , the last week of rehearsal, the last week of Claire. I lay in bed, not in a confused state but very eager to slow down time. I thought of the night before with Claire and our new intimacy. I wanted her with me now, in my arms talking with me about the week of rehearsals, making love with me, telling me stories about growing up in France and going to school in London, listening to my fears of failure and reassuring me of success; me telling her family stories and what it's like my growing up in a family of artists, revealing how difficult it is to escape Dallas and get to New Mexico or New York, looking at her startlingly beautiful face and skin, putting my arms around her and pulling her to me again.

I wrote in my journal for an hour. It was becoming a book about directing this production. I had had no idea it would become so long, over a hundred pages now. I stopped and wrote a poem about Claire, a poem, a first for me, well, the first in a long time and never about a girl or love.

A knock on my door. It was Mom wanting to know if I wanted a late breakfast, and bringing me a cup of coffee. I told her I would be in after I showered and shaved. I sat quietly with the coffee for a few minutes thinking of nothing, just clearing my head for the day and evening ahead.

I sat in the kitchen in my robe, ate, and talked with Mom. She was interested in my plans for the week on stage. I told how I was going to light the backdrops she and Daniel had painted. She approved. She hesitantly asked of plans this week with Claire.

"Just being together as much as possible, Mom, just together."

"It would be nice if we could see more of her this last week."

"You will."

Jeordie had left a note for me telling about his plans for photographing the play, and Mom had given him special permission to stay up late and work at the theatre. After Mom and I talked for awhile, Claire called.

"Timmy, when did you plan to go to the theatre? Would you like to come over here earlier? Marilee and Daniel are out for the day. I could fix us something to eat before we go to the theatre."

"I think I'm really finished with any work I need to do alone. I could be over in less than an hour. How's that?"

"I wish you were here now, Timmy, but that's fine."

"I'll be there soon. Bye."

I hung up and smiled at Mom. She hugged me and sent her love to Claire. I rushed out to my apartment, feeling very excited about being with Claire earlier than expected and alone. I wanted to hold her as much as I wanted to talk with her.

I put on a bit of cologne, combed my hair, brushed my teeth again, and gathered up everything for the evening with a couple of extra books. I felt very classy carrying the new shoulder bag Claire had given me along with wearing my barn coat. On the way I made one of those embarrassing trips to the drug store to get some prophylactics, not that I expected anything to happen today, but I was never going to be unprepared again, and I certainly wanted to protect Claire from any fears if she decided we could make love.

As I drove up to Marilee's, Claire came out to meet me. She hugged me and walked me into the house. We went into the den, sat down in the cushy couch, and just sat there for a minute, looking at each other, "Hal-lo Timmy, I love you. Do you think you really do love me?" Claire said.

"Yes, Claire, without any doubts, I do love you."

She snuggled over into my arms. Her hair was scented with Rosies or some beautiful essence. I just held her.

"What time do we have to be at the theatre?"

"I should get there within the next five hours."

"That's good. Do you have any more work to do before you go?"

"Well, there are some real problems to solve this week, so tonight must really be a good rehearsal...to kind of set up for the rest of the week."

"What are you most concerned about?"

"How the poetry lines sound. It just doesn't work yet...or not the way I think I want it to sound. In the early rehearsals, when I was asked the question about how to do them, all I said was that we just do them. I didn't want them to be sung, unless the script actually calls for it, or chanted, but where necessary said together in perfect unison as if they were lines of dialogue. The cast is just about there with the perfect unison, but not quite sounding like dialogue or an overlay of emotional reaction using a different way of reacting to the action or the character's situations. There are several sections where the poetry is behind the action or it's announcing something like a new life."

"Where in the play are you talking about?"

"In act two, scene one, where it's described in the text as singing being heard at first, probably off-stage but getting closer, saying for the bride to awaken; and then several other characters coming on stage continue the refrain. It's very complicated staging and Eddy has composed some music for it that works fairly well, but it's not yet anywhere near what I think I want. Right now it has almost a Greek chorus sound to it, and I want it to be more lyrical. And act three, scene one is almost dominated by the poetry, but I think it's working better."

"Watching you work with the cast on these parts, I knew you weren't satisfied with it. But it sounds better than you probably think it does. Every time I watch it, it gets more beautiful. I mean the whole play together. You've told me several times that this last week was the most important."

"It is. I'm pleased with almost everything-the set, the lighting plot, the costumes, and the acting in general; it's just the poetry that troubles me the most. Of course, it's not ready for production as it wouldn't be a week, almost, from opening. I believe my directing has got to go up several levels for it to be as good as I want it to be, and that's real scary."

"Is there anything I can do to help? I mean as a friend who believes in you."

Well...just be Claire. I don't think I could have gone as far as I have without you. I'm not sure you realize how important our being together has been for me, and I don't just mean as a director, but as a man. As a director you've inspired me every day. Sometimes it's as if you help to open new windows in my mind. I've never thought more clearly or with as much imagination. Well, there is something you could do occasionally, and that is to just hold me and say everything is going to be alright."

"I would have done that without you asking. Timmy, you've changed me too. I don't mean just in our closeness, our almost lovemaking; but also in the way I think. It's difficult to describe but I'm different. I was always frightened of the future. I'm not now because of you. We know I'm leaving to begin a life away from here. There are things that you wouldn't understand. My parents are of the old country and the old ways, and I'm beholden to them. Perhaps...well, that may change someday, but I can't desert them now. Tradition to them is everything and I'm a part of that. Do you understand me a little bit?"

"I do understand tradition, or I think I do. But I believe there can be new traditions brought about by new situations. Don't you?"

"I don't know. Some traditions are very difficult to change. This new life here in America is changing me, I just don't know how much yet. But I do know I love you, and that will not change."

"And I love you, Claire. Neither will it change in me."

We talked for another hour about the play and the coming week and how much my parents wanted to see her again, and how much Jeordie was using his camera, and how we wanted every day and evening to be special being together and with other friends and family members. We set a plan for one afternoon to visit Uncle Willy and Aunt Rosie. Dick and Camila wanted to see us one evening after rehearsal. Camila had actually joined the cast in the wedding scene so we would just take her home and join Dick at their place.

And then, "Timmy, would you like to go upstairs to my bedroom for awhile before I fix us some dinner?"

"Yes, more than you can possibly imagine. I was hoping you would suggest something of the sort."

We went by the kitchen, got Dr Peppers for both of us, and walked upstairs holding hands. All of a sudden, we were shy about being together like this alone during the day. I suggested we pull the shades on the windows. Claire giggled and agreed. We left the light on by the bed. I went to her, wrapped my arm around her, and kissed her neck. She cooed and kissed me back.

"I'm a little scared Timmy. Well, maybe just nervous, but happy to be alone with you, and I feel safe."

"I want you to always to feel safe and secure with me. I don't think I've ever had such protective feelings about anyone as I do for you, Claire."

I took her hand and guided us to the bed. We lay down on our sides and looked at each other for a few minutes. I stroked her cheek, kissed her forehead and ran my hand through her hair. The softness of it still amazed me and I told her so. She told me she liked my strong arms and shoulders."

"I've wondered how you got such strong arms, Timmy."

"Well, I was too small to play football, so I did gymnastics. I wasn't a very good tumbler, but I did the parallel bars and flying rings. It changed me real quickly. I only did it seriously for about three years, then theatre took over. I thought I would shrink back down to skinny, but I didn't. For awhile I thought I looked a bit grotesque, but I'm not as big as I was, thank goodness."

"I think you look wonderful, Timmy."

"Thank you. And I think you are the most beautiful woman in the western hemisphere."

Oh, you know that's ridiculous, but I thank you. It's how you looked at me when we first really saw each other here at Marilee's. It was the first time a man looked at me like that. It was so sweet, and it made me feel so good. And I thought you were so handsome. That was a good beginning, wasn't it?"

"Yes, it was, but at that time I didn't know all the other special things about you."

"Our love for each other is the most wonderful surprise in my life."

"Viva sorpresas buenas. Si?"

"Si, mi amor!"

Claire kissed me, and we drew close. I pulled back and asked if she would like to undress and snuggle under the sheets.

"Would you undress me slowly, Timmy? I don't won't to rush making love."

I kissed her and started to unbutton her blouse as she did the same to my shirt. I ran my hands over her bare back and undid her brassiere. I pulled it up and kissed her breasts. She held my head to them as I gently sucked her nipples, and they rose, erect.

"That feels so good, Timmy. May I hold you?"

I nodded as she unbuttoned my trousers and took me in hand. I reached under her skirt and into her panties. She spread her legs a bit for me as I touched her. She was already a little wet, and I pulled down her panties and undid the buttons on her skirt. I raised up and took off my shirt, and she then pulled my pants and underwear down. I pulled the sheets down as she turned off the bed lamp. We got under the covers and continued to explore each other slowly and gently. She kissed my chest as I ran my hands over her soft round bottom. We lay back very close. We were almost making love like this as we were both moving with each other.

"Ti-mo-thy, do you think it's wrong if we make love?"

"I don't think so. Do you?"

"I'm not sure that it matters at this point. I do so want to be as close to you as possible. It feels so very right with you. You make me feel like a complete woman. I didn't know if I would feel like this, and I don't know if I ever could with anyone else; I don't mean just to make love, but to want someone so much. Yes, I want to make love with you. Please do. I want to feel you inside me."

"Yes, sweet girl."

We kissed and I touched her. She spread her legs more and I gently rubbed her. Claire reached down to me, pulling me to her. I stopped everything, sat up and reached over to my trousers for the prophylactic and opened it and placed it on me. She moved under me and took me in hand, guiding me to her. I felt what felt like little electric shocks as I entered her."

"Oh my goodness, sweet Claire."

"Yes, Ti-mo-thee. Please go slowly."

Claire shivered and cried a little and laughed a little at the same time. I moved slowly as did she, holding me tightly.

"Oh...oh..kiss me, Ti-mo-thee."

We kissed and made love noises. I bent down and kissed her breasts.

"Yes, yes, please suck on me a little."

We moved faster with each other and she wrapped her legs around me. I was shaking and trying to thrust gently.

"Please don't stop, Timmy. It's so very good, yes, yes."

We both reached our climaxes together. I yelped and ooed. Claire was crying out loud with happiness as I collapsed on her.

"Don't leave me, Ti-mo-thee."

I didn't and after a few minutes I started moving slowly again inside her. She held me tighter as we slowly both reached another climax. I didn't have any idea I could do that or that making love could be so completely a beautiful union. Being in love was such an extraordinary experience. Claire was so wonderful in such a new undenying way. Suddenly she squeezed me. I reacted by kissing her neck and moaned in her ear.

"Did you feel that, Timmy?"

"I certainly did."

I didn't want you to leave me yet, so I just tried to hold on to you. I didn't know I could. Is it always so beautiful the first time you make love with someone you truly love?"

"I don't believe it's that wonderful for anyone anytime."

"I was so afraid that our first time to really make love would be kind of painful and clumsy. Well, it was a little painful for a few seconds, more like a sting. Did I bleed a little bit?"

I looked down, "Yes, but only a small amount, not even enough to stain the sheets."

"Oh, thank goodness, I couldn't tell. I had heard that you did bleed the first time. I was sure I would do something wrong or that I couldn't do it at all; but it certainly wasn't that way at all."

"No, Claire, you were and are the most wonderful lover for me that I ever imagined possible. Are you alright?"

"Yes, my magnificent man. I'm very alright. I don't even feel any guilt or anything negative about our being together like this. I don't even know if I should feel anything bad about us because I love you so much, Ti-mo-thee Sart."

"And I love you, Claire Levant."

Claire suddenly held onto me tightly and began to cry in great sobs.

"Claire?"

It was a few seconds before she attempted to answer, "Oh...Timmy, I'm so happy it was you and not someone I didn't...well...really love," she said softly mixed with sobs, "You took me through a...uh...is the word threshold, like pasaje, in Spanish?"

"Yes, threshold, I think we both went through a threshold together," I whispered.

We calmly wrapped our arms around each other and didn't talk for a while. I kind of naturally came out of her and she moaned softly. We were both almost soaking wet. Her hair around her forehead was dark with sweat. I looked at her and she was a new sort of beautiful; that was a shock. She looked at me with a total look of love, a new softness in her expression.

"At this moment, I feel like a very lucky woman, not a girl, which I think I was before I met you, Timmy."

"I wasn't a boy when we met, but I'm certainly more of a man now. We both have read about love and seen films, but they can't touch the true experience of it."

"Yes, I agree. I thought all of my reading and travel had made me rather worldly, but I guess it takes something like us."

"I also always thought there would be a kind of a silence about love, but we seem to need to talk about it all the time, and I like it. It sometime feels as if we're taking a boat ride down a beautiful river and we want to share our reactions to it. Around every bend, there's a new wonderful surprise."

"Bien dicho, mi amorcito."

We talked awhile longer. We laughed and teased each other in sweet ways. Then we were quiet in each other's arms.

"I must take a shower, Timmy, before I fix us some dinner and get ready."

"Alright, I'll read and then take my shower when you go down."

She jumped out of bed and turned to me shyly, knowing I was looking at her for the first time in the light. She gave me an almost scolding look then giggled and went into the bathroom. I had brought my bag up with me and started going over Stanislavisky's index again trying to tie every thing to tonight's rehearsal. After awhile Claire came out in a dressing gown and gathered her clothes for the evening, came over, kissed me and disappeared again. Claire went downstairs to fix our dinner while I showered and dressed. I joined her for lamb sandwiches and iced tea, which had become a favorite for her followed by Dr Pepper. We laughed and talked about the coming evening and looked at each other in a new and wonderful way. We finished and she reached for my hand across the table.

"Thank you." She whispered.

"For what?"

"Just for being."

"Oh, well, you're welcome. And thank you for coming into my life at such an exciting time."

"This is an exciting time. Isn't it?" I wonder what would have happened if you hadn't been directing *Blood Wedding*"

"Different, but with the same outcome."

"Do you truly think so?"

"Yes, if we had had the same opportunity to spend time together. Marilee would probably have arranged it."

"I'm still amazed at her knowing we would have been attracted to each other. Well, I guess she...just knew something we didn't, that is until we met."

"Daniel has said many times that she sometimes has a kind of psychic ability. She certainly did with me about the play when I was having doubts in the beginning."

"You had doubts? About doing it...or what?"

"Not really about doing it, I was committed to that, just about how I was going to do it. You've seen the way I've been working and I've told you it was a new way for me. Well, Marilee was the one who got me started thinking in a new manner."

"I knew she had been an influence for you, or an inspiration. And right from the beginning?"

"Yes, very much so. Especially in...uh...secondary visualization and a logic for art."

"I remember our conversation about that and my own reaction to it in school. Anyway, thanks to Marilee...and Daniel for giving us this day."

"Yes many thanks. Let's get going, sweetheart. I want to get there a little early. Are you ready?"

"Just let me clean the kitchen a bit and I'll grab my drawing bag."

We walked to my car with my arm around her and her's around my waist. I had thoughts of getting to the theatre and also of going back upstairs and I told her so.

"Me too, Timmy, for hours and hours...but."

"Yes, but..."

I opened the door for her and actually patted her bottom.

"Now, now, Monsieur Sart," she laughed and smiled.

I got in and she reached over and hugged me. "Sweet day. beautiful day, mon amour."

When we arrived at the theatre an hour before rehearsal was set to start, everyone was there. Ginger met us and hugged Claire, as they had become fast friends. The actors also seemed concerned about the poetry and were practicing in their groups and trying new things with it, which was great. My encouraging them to constantly experiment with it had worked. On stage the set was complete and ready for us. Ginger's crew evidently had worked all day to get it ready. The lighting designer found me for a conference and showed me his latest work on a light plot and gave the signal to the booth to run through all of the cues. It was even better than I had hoped. Eddy and Aurora showed me their new work added to the wedding scene. I thought it was a bit long, so they edited it quickly. The cast broke from their various rehearsals and went downstairs to get into their costumes for the first time. I knew this would take some time, so Ginger and I went over my notes and I explained my worry about the poetry. Ginger reminded me of some earlier notes I had made. I had completely forgotten them, even in my discussion with Claire in the afternoon. They were very early in my notes, going back to the first week of rehearsal. The reason I didn't remember them, I thought immediately, was that they were so simple in description, but exactly what I was struggling with. I think I had dismissed them as only a spare idea at the time. They had been a reaction to a question a cast member had asked me about how would we deal with the poetry.

My answer was that we would just do it. At the time, it seemed like the answer of a director who didn't know yet what he was going to do. But as I had written in my notes it was to be treated as straight continuation of the script and not some complicated theatrical device. Of course, this wasn't a complete answer but it drew me back to the simplicity of my idea. Where it was written as a chorus, it would be done so, but from different parts of the stage and spread out, not grouped as I imagined the Greeks may have done it. I felt I wanted the lines to bounce around the stage just beyond an echo and overlap a bit. I heard it working in my mind. I hoped I could describe it well enough.

Barney interrupted our conference, asking to have a word with me in the lobby. I said I would be there in a minute and finished the discussion with Ginger. We were ready for the evening.

I joined Barney in his office. He said the advertising in the paper and a small article Rosenfield had done about the play and its history had given us the best presale of tickets we had ever had. We were sold out for the first two weeks. This was both exciting and scary. The fear that always haunts a director raged in my mind. Was the production going to be worth asking an audience to actually pay money and sit for two and a half hours and observe our or my work? Would they stand up and scream insults at the stage as the audiences did in France when Stravinsky first performed "The Rite of Spring?" Such thoughts lasted only about ten seconds. I had asked him to get a picture of the program cover enlarged and framed for Claire. When he showed me the result, I stared at it for a minute realizing there were tears in my eyes.

"Do you like it, Tim?"

"Uh...I love it, Barney, and I'm sure she will."

We discussed theatre business for a few minutes but I refused to talk about the rest of the season, saying this production was too overwhelming to even think about the future. He understood and asked about rehearsals.

"It's the last three days and it's a difficult piece, so they have to go well."

"I've never seen you so concentrated, Tim."

"Yes, I know. This production has been quite an experience, Barney. I want to thank you for the opportunity. I feel very good about it, if only as a learning experience, but let's hope its been more than that."

"Well, I've never seen a cast so committed and what your family has done for it certainly gives it a beautiful professional touch. It surely looks like a piece of art."

"Their help has been a revelation and an inspiration. I just hope the stage work lives up to the design work."

"It will. I've slipped into the back during several rehearsals. I'm very excited about it. This is a first for Dallas and the Civic Theatre, a US premiere. We're not counting that university production in the east. Oh, by the way, a friend of mine at Yale called to say they postponed their production for two weeks, so we are going to be the first to open."

"Great! Now that is good news, I think."

"It is, Tim. You've fallen in love with this play, haven't you? And it appears not just with the show. True?"

"Is it that obvious?"

"Yes. I've never seen you so happy and, as I said, so concentrated. I guess it's true that love can be an inspiration."

"Bien dicho."

"What?"

"Well said, Barney. But she's leaving at the end of the week."

"Oh my! That's not good. Why?"

"Her family in Los Angeles demands it. She doesn't feel as if she has a choice, it seems."

"How does she feel about leaving?"

"The same way I do, but...well I don't understand it and I may never."

"Well...I don't know what to say except that she is a very special lady. I'm sorry, Tim."

"So am I, and yes she is a very special lady. Thank you for framing the picture. Well...I'd better get back to rehearsal. We're getting ready to start the costume parade. Come join me if you'd like."

I went back to the theatre, thinking that was the most intimate conversation I've had with Barney and I wished I hadn't had it. Knowing Barney's attraction to me, it was uncomfortable at best, but I knew he liked Claire and he seemed sincere.

When I got onstage the cast was assembled in their costumes and they looked great. I was taken aback at how my original concept conferences with the costumer and approval of the renderings and color sketches had turned out so well in the final results. This was really my first experience in a costume play with no precedents, and I had been worried about my ideas and about the collaboration with designer actually working. I had heard stories of directors coming to costume parade and seeing grotesque parodies of their original concepts, but this wasn't like that at all. Even the colors that were brighter than I had asked for were better ideas.

Artistic collaboration was amazing when it worked to this extent, when a fellow artist takes your ideas and makes them even more so. I went halfway into the house and watched them go from scene to scene with the changes. I made a few notes on some small changes, to which the costumer quickly agreed. The lighting designer even gave me the lights to give the color contrasts. What I feared would be a difficult tech for three days ceased to exist. I seemed to gain needed hours of stage work with the success of these elements. I told the cast to get into their first scene costumes and set up on stage for notes and critique.

Claire had been close to the stage to draw the parade and do some quick portraits of the cast. I came down and joined her.

"I'll be sitting in the audience once we start the run-through. Would you like to sit with me?"

"Yes, if you don't think it will distract you."

"It won't. I'm sure I'll be taking notes furiously and occasionally stopping the action for changes or even let them continue with some close-in side-coaching."

"Will you mind if I continue to draw?"

"I hoped that you would and it would be good to have you close."

"Did you notice the table Ginger set up for you was a little longer? She said that if we did sit together, there would be room for me to use it."

"I hadn't noticed, but that's great."

I squeezed her hand and went up on stage. The cast came on stage and gathered in a crescent for notes. All of them had their notebooks ready for individual critique and general changes and advancements. I asked them how they felt about their work so far and what they felt we should concentrate on tonight. The actress playing the Wife was concerned about her run-in during the wedding scene carrying out to the audience the urgency of her message. I told her it wasn't her projection, which was strong, but that everything had to stop-the music, the dancing, and any side conversation. It had to be a precision moment; everyone on stage had to freeze and be drawn to her. Her gestures were a signal in that she enters with both hands up then very dramatically points off-right. The rest of the cast understood that it had to be a shocking moment with her announcement that Leonardo had run away with the bride. The difficulty was going from high gaiety to a sudden stop with no slide or overlap. I said that if necessary we would go through it several times.

The next question, from Carolyn Carothers, was one I had expected. "is the poetry working?" Everyone chimed in that that was their main concern also. I said it was almost there but still had to sound more like dialogue, as if the play suddenly changed from a dramatic piece to a poetry piece, and still keep the same feeling of continuity. I didn't want it to sound as if we stopped and went into another form of drama. The part being sung with the music at the wedding preparation scenes was working, but the criss-cross work in the blocking was still not as interesting a picture. It had to have a weaving effect in a stylized manner, or a self choreographed blending from stage right to stage left.

"It may work better if you work in staggered line-ups as you cross through the group advancing toward you. Now it seems too lined up with a one-two-three-start effect. Don't let the movement cue be visual but on the line. When you reach the opposite side of the stage, blend into the scene then re-cross in a different formation. It really is just about there. Just don't anticipate. Play the moment of excitement of the coming wedding and concern about the bride. The waking of the bride has several different interpretations which depend on your raising and lowering the lines and the beginnings of new poetry passages as we have rehearsed. Don't let it seem too complicated; with what I just said, the blending of line and movement should fall into place."

Carolyn said that was what she needed to hear. We discussed all of the major poetic parts of the play, and what would take it to the theatrical effect needed at this point in rehearsal. I asked then not to let it get static out of doubts or fears but to let it grow or take it to another level each rehearsal.

The two actors playing Leonardo and the Bridegroom were still concerned about the fight scene played behind the scrim even though they had rehearsed it for many extra hours. I told them it was working so well that the only changes would probably be in the lighting. I took some time to discuss the two characters they played, the innocent qualities of the bridegroom and the foolhardiness of Leonardo that had to be so charmingly evil. The older actor who called me El Audazito asked if the passion of the people and the situation was evident. My answer was that it was just about there and that so much depended on the Bride and her disastrous desire for Leonardo. When they were onstage together they needed to burn with a desire that should scare the audience or make them worry about what's going to happen to the bridegroom and the wedding or does he know what's going on behind his back. "I don't want to telegraph the run-away, just rise up to it," I explained, "We won't see the bride and Leonardo sneaking off together."

There were more questions and concerns, which as the others did, went back to the beginning concept and directing sessions but had the quality of "is it working and will we be ready and what do we need to do now?"

I then gave my notes and critique, especially reminding them to use the blocking, which I liked, and to remember their stage technique. They had the freedom and my confidence to advance their movement and interpretation. Stanislavisky's writings on communion and delving into the subconscious influenced some part of my notes. Everything that happened on stage in the play must be as if it were the first time they experienced it. The intense rehearsal, the line perfection, the characters they had developed, were the backbone and their truth for their bringing the play to life, not just an exercise of a moment-to-moment rehearsed representation of the play.

All of the cast knew the scene changes with the wagons and pop-ups would go through changes up until the last rehearsal and they were ready for it with no questions. Our version of "Vachtangov's zanies" had been a good idea so far, and what made it work, other than the dancing set changing cast, was Eddy's music.

I gave them a few last words before the run-through. "An important thing to remember is no one in the audience, with the exception of my friend, Dick Ayers, who saw it in Spain, in Spanish, will have seen this piece before. Everything will be new to them, and that's to our advantage, I hope. We love the play and hope that they do. So we will play it to the hilt for them." The cast cheered, clapped, and rose to go to places.

I sat at my table furiously taking notes with only one stop through the first act. I went up on stage and congratulated the cast on their good work, but they knew the next two acts were the tough ones. They were right, but it went well and the wedding party only needed one stop to get the perfection of the Wife's entrance on the ramp. Eddy's music and Aurora's choreography was almost perfect, and Camila added true beauty to her short solo in greeting the Bride. Claire looked at me and smiled at the act break, letting me know she also thought it was going well. We took a long enough break for me to give some notes to the leads for the last act. They were excited and receptive.

When the lights went down at the end of the third act, the curtains closed for the first time to Eddy's new music with Aurora's surprise addition singing in Spanish the waking of the Bride. I felt a relief and excitement that I had never felt before in the last week of rehearsal. The house lights came up. The cast was assembled on stage. The old actor cheered, "Viva el Audauzito!".

The cast joined him in the cheer. Claire leaned over and hugged me. "Si, mi Audauzito. Bien hecho."

On stage, we all gathered in a circle, the actors still in costume, and I gave my ten pages of notes. They wrote everything down in their retrieved notebooks. I gave slight blocking changes and character advancements and thanked Aurora for her idea. She said she had forgotten to tell me about it before the rehearsal started but decide to try it anyway, hoping I would like it. I talked about the poetry, and how it was just about there. All it needed was the next two nights of rehearsal.

"We have two more times to perfect what we have. Use the notes I gave you and your ideas with them to take the next steps. Let's do the next two nights in full makeup along with any costume additions. I think tomorrow we should run through the last act twice."

I asked Aurora if she had any notes on the wedding party. She gave them and worked very quickly with several actors on the dance transitions. Eddy asked for a critique of the under-scoring. My only reaction was for him not to hold back in any way because it could only get better.

"Please try to get some rest for the week ahead because I don't want the opening to be an exhausted let-down," I said, "I want you to be able to rise up for the new experience for Dallas and our audience."

Liza Farquar said she was too excited to get exhausted. The cast laughed and agreed with her. Carolyn Carothers stood up, "This had been the most fulfilling rehearsal process I've ever almost ever lived through,"
She said.

She then did a fake faint collapse on the stage. Two male actors rushed to her, raising her up in an exaggerated fashion. The cast loved it.

I said in conclusion, "Tomorrow night let's meet again, because this was so much fun."

We shook hands, hugged, and said our good nights.

Camila hugged Claire and me, and reminded us that tomorrow after rehearsal we were joining them at Dick's house.

When Claire and I drove up to Marilee's, she came out to meet us, insisting we join her and Daniel out by the pool for drinks. They wanted to hear how the rehearsal had gone.

Dan greeted me with a Bourbon and soda and a pat on the shoulder. Marilee brought Claire a Martini.

We sat down and Claire spoke first, "It was a complete success. Timmy should be very proud."

"Well, we're not there yet, but thanks sweetheart."

"If the next two rehearsals go as well, or even close, you have created...uh... well,...'living art.'"

I laughed and took her hand, "Wow, living art?"

"Yes, 'living art!'"

"That sounds like a giant compliment, brother, if Claire has the same ability as Marilee to be objective, and I think she does," Dan said.

"Barney told me tonight what you, Mom, and Dad have done has added a new professional look to design for the theatre. It's true. Thanks to you and them."

"Daniel said it was fun to do it and hoped it wasn't too wild for the show," Marilee added.

"Dan, you both showed me what you wanted to do."

"Small rendering to big back-drop sometimes doesn't quite ring true. But good. I think your powers of visualization are even better than I thought."

"Did you get some more drawings tonight, Claire?" Marilee asked.

"I tried to, but it was harder sitting so close to Timmy. He reacts so physically to everything. He was as much fun to watch as the play. But I did get some work done, I think my best in a way."

"How so?" Daniel wanted to know.

"I think I've started concentrating on individual character work rather than an over-all scene view."

"She showed me one of me leaning into the action, that is a me I've never seen. If she will allow it, I want to have it."

"I want it, too, but I'll make a copy for you."

"May I see it?" Marilee asked.

Claire nodded and went to get her drawing bag.

"How are you holding up, Timmy? I mean about Claire?"

"Marilee, your belief in us has been a help, and we both are living each moment we have together. No extrapolating on the future."

Dan nodded his understanding of what I said as Claire returned.

Dan took Claire's drawing, leaning into the light, "My word...damn...this is really good, Claire."

Marilee took it and said, "I think you had better make several copies, Claire, because we want one, too."

"Indeed. No wonder you like it brother."

Claire agreed. We talked more about the rehearsal then Marilee asked if we would like to stay together for some of Claire's last nights.

Claire and I answered "yes" in unison.

"I'll do everything I can to help. Claire, we can solve this tomorrow. With Timmy's approval, of course."

"I trust you ladies, but there is always my place."

"I believe she's thinking of something special, brother."

Claire turned to me and smiled.

I found myself almost dozing off, so I said it was time to go. Claire walked me out to my car. We held each other for a few minutes.

I whispered to her, "A very special day, dear heart."

"Yes, Timmy, a beautiful day...and... a glorious evening of work for you. I'm so proud of you."

I kissed her and was off to a deep peaceful night of sleep. My dreams were filled with gentle images of Claire and of actors moving gracefully on stage. No jarring shocks or reality encounters.

I woke up late the next morning to Mom bringing me a cup of coffee. I wrote in my journal about the few disappointments in the rehearsal process-the actors who had to drop out, the difficulty of making the poetry work, and of course, needing more time. I tried to describe a process that would make the last two days very effective. I saw that the blocking and stage pictures were developing nicely and that their projection was strong enough so I thought I could go back up on stage with them and side-direct in the places where it was most needed. If I could do this without interrupting the casts creative process, it would possibly bring to conclusion the rehearsals needs. No stops, if at all possible. Any major notes would be individual-specific, with an overview critique to finish. I knew that many things could go wrong now because everything seemed to be going too well, and I was worried about the letdown from the intensity in the rehearsals. I knew that we had a show that was different from anything we had done at the theatre before and that, at the very least, was exciting. How the audience would receive it was not a concern now. I liked it and felt good about my work and growth as a director. Claire's support and belief in me had made a major difference in my confidence. She had a sophisticated eye for good art. With those thoughts of her, I stopped trying to write and turned to my thoughts of her and what had happened between us. It was a wonderful mystery of an extraordinarily magnificent sort. I don't know if it would have been different if I had not been directing. Her collaboration with the drawings had been an enormous help that just came from out of nowhere. It had added a new dimension to the process. I could step back out of rehearsal and see the show like a set of flip cards that gave the illusion of movement. And having her to talk to about my work and her reaction to it was a first-time experience. I had always been rather resistant to discussing my work in progress before, but with her, our talks seemed to bring new ideas constantly, that I'm sure I would not have been there or happened without her. I didn't want to think of directing again without her, but I knew it would have to happen.

I broke away from this direction of thinking and went inside to eat a late breakfast. Mom insisted on talking about Claire and how I was taking it, being this close to her leaving. She really wanted to help me not get depressed about it, and I assured her that I was alright and accepted the coming inevitability. I tried to explain to her that it was the best thing that had ever happened in my relationships with women and that, of course, I wished it wasn't going to end, ever. Yes, I was very much in love with Claire and hoped her leaving wasn't truly the end. Mom assured me that her feelings for Claire were also very strong and that she also hoped it wasn't the end. She tried to express how it was for her to accept someone so quickly into the family and how it had been so natural from the very beginning. At that point, Mom starting crying, something I had rarely seen, and came to me with a comforting hug.

"I know I've said it before, but just be strong and love her up to the last minute. Because I know she's very sad about having to leave. There's a family situation we don't understand. She's a European girl with customs and traditions that are very different from ours."

"Yes, I know all of this, and I appreciate your caring, but I don't think there's anything strange about Claire, not that you implied that, but she is a woman who has changed my life in many ways and my way of thinking so I accept this difference that I don't understand. Perhaps I will someday, hopefully soon. Everyone has fallen in love with Claire…so…well."

I left Mom still crying, and went to shower and dress. I went into my apartment and sat on my bed and, for the first time cried about Claire. I wanted to be with her at that very moment and always.

After dressing, I went into the house and called Claire to tell her that I would be by to get her later in the afternoon. She said she missed me and would be waiting. In the meantime, she was going to touch up some of her drawings and go on a short shopping trip with Marilee.

I headed downtown to a jewelry store that Marilee told me about that was close to Sanger's and not far from the courthouse. It was long and narrow, with cowboy and western art on the walls. It specialized in Indian jewelry from New Mexico. I wanted to get a ring for Claire that was special and unusual. Marilee had helped by getting Claire to try on one of Marilee's rings so she could get her size. I want it to be unique and something she could wear almost all the time. The jewelry in all the cases was beautiful. The owner brought out a tray of rings, and I found the one I wanted almost immediately. It was silver and delicate with a spider web turquoise center stone and very small pieces of coral on the sides with circle zig-zags around them. I said it had to be about six-and-a-half and, in what seemed like a quirk of fate, it was. The owner said it hadn't sold because it was so small. It was by far the most expensive gift, or anything, that I had ever bought, but that's what savings are for. He gave me a pretty little ring box and then asked about Marilee. As it turned out, she had called to tell him I was coming. She had been a customer of his for years because she had a real love for Indian art and jewelry. I thought her tastes had changed since meeting Daniel, but she still watched for the best Southwestern work.

On the way back to my place, I dropped by Uncle Willy's shop. He was busy with about ten things at once in the machine shop and went back and forth to his Auburn acquisition. His four workers were hard at work on a new contract and a new mechanic was dismantling the Auburn for a total restoration. He dropped everything and came out to greet me. We went into his office so he could show me how he had framed and mounted the racing posters Claire had given him, and they looked great. He asked how the show was going and then about Claire. Rosie was doing fine but going through unpleasant sickness of early-pregnancy.

"It seems that life has changed for both of us, Tim-boy. You and Claire, and Rosie and me having a baby. You know, I've been a kind of independent spirit all my life. I didn't even expect to ever get married, but then Rosie came along. That's been about ten times better than I could have imagined, and now a baby. You've only seen me get excited about cars, racing, and telling you about China, but now I'm so damn excited about being a father...well...I'm already thinking differently. Rosie thinks I'm obsessive about being so protective of her and the...Yes! It's kind of strange for a guy who's never been religious to pray every day that she and the baby are going to be alright."

"It sounds like a good life change to me, Uncle Willy. You know, if it were later in the afternoon and I didn't have Claire to be with and no rather important rehearsal, we would be having a drink of that good Bourbon you keep in your desk, but I don't believe we'll being doing much of that any more. Right?"

"Probably not...well, maybe occasionally, but I don't think Rosie will be as tolerant about our man talks now."

"Occasionally, or even rarely, is good enough for me," I assured him.

"It's funny, but I think my work is getting better, or my concentration anyway. Everything is more important."

"I've been experiencing that too, and there's no doubt it's been Claire. Love is strange."

"Yes, it is, nephew, but ain't it wonderful?"

"At the very least, Uncle."

Because Uncle Willy seemed to understand more than most about Claire's leaving, he didn't try to talk about how I was feeling. He hoped that we could all get together but there wasn't really an evening free unless they came over to my parents for the early dinner on opening night. He said he would call Mom about it and see if it was possible, which, of course it would be. As I left he gave my car the once-over, saying it was time for him to redo it; engine, brakes, etc. "Soon," I promised.

Back at my place, I sat for a while going over my notes, writing down some new ideas, and putting a bit more into my journal. After a couple of hours, I went inside the house and called Claire. She and Marilee had just gotten back, and she asked if I could give her another half hour to get ready. She also asked if I wanted to eat there, or go out. I said I didn't want to go out, as I heard Marilee was saying in the background she would fix us something special. I laughed and said I would be there in 45 minutes. Claire said 35.

Daniel met me at the door and said the girls were in the kitchen. Claire greeted me with a kiss, making me feel like we had been together for months instead of weeks. We sat around the breakfast table and chatted about rehearsal and the weekend.

"Timmy, Claire, how about a suite at the Adolphus for Friday and Saturday nights?" Marilee asked.

Claire and I looked at each other and smiled.

"Uh…it sounds great, but what if Claire's parents call?"

Daniel had the answer for that. "On those days, I will answer the phone. If they did call, I'll tell them that Claire and Marilee went fishing at a friend's ranch for the weekend and there wasn't a phone, that everything was alright, and that she will be back in plenty of time to catch the train Sunday evening."

"It's almost like a conspiracy, but I like it. Don't you, Timmy?"

"Yes, I do sweetheart. Thank you, Marilee, Daniel."

"Well, brother, we have been plotting for a couple of days to figure something out for you. A bit of sanctuary for two special people can be a real impetus for an idea. If you didn't have the theatre to go to Friday night, it could have been something really nice like…Ft. Worth."

I laughed and Claire asked what was funny.

"Ft. Worth is not usually considered some where really special for Dallas folks to go to," I explained.

"Oh. Well, I like it that we'll be at the theatre Friday and Saturday night. But it would have been nice to have the whole weekend alone …sanctuary."

"We'll eat in about 45 minutes, folks. Claire you don't need to help me. You two go off somewhere in the house."

"I'm going to disappear into my studio. Just whistle for me," Daniel said as he gave Marilee a flirty pat on the bottom.

"You rascal, I'll get you later, perhaps." Marilee then whistled with her arms open.

Daniel turned back to her with a hug and kiss. "You two are a bad influence on us," he told Claire and me.

Claire took my hand and pulled me into the living room and the big fluffy sofa.

"Hallo, Timmy. I missed you this afternoon."

"Me, too, baby."

"Baby?! You've never called me that before. I like it. You sound like a movie star talking."

"I don't believe I've called anyone 'baby' before, it just came out; perhaps because I love you, dear girl."

"Good, baby." She said and laughed. "Hold me a minute, please, Timmy. Just hold me."

I did, not saying a word. Then we both started shaking a little bit and realized we were both crying softly.

"Oh, my God, Claire."

"Yes, I know. I've never been so happy and so sad at the same time."

I kissed her gently and leaned back in the sofa with her head on my shoulder and my arm around her. She looked up at me and kissed my chin.

"Did you get some good work done today?"

"I think so. I've had some new ideas about my last critique sessions. I'm not really worried about the show…I guess I'm just kind of excited. Last night was a really good evening."

"The afternoon was good, too."

"Indeed it was."

"So beautiful that I feel like I'm still there."

"I think we both will be there, in those moments, forever."

"Yes, forever, Timmy."

"Will you come home with me tonight, Claire?"

"Yes, I will, mon amour. And I think I will go call my parents so they won't think about calling me later. They've only done it once, but there's no reason to take a chance about it."

"A good idea, sweetheart." And she was off to phone.

I went into the kitchen to see Marilee.

"Well, Timmy, where's your lady?"

"She's calling her parents."

"What's going on?"

"I've asked Claire to spend the night with me at my place. What do you think?"

"You certainly don't really need my permission at this point. When it comes to you and Claire, I've become a free thinker of the first order, though I wasn't very conservative before you two, considering me and Daniel not being married and all that."

"Well, I wasn't really asking permission…well, maybe approval or something, I don't know. I don't want her to get into any kind of trouble with her parents."

"It looks like she's taking care of that, doesn't it?"

"Yep, it does. Thank you, Marilee…for introducing us…uh…bringing us together."

"You're most welcome. Thinking back I don't know why I felt so strongly about you two, just intuition I guess. It's good to know I was so right. Timmy…are you alright about everything…you know what I mean?"

"Yes…in a way. At times I do…well… 'look upon myself and curse my fate.'"

"The old bard is speaking in the extreme there, Timmy. There is no curse, though bitter people may have described it, love, that way."

"I don't want to sound as if I'm feeling sorry for myself, and our falling in love is the best thing that could have happened, it's just that…"

"We are all feeling it, though not in the same way you two are. Hey, you're both still young and the future is not written in stone. Right?"

"I hope not. Marilee, I've loved you like a sister from the very first, but now, Wow!"

"These past weeks have been fun for us, too, Timmy. And seeing you so happy…and so serious about your work. Sit down there, I'm going to whistle Daniel in. I think I want everybody around me right now or I'm going to start crying," she said.

"Well, get him in quick. Too much crying going on around here."

"What?"

"Yes, me and Claire just went through a session of it," I admitted.

"Oh, my, Timmy."

She went to the back door and did that fingers-in her-mouth incredibly loud whistle.

I sat down and within a couple of minutes Daniel came in.

"That was quick. Is the food ready so soon, honey?"

"No it's not. I just wanted you in here with me, that's all."

"Is everything alright?"

"No it's not." Marilee went over and hugged Dan breaking down into loud sobs.

"Oh, sweetheart. What's happened?"

"Nothing. I don't want Claire to leave either."

All I could do was sit there as Daniel comforted her. Soon Marilee pulled out a handkerchief and dried her eyes.

"I'd better get this food going since you do kind of need to get to the theatre."

"I have another hour and a half for even an early arrival. I'm doing fine."

Marilee talked about the production and how excited she was about it. She said she even put up posters at the country clubs, Dallas and Brook Hollow, and had been calling friends about it. Dan said he had put up a poster at the museum. I told them what Barney had said about being sold out for two weeks. In twenty minutes, or so Claire came down carrying a small bag plus her drawing satchel.

"Hallo, all of you. Marilee, I just called my parents, well…because I'm going to…" she started to explain shyly.

"Yes, I know, Timmy told me. That was a smart thing to call them."

"Is that alright with you? I mean going home with Timmy tonight?"

"Of course…hell, I'd buy you both tickets to South America if I thought we could get away with it. But for some strange reason, I think it would harm the friendship I have with your parents and would kill the possibility of your father coming to work for me."

"Yes, probably so, but the sentiment is a sweet one. They told me to say hello."

"Anything else?"

"No, just that they're excited about seeing me soon. They wanted to talk about the arrangements for the train, but I assured them it had all been taken care of a long ago. I did tell them how much I like Dallas and being with you and that I think of you like a sister now."

"I guess this is my 'sister' day."

I quickly added, "I told her the same thing a few minutes ago."

"Hey, brother, I thought you've felt that way about Marilee for a long time."

"I have, Daniel, but more so now."

Daniel turned to Claire, "You have changed this family, dear Claire."

"And you've changed me. I vaguely remember the Claire Levant who came here five and a half weeks ago. To gain a new family is…well…a happy event. I didn't know it could be except by a forced tradition…I mean…"

"I understand, Claire, you don't need to say anything more." Marilee said, turning to me and subtly shaking her head, which I immediately knew meant I shouldn't ask a question.

Claire went to her drawing bag and pulled out a new piece.

"Look what I did this morning, Timmy."

It was an absolutely beautiful colored drawing of the marriage party dance scene.

"I did it from memory and my other drawings."

Daniel took the drawing, "This is really good, Claire. May I buy it from you?"

"No you may not, silly Daniel, you may have it. Is that alright with you, Timmy, if I give it to Daniel and Marilee?"

"Yes, I haven't seen Daniel react to anyone else's art like that, ever. It is beautiful, sweetheart. I certainly will get to see it often if Marilee hangs it in the house here."

"You bet I will. I like it as much as Daniel does," Marilee enthused. "Claire, you've really exploded in growth with your work. I liked it from the first, but this is…Wow!"

"I've been inspired by someone," Claire said as she took my hand and kissed it.

"And you me, my muse from France."

Daniel put the drawing up on a low cabinet by the breakfast table so we could all see it.

"I believe we're about ready to eat here." Marilee said as she returned to the stove. "Salmon filets are the specialty of the house tonight with a salad. Good. No?"

After dinner, Claire and I jumped in my car and headed to the theatre.

"Claire…?"

"Yes, Ti-mo-thee?"

"Your going with me to rehearsal makes everything so exciting. In the past I've always been rather anxious and worried, but now I look forward to being a director with no doubts about my work and the coming night. It's a great feeling."

"I'm excited, too. What you do is so different from a painter, or a sculptor, or even a film maker. It is living art, and so ephemeral. It's like being in a painting that starts, moves coming alive, and then is gone, but it's not because it makes pictures in the mind that don't go away."

"Bien dicho, mi amor."

"Gracias, mi vida."

We walked in the back door of the theatre to be greeted by a beehive of activity. There were greeting and hugs all around. The old actor called from across the stage.

"Bienvenido, el Audazito!"

I laughed and waved. Eddy and Aurora were playing and dancing. The cast was going through the poetry and scenes. The two leading actors were rehearsing their fight scene. Liza Farquar was going through her run down the ramp and practicing her extended gestures. Camila waved and came over to remind us of our being with her and Dick later. I assured her we hadn't forgotten. Claire went into the lobby to check on the hanging of her drawings and Ginger took me by the arm for our pre-rehearsal meeting. Never had I experienced this sort of excitement before rehearsal and with everyone here much earlier than required.

The lighting and costume designers came with us. We met in my little office downstairs and went over things for the evening's work. The costumer said she was making some changes for the night, primarily in fittings that weren't quite right yet and a few new colors for me to see. The lighting designer had some new ideas for me to see that were inspired by the last two rehearsals. I told them I was happy that they were still having new ideas, and they left to finish up their changes.

Ginger and I went over the notes from the last night and I asked her how she thought the set change assignments were working. She said they were the hardest part of the show concept and very much needed these last two nights for them to work perfectly. I needed to know if the cast was comfortable backstage, because there were so many of them who weren't on stage a lot of the time. She said it was crowded but just fine. The Green Room had been cleared of most of the unnecessary furniture, and the sound system from stage to Green and dressing rooms was just the answer. No one had missed an entrance yet and the cast had worked out its own traffic problems for getting from off-to on-stage.

"Tim. Ginger began, "I believe all of your innovations for this productions have created a lot of good enthusiasm. There's an excitement I don't think I've ever seen before. I feel it, too."

"Let's hope it translates into good theatre, but one of the best things for me has been your setting me free to work as a director. Usually I would have to solve a million problems that you've handled for me."

"Thank you, but I loved this play from the very beginning and my not having to work this month was a big factor. It has been fun watching you change every week and still keep the show going in the direction you wanted it to. I think your talks with the cast have made the difference, and they believed in your concept from the beginning. They feel like they're involved in an exciting theatrical experiment that could be important, for Dallas anyway."

"Well, I don't know about that, but I knew *Blood Wedding* couldn't be done in the way I had worked before. I guess it is an experiment for me but it had to be tied to a rehearsal process of a few weeks, not the months that Brecht or the Russians take. Well, here we are. Do you feel ready for the next two nights? After that, it's your show."

"I think I am, but I can't imagine you pulling away completely. I don't want you to and I'm sure cast feels the same way."

"We'll see. Lets go up and set up for the evening. I'm eager to see the makeup."

I decided to go into the dressing room which, oddly enough, I had not done before with this cast. They were all busy finishing up their makeup but were happy to see me. I went to each cast member, offering encouragement and praise, and looked at the rather extreme makeup I had asked for. Everyone looked good here, but on stage is the real test. What was good to see was that there wasn't any idle talk but line work and scene speed throughs. I went back up and met with Eddy and who had gotten ready early so we could meet. He played a new piece he wanted to try for a transition between the second and third acts, which had concerned us both. It was much more intense and seemed to set up for the violence that was coming without telegraphing it or giving it away to the audience. It had to be split in two for the intermission, but it was a terrific segue. I had written about my worries of going from the escape of the Bride and Leonardo in the second to three deaths in the third. The cast member who was dancing the part of Death, a recent idea, went through her entrance and exit for me. Watching them work reminded me that everyone would be going through changes and new ideas through out the run of the show.

I left them to go see Claire in the lobby. She was helping the hanging of her drawings, using her obvious expertise and doing a good job making changes where she thought necessary. Barney accepted her rearranging without a word of advice. I had told him of her studies in London, and he had been very impressed. When she saw me she came over and asked what I thought.

"The lobby has never looked better. We've never had pieces hanging that were so tied to a show. Most of the time, there were just pictures of the cast."

"I've saved that wall near the entrance to the theatre for those."

As if on cue, Jeordie came in with his latest prints from last night. They were different from the usual head shots in that they were more like candid character shots that meshed perfectly with Claire's drawings. He had worked backstage, in the Green Room and the dressing rooms. Claire loved his work, saying she would frame them during the rehearsal. We had a large collection of photo frames from the storeroom that we had used in the past. Jeordie said he wasn't through taking pictures, so he helped her choose the shots he had with him that he thought were the best ones. He stepped back to look at Claire's drawings.

"Mom told me about your pictures, but I didn't know they were this good. Do you mind if I take some pictures of the lobby, Barney?"

"No, Jeordie, not at all," Barney smiled, "I would like a record of this exhibit, and that's what it is. I've never thought of the lobby as an art gallery but it is now."

Claire seemed taken aback by Barney's statement.

"I really just started doing them for fun. I didn't expect Timmy to like them as much as he did and didn't know if he could be truly objective."

"Claire, Jeordie and I have been close to art all of our lives, so we do have idea about what's good. Don't you think Daniel's reaction today was a reassurance of the quality of your work? They were good enough to help me for three weeks."

"Thank you, gentlemen. Well, I did think they would be interesting in the lobby after you liked them, but let's not make too much of this."

"You may get reviewed too, sweetheart."

"Ti-mo-thee, please?"

I laughed and hugged her. "I'm going in to start the rehearsal. Are you going to draw tonight?"

"Yes, but not yet. I'm going to do more work here, but I do want to get a better and more dramatic vista of Liza's entrance on the ramp and the third act."

Jeordie joined me in the auditorium.

"I sure do like her, big brother. Mom and Dad can't stop talking about her. I didn't know she was leaving until Mom told me yesterday; I wish she wasn't."

"Me too, Jeordie."

He shrugged as if he didn't know what to say, which was probably better. The cast was gathering on stage and Jeordie joined them to get some close-ups. I got my satchel and retrieved my notes for the opening session. Chairs were pulled out into the crescent, and we started. I realized that Jeordie was also taking pictures of me as I talked to the cast. It didn't bother me, but I suddenly hoped there was one that Claire would want.

The notes session before, the run-through, and the critique afterwards went better than I had hoped for. Claire joined me for the marriage party scene and drew for the rest of the time. The makeup looked fine, needing only a few touchups. I talked to several of the cast members individually. Camila joined Claire and me and we left to meet Dick at his parent's house.

Dick had gotten some very good Spanish wine and had prepared tapas for an evening snack. We sat out on patio. Dick and Camila talked about missing Spain, and Claire reminisced about France and London. I was glad to not talk about the show and didn't feel left out at all because I had so many questions. All three were deeply concerned about how things going in Europe and fearful of the future there. My innocent questions on the situation brought out much information about Nazi Germany and Franco's advances in Spain with the help of Germany and Italy. Camila told me of a letter she had gotten from a friend.

"Tim, she wrote that Lorca has disappeared and he's probably been murdered by Franco's secret police."

"What…!?" I was stunned. "How could they…he's a national treasure?"

"They're doing a lot of that. My friend said that if Lorca had not been a homosexual it possibly wouldn't have happened. But he did insist on staying in Granada and taunting the powers that be."

I had been told that Lorca was homosexual, but it didn't seem to be a part of his writing so I had never given it a second thought. For awhile that put a damper on the evening, but Dick insisted on changing the subject.

"Well, we don't know that for sure and we are here, thank goodness. Tim, Camila is enjoying being a small part of your play."

"She's not such a small part, with what she adds to the dancing scene and the ensemble."

"Working with Tim and Aurora is great. When Aurora asked me to join her, I was afraid Tim would think I was imposing myself into his play."

"No, I was thrilled you wanted to be a part of it," I protested. "And you are a powerful and beautiful presence on stage."

"Timmy's right, Camila," Claire agreed. "I think some of my best drawings are of you and Aurora together."

"Today at Marilee's, Claire showed Daniel and Marilee one of her new drawings in color of Camila and in the marriage party scene and he wanted to buy it. Claire, of course, gave it to them, but anyway Daniel's liking it so much was a true stamp of artistic approval, and you were a part of that, Camila."

"Dios mio! That's wonderful for you, Claire."

"Thank you, Camila, but this is a one-time experience, I mean, how often am I going to be asked to do drawings in rehearsals?"

"How about all of mine, forever, sweetheart?"

Claire jumped up and came to me, "Is that an open invitation?"

She laughed and kissed my forehead, making light of the portent. "Thank you, baby." She turned to Dick and Camila giggling, "It's a new love word he called me. I had heard it in movies, but I never thought any one would call me 'baby.' I like it."

Dick laughed turning to Camila, "I think it's cute. Don't you, baby?"

"Claro que si, mi amorcito."

It was time to leave. Camila and Claire hugged very emotionally, as Dick and I put our arms over each other's shoulders as we walked out to my car.

With Claire's head on my shoulder on the way to my place, she said, "They are wonderful friends, I will miss them."

We quietly went into my apartment and tuned on only the bedside lamp. When I came out of the bathroom Claire said it was her turn. She splashed around for a few minutes then came out in a lacy night gown…. A glowing apparition. I told her to stop as I stood up in my sleep shorts and went to her wrapping my arms around her.

"You are one powerfully good looking woman," I said in an exaggerated

Texas drawl.

"And you are my handsome Texas man."

We stood there for a minute as I kissed her neck, then her lips. I then moved around behind her and stroked her breasts with one hand and moved the other down to her soft mons.

"Oh, Timmy, I love it when you touch me. Please take me to bed and make love with me." We made gentle love side by side and fell asleep in each other's arms.

I woke before Claire and just looked at her for a few minutes then she opened her eyes and smiled.

"Good morning, Ti-mo-thee. Is it late?"

"Ten-ish."

She pulled me to her and whispered, "I love you."

"Me, too, baby. Would you like some coffee?"

"In a few minutes. Just hold me a bit more." Then we made love without any foreplay at all.

I put on a robe and went into the house and made a pot of coffee. We sat on the bed, drank coffee and talked. She asked about growing up with an artistic family saying she envied that experience since her parents were not at all artistic except as minor collectors, which in the last years she had helped with. I told her about the game Daniel and I Played; while Dad played Bach on the piano, we drew what we heard. I had not been very good at it, but Daniel created flowing drawings with the crayons while I struggled with angular trees and mountains, but it was sure good for the imagination. The hours spent in Dad's shop helping him cut and sand wood for his furniture creations. And Uncle Willy's instructions on mechanics, which Daniel had no interest in what so ever. I told her about experiences in my high school with a pretty good Drama department, and how it had headed me to what dominated me now. And how my job at the bookstore made it possible for me work at the theatre.

I was curious about her youth in Europe so Claire told me about growing up in Paris and how beautiful spring was there. She wondered what it was like going to a school with both boys and girls because all of her schooling had been only in girls' schools until she went to university at the Sorbonne, and then in London.

I had known generally about her youth, but she added so much with a sweet nostalgia. She thought she would always be a French girl, but the move to London had not been difficult except for getting used to the academic life in English. She liked New York very much and was disappointed for me that I never been there. I assured her I would get there some day. At that, we paused for a minute because my wish was to go there with her and she knew what I was thinking.

As we finished the pot of coffee, we started making plans for the day. She wanted for us to go to Marilee's where she would make us a big breakfast, and I agreed.

"Hurry up! I'm a hungry girl."

I showered and shaved while Claire looked at my collection of theatre books. I heard her squeal and came out of the bathroom to see what brought on such a reaction.

She had found my copy of Somerset Maugham's <u>Then and Now</u>, which she had never read. I told her it was hers since I had read it twice. She started it immediately, saying that Machiavelli had always been an interesting character to her since she had written a paper on <u>The Prince</u> in secondary school.

Claire was already dressed and curled up on my bed reading when I finished. Just as we started to leave, Claire insisted on combing my hair saying nothing was wrong she just wanted to comb it. I sat down on the bed as she got behind me wrapping her legs around me. She stopped combing and put her arms around me, put her face into my neck, and said softly, "it was wonderful waking up and seeing you first thing this morning."

"I liked waking up before you and watching you sleep."

We said nothing more to each other. Soon she jumped up, got her bags as I got mine and we walked to my car holding hands.

Marilee was in her den working when we entered. "Well, home again, home again, jiggidy, jog. Hey there you two. Good…uh…early afternoon. I actually just made another pot of coffee."

"I could do with another cup. Claire?"

"No thanks, baby. I'll squeeze some orange juice. Marilee, do you mind if I make us some breakfast?"

"Nope, I'll help. I've been at it for four hours. I need a break. Dan's been in his studio all day. He said he was going to paint for as long as he could stand. He even took a sandwich with him, so it's just us."

"Perfectly fine, I won't even go out and bother him," I said.

"I don't think you could bother him. He doesn't mind family joining him as long as he can keep painting."

Claire fixed a great omelet with ham, peppers, and tomatoes. Marilee asked about Dick and Camila, hoping they could keep up a friendship. I assured her that should be no problem because they had expressed similar sentiments about her and Daniel. Claire went upstairs saying she would be awhile because she wanted to take a long shower and wash her hair. I told her I should probably go over to the theatre for a couple of hours but for her not to worry because I would be back soon.

"Timmy, that is your work and tonight is your dress rehearsal. If you need to work all afternoon, perhaps Marilee could give me a ride to the theatre. Would that be too much trouble?" she asked Marilee.

"Claire, please, Of course not."

When I got to the theatre I immediately met with Barney to discuss the needs for the day and plans for the big opening night he had planned. Openings were usually very simple affairs, but he wanted to make this one special because of the response to ticket sales. There would be society writers for the party in the lobby after the show. Barney evidently had been calling people for weeks trying to get our biggest supporters there for the evening. He was concerned that we were on the edge of being overbooked, with more people calling all the time to respond to his invitations. He just wanted to be sure that Claire and I would be there for the lobby party. I assured him we would be. Because of the opening night lobby gathering, the cast party was going to be Friday evening at Liza Farquar's house, co-sponsored by Marilee and Daniel. I told him I would be leaving after the show on Friday for the weekend so not to plan anything.

The technical crew that didn't have a day job were all working everywhere in the theatre, backstage, dressing, and costume shop. Ginger found me onstage checking the set piece wagons with my Dad who I was surprised to see. He felt responsible for the workings so he had come in to check his design for the pop-ups. I hadn't seen him all week. I told Ginger I would meet with her after I spent some time with Dad. We sat and talked about the pressure of this last week. He was surprised how calm I was about the coming dress rehearsal and opening.

"You're usually fairly high-strung about this time, son. You must feel pretty good about how things have been going."

"I do. I've worked harder, studied more, and planned more artistically. Also, Claire and I have had a great time together. She comes every night to rehearsal with me, and works on her drawings. Last night, she set up the lobby display of her work and Jeordie's photographs. Once she was convinced that her drawings were good enough to be seen by the audience, she put a lot of time into making them as good as possible. Yesterday, Daniel offered to buy one of her best pieces."

"Jeordie sure has gotten a kick out of doing the photography. I don't think there's much doubt he has talent at it. That camera Claire gave him was really something. I spent some time in the lobby when I first got here. You were right about her drawings. They are good. She is leaving Sunday? Isn't she?"

"Yes."

"Well, there's nothing to say about it, except that we all wish she wasn't."

"I know. Everyone she's met here feels the same way, especially me. But I have to accept it."

"You're both young and who knows what will happen in the future. Oh, by the way, your Mom called Rosie and Will to ask them to join us for the early dinner tomorrow. Will told her he was just about to call and see if he could join us."

"Great. I visited Uncle Willy yesterday and he mentioned wanting to come. I'm glad Mom beat him to the punch."

"Tim we're excited about your show, as you know, but most of all about how happy you've been in the last few weeks. Try not to let Claire's leaving end that."

"Well, there's always my work, here and at the store."

"Keep that attitude alive," he said as he rose to leave. "Tim, I must get back to my shop but I'm glad we had a chance to talk. I'll see you tomorrow, give our love to Claire.

"I will. See you then Dad."

Ginger was backstage at her desk making a list of things to be done or checked before tonight. I went over it with her, adding some items. She gave me a set of typed notes from the rehearsal, and I went to my office to go over them and prepare for the evening. I read the notes and wrote out plans for the evening with critique and a section on stage technique for the cast to rely on if they found themselves getting flat on stage. I then wrote in my journal for two hours. It was now up to a hundred and fifty pages.

As I closed my journal I had a sudden strong need to see Claire. I went upstairs, just checking with Ginger to see if she needed me. Everything was under control. I almost ran out to my car and headed to Marilee's.

Claire was in the den reading. She jumped up when she saw me and came into my arms.

"I just wanted to see you, sweetheart. Every moment we can have together seems so important."

"I was missing you, too. I came in from taking a walk before you got here. I couldn't sit still for thinking of you, Timmy."

"Do you feel like another walk? Wait, I've a better idea. Let's go for a boat ride. That ought to bring back some memories."

"Let's go," she agreed eagerly, "I couldn't have thought of anything better."

We went down to the dock and set off down Turtle Creek. We laughed and talked about everything we saw and waved at people on the shore. Claire told me of her boat trips in France and parties on the Seine River. Her family had once rented a houseboat in England going up the Thames, though locks, and staying at country Inns. My boating experiences were limited to canoes at summer camp and a fishing trip once down the Texas coast. I told her about fantasies I had about going up the Amazon and traveling the Nile to the first cataract. When we got back to the dock, Marilee was sitting out by the pool going over business papers. She was surprised to see us, having thought I was at the theatre.

"I couldn't stay away from this French girl here," putting my arm around Claire.

"And I'm glad he couldn't. I missed him terribly."

"Do you have to get back to the theatre?" Marilee asked. "Because if you don't, I got some Oaklawn barbecue that sure needs to be eaten."

"I did everything I needed to do and more. Everything is in shipshape there."

"It's supposed to be a very warm night. Why don't you two have a swim after rehearsal tonight? I hope to have a swimming surprise for us."

"Sounds good to me. Claire?"

"You know I would. We haven't had a chance to swim in several days."

"Marilee, do you mind if Timmy comes up to my room while I get ready?"

"No I don't, but don't fall as you run up the stairs," Marilee teased us.

I grabbed my coat and satchel, and we did indeed run up the stairs. Claire pulled the curtains closed and we jumped into the bed, undressing each other as quickly as we could. I pulled Claire to me and kissed her all over the face, neck, and breasts. She responded by taking me in hand and guiding me to and in her. I pulled back fairly quickly and prepared, but that feel of her without a prophylactic was heavenly and electric. We made love with a passionate hunger for each other.

"I wanted you so much this afternoon when you came in the den that I thought you had read my mind from afar," Claire told me.

"I didn't need to, baby, or maybe I did. When I finished my work, I had an overwhelming urge to hold and love you. Our little boat trip was a sweet bit of foreplay."

"Yes, I thought it was at the time."

"Naughty girl," I laughed.

"No, not naughty, just a girl in love. Would you like to take a quick shower with me?"

"Yes, I would, Mademoiselle."

After we had dressed, we joined Marilee and Daniel downstairs for a barbeque sandwich and promised to join them later for drinks and a swim. At the theatre, Ginger was waiting, even though we were an hour early. She was putting up new variations of set changing groups, which I had discussed with the cast last night. She handed me typed notes to go over and took me to the Green Room to see all of the instructions for the cast she had put on the walls. Some of the actors were already getting ready with makeup and costumes. Some were making repairs and changes. The two leading men came in and wanted to show me a new set of moves they had put into the knife fight scene done behind the scrim. I watched them work on stage and approved their ideas. The scene was already exciting and they had taken it to a new level. Barney wanted me to see the final work in the lobby. Jeordie had brought in his latest photographs of the cast. I liked them but was concerned that the cast would feel annoyed that we were not using the usual publicity headshots. I went down to the dressing room and asked them to come look at the lobby before rehearsal started.

Eddy and Aurora came in holding hands and laughing; they had come through the lobby and praised what Claire and Jeordie had done. They said it seemed to go with the show as something different like the show was. I wasn't surprised at their reaction because some of Jeordie's best work was of the dance scene. I thought the best thing about the photos was that they portrayed the cast in their characters. I joined Barney in his office for a quick cup of coffee as he gave me more information on the opening. He was the most excited I had ever seen him. At this point before, he was a nervous wreck fretting over details, but I believe after he had seen some midway rehearsals, he had started to work much sooner on planning. The news about highly increased ticket sales had freed him from the frantic fundraising he usually had to do before an opening. He said that because the play was an American premiere, it needed only moderate critical success to do well for the theatre. That was heartening to some degree but I was hoping for more than a moderate critical success. At this point, I now believed completely in the process I had developed and used.

I walked on stage as the cast was setting up in the crescent. If they had not seen the photography in the lobby, I told them to go now. Some had not so there was a slight delay, which I used for specific work with some of the players. Everything at this stage was mostly praise with some new ideas. I was pleased with all of the acting and character development. When the others got back from the lobby, we resumed a discussion of the photography. Most liked it very much and agreed it fit the show perfectly not to display the usual glossy headshots.

They all knew the importance of a final dress. I reminded them of using technique when they found themselves going flat on stage, to just adjust by raising their chin a bit, extending gestures, and pushing their reach for communion with the other actors. I described again how they must be aware of where they were on stage in relationship to the other players and the audience, and to try not to get in the wrong place for their character. The blocking should hold them, but this piece was so emotional and passionate that they could be pulled into a position that was too strong or weak for their character. After 45 minutes of concentrated work, I set the curtain call. Everyone went into the position they would be in for the end of act three. I wanted the main players to freeze on stage after the curtain closed. The company ensemble would form behind the curtain, and when it opened, they would bow and split left and right. Then the others would step in among them according to their prominence in the play and bow. The four major leads would bow together, them the two couples and finally, the Bride and Leonardo with singles, then together. The whole cast would then bow together. I didn't rehearse anything more, just to repeat it if the audience wanted more.

For the next five and a half hours, we went through the dress rehearsal from hell. Almost everything that could go wrong did. In the first set change, an ensemble actress got her dress caught and she didn't notice it until she had her skirt ripped off. During the dance sequence Camila and Aurora collided, knocking them both to the floor. It scared everybody to death when they were knocked out, but after a few minutes, they were both up and at it again where we left off. When Liza made her run onto the ramp, she fell and tumbled off the back and disappeared. Luckily, it resulted in only a skinned knee. At the beginning of the third act, the theatre went completely dark. Barney came out with a flashlight, went into the basement, and replaced the fuses. Eddy broke a string on his guitar in the intro to the fight, and the actor playing Leonardo broke the trick knife, which led to the Mother holding up a knife handle to cut the Bride's throat with. At the end, there was total silence for a few minutes then nervous laughter and collapse on the stage. The cast didn't even get their chairs; they just sat on the floor. By the time I got on stage, some of the girls were crying, and Camila and Aurora were hugging each other saying they couldn't figure out what went wrong or who was out of place. Liza had a bandage on her knee and was already getting sore from her tumble. Eddy held up his guitar with the string flying, shaking his head. Ginger got the knife, saying she would get it fixed before opening with no problem.

"Well," I said to them, "I've heard it said, from afar mind you, that a bad dress guarantees a great opening."

I gave the best after-dress notes and critique session I had done to this point. I assured them only the accidents were bad, but what did happen was great after everyone started up again and they had taken the play to a higher level. I said this proved that if anything happened in performance, they would be able to continue as if nothing had happened, or as if it was a part of the performance. The actress playing the mother said she would have an extra wooden knife in her skirt pocket, and Camila and Aurora had already countered their collision by adjusting another foot away from each other. Eddy said he would put on new strings every week. Liza said she had started her run onto the ramp a little too far back, which made her misjudge the steps. The actress with the torn skirt was repairing it while I talked. Barney had placed new fuses next to the box just in case. I said the curtain call looked great and for everyone to try to get some rest. It was an emotional parting for the evening, as we all hugged one another and left with a new heightened spirit.

As we drove back to Marilee's Claire was concerned mostly about my reaction to the rehearsal.

"It could be the best thing that could have happened because everything had gone so well for five weeks that this was a wake-up call for what can happen in live theatre. I had almost forgotten how fragile the whole physicality of it is, No one was seriously hurt and the rehearsal was actually very good. I thought it would be a bit flat just from nervousness, but their work on stage was terrific."

"Yes, I thought so too," Claire agreed, "it just scared me for you."

"Don't be. If anything, their concentration will be better and I think without anticipation. They were in the moment tonight. For a few minutes, I was worried about, Camila, Aurora, and Liza, but they jumped right up and went on. This cast has been amazing in their commitment and belief in the show. I think they're going to get better and better, and they're already really good."

"I believe they know they're good, and it's because you are good. They could not have done it with anyone else. They love you and believe in you."

"I love them and believe in them, too, and I hope the audience loves them too."

"They will, mon amour."

We drove up to Marilee's, Claire's head on my shoulder.

Marilee greeted us in her bathing suit, put her arms around our shoulders, and headed us towards the pool where Daniel handed me a Bourbon and soda, Claire a Martini.

"You're about an hour later than we expected. How did it go?" Daniel asked.

Claire and I both laughed.

"If they weren't so damn good, it would have been a disaster. It was a dress from hell."

They both laughed and said for us to change and get into the water. Claire went upstairs, and I sat to finish the much-needed drink. I described briefly what had happened. Marilee and Daniel gasped then laughed when I said everyone was all right. I waited for Claire to come down just so I could see her in the two-piece. I felt the same thing I did the first time when she had come out in it. I stood up and toasted her and went into the cabana to change.

Everyone else was in the water when I came out. As I climbed down the ladder, the warmth of the water shocked me.

"How do you like it?" Marilee called across the pool.

"How did you do it?" I called out, "It's great."

The water was just short of being as warm as a bath.

"Your Uncle Willy did it. When he came over once during the winter, he asked how long the water was cold in the spring going into the summer."

"I told him too long."

"He said maybe he could fix that. He started working on it in January and devised a gas heater for the recirculating water. He just put it in this week."

Claire said, "I wondered what was going on out here this morning, but I didn't see Uncle Willy."

"Some of his shop people did it. They said it wasn't really complicated, just the heater, some new pipes, and using the gas from the cabana heater. He said it was his secret project in case it didn't work," Daniel told us.

"It sure does work. No more shivers after being in too long." I said going all the way under to come up beside Claire.

"Hallo, Timmy." She put her arms around me as we worked our way over to Marilee and Daniel.

"Would you like another drink, Timmy?" Marilee asked.

"I'll get it in a minute."

"No. no, after the evening you've had, we'll take care of you. Daniel, would you also get me another Martini, please, dear heart?"

"A sus ordenes, Madam Grant," Daniel said as he climbed out.

Claire whispered in my ear, "May I take care of you, too, baby?"

"You already do, in a thousand different ways, Mademoiselle Levant."

We all sat together on the underwater ledge and laughed about the rehearsal and how lucky we were that nothing really bad happened, especially to Camila, and Liza. Marilee went in the house and brought some snacks of cheese, bread, and ham slices. After a while Marilee and Daniel went in the house and Claire and I went back into the pool and whispered to each other how nice it was to swim and be close in the pool again. Marilee had turned off the lights when they went in saying we could frolic as much as we liked, and we did, taking off our suits and being close. It was very different and nice being naked together in the warm water. After awhile we wrapped up in towels and lounged in the patio chaise in each other's arms, we both dozed off for a bit, and I realized how exhausted I was and that I had better go home soon and rest. We dressed as I made our plans for the next day. I would go to the theatre early in the afternoon then, come get Claire for the early dinner at my parents house. We kissed and parted wanting to stay together.

I didn't even attempt to study or read. There was nothing more for me to do for the play. I slept in late and had breakfast with Mom, and went to the theatre where everything was on schedule. I spent three hours working on all kinds of arrangements, checking the set, and in a long conference with Barney. Then Ginger and I spent an hour together talking about the past weeks. Both of us had good feelings about the coming evening. She was finally able to laugh about the dress. She said it had scared her to death, but I assured her we only go with what we have and to think about the seeming disaster as a good omen. Before I left, I hugged her and said she was by far the best stage manager I had ever had and that she ought to think about New York, though I didn't want to lose her. She told me it was a great experience for her and that she had learned more about working with a good director than she could ever have hoped.

I decided to go home and get dressed before picking up Claire. I rarely got the chance to wear a coat and tie, but Mom was ready for me with an ironed shirt and slacks. She had actually made me a new hand-painted tie. The jacket Uncle Willy had given me was perfect.

I decided I would give Claire the turquoise ring when I picked her up. I wasn't sure it was the right time, but I wanted to see it on her at our opening night. It was her opening night, too, because of the lobby drawings exhibit.

Claire was waiting for me in Marilee's den. The new emerald green dress she was wearing was stunning.

"My word, Claire, you'll be the most striking lady at the show! That dress makes your eyes glow. Did you know that?"

"I don't know about glow, but it did kind of scare me when I looked in the mirror. You look very nice yourself. Are you excited?"

"I think anxious more than excited. I guess I'm nervous, too. Opening nights are always nerve-wracking. You just never know what the audience reaction will be, and this is my first, as you know, 'national premiere'…Hell, baby, I'm scared to death."

"Well, as you say, 'hold on tight,' because I believe it's going to turn out very well. And since I'll be right beside you, you can hold on tight to me. I dreamed last night that people pointed at my drawings and laughed."

"Between the two of us, I think you're the safe bet."

"That's ridiculous, Timmy," she protested. "What I did just supports your work."

"And you've certainly done that from the beginning. Let's sit down for a minute. We've got time."

We sat on the sofa and I brought out the ring box and gave it to her. She opened it, took out the ring, and looked at me in shock.

"Oh, Timmy, it's beautiful…when did you…?...Oh!"

"Try it on and see if it fits." It did.

"I love it! It's so different."

"A New Mexico Indian artist made it. I thought something from the West would be appropriate."

She turned and hugged me, "I'll wear it always. And I have something for you." She got a small long box out of her purse and gave it to me.

I opened it to find a steel Rolex watch.

"Look on the back."

I turned it over. Engraved was 'Love always, Claire'."

"Well, this is something beyond my…I mean it's, my God! Boy did I need this. My watch is on its last legs, but a Rolex!"

"The best for the best. I hope you're not disappointed because it's not gold. Gold didn't seem right for you."

"No, no, I much prefer this. I've never been one to wear gold." I took off my old hand-me-down Bulova and strapped on the Rolex. "I think I'll roll up my sleeve tonight so it will show."

"And I'll hold out my hand so everyone will see my ring."

We both laughed then kissed our thank yous. She wiped the lipstick off my mouth then redid hers. And we were off to the family dinner. Mom had prepared a lightly spiced version of her curry and the gathering was happy, though everyone was bit nervous for me. Jeordie insisted on taking photos of everyone constantly and Rosie wore her first expectant-mother dress. Claire showed off her ring, I my watch. Even Jeordie was dressed for the night, in a tie and cardigan sweater.

"Jill's parents are bringing her to the theatre. I guess it's kinda like a date. I wanted her to see my lobby photos," beamed Jeordie.

Thankfully, no one mentioned Claire's leaving on Sunday. No sad things on an opening night. Claire and I left earlier than the others did so I could spend time with the cast.

There were some early arrivals in the lobby admiring Claire's drawings. She stayed and talked while I went backstage. The cast was busy, excited, and concentrated. Some were warming up with vocal exercises and sonnets. They greeted me with smiles and confidence. Liza Farquar came to me and whispered, "Thank you, Tim. Don't worry about a thing. We're ready to go." Ginger had gotten roses for me, and I handed them out to all the ladies in the cast. I shook hands with all of the men, thanking them for the hard work. I left for the lobby, now filled, where Marilee and Daniel had found Claire. My family joined us, as did Dick Ayers. When the house was opened, Barney rang a bell and the evening started.

Eddy's playing quieted the audience and the curtain opened to oo's and aah's in reaction to the very different and colorful set. I was so nervous I couldn't sit down so I stood in back with Claire seated in front of me, my hands were on her shoulders. The audience applauded enthusiastically, after the first act. Claire joined the family, but I was headed to the office to be with Barney. He handed me a glass of wine smiling at what he already thought was a successful evening.

In the second act, the dance sequence between Aurora and Camila stopped the show as the audience applauded. As if they had expected it, they froze in place and started up again perfectly as the applause subsided. Liza's run down the ramp and scream of deception brought out sounded reactions of shock, and the applause was greater after the second act. Claire stood up and hugged me across the seat. I went backstage but said nothing, just going around touching and stroking the cast.

When the curtain closed at the end, there was a loud burst of applause. When the curtain opened, the audience stood and demanded three bows. Then, of all things, the cast called for me to come on stage. I had never made any sort of speech to an audience, so I was very embarrassed. The audience quieted, and I thanked them for their response and turned to the cast and thanked them for their hard work. I turned back to the audience and said, "There will be no more plays by Federico Garcia Lorca because he has been murdered by the Franco forces is Spain. This is a major loss for modern literature. There is someone else I want to thank, Miss Claire Levant, for unequaled support and the wonderful drawings in the lobby."

The cast and I stepped back, and the curtain closed. They all started screaming and jumping up and down. I heard, "Viva el Audazito!"

I went to the lobby, where Claire greeted me with tears and a hug. My family gathered around with smiles and congratulations. Marilee gave me a kiss on the lips.

Dick Ayers found me, "You outdid the one I saw in Madrid," he said, delighted.

An exuberant Barney grabbed my hand but couldn't say a thing. Wine was served, and the audience waited for the cast to appear, which they did after about thirty minutes. The celebration lasted for another hour and a half. Eddy set himself up in a corner and played his guitar, with Aurora standing beside him. Barney introduced Claire around as the artist of the drawings. The critics from the two papers had left early but John Rosenfield stayed long enough to shake my hand and greet Barney. I hoped that was a harbinger for a good review.

Before Jordie was sent home early with Jill's parents, they came over to say goodbye. Jill said the play had made her cry. Jeordie's photos were a big hit.

Claire tried to stay beside me, but we were both pulled away several times to discuss her work or my direction. Once, I saw her across the room, and she must have felt me watching her because she turned, beamed a broad smile at me, and mouthed my name. The major patrons seemed thrilled by the show and its prospects for an extended run, which they felt would help the theatre fund-raising potential enormously. From the moment the curtain had gone down after my few words, I had been in a daze and shocked by the audience's response to the show. I'm not sure I carried on any intelligent conversation with anyone in the lobby. Finally, the reception dwindled down to my family and the cast, Claire and I were able to sit down and just be with the family. The cast members came over to us alone or in small groups for a handshake or hug and to thank me for the opportunity. I let them know quickly that they had made the show with their dedication, commitment, and artistry. At last, Barney brought out the framed blow-up of the program cover for Claire; she was taken aback and thrilled by the gesture. She held it up for all to see and they applauded. My Mom was especially touched when Claire turned to her for a hug and a kiss, telling her how much it meant to her that Mom liked her work. Claire had told me earlier in the evening that Mom had asked her if she could have a drawing after the show closed. Claire had told her that they were all for me to keep, and she could probably choose as many as she liked.

Camila and Claire spent some minutes together, wishing they could spend more time together, but knowing Claire's leaving would prevent that. They promised to write and keep up with each other's careers. Daniel and Marilee left, asking Claire and me to join them when I took Claire home. The evening ended with family goodbyes and Claire and I walking to my car with our arms around each other and holding the framed program cover.

In the car Claire, leaned over and kissed me and dug her head into my neck. "I'm so very proud of you, Timmy. It could not have been a better end to all of your work. I knew *Blood Wedding* was very good, but I couldn't really express how much I believed in it because I knew you would think I was just praising from my love for you. I wasn't surprised by the success. It was almost overwhelming and I know you were really unable to understand how important it was for you. You were fun to watch at the reception because you couldn't quite accept what was happening; you just smiled and nodded your head to the compliments. It made me love you even more," she smiled.

"Well...it was a pretty special evening for you, too. Your drawings kind of topped off the night. When the audience looked at them, they were seeing the play all over again. Thank you, sweetheart. You know when you reached back and took my hand during the wedding dance, I felt rushes of excitement that I had never experienced before. I had a funny idea that I wanted us to be watching the play with you in my lap and your arm around me."

She laughed out loud. "Oh, Timmy, I wish we could have."

We were both laughing as we pulled into Marilee's driveway. Daniel greeted us and pointed to the den. Marilee handed us both snifters of Spanish brandy.

"What would be more proper than to toast with what we started with five weeks ago? To you, Timothy Sart, and you, Claire Levant. May these weeks together last in your memories. They certainly will for us. But this is for tonight and those days of work that have brought us here together this evening. I know that sounds a little formal, Timmy, but I believe it will change your life," she finished.

Claire and I both raised our glasses and drank the Villalobos as an elixir. I had tasted it before I met Claire but it didn't become an elixir until her.

"Thank you, Marilee and brother," I said as I bowed from the waist. "Yes, quite an evening. I have no idea how it could change my life beyond what it has already done."

"Well, the change is that you are no longer a young director trying to do good theatre. You are now a very good and innovative director who can direct anywhere, even New York," Marilee pointed out.

"She's right, Timmy. You've done something very special, and it may be only the beginning for you," Dan agreed.

"I don't know about that, a new beginning, I mean. I'm slated to direct the next show, as yet unnamed, but..."

"It was a terrific evening, brother. And I absolutely loved the play. It surprised me, even though I was sure I would enjoy it, I didn't expect the emotional reaction I felt. And Claire, your drawings are a beautiful part of it. I don't know what you plan to do with your art, but please don't stop," Dan urged.

"Thank you, Daniel. You and Marilee added a truly beautiful touch to the production. I don't know if I plan to do anything with my drawing. I'm sure it was watching Timmy that inspired me."

"That inspiration thing goes both ways, Claire."

"I think the best way to describe the evening is a 'triumph,'" Marilee said as she poured us more brandy.

"I don't know how I feel yet about the reaction of the audience. Most of the people there were theatre supporters, so it could be just because it was something new, you know, a premiere and all that. But, of course, I'm just now beginning to take it all in. I guess the run will tell. Barney was certainly happy about it. I believe, right now, that everything went beyond what I had hoped. It would have been a lot harder without you-all, I mean, without your help and support. Marilee, that discussion we had in the parking lot of the Art Fair got me started."

"Brother, I told you she can be a real 'muse.'"

Well…in this case I had two," I said, and turned to Claire. "Dear Claire, thanks for a thousand reasons for coming to Dallas."

"You're most welcome, Monsieur Sart. Marilee, thank you for introducing me to this wonderful man. When you invited me to visit you, I was actually scared to really be on my own and away from my family and now…well, I'm not going to think about my leaving because I'm so happy for Timmy."

"Yes, let's not think about that," Marilee agreed. "Oh, I've arranged a suite for you two at the Adolphus for Friday and Saturday with all the room service you want."

"Great! What do you think about that, Claire?" I asked.

"I like it, Timmy, but Marilee you don't have to…"

"Claire, don't even think about it. Didn't you mention a 'sanctuary' several days ago. You know you would both be welcome here, but why not have it away from all of us, just you two and no one else?"

"I wish I didn't have to go to the show for the next two nights so it could be more like a little vacation with Claire, but, well, that may not be the right word for it."

"That's a good enough word for it, Timmy. I just want to be with you."

Marilee had an idea, "Timmy, why don't you tell Barney you're going out of town for a couple of days-you know, exhaustion from working on the production. After the cast party tomorrow night go to the hotel and stay until you bring Claire back Sunday."

"He won't like it, but I'll do it. Is that alright with you, Claire?"

"If you think it's alright, yes."

"Well, I'm going to call it an evening, and a great one it has been. Marilee are you ready."

"Yes, Daniel, I think it's time to give these two the rest of the night…what there is left of it since it's almost two. Timmy, you're welcome to stay here."

"Thanks, Marilee, but I'm not sure I could sleep anywhere. Is the water in the pool still heating up? I could use a swim."

"It should be almost like a warm bath by now. I turned it on again before we went to the theatre. Have at it."

"Does that sound good to you, Claire?"

"Yes it does, Monsieur Sart, it certainly does. I'll run upstairs and change."

The three of them went upstairs. I poured another snifter of brandy and went out to the cabana and put on my bathing suit. The water was like a bath, which couldn't have better for all of the pent-up tensions I felt. Claire came down shortly in her super-cute two-piece suit. I pointed at the brandy and her glass on the table. She filled her snifter and joined me.

"Are you able to talk about the play yet, Timmy? We don't have to, but it was a real success for you."

"I don't know what to say. I guess it was what all directors hope for, I mean an audience reaction like that. I don't know yet what it means for me or the theatre. It may just mean that things will be the same except more so."

"More so?"

"Well, the expectations of me will be higher."

"But isn't that the way it is for any artist, whether you're a painter who sells out an exhibit or a writer who has a successful book? Perhaps you'll get better with each play. It's not like something that happens, then goes away. I watched you work, and you seemed to gain confidence with each rehearsal. Remember when we talked about the book on art logic? A part of that, as I remember, was being able to visualize the specific conclusion even though it may change as you work towards it. From the beginning, or when I first started going to rehearsals, you had a good vision of where you wanted it to go. I believe that's what being a good artist is. Of course, the artist must have an innate talent. You were a good director before *Blood Wedding,* according to Marilee.

"My goodness, girl. That was really something. Yes, I guess I was a fairly good director before this production, but I never thought of it like that. I was trying to learn with each play, with some success."

"I don't think Barney would have let you direct as much as you have if he didn't believe in you. We had plenty of chances to talk while I worked in the lobby, so I know how he feels. And this show is way beyond some success."

"Still, I don't know what, if anything, it means for me. I hope to keep working at the theatre, and probably the bookstore. I'm not sure there is an up from here or even that there needs to be. Are you saying that perhaps I have a chance as a professional director somewhere else?" I asked.

"Yes, Timmy, I am. You worked minor miracles here with your cast. What could you do with the best actors?"

"I must say it is great to have a lady who is very smart and believes in you. If there is a next step up from here, I believe I'm ready for it. I have a good life here in Dallas, family, the work, the theatre, but these last weeks have changed a whole lot of things. *Blood Wedding* still rages in my head even though my part is done. And you, Claire-You must know you are not short on talent as an artist either. This should not be a one-time artistic thrust; you must continue your drawing and your beautiful water colors."

"You've helped me fall in love with drawing again and I never enjoyed waters as much before. I knew I could do, it but I guess it just took something like working with you to make it happen."

"That goes both ways, sweetheart."

"I don't want you to think you need me to become a great director. No, that doesn't sound right, I mean you are very talented and the inspiration will come from within you."

"I understand that. I know how much you or our love, inspired me. I think it is because I have been so happy with you and wanted you to be proud of me. But I do need you, because I love you."

"I know. Me, too. Timmy we must agree not to be sad about my leaving. Yes, it is sad for me, so very much that I don't even comprehend it. I've never been so happy in my life and the wonderful things that have happened between us were beyond my imagination before we met. What is the word in English? Uh…serendipitous, yes that's it."

"At the very least, 'serendipity' is a good way to describe us. I agree not to be sad or wallow in unhappiness. I believe I want some more brandy, with no qualms about getting a pinch drunk. Is that OK with you?"

"Yes, our own celebration."

During this whole conversation we were up to our necks in the warm water and very close, almost whispering, with our arms around each other. This intimacy between us was now an accepted part of our relationship. When we could be close, we were. Before Claire, I thought love would be sex and a new fun friendship; but this was much more. The sex was a natural and magical union, more than the thrills of passion but a completeness in our need to be as close as possible in the sharing of our physical lives; the friendship was a total trust in each other's intellectual presence. We listened and shared our ideas about everything we discussed. I adored her beauty, often finding myself just looking at her, amazed by the idea that she could possibly love me too. We laughed sometimes just in happiness. Her accent gave English a sound almost Latin in its softening of harsh consonants banging up against vowels. Her well-educated and continental sophistication carried no arrogance or feelings of superiority. Her coloring and figure were so different and striking that she seemed to almost be of another species from a place where humans had evolved into something new that incorporated all of traits of beauty and femininity. All of these thoughts raced through my mind as Claire insisted on getting out of the pool to bring the brandy bottle to us. As I watched her, she turned to me, smiled, winked, and said in an exaggerated accent, "Viva Villalobos, El Audauzito."

I laughed with my head thrown back, hoping I didn't wake the distant neighbors, "Si claro, eso si, mi amorcita Francesa!"

We finished off the bottle and swam around the pool on our backs for awhile then went to the lounge chair and wrapped ourselves in the light pool blanket. We took off our suits and cuddled, whispered intimacies, kissed, and made long, slow love, facing each other side by side, then dozed until dawn. We went up to her room and slept until noon. I awoke with her head on my shoulder to a knock on the door.

"How about breakfast in thirty minutes?"

"That sounds good, Marilee."

I hadn't moved. Claire's eyes were open and she smiled.

"Bon jour, Ti-mo-thee."

"Good morning, Claire. You are a magnificent sight in the morning."

"I don't believe you, but thank you. Don't move yet. Just hold me for a few moments more."

I did agreeably.

"Oh, Timmy, I love you so much, I love waking up with you."

"Strange coincidence, I was thinking the same thing with the emphasis on loving you."

She then jumped up, grabbing a robe to shyly cover herself as the bright noonday sun streamed in. I wished she hadn't, but the giggle and smile almost made up for not being able to see her in the light. As she entered the bathroom, I told her to hurry and let me in there quickly. She came out in a minute and I went in. When I came out, she had laid out her clothes for the day, then returned to the bathroom for her shower.

In a few seconds, she opened the door, "We could save time by taking our showers together. Do you think we could resist morning passions?" Her expression was sexy and cute.

"We could try, but I don't think so." She laughed and pulled me into the already running shower. We soaped each other and weren't able to resist our morning passion completely. We only got out when there was almost no hot water left. I dressed in my crumpled clothes and she in a spiffy slacks outfit. Daniel and Marilee were waiting for us at the breakfast table.

"We haven't been up long ourselves; we got into the celebration spirit also." Marilee said as she poured coffee for us. Daniel smiled and nodded.

"Well, I suppose you should be the first to know...Daniel asked me this morning to marry him and I said yes, then jumped up and down a bit. How about that?"

Claire squealed and hugged Marilee. I shook Daniel's hand. Daniel was a bit subdued about the announcement, a quiet happiness. He smiled and then laughed looking at Marilee with complete adoration. He finally said, "I supposed it was about time to ask, I guess my fear was that she would pooh-pooh the idea and say things were fine as they are."

"Little did you know, my fine man. How many signals did I have to send out? I am one happy girl. We even talked about a family in the future. But...I certainly don't want some semi-society wedding at the Highland Park Methodist Church with a reception at Dallas Country Club. There is no hurry, just this year sometime and probably away from Dallas.

Claire and I shared a look, knowing that we would not be together at the wedding, whenever it was, unless it happened in the next couple of days. We were too happy for them to let that knowledge affect us with any sort of sadness. Claire knew she would always be their friends if even from afar.

Marilee walked to behind Daniel and hugged him with a kiss on his cheek, "Why don't we have a small celebration for the four of us? Our engagement, Daniel's two new paintings he finished this week, which you two must see, Timmy's triumph last night, and Claire's exciting exhibit in the theatre lobby…but mostly for me and Daniel…!"

We all joined in with clapping and laughter, which, of course, meant we agreed to a celebration. Marilee held up her hand for attention.

"I'm going on a quick trip to the refrigerator in the garage."

She left and was back in two or three minutes, holding up a cold bottle of Dom Perignon.

"We'll have Spanish omlettes after this French treat is all gone."

After Daniel did the honors of opening the Champagne, without a drop lost, Marilee brought out some crystal glasses. After the pouring, we toasted them and they toasted us.

"Speaking of French treats, Claire, did this other worthy Sart man let you get any sleep last night?" Marilee teased.

"Yes he did. We fell asleep out by the pool under a blanket and woke up at dawn, then came upstairs."

"Good, I'm glad you stayed over last night, Timmy. This announcement and celebration would not have been the same without you."

"I am too. I just couldn't face driving home after we finished off that bottle of Villalobos and talked ourselves into oblivion before the sun 'done come up'.

"Timmy, always, 'Mi casa, su casa.'"

We drank the Dom Perignon, all four of us getting a bit tipsy and laughing about everything. I talked about all the things that could have gone wrong with *Blood Wedding*, Claire of all the people who had noticed her new ring, Dan about his new paintings that were more figurative than usual, and Marilee about her business in the Far East and Oklahoma. Occasionally, Marilee would go over to Daniel and hug him saying again how happy she was. Both of them were aglow with their decision as if a weight had been lifted from what was already a happy life about to get better. Marilee told about when she had first seen Daniel and knew immediately that something good was going to happen between them.

"He was the first person I had ever met who actually had an aura. It shocked me at first but it wasn't all the time. It isn't bright, but like a glow that happens when he's very happy."

"You've never told me that, honey."

"I didn't want to scare you off thinking I was a babbling witch."

"There was no danger of that happening. You were the most intriguing and beautiful woman I had ever seen. Claire, Tim knows this, when Marilee and I first met we talked nonstop for ten hours, I mean all night long and into the next day, most of the time sitting in my old Plymouth behind the art gallery where we met."

"That night and morning sure changed our lives. It also had what started out as an embarrassment. After about three hours, we both had to go to the bathroom so badly we were in pain. We didn't think we could make it to a bathroom anywhere, so we both went behind the bushes near the alley. It didn't seem to bother us, though. We actually kind of stumbled into our first kiss right afterward and the rest is history."

Claire laughed out loud at Marilee's story. "I don't believe Timmy and I have had any embarrassing moments, well almost, this morning."

"Yes. Similar situation, but we were in a civilized environment. It ended up pretty good, too."

Claire blushed at this but smiled and winked at me. Her winks were a new thing and I liked them. I think it meant something good in her feeling about me. All of a sudden, a rush of reality overcame me for a few seconds; the thought of not being with her much longer, but I pushed it out of my mind, remembering our promise.

Marilee and Claire made the omelets, which were great.

"Timmy, did you know that Claire is a great cook, a really good one?" Marilee asked.

"No, I didn't. She mentioned once that she liked to cook but with no hint as to her greatness."

Claire reached over and poked me. "Did you expect a French girl to brag about her cooking skills? It just comes naturally, amorcito."

"I guess my business skills came naturally, too," Marilee mused. "I mean with my father first then with Grant."

"Thank the sweet Lord for that." Daniel said, "The Sart family is not known for great money knowledge, just barely staying ahead with 'the arts.' Right, brother?"

"Oh, am I ahead?"

"You are now, director and almost brother-in-law." Marilee added to the mix.

"She's right, Timmy. If you don't know you're a special artist, a lot of other people do."

"And you are well ahead, Daniel. I think being accepted by the museum establishes that. Remember that at that gallery exhibit where we first met and every one since you've sold every painting you've put on the wall,"
Marilee reminded him.

"Well, I think…viva Sart men!" Claire cheered, giggling from the champagne.

"Indeed, Mademoiselle Lavant, viva all of us." Marilee laughed.

Daniel stood, "Thank you for the support ladies. Right, brother?"

"Couldn't ask for more, Daniel."

We toasted across the table with our orange juice.

"Now, for the rest of the day." Marilee started, "Timmy, I hope you don't mind if Claire helps. We have a lot of food to get ready for the cast party. Liza is coming over later to help and take stuff over to her house. I promise to get Claire to the theatre before the curtain."

"That's perfectly fine. I want to spend some time with Daniel in the studio seeing his new work and then go for a swim. I'll go home to change and pack a bag for the weekend, which we thank you greatly for, Marilee."

"My pleasure, Timmy. No one deserves it more than you two after the activity of the past weeks."

"I'll call my parents this afternoon and tell them about our fishing trip this weekend, Marilee. I've never lied to them before, but must needs be. Timmy, I'll try to join you for a few minutes in the pool if Marilee will release me."

"I will, but it's rare that I have a real French cook helping me, so not for long…just teasing, I may jump in myself for awhile. As a matter of fact, now would be good to wash away the champagne, or perhaps to enjoy it before it goes away. Let's all go in. What do you say?"

We agreed and scattered to change. We all played in the pool like kids for half an hour. Then the ladies retreated to the kitchen and I joined Daniel in his studio. His new work was large and very different. He had worked figures of women into forest scenes almost hidden by foliage. His new coloring style was even more startling and dramatic, using a pastoral scenic approach. There was no jungle look to it or a forest or woods look but a fantasy world that had places of reality or naturalism that would blend into the extraordinary colors. The women were nude but revealed more as spirit-like wood sprites just on the edge of misty. The paintings were the most powerful thing I had seen him do so far.

"My word, Dan, these are terrific! Where did they come from?"

"I don't know. They just happened. Well, perhaps from a morning I was watching Marilee in our bedroom. She was so beautiful that I wanted to try some magical women that are just barely real. I hadn't realized that was my inspiration until you asked."

"Did it also happen to inspire your proposal?"

"No, that, dear brother, happened on waking up and holding Marilee and all of a sudden we started laughing, I don't know why, then she started crying softly and kissed me, saying she loved me so much. I just couldn't not ask her. Hell, I've been trying to get my nerve up for a year to ask her, and I didn't even have to. It just happened."

"That sounds like a pretty good way for it to happen."

"I thought our getting engaged to be married wouldn't change anything because it was so good anyway, but even though it's been for only a few hours, things are different in a very good way. I'm softly buzzing all over."

"I think Marilee is too."

"Yes, love is good."

"Yes, I agree. Claire is…well, she is love to me."

"We have seen it in the both of you. Have you talked much about her leaving?"

"No, we haven't and we won't."

"I do understand, but you haven't really lost. What you've had together for the past weeks…well, I guess there's nothing to say."

"Nope, there isn't. But, my God, she's a wonderful woman, more than I ever…"

"Yes, but what you have now, is more than you ever expected. What was it like before Claire? Were you happier? No. Even when she leaves, you will be more into your life and your work. She's not leaving because of some terrible disagreement you've had or a bitter breakup. She's leaving because of a very strong family obligation. We've talked about traditions that we don't quite understand, well…I think this a prime example of one, whatever it is. I know this may not help you at all and I'm speaking beyond my own experience."

"Yes, certainly beyond mine, too. You know, in the last six weeks, I've talked more about love than in all of my life before. With you, Mom and Dad, Marilee, and even with Uncle Willy. Of course, mostly with Claire, being it's new experience for us both. We're not total innocents, but what has happened between us has been a new world of caring…and friendship, and a physical love without, I think, a hint of lust, just us becoming closer. We haven't tried to analyze it. We're amazed by it as a wonderful surprise that has enveloped us with a happiness that neither of us knew was possible. I remember you and I talking about Gwen, and my reaction was that she was fun to be with and I liked her, but when she left it was, well Gwen's gone, that was nice."

"And we all liked Gwen, but Claire…we've all fallen in love with her, so don't feel alone in that. None of us wants her to leave, she has become like family. And it's not all because of what has happened between you; she is one special lady. That first day you came over, it was pretty obvious that you two were drawn to each other, 'smitten' as Marilee said. Even if it were just a casual thing between you, we would feel very caring about her. But it's not a casual thing for either of you, Marilee and I do know something about love, and we saw it developing for you and Claire very soon. And it was so real, there was no appearance of two lonely people reaching out. She is a strong independent spirit and you were, and are, very much involved with directing."

"Yes, I clearly wanted no distractions from *Blood Wedding*, but you're right I was involved, and still am, but all of my work was better because of being with Claire."

"For her, too, brother. Her drawings are exquisite, and they wouldn't have happened without you and *Blood Wedding*. I believe my paintings would be good without Marilee, but with her I know I can be a better artist each time I face a blank canvas."

"Claire and I had a conversation one night by the pool about how lucky you and Marilee are, and then we realized how lucky we were. Speaking of lucky, has Uncle Willy ever told you about a lady he knew in Shanghai?"

"No, tell me."

"Well, I don't think I'm betraying a confidence. He told me about a White

Russian lady he met while on shore leave that Claire reminded him of. They met and were together for a month or so for every minute. Because of all the diplomatic complications, there was no way he could bring her back here, no matter how hard he tried. And he had to leave. But he felt he was double lucky because of Rosie."

"Close to home."

"There always seems to be a purpose behind every one of Uncle Willy's stories. This has been good, Daniel, the talk and seeing your new canvases. The concept of a big brother has taken new steps," I said.

"We want you to be here with us as much as you can be. I think family is meaning more and more to us. Marilee is so proud of you and what you've done with *Blood Wedding*. Are you satisfied with how it turned out, I mean we all know it's an absolutely terrific show, but how do you feel now, a day removed?"

"I believe every director would always want a couple more weeks of rehearsal, but this particular process was so intense that it couldn't have gone on any longer. I like the show and love the play, and the ensemble will grow enormously during the run, which is the first time I've been able to say that. Every show gets better, but this one-in three or four weeks, if things go well, opening night will look like an run-through. I'm beginning to actually believe that the way I shaped this production gives the cast more room to grow."

"That's exciting to hear, but I'm not really surprised after all the work you put into it. I guess I've experienced a similar thing in painting this year. I feel a freedom now in my choice of subject matter. I guess there always was a struggle for what will I do next, but I don't sense the inhibiting nature of that any more. I face the canvas, and it happens. Also the loneliness of the studio isn't a part of my existence with Marilee always close. I sometimes envy the collaborative nature of your theatre work."

"And I sometimes envy your being in the studio alone. At times, all of the different people working on a production create a sort of cacophony…but it didn't with *Blood Wedding*. This was different, and a big part of that was Claire…but… well…what the hell. I damn sure better be able to transcend that. Perhaps her presence will continue to be an inspiration."

"Hold on to that idea, brother. It could be the best one of many good ones you've had in the past weeks."

"Think so?"

"Yep!"

"I think I'll go give her a big kiss of thanks, then go to the house and get ready for the weekend."

"I won't see you at the theatre tonight, but I will be at the cast party. The drops Mom and I painted do get me an invite, don't they?" He asked, teasing.

We both laughed then hugged, patting each other on the back, "You darn sure better be there, Daniel."

Claire and Marilee were working in the kitchen. I came up behind Claire and took her hand. I guided her into the den and took her in my arms. She looked at me in a happily surprised manner and I kissed her, holding her tight. She looked at me with such love that I hugged her again, pulling back her hair, kissing her on the ear and neck.

"Oh my goodness, Timmy. What was…"

"Just thank you, sweetheart."

I squeezed her hand, "I'll see you at the theatre. Don't be late."

She stood smiling and waved as I left the den and walked out the front door.

I went by the bank and took out a hundred dollars, which was more than I ever had before. I didn't know what I would need it for, but I wanted to be prepared for anything.

When I got to the house, I went in to see Mom in her studio.

"Well, hello stranger," she said. "It looks like you slept in your clothes."

"I guess I kind of did. How are you, Mom?"

"I'm fine, but a bigger question is how are you after your wonderful success… and how is Claire?"

"I feel great and Claire is also fine, very fine."

Mom laughed. "You know we're proud of you and I expect she is, too."

"She certainly seems to be, and thank you. Are you and Dad going to come to the cast party?"

"We plan to, but it will be too late for Jeordie. "It's almost too late for us! Perhaps just an appearance."

"That's alright. Mom, Claire and I are going away for a couple of days, then I plan to go with her to the train station on Sunday."

"I'm not surprised you two want to get away and be alone before she goes. It's been a rather hectic past few weeks, there's been more socializing than we've seen in years. She sure made life different around here, different good, I mean, especially for you."

"Yes, especially different good for me."

"Try to hold on to the happiness you and Claire have had. I don't want you to go into any sort of deep sadness when she leaves."

"Of course, I'll be sad, but I'm not going to fall apart. It's been too very good for that. We are very much in love, but somehow destiny has overruled us. I don't quite understand it and may never completely."

"That sounds like a healthy attitude. Believe me, no one, with the exception of you, wants her to stay more than I do."

"I know, Mom. Well, I'm going to take a short nap and then pack and get ready for the evening."

She grabbed me up into one of her motherly hugs saying, "Your play is beautiful, son."

I went out and fell on my bed, set my alarm for a couple of hours of sleep, which I did and dreamed of being with Claire for two days.

When I stepped out the shower, Mom came in with a sandwich and several hangers of freshly ironed clothes. She came back in a few minutes with clean underwear and socks.

"Sometimes it's a mother's duty to see that her boy looks good," she said with a big smile and was gone.

I tried not to over-pack but did go a bit crazy with shirts. I put on my one good suit with a solid-color knit tie and was off to the theatre. I got there an hour before the doors opened and went immediately to meet with Ginger backstage. There was a flurry of activity and excitement. The cast was getting ready a little early at Ginger's request so they could have a group warm-up. I found out there wasn't much to say because she was on top of it all. I roamed around the dressing rooms wishing every one a good show. Eddy and Aurora were rehearsing in the hallway, and then stopped to chat and ask if I had any critique. I didn't, saying what they had done in the show had been crucial to its success. Eddy waved his finger then pointed at me and smiled. Aurora nodded and took my hand, giving a gentle squeeze. As I went into the Green Room the old Hispanic actor greeted me with a hand shake and his usual, "Gracias, el Audazito."

He was doing a terrific job in the play, much more than I had expected and I hoped I had a friend for life, but then this was the first show where I felt that way about everyone in the cast. I had no bad feelings or regrets of any sort, which was strange, because usually there were a couple of actors I would rather not see for awhile. But not now.

Liza Farquar came out to tell me everything was ready for the party, and that she and Marilee had sent Claire up to take a nap. She said she had barely made the call but was ready and excited. She, too, was doing great work as the Wife. I had thought, at first, she was too attractive, but it worked.

I met Barney in the lobby, and he was ecstatic about the response. He said the word of mouth was already filling up another week. I suddenly began to think of what John Rosenfield was going to say in his review. I didn't think he would pan us, but I was concerned. A good review could give us an extension on the run. I looked up just as Claire entered, looking glorious in her burgundy dress.

"Hallo, Timmy. Oh my, you do look handsome in your suit."

"You look pretty good too, Baby." She laughed and kissed me on the cheek. She walked around the lobby straightening her drawings on the wall and looking back at me smiling. Shortly, the audience started arriving. They were made up mostly of season-ticket holders so I knew many of them. We talked about the rehearsal period, and I introduced Claire as the artist of the drawings, which were much admired. Several said that they had received telephone calls about how powerful the production was. This was all fairly different, because I didn't usually like to greet the audience or talk before a show, but I wanted Claire to have the chance to discuss her work. Barney was being his usual charming self, promoting the theatre and fundraising at the same time. He was very smooth at it and successful, able to keep the theatre out of debt during difficult economic times. It was always hard to keep up a high artistic quality with an all-volunteer acting and technical force, but he had been able to by drawing on the civic pride of the best in the community. I would have probably been involved without the pay I got except that I did quite a bit more than direct. He depended on me as the artistic fundraiser and backstage organizer when I wasn't directing, but now he was talking about my directing four or five shows a year! I mentioned a pay raise, and he sounded fairly positive about it, though I knew whatever it was would not permit me to give up my job at the bookstore.

The house was sold out so Barney brought out three chairs from the office for himself, me, and Claire which we placed in back of the audience. I thought now I could sit down and watch the show not quite like an audience member, but as a fairly calm director watching his creation and maybe having some new ideas. The audience reaction was even more receptive than the opening. Everything was better; the cast was not nervous but very much into the play. Claire watched like an innocent to the piece and held on to me during the more emotional moments. I envied that ability of hers to separate from experience and see it anew. But I found myself falling into the story, especially Eddy's playing and Aurora's dancing, which stopped the show again.

During both intermissions, Claire and I retreated into the office and had a glass of wine. There was another standing ovation. As the cast took their bows, I was in a state of shock. Perhaps the show was really that good and I had developed a process of directing that truly worked for me, but I didn't know if it would work for every play. *Blood Wedding* had become an ensemble piece rather than the usual cast in process of working through a stage story. There were very few plays that told their story with such a passionate surge of ideas. I thought of Brecht, which was different, but relied on the extremes of human emotions, or I thought he did, anyway. What could I do next to even come close to what I had experienced with Lorca? And there was going to be no more Lorca. Well, at least I had weeks to think about what to direct next because I decided I wasn't directing the next play in the season…thank goodness. An older director in the community was going to do a tried and true comedy. I wondered if Somerset Maugham's plays would finally be right for me, and could I do one in a similar manner as to the Lorca. I guessed I could adapt the process…Claire startled me out of my thoughts by putting her arm around my waist.

"Do you believe it now, Ti-mo-thee?"

"Well, I'm beginning to. It appears this was the right play for me to do. I was just thinking where do I go from here?'"

"Dear Timmy, that is the least of any worries you have now, but where you do go right now is out to the lobby to meet the audience and then to the cast party. And after that, to our sanctuary that Marilee has given us."

"Yes, you're right," I laughed. "I guess that was a quick case of negative anticipation. Thank you for pulling me out of it. Let's go."

Claire took my hand and we joined the lobby crowd. There were a lot of congratulations and questions about how I did it. Claire was drawn away with questions about her drawings. There were even good comments about Jeordie's photographs. Finally we were able to leave and go to Liza Farquar's house for the gathering. Her house was an elegant modern Highland Park two-story. The circular driveway was almost full, and more folks were pulling in behind us. I knew that Barney had invited several of the more prominent theatre patrons, which was unusual but he felt that this show warranted their presence. The house was as beautiful as a house gets in Dallas with the design being highly influenced by Frank Lloyd Wright. The party was primarily out on the large rear patio that led to a large swimming pool. There were tables laden with food and a bar with one of the bartenders from the Dallas Country Club doing the honors. Liza had set up tables that extended out into the yard. Mom and Dad had arrived just before us and joined us immediately. Mom hugged Claire and took her over to Marilee and Daniel, who were waving and throwing kisses. Dad and I went to the bar. Both of us got Bourbons and I got a Martini for Claire. We joined the other family members at a table. Liza joined us for a few minutes, then returned to her hostess role. I had been to many cast parties but never one this happy and elegant. When Dad and Mom left early, Claire and I made the rounds. Eddy decided he would play his guitar, which turned out to be a great idea and really set the mood.

One of the patrons from Lakewood took me aside to tell me that I had taken the theatre to a new level artistically, which he thought was very good for Dallas. He asked if I planned to stay in Dallas, which I thought was strange because I had no thoughts of going anywhere else. He said he believed my horizons had broadened a great deal with my work on *Blood Wedding*, but he hoped I was going to be staying longer. I didn't know what to say about plans because I had none. This sort of praise was becoming confusing as other patrons and even cast members asked me the same questions about leaving Dallas. I tried to express the idea that one "success," if it was one, did not build a new career somewhere else. Barney and I walked out around the pool and talked about the last two nights. I told him I was totally unprepared for the reaction so far. It was more than just a surprise, but a shock that I didn't know how to deal with right now. He told me to get used to it because it wasn't going to stop. I then told him that I was leaving town for the weekend and wouldn't be there for the Saturday performance. He didn't like it but had to accept it.

"Tim, *Blood Wedding* will go a long way towards supporting the rest of the season of plays. I hope you'll be able to direct at least two more plays, later this summer and one next fall."

"I don't know, Barney. That's more of a challenge than I may be ready to accept. Have you thought about the raise in pay?"

"Yes, and more. You know that in the last couple of years, I've been trying to build an endowment for the theatre with some success. If it progresses as much as I hope it will, I think I can, with the help of several donors, raise your salary so you are a full member of the theatre staff. How does that sound?"

"Good, and very exciting, but let's see how my next show does."

"It would take that much time anyway, but I don't have any real doubts about it being possible. And it would give you the chance to hone your rather exceptional skills even further before…well, before you decide to leave Dallas."

"Why is everyone talking about my leaving Dallas?"

"Please, please, dear Tim, because everyone thinks you're ready for real professional theatre. Most of those concerned have thought that way for a year or two and *Blood Wedding* proves it. Of course, my motives are selfish; I want you to stay here, at least for a couple more years."

"You're talking about New York, and that scares me to death. I don't know if I'll ever be ready for that."

"I want to give you the time to get ready, because if you continue the way you're going, New York will call you."

"Thanks for your belief in me, but I've got some other things to think about now."

"You mean about Claire leaving?"

"Uh…yes, that, among other things." I took a big breath and said, "If you believe in me that much, double my salary starting this week plus a directing fee for every show I direct until the full-time salary comes through, if it does."

"I believe *Blood Wedding* will finance that along with the fundraising it will bring about. I don't think there's any doubt we'll have to extend the run for at least three weeks. It will change the season some with new dates for openings but that's alright. Yes, it's a deal, and we'll negotiate your directing fees."

"Good, I accept that."

I had spoken with a confidence I didn't know I had. We shook hands and went back to the party. Daniel saw I didn't have a drink as I walked towards him. He guided me to the bar and ordered me a double Bourbon and soda.

"Whoa, big brother, this is not a night for me to get even close to drunk."

" I know, sip it and enjoy the evening. Besides that was a lot of barbeque you ate at the table. You'll be alright. Revel in the success some."

Daniel smiled at me and slapped me on the back.

I roamed around talking to the cast and crew then joined Claire and Liza. They were speaking French, which was a surprise to me. They looked at me and laughed.

"Tim, my major in college was French and I studied at the Sorbonne for a year," Liza said.

I then remembered it from her resume.

"I rarely get the chance to speak it here, except at the French bakery in the Village. But for your sake, we'll switch to English. Don't think that was a slight because I know how well you speak Spanish and I wish I spoke it."

"No slight taken, Liza. Claire hasn't had much chance to speak it here, either. It's been more Spanish than French."

"I was telling Claire what a great experience the play has been and what a first-class director you have become. You always were good, but this time, Tim, you made us feel like a professional company."

"And sadly enough without the pay, because you were a professional company. We couldn't have brought in a stronger group from New York," I protested.

"You're going too far, but thank you, from me and the other cast members. You're the one who got us there."

Liza left us with kisses and hugs. I looked at Claire and asked her, "Are you ready to leave?"

"Yes, I am. I think I said goodbye to everyone. It was sad to say goodbye to your parents. Your mother cried, your Dad kept hugging me. I love them very much. Yes, let's leave. We'll have to get my bag out of Marilee's car."

We waved our goodbyes. Marilee and Daniel walked out with us. Marilee gave us last-minute instructions about the hotel as I got Claire's bag out of the trunk.

"We'll see you Sunday afternoon. Claire, don't worry about your parents calling, Daniel will handle it."

I put her bag with mine, and we jumped in and headed downtown.

We arrived at the Adolphus at close to 1:30. At the desk, they addressed me by name as I signed us in as a couple. I asked that a paper be brought to our door in the morning, and said that we would order a late breakfast from room service. They assured us that everything was in order and pre-paid. I was surprised at how luxurious our suite was-large bedroom, small living area, and a dining room. It looked our over downtown Dallas and Main Street. We unpacked, sat down in the living area, laid back on the sofa, and looked at each other. Claire started giggling, and I laughed, both of us realizing we were too exhausted to even carry on a conversation. We marshaled our strength and went into the bedroom. Claire went into the bathroom with a wrapped bundle, and I changed into the bottoms of the new pajamas Mom had made for me. I pulled back the bedclothes and climbed in bed to wait for Claire. Soon she appeared, her hair shining and her skin glowing. She was wearing a new nightgown that was just this side of sheer enough to see through. I think we were both a little nervous and excited about being together in a secure place with no interruptions expected. I could feel my heartbeat rising as I looked at her. She was a sylph-like apparition of beauty.

She did a little dance in a circle, "Do you like this, Timmy?"

"Boy, do I ever!" She filled out a loose fitting gown in the most sensual manner. "Please climb in this bed beside me."

"Just a minute, I want to look out the window. Oh! Look, there's a flying red horse on that building down the street...a Pegasus?"

"Yes, that's the first thing you see when you drive into Dallas at night. Now, come over here."

She did, and we snuggled close. We kissed slowly, gently, and in no hurry to go further. Our kisses had become a beautiful communion. As we kissed, we explored, touched each other, and were almost out of our pajamas and gown. I kissed her breasts as she eased me into her. With almost no foreplay we were both needful and ready to make love. Claire wrapped her arms around me to hold me tight. Then I realized I hadn't put on a prophylactic. I quickly pulled back.

"What are you doing, Timmy?"

"We can't go on without any protection."

"Wait just a moment," she wrapped her legs around me.

Soon she let me move away. In a few seconds, I came back to her but didn't proceed with complete lovemaking. I nuzzled and sucked her breasts then kissed her stomach. The scent of her was as a different sort of perfume. I moved down, kissing and tasting her.

"Oh, Timmy, what are you doing...I never thought...Timmy..."

I lifted up, "Do you mind me being this intimate with you?"

"No, I don't think so...if you..."

I kissed and made love to her with my tongue and lips.

"Timmy...I...oh..."

She was soft and sweet in a way I didn't know was possible. I realized that I may have frightened her, but it was not planned. It had happened before I even knew. This had nothing to do with any previous experience, but was a part of Claire and me that had grown so steadily to being this intimate. I was almost dizzy with the gentle passion I felt with her. I reached and touched her with my fingers.

Claire started shaking and whimpering then reached down and held my head to her. As she seemed to reach a climax, she squirted a little bit of warmth on me. When she stopped moving to me, I raised up and kissed my way up to her face as I slipped into her. Our lovemaking was long and gentle, with a sweet, passionate ending. She moved into my arms, breathing in a soft panting manner.

"Timmy, that was a surprise. I didn't know people really did that. Did I wee-wee on you? I don't know what happened. I read about it in an Anais Nin novel, but I didn't know if it was real or not, but it certainly was real for me. I guess I thought it was sort of nasty when I read it, but I was very young, eighteen I think. I didn't know I could get that wet, I'm sure glad I cleaned myself a little bit when I changed. But for you...?"

"Claire, sweetheart, it was wonderful for me to be that close to you. And no, you didn't wee-wee on me. I guess it was a passion surprise, but it was beautiful. I remember you once said you couldn't get enough of me; well, I feel the same way. It seemed the natural thing to do because I felt so much love and desire for you."

"I thought we were too tired to be close like that but once I got into your arms...well, I became so...uh...aroused. Oh, Timmy, I love you so much, I do. I don't want to...I...just hold me."

I couldn't say anything because I thought I knew what she was thinking. We went to sleep, her head on my shoulder.

I awoke suddenly in the middle of the night, dreaming Claire wasn't beside me. I sat up and Claire stirred reaching up to me.

"I'm here, sweetheart," she murmured as if she knew what I had been dreaming. I finally went back asleep.

We both woke up at eleven. I called for breakfast and coffee. Claire took a quick shower as I put on a robe and went to the door to see if the paper had been delivered, and it was there. I sat up in bed and opened the paper with trepidation. I turned to the entertainment section for John Rosenfield's review of *Blood Wedding*, and was surprised by a photo of me above the review. I put the paper down and waited for Claire. Soon she came out in her robe and sat beside me.

"Does it have the notes about your play?"

"Yes, but I waited for you before I read it."

"Well, read it to me. I can't wait to hear."

It was as solid a rave as I had ever seen. He liked everything about the production saying it was a new standard for Dallas and the Civic Theatre. He said the musical underscoring of the play was a revelation and the dancing magnificent. It was the best ensemble production he had ever seen equaling some of the best he had experienced in New York. The acting and directing were inspired with a passion rarely seen on any stage, he went on to say. The last third of the review was about me and my family and coined a reference calling us the artistic 'DallasSarts,' saying all of us brought artistic honor to the Dallas scene. His last statement was that he planned to see the play several more times just to see it grow and to spend some time with the art in the lobby by a new artist who had painted scenes from the rehearsals.

"Timmy, I don't think it could be any better for you. This does mean the play will do well for you and the theatre doesn't it?"

"Yes it does. When Mr. Rosenfield writes good things about a play or concert series, it certainly does help. I had hoped he would like it, of course, but this review is beyond all of my expectations. I'll bet old Barney is dancing around his house like a mad sailor. Yes, this is good."

"Do you think you should telephone someone?"

"No, not really. Right now I'm enjoying being away from it and being with you. There will be plenty of talk about it later and about this new artist who painted during rehearsals. "

"I suppose I will be a mystery. 'Who is this Miss Levant?'"

"I wonder if your parents will find out about your new fame."

"I don't think so, and you're the one with a new fame, not me. If they did see the paper my name isn't mentioned."

Breakfast arrived, and we settled down in our little dining room. We lingered over coffee and Claire read the review aloud again. It sounded better with her accent. We laughed and talked about the past weeks, not mentioning tomorrow. I said we should tour downtown Dallas because Saturday is a big day for shopping. She liked that idea so I showered and shaved as she got dressed. We walked out into the late spring. Claire wanted to walk through Neiman's one last time. She insisted I help her choose another nightgown to wear tonight. I was almost embarrassed at the idea, but it ended up being fun because the one we chose was exquisite and I couldn't wait to see her in it. She decided I should have some silk pajamas but I said that was too expensive added onto the night gown.

"Timmy, I told you I am able to buy some things and the money I brought with me has been barely used."

I gave in, but felt uneasy about her spending her parents money on me.

"This is not my parents' money. I have some of my own, and if I want to spend it on the man I love, I can."

I accepted that with a hand squeeze and chose burgundy ones that almost matched her nightgown. She wrote a check with an approved account number on it. She showed her passport for identification and we made arrangements to pick up the packages downstairs in several hours.

We walked over to Elm Street to see the movie houses. We stopped in front of the Melba to view a poster for a Tarzan movie that was playing. "The New Adventures of Tarzan," staring an actor named Herman Brix, he had been an Olympic hero several years ago. I had read all of the Tarzan books and had seen all of the previous movies, but this one sounded like something completely new because Edgar Rice Burroughs was listed as the producer.

"Oh, Timmy, I love Tarzan movies! Let's see it." I had always been disappointed in the movies compared to the books, but I was interested in seeing this one. We got seated just as the movie was starting. It was terrific. The story was strange and disjointed, but it was the first time the actor playing Tarzan was just like the Tarzan in the books. He was more articulate and classy than a super person in the jungle. It began in Africa and then went to Central America on an obscure quest for a secret explosive and ended at a costume party in what looked like England where everyone was dressed as Gypsies, including Tarzan. We both loved it. Claire squealed at all the daring-do. It even had a comic character who was genuinely funny. We walked out laughing and almost skipped down the street to barely make it to Neiman's before they closed to picked up our packages. I told her there was something I wanted her to see.

The Baker Hotel was across the street from the Adolphus and it was the bar there I wanted to show her. It supposedly was more like a New York bar than any other place in Dallas. We sat at the bar, and I pointed at the mural behind the bar. It was Daniel's first big commission a couple years ago, a mysterious woods scene with wild panthers and a hunter. Claire was thrilled to see it. We ordered Martinis and toasted the day and our review in the paper. After two drinks, we then strolled back to our Adolfus. I made reservations for dinner, and we went upstairs to dress. The dining room was one of the classiest in Dallas so we dressed up for the occasion. We had a lovely meal, with wine and brandy afterwards. There was a small band playing, so we danced three nice slow dances. When we got back upstairs we were both slightly tipsy. Claire went to her bag and brought out a candle in glass holder and a bottle.

"Marilee had an idea for a romantic evening activity which I thought I would be too shy to even consider, but I'm feeling a little brave. In this bottle is some very special bubble bath. Would you like to take a bubble bath with me by candle-light?"

"Indeed, without any qualms whatsoever, because I'm feeling a little brave myself."

"You wait right here while I prepare things," She said as she turned to go into the bathroom, but came right back out to bring me a towel, telling me to get undressed. I heard the water running and after awhile she called me to come in. The candle was burning beside the lavatory and Claire was in the bathtub covered with bubbles up to her neck, her hair piled on top of her head. Against the white bubbles and porcelain, she glowed in the soft light of the candle.

"Timmy, get in with me, please."

"Yes, ma'am, I'm on my way."

I dropped the towel and eased into the hot water at the opposite end of the tub. Nervousness and any tensions were immediately gone. Claire smiled and tickled me with her feet. We both just lay back and enjoyed the warmth saying nothing.

Claire sat up and turned around and handed me a washcloth, "Wash my back, Timmy."

I took the washcloth and rubbed her back, then her neck. I dropped the cloth and reached around to her breasts. She cooed, and turned her head around to kiss me as I moved my hand down over her tummy to the softness between her legs.

"That feels so good when you touch me. I think the warm water makes it even better. Let me hold you."

"Please do, sweetheart."

She turned around to face me. The bubbles on her breasts were a startling vision of loveliness. She took me with her hands as I touched her. We kissed, and I put her legs up and around me, getting as close as we could. We rubbed our chests together, rising to a warm passion. We kissed each other all over our faces and necks. I pulled her up onto me and entered her. We stayed very still, feeling the new sensation of the warm water. She began to move very gently and put her arms around me saying, "Timmy, Timmy, hold me, don't leave me, don't stop being inside me. I don't want to ever forget this moment."

"Are you sure, Claire?"

"Yes, I know it's dangerous, but at this moment I want to feel you inside me this way."

"Oh, Claire, I don't want to stop either. Oh my God, did you know you're squeezing me so good when you move."

"Am I? I just feel like I'm kind of quivering with little electric shocks."

I reached down a touched her as she moved on me.

"Ti-mo-thee, I'm…yes, touch me more, please…Oh!"

She kissed me then threw her head back, making soft sounds and sighs then a long, "Oh…" then "Timmy…I'm going to…yes!"

I felt like I was going to cry out, but remembered where we were. We both climaxed at the same time, holding each other tightly.

"Oh my, my wonderful man, how nice, how sweet." And we untangled and lay back in the water, letting the bubbles cover us up to our necks. We were very quiet for a few minutes as the water cooled down. We sat up and soaped each other. Claire pulled the stopper and we stood up and turned on the shower to rinse off. We toweled each other, and I went into the bedroom and put on my new pajamas. Claire came out in a few minutes in her new nightgown, holding the still burning candle.

I turned off the bed lamp and Claire placed the candle on the dresser across from the bed.

"I don't believe the hotel people would like it if they knew we had a lighted candle in here, but 'tis our secret and it's extremely romantic. Don't you think?"

"Indeed I do, as you would say, Monsieur Ti-mo-thee Sart."

"Come over here and lay yourself down beside me, Mademoiselle Claire Levant."

"In two shakes of a lambie's tail, I heard Marilee say that once and I thought it was a cute expression."

"I never thought of as being cute until you said it."

She took a minute to put on some perfume. "Coco Channel will join us tonight."

She came to me and leaned over close, "Do you like it?"

I took in the scent, "Very much."

She lay her head down on my arm, "This has been a special day and night in my life, Timmy. It was so much fun this afternoon and the last hour. I believe we discovered a new togetherness, don't you?"

"Yes, I didn't know making love could be like that. I do hope you're not scared of getting pregnant."

"Perhaps I am a little bit, but it was so beautiful I'm not going to think about it, and I did try to clean myself before I put on my nightgown. Oh, do you like my new gown?"

You look like some extraordinary ancient princess in it. How about my pajamas? They feel great."

"Yes, I like them on you. In the candlelight, you are extremely handsome. Timmy, I don't want to go to sleep tonight. I want to be beside you and look at you and kiss you and talk with you."

"Me, too. I want to stretch out this night as long as possible."

"What are you going to do now…now that the play is going? What are you going to do next?"

"Well, Monday morning I go back to work at the bookstore. My boss has been holding off inventory until I got back, so I will be very busy there. And I'll go to the theatre after work for a few hours. When the play is running, I'll be there for the performances. I'm not directing the next play so there will be a lot more time off unless what Barney has proposed works out."

I told her about Barney's idea of me being at the theatre fulltime and about the new raise that started this week.

"That's wonderful, Timmy! When did this happen?"

"At the cast party. I haven't had a chance to tell you until now."

"Do you believe it will really happen? When? You said it was an idea."

"I don't know. It depends a lot on fundraising. I got the idea that Barney is afraid I'll leave the theatre and go elsewhere. But the only other elsewhere is New York, and I know I'm not ready for that yet, or maybe I'll never be."

"I believe you can do anything you want. You just proved yourself to be an excellent director."

"I don't think one good show puts me in that category yet."

"From what Marilee told me, you have many good shows. Yes I know *Blood Wedding* is something very special, but it does prove how good you are. I don't think you should have any doubts."

"I guess doubts are the thing, and self-confidence."

"That's one of the nice parts about you, you're not conceited or arrogant.

Most directors that I've met are."

"Claire you've made me feel more self confidence than I've ever felt before."

"Oh, Timmy, don't say that. You don't need me for that."

"No, I need you because I love you."

"And you know I love you, too."

Our conversation stopped for a few minutes. A painful moment for both of us.

"Uh…what are you going to do now, I mean when you get to Los Angeles?"

"I suppose, first, I will get used to being there. I'm sure it's very different from being here in Texas."

"There is no doubt about that. Very different."

"My parents have bought a large house up in the hills overlooking the city, and my mother says you can see the ocean in the distance and even the mountains to the west. My father has arranged several interviews for me. The one I'm most interested in is at the Los Angeles Art Museum. He said they were impressed by my studies in London and at the Sorbonne. But beyond that, I don't know. Oh, Timmy I don't want to…well, I guess it will be a new life of some sort."

We talked for several hours. She told me about London and the museums and theatre there. And about the Comedie in Paris and how beautiful Spain is. I told her about a trip I took last year to the deep woods of East Texas and about the West Texas plains. I told her how much I enjoyed working with Uncle Willy in his shop learning about cars and hearing his stories about China and going up the Yangtze River, about the places I would like to go and see. I talked about theatre and how much I liked the collaboration and seeing it come alive on stage. I tried to describe how impossible every play production was, that it was a miracle with so many people involved that it ever happened at all. And how exciting it was when a real acting breakthrough happened and one of my ideas really worked. We talked about the weeks of rehearsal we had shared and the new friends made. She wished she had had more time to learn how to drive better, but said her father would be surprised at how much she already knew. She told me about her favorite artists, and it was a surprise we both like the Pre-Raphaelites, especially Rosetti. We realized we had brought a bottle of Villalobos brandy Marilee had given us. We sat up and toasted the evening, and us. We laughed about having gone swimming so much, she said more than she had ever before. We toasted Marilee and Daniel and talked of how much we loved them. Daniel's paintings dominated our talk for awhile. Claire thought he was an exceptionally talented painter and would soon be recognized beyond Dallas.

We lay in each other arms and kissed, crawled under the covers, and made gentle love for a long time. We both dozed off, though we trying not to.

I awoke before she did and went into the bathroom taking the bottoms of my new pajamas. When I came out she was stirring, then jumped up and dragging her nightgown. I ordered coffee to be sent up, and I was sitting up in bed when she came out in her gown, brushing her hair to a shine. The coffee arrived, and we sat up in bed drinking it, not saying a word. We knew we had about five hours before we needed to leave for Marilee's. We looked at each other as if trying to remember everything about how the other looked.

Suddenly tears started streamed out of my eyes, and then also hers.

"Claire, I don't want you to leave."

"Timmy, I must."

"I don't mean your staying with Marilee and Daniel but with me…I want you…to…"

"Do you mean marry you?"

"Yes, will you marry me?"

"Oh, Timmy, don't ask that of me."

"Why not? We love each other. I don't want to be without you."

"Yes, I do love you, I do love you, Timmy. But…I…I can't marry you."

"What are you saying, you can't marry me? Can't? Why? Please tell me."

"Timmy, there is something you don't know about me. Marilee and Daniel know, but I swore them to keep it a secret until after I had gone."

"What is it? Now you have got to tell me. Now."

"I'm Jewish, a Jew."

"A Jew? What difference does that make? Why would I care if you're Jewish?!"

"I'm an Orthodox Jew, and my parents are very religious. I would be disowned by them if I married a Gentile. I would shame them. They would never speak to me or see me again."

"A Gentile? Am I a Gentile?"

"Yes, you're a Christian. Aren't you?"

"We've always gone to the Unitarian meetings, but I haven't for a long time."

"Unitarian? What is…?

"It's kind of like being a Christian, I guess, but without the supernatural stuff. Jesus is more like a teacher, a guide to a way of living."

"Oh."

"Do you think if your parents got to know me?"

"No, that wouldn't make any difference, even if you were willing to convert."

"I don't think I understand. There was always something about your leaving, as if you would disappear, like this was all a dream. But it hasn't been a dream. You've made me happier than I've ever been in my life. I want to spend my life with you. Do you understand that?"

"Yes, I do, and if things were different I would. Before we left London, my parents had found a matchmaker. Do know what they do?"

"Other than the obvious, no."

"They search for a suitable match for Orthodox women. It has nothing to do with love. If a match is found to the approval of the parents, a marriage is arranged with very little contact between the couple."

"But that was in London and it didn't happen."

"No, we left London to come here. Terrible things are happening to Jews in Europe, in Germany and Poland. We didn't know what Americans felt about Jews. Marilee assured my father it was different here. But is it?"

"As far as my family is concerned, it is. We've always had Jewish friends. Barney told me his parents were Jewish. Is Orthodox so different?"

"Yes. Timmy, everything that has happened between us is considered a major sin. And it is also very important that I must be a virgin before marrying. I don't know how I will get through that, not being a virgin. I suppose I will just lie. But things happened here that I didn't expect. Meeting and falling in love with you altered my perception of existence. This has not been a flirtation for me. I have fallen deeply in love with you but, I have to go back to my life as a Jew. I have no choice, it's...my destiny. My father told me last week he has contacted a famous matchmaker in Los Angeles. The process will start up again. I eventually will be forced into a loveless marriage to someone I don't know. I will be required to be subservient and produce children. Do you hear what I'm saying...forced into a loveless marriage!"

"Yes, I hear you, sweetheart and I don't like it."

"Please, dear Timmy, don't think I do. I can feel my heart breaking. I didn't want to have to tell you all of this. I knew how hurt you would be, as I am by this destiny thing. I don't know how I can face going there. But my parents are..."

"My family loves you and would welcome you as my wife. There's the difference."

"Yes, and I love them. I've told you that I've never felt such warmth from people. I already feel as if they are family. Your Uncle Willy and Aunt Rosie are wonderful. I want to see their baby, I want to watch your mother paint, I want to see Jeordie become a fine photographer. I want your father to make furniture for us... Timmy, many nights I've cried myself to sleep over the sadness of leaving you. You know my feelings for you scared me at first because I didn't believe you could feel the same way about me, but you did...of course I would marry you and know that we would be happy...but..."

"I don't know what to say because I'm very confused by the religious part of this. I don't know, evidently, about Judaism and how restrictive it is. To me it seems unnatural to keep apart people who love each other..."

"Yes, it must seem that way, but we, or I can say now, they, we, have a different view of marriage. My parents came together through a matchmaker and my father says that love is something that grows from the union, not before it. I guess I always accepted that because it seemed so far in the future. I was horrified when my parents told me in London that a matchmaker had been contacted. When they made the decision to come to America I hoped that the freedom here would change their minds, but it didn't. I suppose I'm not a very good Jew to even question it. I had many talks with my father and mother about this, but they didn't understand my questioning it or even discussing it with a negative attitude. I know it frightened them. It took Marilee a month to convince them to let me come here for a visit. If they knew about what has happened between us, they would blame her for not protecting me. I'm sure they would consider me weak and vulnerable and exploited. And I'm just referring to our seeing each other, certainly not any of the intimacy we've shared. That would shame them to the point that I don't know how they would deal with it. Perhaps there is a ritual cleansing that I don't know about, but I doubt it."

"This is beginning to sound slightly primitive, I can't imagine marrying someone I didn't know or love, hoping that love would grow."

"Yes, it's sounding that way to me also, but to lose my family…Timmy, I don't want you to believe I feel any guilt about us or anything that has happened. I was not innocent,…well in some ways…or vulnerable, everything that we have shared I was a part of and it was and is the most beautiful experience in my life. In London, I had a freedom my parents didn't know about. When my father traveled, I went to parties, even went on secret dates, danced, and drank beer and whiskey in artists' flats. I kissed boys that I was sort of attracted to. I almost made love but knew it wasn't the right person so I didn't. This has been so very different…the time, the weeks, we've spent together seem like a year. I feel as if I truly know you."

"Will I be able to write or call you?"

"Not to my house. Perhaps I can arrange something when I get work, or a postal box. Of course, I don't want to lose contact with you as painful as it may be because I will miss you very much, every minute of every day. This so hard to talk about…but perhaps it's better that we have. Oh Timmy, let's not talk anymore, just hold me a little bit. I'm beginning to be frightened of not being able to be with you."

I moved towards her, then dropped down on my knees and put my head in her lap. I was shaking and holding her around her waist. I began to cry, then sobbed out loud, soaking her with my tears. She pulled me up as her crying turned to sobbing. We held each other tightly. We kissed each other's faces, still shaking and crying. Finally, we calmed.

"Timmy, oh, Timmy, I hurt in my heart for us. We must…"

"I know, I just…I've never in my life known such a sadness, such a feeling of despair…of loss. The thought of you being forced into being with another man…when there's us…I can't…"

"Hold me, I'm frightened of what we are feeling."

And I did. There was no more crying, just being close. And there was really no more to be said by me. I only understood from all that was said and felt, that we were not going to be together, possibly never again, but I refused to believe that and said nothing.

"Claire, are you hungry?" I asked after awhile.

"I think so. Are you?"

"Yes, let's have something special. I saw that they have Eggs Benedict. Does that sound good to you?"

"It does. You call to order and I'll take a shower."

She jumped up looking back with a weak smile. I called and asked how long it would be. When they said there was a backup on breakfast, about 25 minutes. I went to the bathroom door and waited to hear the shower. As it started I opened the curtain and asked if I could join her in the shower."

"Please do."

We scrubbed each other's backs and I washed her breasts from behind. When I moved down, she said that wasn't fair and for me to turn around. I did and we washed, and laughed for the first time that day. She was so lovely to touch, it was hard to stop especially since she had rather aroused me with her attentions.

"After we eat, will you make love to me like you did before, Timmy."

I nodded and kissed her.

"Now you get out of here and let me finish."

"Yes, ma'am."

I dried off and got into my silk pajamas and robe. The food came just as she came out in her robe. We ate the terrific eggs and had more coffee. We finished and she went in the bathroom to brush her teeth. I finished my coffee and did the same. When I came out, she was standing, looking out the window. She turned and came to me. I undid our robes and moved close to her. As her robe dropped, I moved behind her and reached around to touch her beautiful breasts with one hand and with the other, reached down to her soft downy area. She turned her head and kissed me.

"Touch me inside, Timmy."

She was getting wetter, and it was easy to touch inside her and stroke her. Feeling her breasts respond to me and touch her at the same time with her kisses was a new kind of closeness.

"Timmy, I want to hold you, come around in front of me."

I did, and she undid my pajamas and took me in her hand as I touched her wetness.

"Claire, that's too good when you hold me like that. I won't be able to hold back much longer."

"For me, too."

She took my hand away from her and started kissing me down my chest, going lower. She put me in her mouth very innocently.

"Claire, you don't have to do that and it will be too good for me to hold back."

She looked up at me, moved away and said, "Timmy, I want to taste you like you did me."

She put her mouth on me again moving up and down my erection. I was shivering with the new sensation.

"Wait, sweetheart, I want to taste you at the same time."

She pulled back, breathing heavily, "How...can...?"

I lifted her up still shaking from her touch and guided her to the bed. I lay down beside her with my head close to between her legs and kissed her wet, soft pillow mound and reached to touch inside her and moved my tongue on her rising bud. She then put me in her mouth again, moving up and down on me. I shifted up on top of her to get closer to her. I could feel her beginning to climax, and I couldn't hold back any longer. We both had rising climaxes, shaking with the electricity of it. She squirted a little bit on me as I pulled away. She didn't want to take me out of her mouth so she could get ever last bit of me. I couldn't take any more of the feeling as I pulled out of her. I kissed up her stomach to her breasts and sucked her nipples, and then went up to her lips and tasted both of us. She pulled me on to her and guided me into her. I raised up on my hands to look at her as I moved inside her. She reached up and held onto my arms moving with me, looking at me.

"Timmy, I'm going to again..."

"Me too, Baby."

Afterwards we lay in each other's arms under the sheet almost unable to speak, still both breathing heavily and shaking from our passion.

Finally, "Claire, I'm sorry I didn't protect you, I just couldn't stop or even think."

"I didn't want you to stop...it was so...Oh, Timmy, if that was our last time to make love...it was so beautiful. I thought we couldn't be closer than before...but we were like a complete part of each other, or...Do you understand what I mean?"

"Yes, I was unaware of anything except you. My, God, Claire, I don't know about being without you...I...how I can..."

"I don't know either. Perhaps our not being careful will solve that, but I don't want us to be forced together, but then...well we, I think we will always be together in a way, even if we're apart. Do you think so?"

"I do, but I would prefer really being together."

"Timmy, you must, as I have, accept that I'm leaving without being so sad that you can't go on. We must go on...I love you so much and I must know you are alright."

"I will be, I'll have to be."

"Do you think the passion between us has been a bad thing and will make it harder for us to part?"

"I don't think in any way it's been a bad thing except for any feelings you may have about betraying your beliefs-maybe betraying is the wrong word. You said it is considered a major sin, but I don't how it could have been any different unless we had resisted it completely, but I believe we both tried...I know I did. It was all so natural, or it happened without us being able to not being as close as we have been in our lovemaking. I began to realize how much I felt for you. I didn't want to frighten you or feel later that I had taken advantage of you."

"When we talked about our feelings before, my leaving seemed so far away, I tried then to express that I had some of the same thoughts about my taking advantage of you...I mean I didn't want you to think I wanted to use you to experience something I never could anywhere else. Oh, I don't know how to say any more. I believe now, right this moment, that our meeting was as much destiny for us as my having to leave and return to a life that is almost foreign to me after us. I told you it was difficult for me at times in London, but now, after us...I ..."

Claire started crying very hard and leaned into my arms.

Then, through crying and sniffling, "Let's not talk about it anymore, dear Timmy. How much time do we have?"

"I guess about two or three hours."

"Oh. What time is it?"

I reached for the watch she had given me, "1:30."

"We need to leave about 3:30 to go to Marilee's, then to the train station."

"I just realized, Timmy, we've never had a disagreement about anything... well, except for my religious obligations."

"That's your disagreement, not mine. I don't care about your religion. But you're right. The important thing is that you're the best friend I've ever had, and you were a friend first, then the love happened."

"I know. At first, I wanted to talk to you about everything and all at once our first kiss happened. That was so...well, we were in that boat talking, then leaned towards each other and it was my first kiss that just happened. I wasn't thinking about kissing you...it..."

"Yes, it...I was so intimidated by your beauty and intelligence that I knew I would be too shy to try to kiss you."

"I've always been shy about kissing. Well, how about you kissing me right now? Then let's take a shower, get dressed, go downstairs have an afternoon Martini, and eat something before leaving. If we're a little late, it will be alright."

I laughed and brought her into my arms for a sweet long kiss.

We drove up to Marilee's house and sat in my car for a few minutes, holding each other. Marilee came out to greet us and say that she had done the rest of Claire's packing, leaving out a choice of traveling clothes. We went in and Claire went upstairs to change and finish her preparations. Dan, Marilee, and I sat in the den to wait. Marilee asked how our weekend was.

"It was very nice, fun, and sad. And thank you for the room and everything else."

"How are you holding up, brother?" Daniel asked.

"It's one of those times you hoped would never get here. I don't know yet. This is hitting both of us harder than we thought. I asked her to stay, and she told me why she couldn't."

"I promised her I wouldn't tell you, I know it seems wrong now, but none of us knew what would happen between you two. Claire and I talked several times in the last couple of weeks about her decision not to tell you now but later in a letter or phone call. You didn't know that several Saturdays I took her to temple. But you were spending so much time together, she gave it up to be with you in the last weeks. It's been very hard for her not to tell you the truth. Uh...you asked her to stay?"

"Yes, I mean not just stay, like with you, but with me."

Marilee leaned into the question, "You mean marry you?"

"Yes."

"Oh my!"

"Yes, oh my!"

"What was her response to that?" Daniel asked.

"That she loved me, and that she would if she could, but..."

"She can't, right?" Marilee was starting to almost break down with this development. "I don't know why I should be surprised you would ask her."

Claire came downstairs at this point, seeing we were in serious conversation and Marilee's reaction. She was bent over with her head in her hands.

"Timmy, you've told them you know and what you asked?"

"Yes, sweetheart." I stood up and went to her. She leaned on me and put her head on my shoulder, crying softly. "I thought we would talk about it after you left but...well, it just came out after Daniel asked how I was holding up, which is not well, but I'm alright, Claire."

"That's alright, Timmy. I guess neither one of us is doing too well."

Marilee stood up, "I suppose we should start for the station."

Claire went to Marilee and hugged her, "Oh, Marilee, I don't want to go. I want to be with Timmy, but my parents..."

"Yes, I know, and I think Timmy understands more than we think he does."

"I don't like it, but I do understand the consequences. I can't ask her to give up her parents, which is evidently what would happen."

We loaded Claire's luggage into the back of Marilee's station wagon and drove to Union Station. On the platform, Claire said her goodbyes and thanks to Marilee and Daniel and then to me.

"Timmy, I do love you so. Please don't forget me but go on with your life. I wish I could see *Blood Wedding* one more time. I don't know how I'm going to explain the framed poster. You're such a fine director and a wonderful man. Thank you, my Timmy."

"Yes, I am your Timmy, and I won't forget you sweetheart, ever..."

We were both crying openly and holding each other in a desperate fashion. She kissed me long and sweetly then got on the train and in a matter of minutes, was gone.

Chapter 14
Despues que se va la Aparicion

When the three of us got back to Marilee's, we went out back to the patio.

"Could you use a Bourbon and soda, brother?"

"Indeed I could, Dan. The first of several."

Dan went to the bar, mixed a Martini for Marilee and our Bourbons.

"That was a little hard to watch, you two in your last kiss, Timmy. I thought any moment I would start bawling out loud."

"At that point, I was beyond crying Marilee. Claire was leaving and that was that. We had talked about it so much that the reality of was a sort of swish in time. So sudden. And she has that long train trip to L.A. all alone...I feel like I've experienced a death in the family."

"No, Timmy, don't let that sort of emotion take you over. It's not a death. No one has died, especially not Claire."

"I know, but my life now just doesn't feel...well, it's as if something has been ripped from me. It ran through my mind that I should get on the train with her. I knew she needed me to be with her, but I think Daniel would have put a stop to that."

"Yes, I would have, even though I would have understood the sentiment. I believe she's strong enough to deal with it. Hell, I didn't like her leaving either; and not just because of you, Tim. It seemed a natural situation, her living here with us."

"It was the first time I had the feeling of almost having a younger sister," Marilee agreed. "I don't believe I've ever been that close to another woman."

"When I first met her that night at the theatre, in near darkness, she seemed to glow. I had never seen anything like her, I mean I thought I could see her aura. I know that sounds ridiculous, but I'm serious. She was beautiful in such a different fashion and as we grew closer, she became more beautiful to me every day. An apparition that stepped into my life and changed me and is now gone," I said wistfully.

"Timmy, there's no doubt that you changed her too. I watched it happen," Marilee said.

"We both did, Tim. You know, I think the love you two felt rubbed off on Marilee and me. We know we were very much in love, but seeing you and Claire fall in love right in front of us kind of helped us to realize how much we really have. It made me believe even more strongly how I never want to lose Marilee. And do you remember me saying that Marilee has been, quite often, my muse? Well, I think Claire was for you."

"Yep, there's no doubting that. I didn't completely understand it. The passion that Claire and I developed gave me new perspective on it. Have I told you how much I've written about directing? It's gotten to the point that it's a short book. Every night when I left Claire, I could write for hours and I know I couldn't have done that before."

"That little book could be something, Timmy. Do you think you've finished it?"

"No, but I'm going to. Hey, brother, I rushed through this drink. Do you mind if I fix another?"

"Yes, I do mind. Give me your glass. Marilee?"

"Just a half, Daniel."

"I thought at first I wanted to get a little drunk, but now I plan to write some tonight," I decided.

"That's going to be after the dinner I'm going to fix fairly soon," Marilee said.

"Why thank you, soon-to-be-sister-in-law."

"Not too soon for me, Tim," Daniel laughed, turning to Marilee. "Eh, mi amor?"

Marilee went to Daniel as he was bringing our drinks and kissed him on the cheek, "I wish it was yesterday, so Claire could be with us."

"She's still going to be with us in many ways, I know for Tim, but have you seen the drawing she gave us now that it's framed? It's going up in the den where it can be seen all the time."

"Jeordie did some really good portraits of her, some while she was drawing and coloring in the lobby. I think Jeordie fell a little in love with, her too. When I told him she was leaving he didn't believe me, saying he would have to talk to her about that. I put a quick stop to that idea."

We talked a little longer. Daniel and I stayed outside for a little long but soon joined Marilee in the kitchen. I got home before ten, had a tot of the Spanish Brandy, and started writing. I wanted to make as clear as possible how I had worked up close with the actors on stage, using intimate directing ideas, shaping the character development, and smoothing the blocking. An important process I used was helping the stage pictures flow instead of becoming static going from freeze to freeze. I had used Claire's drawings almost like flip cards in my mind to create a cinema effect. In the last weeks of rehearsal for warm-ups, I had asked Aurora to lead the acting company in flowing dance-like moves as they recited the sonnets they had memorized. The actors had loved it, saying it helped them get focused. I thought, at the time, that other directors could use a variation of it to start rehearsals. But this was my journal, not a book on directing, more a story of a play in the process of happening. I knew it would never go any further than me, but I couldn't stop writing it because it was going to be my escape from my loneliness for Claire. I quit at midnight and tried to read Maugham, but couldn't concentrate. I finally slept, softly crying with Claire's image and touch in my mind. My dreams were filled with erotic visions of our lovemaking.

The next morning, I woke up early, knowing I started back at the bookstore today and ready for a long inventory. I went into the house for breakfast with the family. It was both happy and sad because everyone wanted to reminisce about Claire. Jeordie showed me some of latest developed prints, about half of which were of her.

They were terrific, but hard to look at. Jeordie was upset that he hadn't seen her again before she left.

Mom gave a pep talk on being strong, which I just didn't want to hear. I went back out to my apartment with a cup of coffee to sit and prepare for being strong. Work was the answer; but I wasn't directing the next play so writing had to substitute, along with fundraising for the theatre and a permanent position.

I arrived at the bookstore on time and was greeted with major congratulations from Mr. Franklin. He had seen the play on Saturday and was disappointed I wasn't there to talk to afterward. He surprised me by asking if any of the drawings in the lobby would be for sale because he wanted to hang one in the store. We started inventory, with the store closed until we were finished later in the week. I had my lunch alone, eating the sandwich Mom had prepared for me and reading a new book on Brecht the owner had found for me. After work, I went to the theatre to see Barney, find out about reservations, and check the set.

Barney was very excited about the past weekend and said he wished I had been there Saturday for the audience, because there was a lot of excitement. Ginger was backstage working on the set and cleaning up the dressing rooms, and I went back and joined her after I finished talking to Barney. I found her arranging the makeup and cleaning mirrors, she stopped working to talk. There had been another gathering after the play Saturday, she said and I had been sorely missed, but most of them knew Claire and I had gone off to be together before she left. A big question had been what Claire had said about all of the drawings in the lobby because several actors wanted to buy one. Claire told me they were all mine and to do whatever I wanted to do with them, I said. I would consider selling some of them but would just choose the ones I wanted to keep.

The set seemed to be in fine working order. Dad's design was holding up well. Barney came backstage to get me for a conference in his office. He said both papers wanted to interview me for the next weekend edition. This was a big surprise, and a first for me. Barney was thrilled because of the box office and fundraising potential. I had a brief surge of shyness and hesitancy thinking of the interviews. Barney said they both would be here tomorrow afternoon; the Morning News at one and the Herald at four. I immediately thought of the bookstore, but knew Mr. Franklin would be supportive, as always, even though it would probably mean keeping the store closed for another day.

Ginger soon joined us, and Barney poured us glasses of wine. We sat around his office and discussed the coming weeks and possible schedule changes. Ginger agreed with all of the changes, but said, as I had, that the actors had to agree to added days and show extension. We ended with Ginger asking me to join her and her boyfriend for dinner at a steak house on Greenville Ave. It had been a family favorite for years, so I quickly agreed. I had the time to go home, take a shower, and change. I was thankful for the invitation because it would have been my first evening without Claire in weeks and spending it alone wasn't a pleasant prospect.

I went in to see the family and tell them about the interviews. To my surprise they already knew about them because John Rosenfield had called them to say he also wanted to interview them because his article was going to include the whole Sart family. Thankfully, neither Mom nor Dad mentioned Claire. Both parents had gotten new commissions in the past week, so things were pretty busy around the house. They wanted a family dinner, but I gave regrets and went to my apartment to shower and dress. I arrived at the restaurant just after Ginger and her boyfriend did. He was an attorney in a large firm downtown, so we were able to have cocktails in the private club part of the restaurant. I had met him several times, but this would be our first chance to really have a conversation. I had liked Randol from the first meeting because he seemed so perfect for Ginger, a smart country boy from East Texas who had gone to Yale and loved the arts. We talked about the play and Ginger's commitment to it. He didn't seem to resent the time she spent at the theatre as long as they had weekends after the shows and Sundays and Mondays. Ginger told me the evening had been tentatively planned because she knew I would be alone and Randol wanted to spend some time with me after seeing the play and enjoying it so much. I mentioned that I was a bit taken aback by all of the reaction to it. He laughed and said he wasn't at all surprised because it was by far the best work he had seen in Dallas. That was, of course, great to hear because I knew he had seen a lot plays in New York.

The conversation then turned to Ginger's concern about my staying in Dallas. I told them about Barney's potential offer of a fulltime position at the theatre in what I supposed would be a sort of artistic director capacity. She was thrilled at the prospect, hoping we could work together many times in the future. I promised that would always be the case and that I would try to pay her for each show she did as stage manager, a by-the-play contract knowing I would never find a better backstage leader.

We left the club area and went into the dining room for great steaks and talked about Lorca. We finally got around to Claire's leaving. I said I was still in a slight state of shock about it but hadn't had time to really think about it and would try to stay busy enough to not to let it bring me down. Randol said I shouldn't spend too much time alone and that I surely didn't need to with my newfound fame. I hadn't even thought, dating or seeing anyone new. I thought it would be a long time before I could even consider it or be interested. Being alone seemed the right choice, as it had been before Claire...well, except for the weekend with Gwen, which looking back was the best thing that could have happened. Now, it seemed as if Gwen had known I would meet someone like Claire and needed to be prepared for it.

When I got home, I sat up in my room had a couple of snifters of Villa-Lobos and looked at the portrait of Claire Jeordie had taken. I eventually got to bed and tried to read; no writing tonight. I dreamed of Claire in passionate ways that dreams had never taken me to before.

One week after Claire's leaving, I received the first letter from her. It was long, sweet, and sad. She had started having interviews and felt that her best chance was with the Los Angeles Museum of art as an assistant curator of European art. They were very interested in her training and European background. Her parents had contracted a well-known matchmaker, totally against her wishes, but they said it must be. She missed me terribly every minute of the day and I filled her dreams. Her family's house was a beautiful place in the hills overlooking Los Angeles and even had a swimming pool. Her brother had started school and wasn't very happy with it because it was a religious school and he wanted to go to a regular school. But the parents insisted that it was the best thing for him to be there. Her father was "teaching" her to drive and was surprised how quickly she took to it. She asked about the family and how the play was doing. There were two separate pages that must have been written later, about her feelings for me and how what we had made her think in a completely new way about her life. She was trying to adjust to this new life, but it was extremely difficult. It was her home but Dallas was in her heart. As soon as she found a job, she would arrange a way for me to write to her. The letter ended with a pledge of her undying love.

I read the letter several times.

The next weeks were a blur of store work and the theatre. The newspaper articles had been very good. Rosenfield's had included pictures of the whole family; Daniel and Mom in their studios, Dad in his shop, and me on the front page standing on the theatre stage. He titled his story <u>The DallasSarts</u>. The Herald's article concentrated on the play and me. And there were constant invitations to social gatherings. I also started spending more time with Dick and Camila Ayers. And several things happened in the next week that caused big changes, one that almost alienated me from the theatre.

One evening after a weekend show, Barney held a cast party at his little house in Oaklawn. It was the first time since the first week of the play's run that I had a chance to spend relaxed time with the cast. We drank and laughed late into the evening. At one point, Liza Farquar sat down beside me with a new Bourbon and soda for me. She had proved to be one of the finest actors in the play and got better with each performance. She was a strikingly beautiful woman and had always seemed extremely happy, but something was wrong that she couldn't talk about.

"Tim, I understand more than you know about your feelings on Claire's leaving. I think I was the first one in the cast to see that you had fallen in love, and how happy it had made you. Besides everyone loved Claire but didn't know she would be leaving. I well…I…"

I knew that her husband was working in Java as an engineer on an oil-drilling project.

"What are you saying you understand more about…?"

"The loneliness, Tim, and what do I do about it. Being in the play has been a lifesaver for me. I want to thank you for that. This is a great bunch of people. I doubt if there's been a cast in any show at the theatre that has gotten along so well and works so hard. I don't think we'll ever get tired of doing it. I'm glad we're going to extend the run and do an extra performance each week. Do you think the show has grown?"

"Without any doubt. Actually much more than I had hoped," I admitted.

"The sessions of critique you have had with us each week have helped. I've never seen a director do that before. Usually, they feel they're finished after the show opens."

"I didn't know how receptive you all would be if I stayed with the show."

"I hope those doubts are gone because we look forward to your new ideas and refinements. Everything you've said has helped us to be even stronger and it was a good show from the beginning, but now…"

"That's good to hear, Liza, but how about you? There's something going on with you that has nothing to do with *Blood Wedding*, right?"

"Yes, but it's not something I want to get into yet. I'll get through it… somehow."

As she said that, the actors playing the bride and Leonardo came over and joined us, sitting on the floor. They had also fallen in love during the rehearsals and seemed to be even more so now. It certainly helped them express passion on stage. We talked about the past week and the continued audience response. Slowly, the party began to wind down. Liza left me with a kiss on the cheek and encouraging me to stay strong.

As the last folks left, Barney asked if I wanted to try something special. I agreed with a bit of trepidation. He went into his kitchen and came back with a bottle of a clear liquid.

"What the hell is that?"

"It's a rare drink that a friend from New York sent me-It's Russian Pepper Vodka. I keep it in a block of ice."

It sounded a little dangerous but I agreed to try it. He brought out a couple of small glasses and poured us each a full glass. He tossed his back like a Cossack. I took a sip and was shocked at the hot taste and strength.

"Take it all in one quick drink, it will do you good. I've seen how sad you've looked all evening. Missing Claire, huh?"

"Yep, in a big way"

I drank it down quickly and he poured me another. We talked about the evening and what a good group it was. Then I realized that I was very drunk, slurring words and feeling numb.

"How strong is this stuff?"

"Quite. One hundred and ninety proof."

"It sure has hit me hard," I said as I leaned back on the sofa. "I don't think it mixes too well with the bourbon I had."

"You'll be alright, just lay back and relax. I'll go and try to clean up the kitchen."

I felt myself drifting off, passing out slowly. It was, in a way, a very peaceful release. I tried to keep my eyes open. Barney had put on some more records, and I drifted off to the music. I started to half-dream of the play and the people who had been at the party. As I began to sleep deeper, I began to dream of Claire. We were on the boat again behind Marilee's, then in the swimming pool, in the museum together looking at Daniel's painting, in Uncle Willy's back yard laughing with my family. We were alone in the dark and back at the hotel slowly beginning to make love. We kissed and touched getting more intimate whispering our love words of commitment saying "forever" to each other many times. Claire pulled me to her, urging me to be inside her. I touched her soft wetness, and then we were making love. It began to feel very real as our passion grew. I could feel myself rising to a climax as she held me inside her. I tried to force myself awake as the feeling increased. Then I was having a climax.

"My, God, what's…?"

I woke up enough to look down and see that Barney was sucking on me. It shocked me awake as I pushed him off of me.

"I'm sorry, Tim, I couldn't stop when I saw you were having a dream. You were moving like you were making love. I've always wanted to…"

I tried to speak clearly through the liquor, "Don't say anything else, Barney."

I struggled up and staggered to the door.

"Don't leave, Tim. I guess I was too drunk to know what I was doing."

"You knew exactly what you were doing. I said don't say anything else."

I got through the door and slowly and carefully made my way to my car slowly and carefully. I leaned against the front fender and threw-up for what seemed like thirty minutes, but was probable more like ten. I was able to get the door open and get in., but I knew I couldn't drive, so I locked the door and laid back. I slept until just before dawn then drove home still feeling the effect of the strong vodka but sober enough to drive. Thankfully there was no traffic.

I slept late into the morning, very glad it was Sunday with no work and no show. I woke up, suddenly remembering what had happened the night before. I was furious with Barney, knowing he had taken advantage of me in the worst way. I didn't feel any shame or embarrassment, just anger. I had always known Barney was attracted to me and thought I had made it very clear that I wasn't interested. I knew that our next words together would be serious. I immediately began to have doubts about being at the theatre, but I put that reaction out of my head because the theatre was my future, I just needed to set Barney straight and never again get drunk around him.

I didn't go back to the theatre until Tuesday after work. I went in the office to confront Barney. He was very ill at ease.

"Please don't hate me, Tim," he cried. "I'm very sorry for my actions. I…"

"I don't hate you, Barney, but I do resent the hell out of what you did. Did you give me that Vodka hoping something like that would happen?"

"No, I don't think so, but when I saw you having that passionate dream I couldn't resist doing what I did. You must be aware how I've felt about you for a long time. Aren't you?"

"Well, I didn't know it was that strong. But I'm telling you now, get it out of your head. I'll take it as a compliment but from afar. Do you understand? If you have any thoughts of me staying with the theatre, forget about it. Understand?"

"Yes, I understand. Are you going to stay for the show tonight?"

"I'm not sure yet. Is Ginger here?"

"Yes, she came in right before you did. She must be in the dressing room. Again, Tim, please forgive me, I don't want this to ruin our working together."

"That will take some time, Barney, but we should be able to work together if you control your thoughts about me," I said, leaving abruptly.

I went to the dressing room to join Ginger. We went over notes that I wanted her to give to the cast since I felt it was her show now. I would come in for critique only if I had some big ideas. I was beginning to believe that the way I directed the play had given the cast the freedom and incentive to grow on their own creative drive.

We talked about the cast party at Barney's and the evening we had dinner together. I left to go home, shower, and dress for the performance. Mom called me in as soon as I arrived. She handed me a package that had arrived in the afternoon from New York. I opened it to find a beautiful tan suede sport coat from Brooks Brothers from Claire. It fit me perfectly.

"How did she get this so right?"

"Well, Tim, I gave her your measurements. Do you remember when I measured you for that shirt I made you? She asked for your size before she got you that barn coat and I gave her your sleeve lengths, too. It is a gorgeous jacket."

"Yes, it is. Claire's presence does go on."

Before I went out to my place, Marilee called to ask if I wanted to come over for steaks on the grill. I accepted, cleaned up, and got there in thirty minutes wearing my new jacket.

Marilee's first words were. "It looks even better than in the picture. I'm glad it arrived. She found it in one of my catalogues and couldn't resist it. Come here, Tim, let me hug you. We haven't seen you in a couple of weeks."

Daniel called from out back, "Get out here, brother, and have a drink with me."

Marilee and I joined him, she with her arm around me.

"We've missed you, Tim," Daniel said as he hugged me, "When I've finished getting the coals ready here I want to show you my latest painting. I walked away from it only an hour ago."

Marilee mixed me a Bourbon and soda and poured herself a Martini.

"How are you holding up, Timmy? I'm sure that jacket brings it all back."

"I didn't need this great jacket to bring it all back. That happens every morning and in a very nice manner. I miss her. She's written me, and I hope soon I'll be able to write her. She's going to arrange a post office box or something. You know this jacket, Jeordie's camera, and all the other gifts are all rather extravagant. How is she able to do that?"

"Don't give it a thought. Believe me, she's able to do it."

"Uh...alright, I'll accept that, but..."

"But nothing. Don't worry about it, Timmy."

"'Nuff said, almost sister-in-law."

"Let's go out to the studio, folks." Daniel gestured for us to follow him.

His new painting was large and both pastoral and figurative, using the brilliant colors of "Flood Zone" and the other recent works. It was much more sensual than any other of his figurative pieces because the women were nude and seemed to be wood nymphs. I thought it was absolutely magnificent. I couldn't say anything for a few minutes.

Finally, "You know, Daniel, I've always liked every thing you've done but this one is…well, exciting. I can't think of any other words. Of course, it's beautiful, but much more than that. Watching it, the figures seem to come alive. It's almost scary…in a good way."

"I think so, too, Timmy. If you've wondered where I've been for the last couple of weeks, it's been out here posing. The women are not quite me, but they are. Do you recognize any other faces?"

I looked closer. "My God, that's Claire in a way, and…a younger version of Mom. I hope you don't plan to sell this one."

"I don't believe Marilee would let me. She wants it right here in the house, but I don't know where yet."

"No, he's not going to sell it. I'm thinking it could go in the library over the fireplace. It would mean taking down another favorite of mine of his from a couple of years ago, but that one can go in the bedroom on the same wall as that fresco portrait he did of me."

"I think the fresco should come downstairs to the den, sweetheart."

"I agree, Daniel. Marilee, that portrait makes you look like a renaissance princess in the style of Botticelli."

"Mom hasn't seen this one yet, but I think she will like being young again."

"No doubt. Daniel, this is a truly a big-time painting. What next?"

"Well, I'm going to try a variation of this one that's not so personal."

"It seems the way your work is going now, a variation will be another big step, big brother."

"Does this mean I'll need to pose some more, Daniel?" Marilee teased.

"I hope so. Looking at you is one of the great joys of my existence."

"My word. Do you think he likes me, Timmy," She asked archly.

"He's kind of given me that impression over the last few years."

"Have I? It must have been an unconscious intention."

"You Sart men are getting silly. Let's go back out, have another drink, and eat… eventually. What say?"

I had a hard time pulling away from the painting. I requested a lighter drink, knowing I would get to the theatre some time this evening. I didn't need to be there for the curtain but wanted to see the dance sequence.

As Daniel was serving the steaks Marilee said, "I've receive a couple of letters from Claire. She told me she had written you and about what was going on with her family's plans for her. She isn't happy at all about the prospects; and I don't blame her. I understand tradition and all, but a forced marriage is more than I can accept, especially for someone I care for as much as I do her."

"Well, there appears there's nothing that can be done about it. Oh, hell, the thought of it literally tears my soul apart, but I…can't think about it too much. It's bad enough missing her the way I do with no hope."

"There's always hope, Timmy."

"A pretty damn slim bit of hope. It sounds like her family is moving rather quickly towards selling her off."

"Yes, it does. I know her parents very well and this is a side of them that surprises me, but then I'm not Orthodox Jewish."

"It looks like she got that job at the L.A. museum. The letter I got this week was a sad one concerning the family situation, she sounded happy about the job. She believes that may give her some independence."

"Well, we all miss and love her. There's not much more that can be said about it. Timmy, I thought the articles in the paper were terrific, didn't you?"

"They sure have helped the show and I'm glad Rosenfield made his piece bout the family. Mom and Dad were thrilled. That was a neat picture of you and Mom, Daniel."

"I was surprised at how well it turned out, but you were the star."

"I'm not sure star is the right word. I'm a bit embarrassed by the attention."

"No one deserves it more than you, Timmy. Oh, by the way, Daniel and I are going to Taos in a month or so, and after that New York. We need someone to take care of the house. Could you stay here for several weeks?"

"You bet. That would be a nice step up in lifestyle. Thank you, of course, I will."

"I'll leave a substantial house budget, and you can use the Packard anytime you wish. We're driving the station wagon out there. I didn't believe you'd mind, and we'll feel much more secure about the house with you here."

"Your lifestyle needs a step up, brother. I would think your little room is getting a bit cramped."

"Yes, it is, and thank you both for the trust."

"Timmy, please, you are family. There's room for you here even after we come back. What's happening with the fulltime situation at the theatre?"

"It looks like it's going to happen, but I don't know for sure yet. I wish there was another option, that is not staying in Dallas…forever."

Daniel was alarmed by this. "What did you have in mind? Aren't things going well there?"

"I don't have anything in mind really, and everything's alright at the theatre. I shouldn't have said that."

"I don't believe you will stay in Dallas forever, Timmy. *Blood Wedding* will probably give you opportunities you can't envision yet.

"I think it's going to take more than this play."

"Are you still writing your journal about the directing experience?" Daniel asked.

"Yes, I try to every night. It was hard for the first week after Claire left but I've been back at it for two weeks. It's actually more than a journal now. It's turning into a book about the way I directed the play and other new ideas on the process. It's well over two hundred and fifty pages now. I don't know what could be done with it, but it has been a good exercise in discipline."

"It sounds you may be a writer and a director, brother."

"Could be, I sure like doing it. Well," I said standing, "I think it's time for me to make an appearance at the theatre. Thanks for the evening and everything else. Dan, the painting is a fine piece of art; I hope it's up when I stay here. And Marilee, I promise to take good care of the house."

"You're most welcome, almost brother-in-law. But we certainly plan to see you many times before we leave."

"Tim, we're coming to the play this weekend and bringing some people. We'll see you then, and if we go somewhere afterwards, we insist you join us."

"Agreed. Good night, dear folks."

I arrived at the theatre for intermission. The lobby and recently opened upstairs patio were filled. Several patrons I knew greeted me. It was an overwhelming whirlwind of attention. Barney entered intent, it seemed, on hugging me. I held up my left hand as a signal to stop and held out my right hand for him to shake. There was a hurt look on his face, but he accepted the new distance between us, and introduced me to new audience members. All made some glowing comment about the show, and some wanted to talk about the future of the theatre. One of the volunteer ushers soon came around ringing the bell for the second act to begin. As I went in, Barney gestured for me to speak with him for a minute.

"Tim, we've raised almost the complete amount for your salary as a permanent director. With the run extended there's no doubt it can be done, and more. I want it to run for a three-year contract. How does that sound?"

"That sounds good as long we understand each other."

"Yes, Tim, I understand what you're saying. I agree. Please trust me."

"I do on theatre matters but beyond that, I'm not sure."

"I'll prove that trust and more."

"If you feel that sure about the position, what will my title be?"

"Does that matter?"

"Yes, I want it to be artistic director. You handle the business, and I'll handle the art."

"I can accept that, but there are a lot of things that we will need to collaborate on."

"Of course. If there's nothing else, I want to go in and see the second act."

"No, that's it."

I enjoyed watching the show more than usual. The marriage party and dance sequences had actually gotten better. Aurora had come up with some variations that made it even more exciting. I was glad I had given her the freedom to do it. She hadn't varied from the style I had set, just enhanced it. The audience applauded the solos by Camila and Aurora and groaned when the Wife ran out on the ramp telling of the runaways. When the second act ended, I ducked backstage and joined the cast. The dressing room was bustling with act change rush. There were waves and greetings from everyone, and Liza kissed me on the cheek. In the Green Room, the first thing I heard was, "El Audaz, bienvenuto." The old actor smiled and bowed laughing."

"Hey, old pal, it's good to hear you've dropped the diminutive."

"Tim, my friend, that ended half way through rehearsal. We all have grown doing the play. I believe the show gets better every performance. Don't you?"

"Sin dudo, amigo."

He laughed and went off to touch up his makeup. Aurora passed by. I touched her arm because she hadn't seen me.

"Oh, Tim, there you are. Eddy told me you were here somewhere. What did you think of the new movements? I wanted to show them to you before the curtain but you weren't here."

"I liked them a lot. I wasn't concerned about seeing them before you put them in. And it was better to see them as a part of the scene."

"This play, and the way you directed it, seems to have given all of us an imagination boost."

"Thank you. All of you affected me the same way. The perfect cast. A director's dream."

"I think so, too. Have you talked to Eddy?"

"No. I saw him as he went out to set up for the last act. We waved, but haven't had a chance to talk. Did he need to?"

"Oh, no, not at all. We're having a great time working together and the other part of our life is great, too. Are you going to stay for the third act?"

"Yes, and looking forward to it."

"Good, we'll see you then. I think the cast really likes your idea of joining the audience after the show."

I spoke to a very busy Ginger for a minute and went out to lobby for the last few minutes before curtain. After the performance, I rejoined the audience, who seemed excited about meeting the cast. Barney had worked out a legal way for us to serve wine after the play if we didn't charge anything, just took donations. The cast came out shortly charged by the standing ovation that had become a part of every performance. Dick Ayers was there to pick up Camila and he joined me, juggling three glasses of wine. Camila soon came up to claim hers, and he handed me the other.

"Great idea Barney had about the wine. I'm sure he's bringing in more than enough to pay for. How have you been?"

"Pretty good. Sorry we haven't a chance to spend any time together."

"Do you have to come to every performance? If not, why don't we go out for dinner tomorrow night? I have to make it back by the end of the show to pick up Camila, so you could, too."

"I'd like that."

"I'll call you at the bookstore for final plans. I hope all of this success hasn't gone to your head," Dick joked. "Although I think some of it should. No need to be the humble, shy director anymore."

"I'll try to keep it in check."

"Camila is loving doing it, and it makes Sunday and Monday nights more special than usual."

Camila had walked off to join Liza, but they soon returned.

Liza surprisingly put her arm in mine and said, "Gentlemen, it's Tuesday night. Let's go up to the patio with more wine."

"Better still, I'll donate enough for a couple of bottles." Dick said as he headed for the wine table.

We laughed and talked for another hour. Liza seemed less distracted, but occasionally stared off for a few seconds. Evidently, she wasn't yet ready to get into what was bothering her.

I got home after midnight, didn't write, didn't read, just went to sleep with an apparition in my arms.

The next night, I joined Dick at the Lakewood Country Club for dinner. His leg was getting better, but was still painful at times. He and Camila were trying to find a school where he could study law and she could finish her medical degree. He thought they would have to go east though he wanted to stay in Texas. It was a great evening with an old friend who probably would be gone soon, as all of the special people in my life were. Dick had asked about Claire, but I found it harder to talk about than usual, perhaps because all of the couples I knew were so happy.

I decided not to go to the theatre, but to go home and write. Seeing the show the night before had given me an impetus for new ideas. I went to sleep reading my Russians.

I went to every show for the rest of the week. Saturday night, I arrived early because I wanted to spend some time alone looking at Claire's drawings. I stopped at her dance sequence group and realized I was crying for the first time since she had left. It was an ongoing shock how much I missed her. The drawings were more beautiful to me than ever. The memory of her and her work must continue to be an inspiration. I was suddenly sorry I had promised Marilee I would be here tonight, but I knew it was for the best; with this surge of emotion, I shouldn't be alone.

After the performance, Marilee introduced me to the people she had brought to the play, all of them prominent Dallasites. She had arranged for a late evening at the Mexican restaurant where we had had the family gathering. She asked if I would mind if Liza was included. I certainly didn't. It would be good to have a friend to escort. During the evening, Marilee and Daniel became primary fundraisers. She talked about setting up an endowment for ongoing expenses and my salary. It was handled in the most persuasive and discreet manner I could have imagined. All of the guests had loved the play and seemed happy to have a cast member and the director with them for the evening, though Liza knew most of them from the Dallas Country Club. After a very successful dinner, Daniel and Marilee drove Liza and me back to our cars at the theatre.

Standing at Liza's car, I asked, "Are you ready to get into it yet?"

"No, not yet, but soon perhaps. Do you really care?"

"Of course, I do! To see that look of total sadness come over your face at times is...well, we are friends. You don't have to tell me anything, I'm just saying if you ever need to talk with someone, God knows, I surely do. I had an encounter with loneliness in the lobby tonight looking at Claire's drawings before the show. I thought I had gotten fairly strong, but it hit me like a ton of bricks."

"It only hits me like that occasionally, mostly it's little flashes of it."

"Yes, well, I get that, too. I enjoyed the evening, Tim. It made it better you being there. Remember, anytime. Perhaps it would be good for both of us."

She smiled, got into her car, and drove off. When I got home and prepared to write, I thought about how strange the evening was. Marilee worked very subtly to help the theatre and my future. I must have answered a thousand questions about the play, the theatre, and my being a fulltime artistic director, which they all appeared to support. And Liza. She was sure going through something extremely difficult but holding on tight. Even so, she was still a charming companion.

I was able to write for an hour, but it was a letter to Claire. I tried not to whine about the loneliness and how much I missed her, but I did write as romantically as I could about the theatre and how her drawings had re-inspired my writing. I tried to describe Daniel's new painting and how she was a part of it, albeit naked, and quite nicely, too. I related the growth in the play, the added night, and the extended run. My coming lifestyle change of moving into Marilee's was almost fun to write about. I ended with a clumsy attempt at writing a poem, quit that, and wrote out Shakespeare's Sonnet 40, which seemed to say the right thing. When I finished, I put the letter with the four other long letters I had written waiting for an address. I went to sleep with her on my mind.

Mom knocking on my door with a cup of coffee awakened me the next morning late. She said they would be eating in about thirty minutes and for me to come join them. I sat up in bed looking at Claire's drawing hung across the room. Jeordie had given me several prints of photos of her I hadn't seen before, and they brought back all of the feelings from the lobby experience. I slowly got up, showered, and shaved. When I arrived, the family was seated around the breakfast table. We talked about my full time position at the theatre and my staying at Marilee's house. Jeordie immediately said he wanted to move into my apartment, but he was disappointed when I informed him it wasn't a permanent situation and that I would surely be coming back home when they returned. Dad asked if I had heard from Claire again and how she was doing. Mom thought the museum job would be great for her and Jeordie, of course, asked when she was coming back. He couldn't believe it when I related her situation. I left out the religious ramifications, fearing his confusion. Dad said he had talked to Uncle Willy this morning. There weren't any races this afternoon, and Uncle Willy wanted to see me at the shop. Rosie was spending the afternoon with her sister in Sherman. She had taken the Interurban train at nine this morning and wouldn't be back until six. I couldn't think of any better way to spend a Sunday than with my favorite uncle.

When I arrived at the shop, Uncle Willy was working on his Auburn. He hugged me, saying it had been too long since we had spent an afternoon together. We went into his office and settled in for good conversation. The expected reminiscences didn't come. He wanted to know how the show was going and if had I heard from Claire. I hadn't had a chance to tell him her situation. His reaction to the matchmaker was almost violent. He stood up and walked around his office, cursing. My marriage proposal almost brought him to tears.

"This calls for a drink, don't you think?"

"It's little early for me, but it sounds good."

"I didn't say let's get drunk, just have a drink. Rosie would kill me if I overdid it."

I laughed at that. He reached into the big drawer in his desk and brought out a bottle of fine Bourbon and a couple of glasses.

"This is a good eighty proof, so it won't hit us hard at all, especially with a good dollop of water."

He had a water dispenser with a big bottle upside down on top of it. The Bourbon was good and immediately relaxed his anger over Claire's dilemma.

"I know she said she was leaving, but I hoped she would change her mind or at least return after awhile. Her family must really be old-country Jews. I know her father is one of the best petroleum engineers around and had studied at A&M, so this tradition they follow is a surprise. What does Claire think about it?"

"She doesn't like it but feels she has no choice."

"Of course she does-just not do it."

"She says it would shame her parents, and that if she had stayed here or came back to me, they would disown her. They're a close family with a lot of love and support. I don't believe she could stand their total rejection. Yes, it's hard to believe, but it's true, and she's gone. I miss her, and she misses me. Everyone says there's hope, but I don't think so. It was so good being with her that it's difficult to comprehend her not being here."

"It must be. It was pretty obvious that night at the house that she loves you. She must be having a hard time, too."

"She is. Her letters are evidence of that."

"Are you able to write her?"

"Not yet. But she should have a post office box this next week."

"Well, that's good, don't you think?"

"Yep."

"When you write her, send our love."

"Of course I will. You and Rosie are very special to her, but then the whole family is."

"I think there is hope, there always is. You remember my telling you about the Russian girl in China? Well, that was a no-hope thing, but yours is not. Go on with your life, but don't give up."

"I'm not going to, at least not for a long time. I guess if she was in an arranged marriage, that would be the end."

"Probably, but it hasn't happened yet, so maybe it won't. Tell me what else is happening with you. I saw in the paper that your play added extra nights and the run has been extended. That's certainly a big approval of you work. Oh, I thought the articles in the paper were terrific! It was funny to be mentioned as a part of a family of artists."

"It seems to be the beginning of acceptance into artistic circles here. I liked the family one best; the other one was too much me."

"No, it wasn't too much you. I didn't think it was enough. That play of yours was the best, by far, of anything you've done. Rosie even says she wants to see it again. Do you think you could get us tickets in three or four weeks?"

"Done, and they'll be complimentary. It looks like I'll soon have a fulltime job at the theatre with a big salary jump."

"Now that's good news, Tim. It doesn't make up for Claire, but it's a start."

"I suppose. How is your work on the Auburn going?"

"Slow but steady. It's not a moneymaking project so it has low priority. Come on, I'll show what's going on with it."

We went out to the shop. The Auburn was a beautiful convertible coupe in need of some bodywork and a paint job. The engine had been taken out and was up on a workbench.

"I'm not sure yet about the engine. I think I'll forget about overhauling it and put something else in it. It's going to take something big and strong to power it, I'm leaning towards a Cadillac V8 that I could modify. But it is a beauty, isn't it?"

"It sure is. Is it going to be Rosie's or yours?"

"Hers, she loves it. For me, my next project is that sports roadster in the European fashion, but all American. But I think my in-between project will be your car. When can I have it for at least two weeks?"

"I'm going to be staying at Marilee's house while they go to Taos and then New York, and I'll have the use of her Packard. It'll be in a month or less from now. Would that be a good time? And by the way, what are going to do to my car?"

"The Packard, huh? After that, you may not want to go back to your Ford, no matter what I do."

"I don't think so. I'm sure I'll feel pretty pretentious driving her car, and besides I love my car."

"I'll do a whole bunch of stuff: brakes, suspension, and a new engine that'll be more powerful and dependable. And I'd like to do some bodywork I want to try. You'll like it. Consider it a present for your good work at the theatre."

"Whatever you think, Uncle. It sounds great."

"Good, let's go back in the office."

We had another light Bourbon and talked about his coming fatherhood and how excited he was about it.

"Rosie gets more beautiful every day, which I didn't think was possible. And she feels pretty good, too, no real sickness now, but growing fast. She's going to keep working right up to the time for the baby. I'm trying to change her mind about that."

I left late in the afternoon, allowing Uncle Willy to get to the station in plenty of time. I got home to Mom's announcement that she had fixed lamb curry. She knew that would cheer me up, and it did. After dinner, Mom asked if I would like to go to a movie with them. She wanted to see the new Fred Astaire at the Majestic. Jeordie wasn't disappointed he couldn't go because he wanted to work in his darkroom and then had homework to do. The film turned out to be more fun than I expected, and we went for ice cream afterwards. Back home, I settled in for the night and started writing, having a glass of the Spanish Brandy. Just before midnight, there was a gentle knock at my door and I opened it to Liza Farquar.

"Hi, Tim. Have I come too late? I feel a great need to talk to someone."

"No it's not too late, and never would be. Please come in. This is a surprise but a good one."

She had a bag with her. She opened it, taking out a bottle of Bourbon, a spritzer bottle, and some chopped ice wrapped in wax paper.

"At home, I had decided to have a drink, but thought it wouldn't be good to drink alone. Will you join me?"

"Yes, I will. I just had a little brandy, but a bourbon would be good. I couldn't have slept anyway. You too?"

"No, I haven't been able to sleep much at all for a couple of weeks."

"It sure hasn't shown in your work on stage."

"I know, I'm able to forget about, or not think about...well, things."

"What things?"

"Are you sure you want to know?"

"Do you want to tell me what's going on? Didn't you come because you know you can trust me?"

"Yes, but let's have drink first. Alright?"

I nodded and she fixed us two rather stiff drinks. I really only had one comfortable chair so I told her to sit up on the bed and I'd take the chair. We sat quietly for a few minutes."

"Tim, are you missing Claire?"

"More than I ever thought possible to miss someone. She is with me every waking moment and then I dream about her."

"Do you believe you'll see her again?"

"I don't know."

"Why did she leave when she was so obviously in love with you?"

I told her the whole story. She listened with an almost tearful expression.

"I almost understand. My mother was Jewish, and it evidently caused a lot of trouble for her when she married my father. But my grandparents weren't Orthodox, and when my parents had my older sister, then me, all was forgiven. They were wonderful grandparents. I didn't even know they were Jewish until my mother told me when I was about ten or twelve and it didn't mean much to me. My parents had joined the Highland Park Presbyterian, and I was much into Sunday school."

"It's good your mother didn't have to go through what Claire is. Now you tell me."

"This will be hard, but here goes. You know that my husband is in Java working a drilling operation and has been for a year and a half. Well, two weeks ago I got a telegram from him saying he was staying for another year. A week and a half later, I got another letter from him. He told me his staying would give him enough money to start his own business when he gets back. He's gotten very interested in something called sysmagraphology and wants to eventually move to Tulsa. This, of course, was all new to me. He had promised he would stay no longer than the first year. Then there was the six-month extension, now another year. Two years ago, I wanted to start a family. Well, here I am waiting for him, and waiting. It was just a shock, not a surprise, but a shock. At times, I think he'll never come back. Maybe he's fallen in love with living in the Far East. I don't know what to think. He says I can't go there because it's too rough. Hell, I was a Girl Scout, I went to camp, all that stuff, and it's too rough for me there? Well, it's getting pretty rough here. Maybe he has a beautiful native girl who wears a sarong around all day and takes care of him...in every way. That's why I've seemed a bit distracted."

"Damn, no wonder you've been...well, I didn't know what you were feeling... sadness, some family tragedy, serious loneliness or...I guess it's kind of all that. Boy, aren't we a pair? Have you heard the stories of the Penitentes in Mexico? They parade through the streets covered in robes and whip themselves until their backs are bloody. Maybe we should do that."

Liza threw her head back and laughed.

"Tim, I thought it would be good to talk with you, but I didn't know you would make me laugh."

"Laugh, Hell! I'm serious." Then I was able to laugh for the first time in several weeks. "Let me fix us a drink" I said.

"You know, I think I felt I could talk with you because I knew that you were suffering about Claire. And I didn't want any comforting words, just talk. My lady friends would ooh and aah, saying poor baby, poor girl. My minister at the church would tell me to pray and be strong."

"I know what you mean. Everyone tells me to be strong, though no one has told me to pray yet. But I guess we all do though, even if unconsciously, that we wish everything will be alright...you know, please let them come back to us now or please let me stop being so sad."

She laughed again, "Yes, exactly."

We talked another hour about everything-the play, her acting, my writing, my job at the theatre.

As we both begin to fade, Liza asked, "Tim, I don't think I'm in any shape to drive home. Can I stay here with you? I don't mean anything intimate, just sleep next to someone."

I wasn't taken aback at all, "Of course you may. I would much prefer that to a whipping."

She got up and hugged me, "Me, too."

We turned out the lights, pulled down the covers, stripped down to our underwear, and got in bed. She put her head on my shoulder.

"Thank you, Tim."

"You're most welcome, and thank you, Liza."

There was nothing really erotic or sexy about it just two lonely folks needing to be with someone. Liza and I became very close friends. I became her escort and she my casual date when we needed. She began coming over several times a week, and we would spend the night talking, then go to sleep in each other's arms.

One night, Liza took off all of her clothes before crawling in beside me. She moved over beside me, put her hand on my chest, and kissed my cheek.

"Liza? What...?"

"Tim, if I'm making you uncomfortable, I'll stop."

"I don't know what you expect...but..."

She moved her hand down to touch me, and I felt nothing. I knew she couldn't arouse me, though she kept trying. Nothing.

"Is it me, Tim?"

"No, of course not, you're a beautiful, desirable woman, it's just that..."

"Claire?"

"Yes, I think it will be a long time before..."

"Please don't be upset with me. I've been lonely a lot longer that you have and you are a most desirable man. You must have known that I had feelings for you."

"Yes, but not like that. You could have any man you want...I mean."

"I don't know about that, but this has more to do with me wanting to be very close with someone I care about."

"I...I'm deeply complimented, but..."

"Do you mind if I don't give up, trying to seduce you?"

I laughed, "Liza, can you imagine how many men would give a year of their life to have you say that to them."

"Well, do you mind?"

"No, but don't expect me to..."

"Tim, do you want me to go home?"

"No, I do not. It's very nice to hold a beautiful woman. Put your head on my shoulder and sleep sweetly in my arms."

She didn't stop her attempts in nights that followed.

A week later, I received a letter from Claire. She gave me a post office box, close to her new job at the museum. Her letter was loving, sad, and sweet. She was evidently going through the same thing as I. Her new job was challenging and exciting, but she missed me terribly, pledging undying love. I finished the letter I had been working on, placing it with others I had written plus copies of the newspaper articles. It was an enormous relief to be able to write to her, but in a way it was like writing to a ghost.

At the Saturday performance after the show, a man introduced himself to me as Dr. John Miller the Chairman of the Speech and Drama Department at the University of New Mexico. A friend of his in Dallas had seen the show and sent him the reviews and articles. Out of professional curiosity, he had come to Dallas to see for himself.

He asked if we could sit down and talk. The production had impressed him a great deal, and he asked if I would be interested in coming this summer to Albuquerque, then Santa Fe to direct a production of Lorca's *Yerma*. Evidently, the person scheduled to direct it had gotten ill and had to pull out. I was stunned by the offer but explained that I didn't have a college degree and had never directed outside of Dallas. That didn't seem to bother him, and he expressed his feeling that my production was an exceptional rendition and interpretation. He had only heard of *Yerma* and only recently gotten the rights to produce it. I asked if there was a chance to be paid, as I had nothing to fall back on except a rather small savings account.

"Yes, there will be a nominal weekly salary and room and board provided. Have you done any writing about the process you used?"

I described my journal and how it had reached almost two hundred and seventy five pages.

"Would you consider pulling it together into book form to see if it's appropriate for publication by the University Press?"

"Yes."

"If you would like to consider getting a degree, I'm pretty sure I could get you a full scholarship. Mr. Sart..."

"Tim, please."

"Tim, I don't think there's any doubt that you are a special talent, I would be very happy for you to join us in New Mexico."

"This is rather sudden. I'm...well, complimented. Do you need a commitment right now?"

"Only a tentative agreement to come out and direct in the latter part of July and through August. The production date is set for the first week in September. That would give you a chance to consider the other things, publication, and a scholarship."

"More than a tentative yes, I would be most happy to come out and do another Lorca. How soon could you get me a script?"

"Within two weeks and I'll send a contract for the direction fee."

"Excellent! This couldn't have happened at a better time. Thank you, Dr. Miller."

"John, please. Tim, I must rush to catch my ride to the hotel, and I have an early train in the morning. Will you be coming alone?"

"Yes, I'm certainly alone. And I'll get to work on my journal immediately."

He nodded, smiled, and was gone. I stood there, almost unable to move, then looked for Liza. I didn't have to look because she found me.

"Tim, what's happened? You're grinning from ear to ear."

"I'm going over to Marilee's for a late drink. Will you join me? I will tell you there."

"Yes, I'm dying to know what it is. I'll meet you there."

Over the past weeks, Marilee's house had become a second home. I had spent some of the most important hours of my recent life there, especially with Claire. Their support for me and Claire and their belief in my work had given me a closer relationship with them. Daniel and I had taken our brotherhood to a new level, and Marilee was like a sister to me. And they just kept giving. Their message for me at the theatre was a welcome release from loneliness.

Liza drove up behind me, and we went to the door together. Marilee greeted us welcoming Liza as a happy addition to the evening. They had been friends for several years, having met in high school at Hockaday.

"Daniel, two of the loneliest people in town are here," Marilee yelled. "Yes, Timmy, Liza finally broke down this week and told me about her situation. I even told her I most heartily approved of you two being friends after she confessed about your evenings together. Nothing wrong with a good platonic relationship to get you through hard times."

Daniel joined us, "Hello brother, and Liza, you're a pleasant surprise. It's a beautiful night, let's go outside."

"Great, it's good to see you two." Liza smiled. "Thanks for the welcome. Tim found me after the show grinning like a fool. He said he would tell me what that was about if I joined him here."

"My goodness, Tim! Only something very special would make you smile like that. Come on, let's have an evening toddy and hear whatever good news you have." Daniel said as he put his arm around my shoulder.

Liza and I sat at the table by the pool as Marilee lighted candles and Daniel asked what our pleasure would be.

"I know Tim wants a Bourbon. Liza?

"The same, with soda."

"Well, Timmy, there's something in common," Marilee noted.

When we all settled in, I told them about the meeting with Dr. Miller and my acceptance of the directing job and the possible scholarship along with a potential book-publishing offer.

"Timmy, Timmy, Timmy, this is wonderful! I knew *Blood Wedding* would change your life," cheered Marilee.

Daniel reached across the table to shake my hand in congratulations. "A directing job and a book! Do you think you'll take the scholarship if offered?"

"I don't know. I guess it depends on how well the play turns out and if I want to stay there since it's pretty much for sure I have a permanent job here at the theatre."

"Tim, you can always come back to the theatre. This may be too good to turn down. I couldn't be happier for you," Liza added in support.

"What play is it, Timmy?"

"A Lorca named *Yerma*, Dr. Miller seems to believe I have a way with Lorca."

"When would you go out, brother?"

"The last week in July. The opening would be during the first week in September."

"That gives you almost two months at 'The Finca' in Taos. You could study and write."

"I hadn't thought of that, Marilee. Won't you two be there at the same time?"

"Perhaps, but only for part of the first month. I've been painting up a storm. I should have enough canvases for New York before long. I think ten or twelve should be fine."

"Oh, we're leaving next week," Marilee said. "Can you move in here then?"

"Absolutely! I'm looking forward to it. Uncle Willy said he wanted to work on my car for a couple of weeks. Do you mind if I use the Packard that much, Marilee?"

"No I don't, use it, and I want you to charge the gas to me at the station in Snyder Plaza."

"Not necessary, but thank you."

"Do what she says, brother, and enjoy the car, it's a dream to drive."

I laughed, holding up my hands in surrender. We all had one more drink. Liza seemed to be especially happy for me, knowing it would help to bring me out of the doldrums. When I walked her out to her car, she hugged me and kissed me on the cheek.

"Tim, everyone in the cast knew something very good would happen for you. You were amazing. We all adore you."

"That's a little much, but thank you." She drove off and I went home to write a letter to Claire, telling her about New Mexico.

Chapter 15
Antes Del Viaje

After the show was under way, I thought life would settle down into a slow passing of the days, but it didn't turn out that way. I worked more hours at the bookstore for extra money, spent the evenings at the theatre, wrote as much as I possibly could, trying to finish the journal and decide how to turn it into a book about directing. I wasn't seeing Marilee and Daniel as often as before, but at least two or three times a week. I wasn't looking forward to them leaving but happily anticipated staying at their house. Seeing Liza was turning into a real pleasure. She was charming and fun to spend the time with. She had me over to her house every week for dinner, drinks, and good conversation. We tried to stay away from discussing Claire, her husband, and her gentle, continuing seduction attempts.

Claire's letters were a godsend. They seemed to ease the loneliness and to keep up the hopes for our being together again, even though they didn't imply anything of the sort. She loved her new job and was, in a way, getting used to Los Angeles. She missed the intimacy of Dallas and my family, especially Marilee and Daniel. There didn't appear to be any new women friends to replace her closeness with Marilee. They had been writing each other, but she longed for the real conversations they had had every day. I felt no distancing in her words because of the expressed passion for us. We didn't need to write of sensual delights but caring words of emotional needs that had been so completely satisfied between us. I felt that she was even lonelier than I was because I had the theatre, all of my family, and Liza. She did write of her meetings with the matchmaker, and how disorienting it was to discuss finding other men because she was so much in love with me. Some of the letters were long descriptions of her day's activities from morning to night and others were short notes of love written just before she went to bed. I was writing her three times a week, staying up late into the night filling pages with my love for her. Her reaction to the New Mexico directing job was that she wasn't surprised by my success at all because she expected something good to happen for me, but that she wished she could share it with me. My writing was what she wanted me to concentrate on the most. She believed the education possibilities were a deserved lagniappe.

One morning, my mother presented me with a notice about a package waiting for me at the post office. On my lunch break, I picked it up. It was fairly large, heavy, and from Claire. I opened it in my car to find a very good Smith-Corona typewriter. In one of my discussions with her about my high school experience, I had mentioned taking typing in a class filled with girls. I was thrilled by the machine and surprised she had remembered it. That night I put it to work transcribing my journal and trying to change it into a book. The extravagance of this gift was, I knew, beyond what she earned at the museum. I guessed her father's success was a satisfactory explanation but I was sure he didn't know what she was spending her allowance on. My fear was that he would find out about her boyfriend in Texas, and that it would cause problems for her.

Barney had somehow gotten wind of my New Mexico offer. He called me at work, wanting to meet with me to discuss it. I sensed a fear in him that I was going to desert the theatre and not take the artistic director's position. I had held off telling him until I was sure about my going to New Mexico. We met in his office, and he was very nervous about my reaction to having any important conversation with him after the episode at his apartment, especially since I had been steering clear of any closed-door meetings. He started off with a hope that we could still collaborate closely, and he again apologized for his actions that night. I assured him that everything was fine and that I had almost forgotten about it equating it to drunken error in judgment on his part. He said the money should be available for my position at the end of the summer or early fall and asked what my plans were concerning New Mexico. I minced no words, stating my commitment to direct *Yerma* in Albuquerque and that it would be completed in September. I didn't mention the scholarship or book because one wasn't offered yet and the other could be done no matter where I was. He thought it would be important for me to sign a letter of intent about the artistic director position because the patrons pledging the endowment needed to feel secure about my willingness to stay at the theatre. My answer was they should trust my future decisions and no matter what happened, the endowment would be good for the theatre and I wouldn't sign anything until the money was there. I knew those potential grantors were aware my family was here and that I felt a deep commitment to the success of the theatre. I thought I would return to Dallas even if the New Mexico experience lasted several years. The idea of coming back a couple times a year to direct was certainly a possibility, though I didn't believe Barney needed to hear that. The meeting ended with Barney feeling fairly secure about me, but disappointed he would have to find a director for the second summer production. There was no doubt it would take awhile for our relationship to get back to where it was before.

As the regular run of *Blood Wedding* ended and the extended run started, I moved to Marilee's house, borrowing Dad's station wagon to carry my things. I had spent the evening before with Daniel and Marilee getting all of the house and swimming pool instructions, keys, fuse box location, and having a fine dinner with them. We discussed their Taos and New York plans and Marilee told me she had received a long, sad letter from Claire. It seemed the matchmaker situation was getting more serious in that she was having to meet men to see if they approved of each other. Claire hadn't told me about this, I was sure in an effort not to hurt me. It was not something I wanted to hear but Marilee wanted me to know what Claire was going through. Actually, I wasn't too surprised because I had known it was coming, but that didn't ease my pain for her. Marilee insisted this wasn't the end and not to give up hope.

"I shan't do that, but it's getting difficult to keep it up."

"Tim, old pal and brother, you know the stay here and New Mexico will hopefully give you a new outlook and possibly some opportunities lady-wise."

"I'm not sure I'm ready for those kinds of opportunities yet."

"That's right now, and you will be ready eventually, I guar-ran-tee."

"If you're that sure, you may be right, Dan."

"He is right, Timmy. And Claire is not married to anyone yet. Actually, your life is rather exciting now. Don't you think?"

"Yes, it is. There's a big minus, but it's really pretty good. Having a friend like Liza helps."

"I know, for a fact, she feels the same way. You two have helped each other when the need was high, Marilee added.

I left them, knowing I would see them in the morning before they left.

When I drove up the next morning, they were finishing loading of their Chrysler wood-flanked wagon. Dan stopped to help me as Marilee finished her part of the work.

"How far are you planning to go today?" I asked Daniel.

"We're in no real hurry. Since we're taking the highway to Sweetwater, then Abilene and Lubbock, I think we'll be lucky to get to Sweetwater."

"Are you going through Clovis or up to Amarillo?"

"Clovis, we both think it's a prettier drive from there up to Santa Fe. We've agreed to skip Albuquerque."

"Well, I'm right behind you, in a few weeks."

"You better be, brother, it'll be good to have at least a week together in Taos."

"I'm taking my car over to Uncle Willy's later this afternoon, then having dinner at their house. I have no idea what he's going to do to it, but he wants to change it into something more so, as he says."

"We saw them a couple of nights ago. Rosie looks great and is starting to show. Uncle Willy is already beginning to act like a proud father. You know, I don't believe we could have asked for a sweeter family."

"Did you have a chance to see Mom and Dad?"

"Yes, last weekend. We spent Sunday afternoon with them. Mom is painting some fine canvases. Dad being a finalist in that New York chair design contest has really lifted his spirits."

"It sure has. He kind of floats around the house on a cloud."

When Daniel and I finished with my heavy stuff, which was just four boxes, they were ready to leave. We hugged and kissed and Marilee handed me an envelope.

"Open this after we leave, Timmy. It should help now and then get you to Taos."

As they drove out the gate, I waved and then opened the envelope. It contained fifteen hundred dollars. I had never held that much money in my hands before. There was a note in it that said she had hit a new well in Oklahoma last week and she wanted to share the profits with the family. This was the first payment of hopefully many. Marilee's giving never seemed to stop. Later that day, Uncle Willy told me about his gift from Marilee, twice what mine was, as was appropriate.

Not long after Uncle Willy drove me back home in the early evening, Liza knocked at the door.

I had forgotten that I had invited her over for an evening swim. She hadn't said that she would, so it was a happy surprise. We went out to the pool patio, and I mixed us drinks. I wasn't worried about the lateness because I had Monday off to get settled into the new living arrangements. We talked for awhile then she went into the cabana to change into the bathing suit she had brought with her. When she came out shortly in a two piece, I was astonished by her beauty. She had a figure like one of the paintings of women in <u>Esquire</u> magazine.

Liza laughed, "You're staring, Tim."

"Sorry, well...you are rather statuesque."

"Thank you, I think."

I went to change, still taken aback by Liza. I wasn't having erotic thoughts about her, just admiring her feminine beauty. She was in the water as I walked out.

"Well, look at you, handsome man. You're pretty statuesque yourself."

"I think squatty would be a better description." She laughed her uninhibited laughter, which was always an unexpected surprise from such a classy lady.

I fixed us another drink and set them beside the pool. I eased into the delightfully warm water. It was a cool spring evening so a light steam was rising from the water.

"Marilee told me about the pool heater," Liza said "and I've wanted to try it ever since. I love it."

"I do too, but when the real summer hits it goes off. Now it's as relaxing as one could hope for after a long day. The drinks aren't bad either."

"Did you get moved in completely?"

"I think so. I'm sure I forgot something, but nothing essential. How was your day? I was surprised you decided to come over."

"It was terrible. I got a letter today that didn't help. My husband says he's working hard but enjoying the life there. He goes into town twice a week and says the nightlife there is great. Exotic, different, but exciting. That was good to hear. Another year of exotic, different, and exciting."

"Try not to make too much out of it. He's probably leading a very pure life."

"Perhaps, but...hmmm. I don't know. My life here certainly isn't exotic, different, and exciting. Well that's not completely true, our friendship is different and sometimes kind of exciting and, of course the play."

"Tim Sart, different and sometimes kind of exciting. I was hoping to be a bit exotic, but then this is Dallas." I said in an almost silly way.

"Tim, you're an exciting man all the time. I meant that I'm not used to having a good close relationship with a man that I'm not...uh...involved with."

"I'll accept that. My involvements have been limited. Claire is by far the most involved I've ever been."

"Before *Blood Wedding,* you were thought of as kind of a loner except for that fiery actress last year."

"That experience turned me into a loner."

"I know you miss Claire desperately, but you can't let that keep you from enjoying all of the good things that are happening for you. You're a very special man who shouldn't be alone or without a loving relationship. Don't get bitter or resentful over the loss of Claire. The letters you're exchanging cannot replace real life. So how is she doing?

"She seems to be handling it fairly well. She does love me, but knows there's little hope for us with the plans her family has made for her. The matchmaker situation is getting more serious and it's hard for her, but has accepted that it is to be her life. I certainly don't beg her to come back because I know it would make it harder on her. I do assure her of my feelings and that they will continue, but the whole thing about the Jewish tradition is incomprehensible. At this point, I think it's cruel and almost primitive in the modern world. But I guess there are worse traditions, though they haven't affected me like this one has. One would hope that her parents could accept our love, but that is evidently not to be."

"Well, that sure does answer my question. I've been experiencing a year and a half of letter love, so I know it's hard. In no way does it replace the real thing. I miss my husband but in a different way than I did for the first year. He's far away and the letters are few. I'm more than lonely...I want...well, I think you understand."

"Uh...yes, I do."

"Tim, it's time for me to go home. Will you walk me to my car?"

I nodded, and we both climbed out. She came to me.

"I'm sorry, Tim. I don't want to spook you, this is such a sweet thing between us."

I laughed and said, "Come here, girl, you don't spook me."

I hugged her and kissed her forehead. Barefoot, we were exactly the same height. I walked her to the car.

"Thank you, Tim, for being...you." And she was gone.

I went upstairs to my new quarters. I had decided not to sleep in the main bedroom but in the one that Claire had slept in and the first place we had made love. I yearned for Claire as if she had left yesterday. Before sleeping, I wondered about the evening with Liza. I was quite sure I knew what she had meant about wanting. She was an extremely attractive woman, but only a friend, actually more than that. I guess what I wasn't sure about was whether she was really attracted to me or just very lonely and needful of physical love.

I spent Monday arranging the room and getting used to the house. I hung Claire's drawings in my bedroom and put out the pictures of her. I cooked and wrote. The new typewriter had proved to be a great help. I also made carbon copies of everything I did. I went swimming in the afternoon and grilled a steak for dinner. I called home to see if there was any mail for me, and there was. I drove the Packard for the first time to pick up the letter. Mom and Dad said they missed me and that Jeordie had moved into my apartment. After I knew I was going to New Mexico, he had persuaded me to let him use it.

When I got back to Marilee's, I went to the den and opened the letter. It was tear-soaked with loneliness for me. The matchmaker had found several men that Clair's family had approved of. It was moving too fast for me and Claire to deal with. I couldn't believe they were so desperate for her to get married. Perhaps they were afraid of the openness of America, and this was a way of protecting her from it. It sure appeared to be making her miserable, but maybe she wasn't revealing that to them, just being the dutiful daughter. The image came to me that it was like watching someone you love being sold into slavery. But perhaps it wouldn't be that bad for her. The man chosen could turn out to be a good person and loving enough to help her forget about me. It would take someone awfully powerful to get me to forget about her.

The run of the show had been extended for three weeks, and it looked like three more could be added. This meant I needed to be at the theatre for almost every performance. I was amazed at how many of the ticket holders wanted to talk to me after the show. Having the cast come out to join the audience after curtain had become very popular; every evening was a celebration. Barney even made a profit on the "free" wine. Eddy enjoyed it so much that he played in the lobby or out on the second floor patio. People started coming who hadn't even seen the play that night to enjoy its success and be with the cast again. Word of mouth had given us the most successful production in the theatre's history. I had slowly become acclimated to being a favorite of the patrons and each evening's audience. My shyness was being worn away. The most asked question, was whether I was going to stay with the theatre and if I had come up with anything to follow *Blood Wedding*. There was no real answer to either question, so I got very adept at just talking about the continuity of the theatre with donations and about the many plays I was interested in, especially musicals like *The Three Penny Opera*. Several patrons had heard about my desire to do a Somerset Maugham play, and they were excited about the prospect of a stage adaptation of Rain, which was one of my favorite stories of his, but a stage version would be difficult. I still leaned toward *The Constant Wife*. All of this was more just theatre talk than a reality of my future, which was very much up in the air.

After receiving the copy of *Yerma,* I immediately went to work on it. It was a terrific Lorca and with the right cast, it could be an exciting directing project. Dr. Miller had written saying he thought I could cast the play to my complete satisfaction, but that really didn't make much difference because I was going to do it and try out the methods I had used with *Blood Wedding*.

One of the most difficult encounters was with Mr. Franklin at the bookstore, but he was very supportive and thought the New Mexico adventure would be the start of a good theatre career. He was disappointed I was leaving the store but he knew it was coming because I had hinted at the possibility of a permanent position at the theatre. He surprised me with the offer of two weeks pay without working before I went to Taos. That was a month away so I would have two weeks free before leaving. Other than loneliness, things were going great and fast.

I decided to use the house every weekend as a cast party location. The actors and crew brought their own drinks, and the ladies prepared a big buffet on two Sunday afternoons. Marilee had suggested doing this before she left and though I had doubts, it turned into an ongoing reward for the cast. The neighbors didn't even complain about two late-night swimming parties.

In the third week of June, I received a letter from Claire. The matchmaker had found a potential husband for her that the parents approved of. It was more than a sad letter; it was desperate and fearful. He was a very wealthy man, in his thirties in the film industry. He was tall, dark, and he gave her that look "what a strange young woman" look that Claire had mentioned to me. She did not approve, but felt it could have been worse and there was going to be a six-to nine-month get-acquainted period.

The letter was a shock. And all hope seemed to disappear, but Claire insisted that we stay in touch because anything could happen. Of course, I wanted to keep writing her and hearing from her, but the idea of hearing descriptions of the developing relationship was not appealing. If anything, the new event helped her to realize how good it was between us, but to no avail. My sadness at her leaving was nothing to what I felt after reading this letter. I had believed that her family would change their minds and let us be together, but now that hope was smashed and I spent two days alone. I wasn't able to write and didn't go to the theatre. I sat around the pool, sometimes crying, sometimes drinking too much. I was leaving for Taos in a week and a half, so my work at the bookstore was finished.

Friday afternoon, the week before the show was to close, Liza called me to ask where I had been and what was going on. I told her I had received a letter from Claire that closed off all of my hope for us to reunite. I didn't give any real details, but Liza understood without my telling. She said she also had received a letter that had deeply disturbed her. A strange quirk of fate for both of us. Liza insisted that I come to the show and afterwards go to a blues joint in Deep Ellum. Some people were playing that she had heard before, and she thought it would be good for both of us. I told her I would pick her up before the show in time for makeup and pre-show preparations. Uncle Willy hadn't finished my car so I was still driving the Packard. It was small consolation. I decided to put the top down which, always pleased Liza. Her mood was obviously down from the usual open attempt to enjoy life even though it had become more difficult for her to accept her husband's decision.

The show was very good having improved enormously since its opening. Afterwards we headed downtown. On weekends, Deep Ellum was lively and a bit scary, though exciting. The joint was small and crowded, but the music was terrific. It was a happy mixed group of whites and Negroes. Before we left, Liza talked to the musicians and we left for Marilee's because Liza didn't want to go home yet, which was certainly alright with me. I didn't look forward to another evening alone. We went outside and decided on brandy.

"So, tell me, Tim, about your letter and I'll tell you about mine."

I related the whole matchmaker thing and the found match, and Claire's sadness but acceptance of her fate. Then Liza started her story.

"I think he must have written the letter while he was drunk or he wouldn't say what he did. It was more of a confession than a communication. He admitted to not being innocent or faithful, that the temptations were more than he could resist, but that he still loved me and would be home in a year. He also said he would understand if I wasn't completely innocent, but not to forget about him. That was it, short and a mess. It was probably written a month ago. I wasn't necessarily surprised but I sure didn't want to hear it. Well, Tim, it looks like we're both in love limbo."

"Damn,...yes...'love limbo.'"

"Strange coincidence, no?"

"Would you like some more brandy?'

"Yes, I think so. But wait. When I went up to talk to the musicians tonight, the guitarist handed me something in secret. He said to try it, that it would make me smile."

She opened up her purse and pulled out what looked like a cowboy-rolled cigarette.

"What's that?'

"Marijuana. It scares me, but maybe it would make both of us smile. Do you want to try it?"

"Isn't it addictive...and illegal? It scares me, too."

"I don't really know anything about it, but I doubt if one cigarette is addictive, and it's safe here."

"Well, what the hell! It's that kind of evening. Let's make it a long one. First I'll go in and put one some music and have a bit more Villa-Lobos."

Marilee had installed speakers that worked off of the record player in the den. I put on a stack of jazz records, set the volume, and got some matches for candles and the coming smoking experience.

Our next snifter of brandy gave us nerve enough to light the marijuana. We got close and lighted it. I started coughing, but stopped quickly as if my lungs were getting used to the smoke. Before we finished it, I began to feel light-headed. We finished it and lay back to listen to the music and enjoy the brandy. All of a sudden, I sat up and began to laugh uncontrollably at nothing, and then Liza also began laughing even louder. The laughing passed, we looked at each and giggled for several minutes. The music seemed to surround us, and the brandy tasted better than it ever had.

"Making us smile is kind of an understatement. My face hurts from laughing and smiling," I drawled.

"Me, too, Tim. My God, the music! It's beautiful."

We both lay back, and my mind raced. Every lovemaking experience in my life came back to me, especially with Claire. Then the play...and the music at the blues joint mixed with the records playing. It was not at all like being drunk, no dulling of the mind but a brightening of sensations. Some of the dreamlike thoughts were almost frightening in their clarity of emotion. Liza stood up and began to dance to the jazz. Her movements were the most overtly sensual I had ever seen. I was sure she had never moved like that before. Watching her was hypnotic and arousing. She had let down her hair and was swaying with her arms out and up. I had the vision of taking her down on the patio and making strong, passionate love to her right there, not even considering my previous feelings of distance from sexual involvement with her.

"Come here, Tim, and dance with me."

I did, and then we were kissing and moving slowly.

"Tim, take me upstairs, right this minute and make love with me...no, wait a minute; let's take a quick cleansing dip in the pool. I want to feel the warm water all over me."

I didn't know if I could wait until we got upstairs. Liza took off her clothes, dropping them where she stood. She looked at me and smiled.

"You are one powerfully good-looking woman, Miss Liza." She laughed and jumped in the water. I couldn't get my clothes off quickly enough. She rolled around, splashed, and went under to come up in front of me. I put my arms around her as she gathered in close. We kissed as her breasts rubbed my chest. She reached down to take my erection in her hand.

"You are one ready man. Touch me, Tim."

I gently rubbed her breasts and went down to her soft abundant hair and moved my finger slowly into her.

"Dear God, that feels good! Rub me more, yes, there."

She stroked me to almost a climax but then stopped, "Let's go up now."

"Are you sure?"

"Yes, the water is nice, but I want to lie down with you."

"Fine, I'll get us some towels."

She waited for me, then rose up the steps into the towel. I had wrapped one around me because of my rather astoundingly aroused condition. We grabbed up our clothes and the bottle of brandy, stopping only to put on more music. In my room, I pulled down the covers, turned out the lights, and lighted two candles. She dropped her towel and came to me. We were eye to eye. The music overtook us as we moved to it. We danced onto the bed wrapped together. She reached up behind my head, pulling me into a writhing kiss. My erection was between her legs, and she moved back and forth. I ran my hand down to the small of her back and to her bottom as we moved together.

"Make love to me, Tim. Be inside me," she whispered.

She lay down ready for me as I rose above her on my hands and arms. Liza was smiling with an extraordinary expression of sensuality. In the candlelight, she was a handsome mature woman. She took me in hand guiding me into her. I stopped looking down at her, then lowered and kissed her as I entered her completely. She wrapped her legs around me, moving with growing passion.

"Oh, that's so good, please don't stop!"

But I did, realizing I had no protection on, and pulled out of her.

"No, Tim, no, please...!"

"Just a moment, Liza," I said as I rolled over to get a prophylactic.

"Oh, yes. I hadn't even realized. Hurry! Here, let me put it on you."

Before she did, though, she bent down and put me in her mouth.

"Liza, that's too good," I groaned.

"Oh, my, yes it is." She laid back after pulling down the prophylactic on me. This time I moved to kiss her breasts and worked down to her wetness. I kissed her lower lips and spread them, moving my tongue in and up.

"That's amazing, Tim I'm going to come if you don't stop. I want you inside me."

"I will be." I put my finger inside her and sucked on her rising little nub. She started laughing and moving her hips, then shaking and pulling my head to her.

"Now, Tim, be inside me!" As she pulled my head up to her face to kiss me and put me inside her, her climax didn't stop and I had my first of three that night.

I awoke the next morning very late to see Liza still sleeping beside me. My dreams had been wild, with all three women of the last months mixed in. At one time, I was standing watching Gwen throw a large pot. She was nude, telling me that she was leaving, and she had things to teach me before she left. She pointed to a pallet on the floor across a room surrounded by windows with full daylight streaming. Her hands were covered with clay as she came to me and turned into Claire walking across Marilee's patio in a two-piece bathing suit. Claire was laughing, taking my hand to walk me down to the boat. We paddled onto Turtle Creek, which became a lake. She leaned into me for a kiss, then said she loved me and always would. The lake turned into the river with jungle on both sides from the Tarzan movie. Claire started crying and we were in our hotel room. In sobs, she said she didn't want to ever leave me. She guided my hand down to her bulging stomach from pregnancy. The music from the play by Eddy was in my head as she disappeared and I was sitting in the theatre watching the play, the only person in the audience. The Wife ran out to tell of Leonardo's leaving with the Bride. Liza walked off the stage in performance to come sit down beside me. She handed me a snifter of Spanish brandy and said, "What now, Tim?" I wasn't able to speak, to form words, no sound. The play was happening but in silence as a dance interpretation in Flamenco style. Liza was only partially covered and I hazily admired her form. Spreading out around her was her long chestnut brown hair. She was smiling as from a dream. I thought of my teen years of innocent encounters with girls. Kissing after the senior dance, fearing, to try anything else. I remembered touching one girl's breast, and she never spoke to me again. Clumsy and confusing sexual adventures after high school and two lengthy relationships that held no love or real commitment. Then Gwen and the violently jealous actress, then Gwen again. Falling so deeply in love with Claire, and loving her still though she was gone...gone. Three very different women.

Liza stirred, beginning to awaken. Last night had been something I had never expected, or yearned for, but in a raging passion had overtaken both of us. I realized I loved Liza but wasn't in love with her. A friendship had changed into something that I was sure neither of us understood.

Liza's eyes opened and looked at me. "Tim." It wasn't a question, more like a recognition that she was here beside me after a night of something very new for both of us.

"Good very late morning, Liza."

"What time is it?"

"Almost noon."

"I think I could sleep several more hours. How are you?"

"I'm fine...I think."

"Have you been awake long?"

"No...Maybe twenty minutes or so, lying here thinking and looking at you."

"Were you thinking about last night?"

"Some, but I don't really know what to think about it except that it was...uh... a vivid evening of..."

"Yes, it surely was a vivid evening. I didn't expect anything like that to happen."

"Nor did I...but...it..."

"Did happen. Boy, it sure did happen. Do you believe the drug made it happen?"

"Probably about ninety percent of the reason. And we both felt a real sense of rejection by people we love, and we needed love."

"Sounds like a thirty, thirty, thirty to me; all true."

"All true," I said.

"Tim, I don't want to stop talking, but I really need to go to the bathroom and take a quick shower. I feel sticky, good sticky, but sticky. What are the chances of you making us some coffee and bringing it up? I'll make it up to you by cooking a great breakfast."

"That's a deal. I don't want to stop talking, either. Our friendship has taken a new turn that certainly needs discussion."

She got up without Claire's shyness. She turned to me and said, "Do I look alright in the light of day?"

"Real alright." She looked like a movie star.

I asked her to hand me my robe and I went downstairs to make a pot of coffee. After my own urgent bathroom use, I found the special Colombian beans Marilee kept in the refrigerator.

Liza was sitting up in bed covered by the sheet. I poured us each a cup and joined her in bed dropping my robe.

"My God, this is good coffee. Thank you."

"You're most welcome. Have you been thinking about last night?"

"Yes, but not in any negative manner. I think I'm still tingling a bit from the experience. I didn't think I was capable of being that uninhibited with anyone else besides my husband. We really made love; my whole body was shaking when I went to sleep."

"When I fell asleep, it felt like we were still making love. That drug was too much. Out on the patio when you were dancing, I wanted you with a disorienting desire or lust. It was exciting but not real until we were actually making love. And my word, that was real."

"It had been a very long time for me. I had an awful lot of need stored up. After my husband's admission of infidelity, whether serious or not, it hit very hard. Now, the only guilt I may feel has to do with your feelings about Claire. I know it was a serious and loving relationship, but she should have told you that she wasn't just leaving but about her family and the traditions involved when she realized she was in love with you and that it was to end, no matter how strong the love between you."

"Strangely enough I haven't thought of it in that way. I don't feel any bitterness towards her or that a betrayal happened. Our love was and is real, but it took us by surprise, especially her. I've thought several times that I should go out there and bring her back, but I don't have the means or the certainty that she would leave with me. If we ever do get together again, it must be her move, a breakaway. I'll not give up complete hope until she's married. I don't believe I feel guilt about last night. I'm not going to live like a monk who suffers. I believe you and I love each other, but we're not in love."

"I understand how you feel, even though I don't agree completely with your reaction to Claire's leaving. But it doesn't really matter, and yes we do love each other."

"What now? Or is that a proper question?"

"Well, I know I don't want to stop being close to you. But without the drug."

"That's for sure. There were things about it that were exciting, but if we have to have it to feel passion, it's not worth it."

"Quite honestly, I'm looking forward to making love with you again without it. It was overwhelming and too much. I almost thought I was going to have a heart attack having so many climaxes."

I laughed and poured us some more coffee.

"Do you think you will ever want me again, Tim?"

"Do you have plans after the show tonight?"

Liza laughed her big laugh, "No, I didn't, but I do now."

"People around the theatre accept us being pals, but discretion is important for your sake."

"I don't believe it will be any problem at all. If my husband didn't come back at all and Claire got married, well, who knows what could happen. Tim, I've had a crush on you for several weeks, you must have known it."

"Wow, a crush. Well, I'm glad it wasn't something serious."

Liza laughed again, throwing her head back.

"How about that breakfast you promised?"

Liza fixed two Spanish omelets, bacon, and even biscuits. The hardest subject we discussed was how honest we needed to be, knowing what ever our relationship was it must remain primarily a friendship. It was hard to rationalize two lonely people enjoying a semi-illicit union that would end if there were any possibility of our getting back with the people we were truly in love with, but we decided that no matter what happened, we would remain friends, and no one needed to know about us especially

Claire or Liza's husband. They had made their choices and we ours, albeit influenced by what we had smoked. We knew it wouldn't have happened if we hadn't been attracted to each other, but erased whatever inhibitions I had about making love. It was a new situation for both of us, without any deep discussion of the morals involved.

We went for an afternoon swim, sat on the patio and talked about the show and the cast I said the closeness they had achieved made me envious of pulling back and not being there with them all the time, but I knew a director had to separate himself and let them play the piece without a constant presence. Liza said it wouldn't have mattered if I had been there all the time because they felt I was interfering. She suggested that I spend the last week backstage with them and watch from the wings. I liked the idea and agreed. We also laughed about being together after the show, and we both felt almost shy about it.

I took her to her house with plenty of time for her to get ready and arrive at the theatre early. I went by the house to visit the parents. They were glad to see me in a much better mood, but I didn't tell them why or about Claire's last letter. I explained it as becoming more accepting of her having left and looking forward to Taos and directing in Albuquerque. I didn't mention Liza because their progressive tolerance would be strained if they knew I was having a relationship with a married woman, no matter what the situation. They had gotten a letter from Daniel telling them he was painting up a storm and almost ready for New York. Jeordie showed me his latest photography and Dad his drawings for some new furniture designs. Mom was attempting a style of painting new for her called 'Trompe L`Oeil,' a hyper realistic style that meant, "to fool the eye." Her first one had been a collection of objects that became a portrait of her without the human image. I liked it very much and encouraged her to continue it.

"I'm going to if my eyes hold up, Timmy." Hearing "Timmy" was a sudden flashback to Claire.

Mom fixed me a meatloaf sandwich; I ate it out in her studio and watched her paint. Dad came out and asked about my trip to Taos. He had talked to Uncle Willy, who said my car would be ready this weekend. It had taken him two weeks longer to fix than he thought it would. Dad was as eager to see the results as I was. He said the rare question of whether I needed any money, and I assured him I didn't. I figured my savings plus the gift from Marilee, should last me for six months, and I would be paid for the directing job in Albuquerque.

The theatre was buzzing backstage when I arrived. Ginger hugged me and said, "Welcome home stranger!"

"Do you mind if I stay backstage during the performance?"

"Now that's the silliest question I've ever heard. I think the cast would be thrilled to have you with them. This has been quite an experience for all of us, Tim; and it's all because of you. "

"Thank you, but it's been your show for several weeks."

"Anything I've said had been from your notes, or our discussions. How is your journal-to-book coming?"

"Slowly but surely. It's a hard transition but it's beginning to come together. I don't know how long it's going to take, several months at least. I certainly want you to see the first draft, if possible."

"I hope I can because I feel I was there when it happened. I really believe you developed a style that can be an influence on other directors. If you do get published there's no doubt in my mind that variations of your work will be used."

I went into the dressing room and there were welcoming greetings all around.

"Are you going to stay with us tonight? Please do," said the actress playing the Bride.

"Yes, I'll be here tonight and the rest of the performances, if you don't mind."

"El Audaz, where have you been?" the old actor asked from across the room at his mirror.

"Not here, sadly enough. How are you all a-doin?"

Several cheered out, "We don't want it to end, Tim. Let's go on the road!"

I laughed and found Liza. She stood up and hugged me with a kiss on each cheek. "Hey there, Tim Sart, you made it."

I had almost forgotten how exciting being in the dressing room of a successful show could be. I waved and left them to go up on stage. The house was closed, as it always was an hour before curtain; and the stagehands were getting the set ready and making the necessary repairs to Dad's pop-up set. It had worked better than we had hoped and still looked good in the colors Daniel and Mom had chosen. I took a chair from the Bridegroom's home platform and sat down looking out into the house. A thousand memories began to rush through my mind.

I remembered the first play I had directed here five years ago and how innocent I had been. It had gone fairly well, but many times in that instance and some to follow, I had no idea how to solve many of the scenic problems. When blocking was obviously wrong, I didn't know what to say to the cast or how to fix it. At night, I would move the toy soldiers around on a floor plan until an answer came to me. After one long night of struggling with stage movement, at breakfast Mom had said that theatre was a sequence of living pictures and the problem was making a play flow smoothly from picture to picture. That was a painter's viewpoint and I had to create the flow. Sometimes after a rehearsal, I would stay late and walk through the play by myself, and I began to understand blocking a play. As I began to tackle more serious theatre, characterization interpretation became the new challenge, but constant study helped me garner some expertise. Some evenings after rehearsal I was almost too scared to come back the next night for fear of failure, but I did, over and over. For those first years, I deeply regretted not having the opportunity to go to a fine school and work with quality directors and teachers. I still felt like an innocent in many ways, but *Blood Wedding* was a turning point in my thinking; now I wanted to take on the biggest challenges and write about it.

The first meeting with Eddy had changed so many possibilities for success, and Aurora's joining the company in collaboration with him had turned the dance and music into a driving force. Looking out into the house I remembered looking out from my work on stage and seeing Claire drawing, looking at me, and smiling with love. The evenings spent with her going over her drawings and gaining new insights into the play. I wanted to relive every moment, and yet I also wanted to be right where I was. I put the chair back on the platform and walked out into the lobby to look at Claire's artwork. They were beautiful and touching; they were the play. Barney came out of his office to join me.

"I look at them every night, Tim. We all miss her. In a way, she was a spirit of the play, an ephemeral presence like the play itself."

"Too ephemeral, Barney."

"Come have a glass of wine with me before the audience arrives. Did you know that we've had a waiting list every night for the last two weeks? We're now setting up chairs behind the back row."

"My word! I hadn't heard that. A hard act to follow."

"I have complete confidence that you can."

"Well, it's not to be, for now anyway. But I'll be back, Barney. Dallas is still my home."

"I and the patrons are counting on it."

We sat in his office with a glass of wine.

"I have a surprise for you, the board of supporters has arranged a generous bonus for you. I'll present it to you onstage after the last performance. A real celebration is being planned. Are you alright with that?"

"Yes, I suppose so. I do plan to be here every night this week."

"Tim, this production has been an incredibly good experience, and you are the reason for it. You have proved that you are a fine theatre artist. I'm aware there were some bad moments..."

I held up my hand as gesture not to get into it. "It's all been good for me, except for things we will not discuss, ever."

"You're right. Forgive me."

"I do, within reason."

He laughed, and we stood to go out and face the evening.

Watching the play from the wings provided me with a new feeling of closeness with the cast. As they came off stage, they would touch me or pat me on the back. Liza came off once right into my arms with a big kiss. So much for being discreet! The old actor came over and pulled me onstage when the curtain was raised for their bows. The audience was standing. I bowed with them as tears began to flow out of my eyes. Never had I ever experienced that emotion before-that the audience was applauding the play, the cast, and me. When the curtain closed after two curtain calls, the cast gathered around me with their own tears and demands that I be with them for the rest of the performances. I smiled, laughed, and nodded my agreement to be with them.

The audience and cast spent an hour together in the lobby and overflowed onto the patio upstairs. I stepped into my duties as fundraiser successfully with some very good pledges of financial support. There was a photographer there from the society pages of both papers. I must have shaken a hundred hands and was almost blinded by the flashes of the cameras. Before leaving, I signaled Liza, who mouthed, 'I'm right behind you.'

I was standing at the door when she drove up. We went into the den, and I mixed us two healthy Bourbons with soda. We eased back onto the big soft sofa and talked about the evening.

Liza leaned over and put her head on my shoulder.

"Tim, tonight was the best show we've done, and I believe the cast did it for you."

"No, you did it for the audience."

"Of course that, but your being there made it a special evening. Having you in the wings was an inspiration."

"It was for me, too. It's still hard to believe how well the show has been received. I really felt a part of it tonight, not that usual separation being out in the house watching. That whole curtain call thing was a bit more emotional than I was ready for, but it was great. The after-show gathering was a strange encounter, and it helped the theatre. I wonder if the papers are going to make a big to-do out of it; they took enough photos for a whole edition."

"I hope it will be real big, with you splattered all over it."

We laughed at that and had another drink.

"Tim, let's go upstairs. I want to hold you in a more intimate way than this."

Liza took a quick shower as I pulled the bed covers back and lighted candles and turned off all the lights. She came out, drying her hair with a towel. She sat down in front of me on the bed and leaned in to kiss me. I ran my hands through her wet hair pulling her closer and stroked her breasts. Her clean smell was tremendously arousing, and her kissing was gently passionate. I reached down between her spread legs and she took my erection in her hand, squeezing me softly as I explored her welcoming wetness.

She scooted closer so our bodies were almost touching. The intensity of our kisses grew as we both were close to climaxing together. It was a new way of making love for me and, perhaps, for her.

"Liza, I'm going to climax any second now...perhaps we should..."

She put her hand over my mouth and moved down to put me in her mouth. The sensation was so good that I held her head as she moved up and down on me. I suddenly was climaxing, but she didn't stop. I was moaning loudly as my orgasm seemed to not end. I leaned back as she came off me and moved up my body rubbing her mouth off on my stomach, and then straddled me, guiding me into her. I touched her and pushed up into her.

"Tim, don't stop touching me...yes, there,...oh! I'm coming."

She leaned back, taking my hands and putting them on her breasts, holding them to her.

"I don't want to stop, Tim."

Nor did I. I put my hands on her hips and pulled her body up over mine and buried my mouth and tongue into her. She had her hands up, leaning on the wall behind the bed as I was able to get my arm under her and move my finger into her.

"Oh, my God, Tim...I'm coming again...OH! Please..."

She moved onto my mouth closer and began shaking and crying out in passion. As she eased down, I kissed her stomach sucking her breasts.

"Bite my nipples a little bit," she whispered.

Soon she was lying beside me, cooing, and her head on my shoulder.

"This was better than last night and I hope we haven't finished."

"I don't even remember last night, Liza, after tonight."

"I thought I was an experienced married lady, but he never kissed me down there. I didn't even think about it ever happening. Making regular love was always good, but the way you do that to me...well, it has taking lovemaking to another level. When did you learn to do that?"

"Actually not very long ago; a special lady named Gwen taught me. I had always been shy about making love at all. She decided that I needed to learn how to please a woman and not be reticent about being intimate with someone I cared for. She knew I wouldn't make love to anyone unless I cared for them so I should be as close as possible when I did make love."

Well, I thank Miss Gwen, wherever she is. Were you in love with her?"

"No, I don't think so, but it was a strong mutual attraction."

"Kind of like us?"

"Yes, but different. At the very least, we have a strong mutual attraction. I think it's much more for us. Don't you agree?"

"I most certainly do. I feel we love each other but know we can't fall in love. There's almost a sadness in it, but I like what we have and I want it to grow without the pressure of an entangling commitment. Do you feel that way?"

"Yes, I do, Liza. I like it and I damned sure don't want it to stop. I believe we are very good for each other, without any qualms or doubts."

"You said that very nicely, sir; you make a lady feel wanted and secure."

"Hey, I know it's late, but how would you like to grab a couple of towels, go downstairs, and go skinny-dipping with a snifter of Spanish brandy?"

"Indeed I would. I'm not sleepy at all. Let's go."

We both jumped up, got the towels; I also took a prophylactic, not knowing what would occur when the warm water did its work on us.

I went to the cabana cabinet to pour the brandy. Liza almost pranced over to me, reaching for her glass. Her bouncing movement was sensual and cute. She was beginning to be happy again in a way that was endearing and sweet.

We eased into the water sinking down to our necks.

"Oo...yes, this is just what I needed," she crooned.

We let the water relax us as we talked softly about the evening and past week. Her appearance in the moonlight made me extremely glad she had stepped into my life after the lonely weeks. I turned to face her, just looking at her leonine features in the dark. We kissed as she wrapped her legs around me.

"Make love to me like this, Tim, please."

I reached up for the protection and rolled it on me. She put me inside her as we moved slowly. I stopped and told her to sit on the side of the pool. She climbed up and faced me with her legs spread, as I tasted her surprisingly sweet wetness, leaning back on her hands with her legs wrapped around my head she had a soft climax then slipped back into the pool. We made love in the water for a few minutes before I climbed out and helped her out over to the lounge. We rolled over on our sides and dozed a bit before going upstairs and falling asleep, my arm around her, her head on my shoulder.

The next morning we woke up smiling and took a shower, where I discovered that because of her height we could make love standing up. She fixed another spectacular breakfast with eggs, Canadian bacon, and a hollandaise sauce. She left at noon with a kiss, saying she would call me Monday.

At one o'clock, Uncle Willy called to say he would be by to get me in my car at four. I was having dinner at their house. I went up to the study next to my bedroom where I had set up my typewriter and worked on directing notes for two hours. I took a walk down to the creek and sat in the boat thinking of Claire and all the things that had transpired since she had left. I wondered how she was dealing with the matchmaking situation, and if she was she enjoying her job at the museum, and if she had made any friends. Even with my semi-involvement with Liza, I missed her. I wanted to talk to her about New Mexico and staying in Taos with Marilee and Daniel. I wished she could have seen the play again to see how it had grown. Our sensual relationship was not as important to me now as her presence. I needed her counsel and sophisticated viewpoint. My desire for her would always be there, but her leaving made me realize there was so much more to what we had. We deserved at least a year, not the weeks we had had. I believed that it would have cemented the relationship into an unbreakable union that no tradition could have undone.

I went back into the house and started a letter to Claire. I wanted desperately for her to understand that I loved her and had hope for our being reunited again. I knew this letter would take several days to write.

At four on the dot, Uncle Willy arrived. I went out to greet him and see my car. It looked like a different vehicle. He had done something to the top. He jumped out and struck a pose, "Ta...da"

"What do you think, Tim boy?"

"It's terrific! No wonder it took longer than you thought it would."

"I put the Auburn on the back burner and made some major changes."

"You sure did. What did you do to the roof?"

"I cut it and the doors down three inches to give it a zoomier profile."

"It definitely is zoomier," I marveled. "The wheels? Wow!"

"I got rid of the wires and nickel plated-larger solid ones. The other changes you don't see from the outside, except for the new paint, and the exhausts."

"That's the most brilliant burgundy I've ever seen. Is it a new kind of paint?"

"Sort of. I mixed some metal flakes in the paint and used a darker red with more brown and blue."

"And the exhausts?"

"I made some new mufflers that sound a lot better because I brought out two exhaust pipes, one from each bank of cylinders."

"What don't I see?"

"I redid the whole braking system and used hydraulics instead of the old mechanicals. Now it stops like a racecar. I put in a much more powerful engine with two carburetors; the second one doesn't come on until you really press on the foot-feet. Plus a stronger transmission and a larger radiator. I also put in some new seats, two instead of the bench seat."

"Let me just lock the door and I'm ready to go. I can't wait to drive this beautiful thing."

"I know you can't, but if you can wait just a few minutes I want to check out that pool heating system I put in."

"You go ahead. I'll do several walk arounds of this beautiful new machine." And it did look great. The lower roof really changed its appearance, especially with the bigger wheels. I stepped back and noticed that it seemed lower to the ground. Getting into the Ford was like stepping into a completely different machine. The dashboard was more luxurious, with a polished wooden face and new instruments, and the seats were obviously out of some expensive car.

Uncle came around from the back and climbed in. "Everything seems alright with the heater. Do you like that warm-water swimming?"

"At night, it's great. Well, I guess I like it all the time. I'll turn it off when I leave for Taos next week."

"I promised Marilee I'd come over a couple times a month and check everything out. Have you liked staying here?"

"Are you kidding, Uncle Willy? My little apartment has been fine, but this is luxury, and having all the room is a major difference. The car looks like it's lower to the ground. Is It?"

"I wondered how long it would take you to see that. Yes, I changed the springs and put some blocks on the rear drive shafts. It should improve the ride, with a lower center of gravity."

I pushed the starter and it roared to life and then settled into a mellow burble. I unintentionally spun the wheels, immediately sensing the new power. When I got to the street, I almost threw us both through the windshield because of the new brakes. It handled with a new sureness. The power felt unlimited and it came on with a surge that was unnerving at first, but as I got used to it, I liked the completely new feel of it.

"Is it ready for my drive to New Mexico, Uncle Willy?"

"You could drive it to China and back without a hitch. All you need is gas and to occasionally check the oil, which shouldn't be a problem for a long time, several thousand miles at least. Change the oil out there in a couple of months."

The evening with Uncle and Rosie was a pleasure. The barbecued ribs were outstanding, and Rosie glowed in her pregnancy. They were both excited about my coming adventure in New Mexico. They asked about Claire and I told them about her job, but not about the matchmaker situation.

"Well, Tim, how do you like your 'new' car?" Rosie asked.

"I like it better than Marilee's Packard. It's certainly more me."

"I'm glad he has finished it so he can get back to my Auburn," she said and laughed giving me a hug. "After your success, you deserved something special. We're going to miss you. When do you think you'll be back?"

"I don't know. I may have some opportunities out there that I don't have here. If I don't go to school in Albuquerque, I'll be back in a year at most. It looks like the job at the theatre is going to happen, but getting a degree may change that for awhile or forever."

"I know I can speak for both of us in hoping that you come back to Dallas." Uncle Willy said.

I left them with hugs and then good wishes for my trip, directing, and writing."

I thanked Uncle Willy for the car, saying it was too much of a gift, but he shrugged that off, adding that he wished could have done more. I didn't want to go home so I took a chance by stopping at a pay phone to call Liza to see if she would like to go for a ride in my 'new' car. She was excited that I had called her and said she would be waiting at her door.

She squealed when she saw the car, "It looks like a racing car, Tim. It's beautiful!"

"Get in this machine, girl. A spin is called for."

We drove around White Rock Lake and way north Preston Road for a speed run. It ran and sounded like a demon but was as smooth as the Packard.

Liza asked if I wanted to come in for a drink when we got back to her house. I did and we went out to her sun room. She mixed us two Bourbons and we sat back, still stirred by the drive. We had a couple more drinks, and I loosened up enough to tell her about the evening at Barney's house after the cast party. I tried to tell it in a humorous way, but she got really angry.

"That son-of-a bitch! Didn't you want to kill him?"

"Even if I did, I was still too drunk to do anything, just barely able to get out of there. But I wasn't truly viciously angry, just mad that he had taken advantage of me. I was having a dream of making love with Claire, and evidently he noticed and couldn't resist. He has always had this thing for me which I've made clear didn't interest me."

Liza started laughing and said, "I'll forget being mad at him, mainly because I couldn't resist, either. Your charisma is a powerful force, Tim."

"Will you teach me how to control it, Liza? I don't want to be considered a dangerous magnetic force." We both laughed hysterically and I decided it was time to leave. We made plans for the following evening, and I was off.

The next week was spent getting ready for the trip, spending time with the family, some good evenings with Liza, and the theatre. It took three days to finish the letter to Claire. I tried to let her know that I was here and I loved her and, of course, I wanted to stay in constant touch with her, and that Sart men don't give up easily. Her quote about the look she got from this new guy gave me a humorous opening for a reference to the first time we met; "It was in the dark," so our first looks at each other were secrets. The coming trip was a big part of the letter, wishing she could make the drive with me. The new address was included, and I finished up with ten pages.

Liza surprised me on Friday by asking if she could ride out to New Mexico with me. We were sitting on the pool patio, and she said she wanted to go to her house in Santa Fe for the rest of the summer. I hadn't known they had a house there.

"We've had the place for years. Actually, I inherited it from my parents. It's not very large but it's a beautiful two-bedroom adobe stucco with a terrific mountain view. I spent more time there when I was younger. Frank and I went out about once a year and, of course, not at all for the last three years. I've been paying to keep it up and I want to go there, get away from Dallas. I think being alone in Santa Fe would be easier than here...perhaps. Well, I want to try it. If you let me travel with you, I'll pay for the gas and for my own lodging. You could drop me off and continue up to Taos."

"Are you kidding? I would love to have company on the drive. When can you leave?"

"Is next Wednesday too late?"

"No, I was planning to leave on Monday, but hell! I'd wait another week for your company."

"Great!"

Later that evening we talked about the trip, what route to take, what stops to make, and what we would take. My car didn't have much luggage space so the packing plans were important. I would take more bags because my stay would be longer. Liza said she could buy whatever she needed out there. We then got into a discussion about us and what it meant.

"Tim, how do you really feel about having a relationship with a married woman? Or I think I'm a married woman. I don't know what's really going on in the Far East."

"I haven't thought much about you being married. Obviously, there are the discretion complications, but we're both such private people that I don't think anyone suspects anything, and everyone knew we were becoming close friends. Even if someone did think we were having an affair they knew our situations and would probably accept it or at least be tolerant of it, and we're both committed to other people, even if from afar. My family doesn't know, nor will they. I believe the real question is how do you feel about it?"

"Well, I didn't think anything like this would ever happen. Of course, sometimes I feel some guilt, but what we enjoy in each other transcends that almost completely. I love being with you and our being lovers has been a surprisingly wonderful experience. We haven't had any serious talks about us, and perhaps we don't have to. I do believe we have to be totally honest with each other, I mean about this, our being lovers."

"I agree and I believe we have been, don't you?"

"Yes. I'm not concerned about us getting tired of each other. It has more to do with you possibly meeting someone more eligible than I am...uh...not married. I would understand...I think." She laughed and reached over to pull me to her for a kiss.

After kissing her back, I said, "Since I'm not in the market for someone more eligible, it's not something that should concern you, at all."

"I don't want you to worry about me feeling rejected if it does happen. Our commitment is to enjoying the present. Right?"

"Liza, let me get this straight with you. If there were no Claire or Frank, I would be doing everything I could to win your heart."

"And Timothy Sart, let me get this straight with you, I know now that it is possible to be in love with two people at the same time. If there were no Claire or Frank, you would have won my heart, even more than you have now."

"Ah, affirmation is good. Yes, there's no doubt we've gone beyond a crush."

We slept a little closer that night.

The next morning Liza woke before I did. She was holding me and when she saw I was awake, she moved over on top of me, and put me inside her and bent down to kiss me. Her hair was loose, hanging down, long, chestnut, and curly, almost hiding her face. She rubbed her breasts on my chest as I squeezed her nipples. We licked each other's mouths as our passions increased.

After we both did our toilettes, we went down for breakfast in robes. We took orange juice out to the pool and swam for an hour, then sat in the sun and giggled about the morning lovemaking.

Liza went home in the early afternoon and I wrote for several hours, then prepared for the evening at the theatre, the last performance of *Blood Wedding*.

I stayed most of the time backstage except for the wedding dance. The cast played the show with an intoxicating fervor. At the curtain, the audience rose from their seats with yells and applause. At the third curtain call, the cast and Barney called me out on stage. Barney talked about the run and asked me to say a few words.

"Thank you, for the response to what we have done here together," I began "It couldn't have happened at all without an amazing amount of collaboration-the cast and crew, my family, Eddy and Aurora, and you, the audience, who appear to have been ready for something new and different. I fell in love with Lorca's words only hoping we could do any justice to them. You make me feel we have."

Barney then stepped forward and said, "As many of you know, Tim is going to New Mexico to direct another play by Mr. Lorca and to write a book about this experience. We just hope he comes back to us. Because of the success of the production, the board of sponsors and I have decided, most gratefully, to give Mr. Timothy Sart a special bonus for his work on behalf of the Dallas Civic Theatre and the arts in general for Dallas. Tim, please accept this check for twenty-five hundred dollars as our gift to you."

I was stunned by the amount. I took the check, shook hands with Barney, and bowed to the audience. The curtain closed, the cast was screaming and applauding. There were hugs, kisses, backslapping, and thanks. The cast hurried to change for the party in the lobby and patio. Liza came over and whispered, "Thank you and good morning." I kissed her on the cheek, took a few moments alone, then went out to see the patrons.

On the patio, Barney held an auction for a framed poster and two of Claire's drawings, with my permission and choice. They raised almost two thousand dollars. That left me with ten of her works, one of which I planned to give to Mr. Franklin at the bookstore.

After the theater gathering, Eddy and Aurora, Dick and Camila, and Liza came over to Marilee's for a nightcap. During the rehearsal and production, all three women had become close friends, so they knew the situation with Liza's husband. In addition, of course, they all knew Claire and that she was gone, probably for good, so they accepted the friendship between Liza and me, though the intimacy between us was still our secret. All were sad about the show ending, though Eddy was glad to get back to his students. Aurora was going to dance in the summer series at the Fair Park band-shell. Dick and Camila were going east. They had both been accepted at Harvard. Liza told them she was riding out to New Mexico with me.

"That will sure take the burn off of a long lonely drive, Tim," Dick commented.

"Yes, I've never driven that far by myself, so it's great. I'm dropping Liza off at her place in Santa Fe, then continue up to Taos."

"Liza, try to talk Tim into staying a couple of days in Santa Fe. It's a great town. I toured there with a Flamenco dance troupe two years ago, and I loved it." Eddy said.

"Good idea, Eddy. What do you say, Tim?" Liza smiled and took my hand in persuasion.

"No, no, don't twist my arm, I'll do it. Daniel and Marilee have always raved about Santa Fe, so why not? I'm not under any time constraints; they expect me in Taos sometime during the week, so that's not a problem."

"I wish we could join you, but I don't think we all could fit into that sports coupe your Uncle Willy has created. That is some automobile, Tim. It doesn't look it came from your Ford. Is it as fast as it looks?" Dick asked.

"Faster. It almost scared me at first. He turned that old '34 into a completely new machine. I like driving it more than Marilee's Packard."

"I love the color," Aurora added, "It looks like *Blood Wedding*."

I laughed at that, and Eddy applauded her.

Camila wanted to talk more about New Mexico, "When Dick was going through his convalescence in Spain, he told me about going fishing in New Mexico with his father, and how much he had liked it. I didn't know there was that much Spanish influence in America. I want to see it. Is Taos different from Santa Fe? I know it's smaller, but what else?"

"There's an Indian Pueblo just outside of the town, so it has more of an Indian culture, but it's been an artists' colony for years." Eddy explained. "I believe it's like going to a foreign country and still being in the U.S. I was there for only two days, but long enough to see that it is beautiful. It's surrounded by the mountains and the nights are clear with the stars looking like they're so close you can touch them."

"Would you really like to see it, Camila?" asked Dick.

"Could we, Amor?"

"If Tim could put us up, I'd be willing to drive out if it doesn't conflict with the start of school."

"You bet! Marilee and Daniel are leaving for New York in a couple of weeks; I'm sure they wouldn't mind at all. That would be great," I agreed.

"I could come up from Santa Fe while they're there, if you don't mind, Tim?" Liza asked.

"I do not. I'll be alone there, so company would very welcome."

"I wish we could join you all, but mine and Aurora's schedule won't permit it," Eddy sighed, "Another time?"

"I'll be there off and on for several months, so think about it seriously."

"I believe we'll be even more together by then." Aurora said.

"What? Does that mean...?" I asked.

"Yes." Eddy announced proudly. "I asked her, and strangely enough, she said yes. It may seem like a rush, but we have no doubts about it."

Congratulations came from all around. I mixed new drinks for a toast.

"It could be an after-honey-moon trip. I'm already thinking about it seriously. Thank you, Tim. Could we, Eddy?"

"We could sure try. We'll stay in touch with you out there, Tim." Eddy answered.

I looked around at the solid friends I had in my life. Being with them now and in the future gave me a feeling of belonging that has changed drastically in the past two months. Those years of being an unwilling loner hopefully had passed. These friends and the three wonderful women I had known had certainly made my life a better one.

We talked of the coming changes for Dick and Camila with their acceptance to the best school in the country. They stated very clearly that they planned to come back to Dallas, Dick to join his Dad's firm, and Camila to join the staff at Parkland. Since she had fewer years to finish because of her time in medical school at the University of London, they would get their degrees at about the same time.

We ended the evening excited about our futures. Liza stayed for a swim in the nude and a night of snuggling.

Chapter 16
El Viaje

I realized that there wasn't going to be enough luggage space for two, so I called Uncle Willy on Monday and asked if he had any ideas. He thought he could solve the problem in a day. I rushed the car over to him. Liza came and picked me up, so she had the chance to meet Uncle. They liked each other immediately.

He pulled me aside for a moment. "Tim, it looks like your luck continues in finding very fine ladies." He remembered her from the show. "I thought she was quite a looker when I saw her on stage."

"Just a good friend, Uncle. She's riding with me out to New Mexico, and I'm dropping her off in Santa Fe."

"That's why you needed the extra space, huh?"

"Yep."

"I'd say it's worth the trouble. It'll make the car more usable anyway. I'll have it ready tomorrow afternoon. One of my best men will take care of it. I've already drawn up the design."

"Thanks, Uncle, this may have reached the too-much point in your helping me."

"Now, Tim, that's impossible to reach. I'm not a father yet and you're the closest thing I've ever had to a son, and Rosie feels the same way."

Liza and I did some last-minute shopping on the way home. Later that afternoon, I went by the bookstore to give Mr. Franklin the drawing I had saved for him. He found a place for it and had it hanging on the wall before I left. Afterwards, I went by the parents' house to spend a last evening with them. They almost treated me like I was going off to Europe or on a far off adventure. They listed all the precautions I needed to take, and Mom gave me packing instructions. Dad brought out his maps and suggested the best route through Sweetwater and on to Lubbock. I had thought I would just follow the signs, but that was unacceptable to him. He gave me a good map with a red pencil line marking the route to take. Jeordie thanked me for giving him my room, saying it had improved his life because he had never had any real privacy before. He showed me his latest photography which was getting better and more like art. He had moved from portraits to nature and architectural pictures. He assured me that the camera Claire had given him made the difference. He surprised me with a sepia-like print portrait of Claire I hadn't seen before. It was framed in carved wood crafted by Dad. Seeing it brought to the surface my feelings. I felt haunted by her image. Jeordie had evidently taken the photo while she was looking at me. The smile was the one she always gave to assure me of her love. I left them later than I had expected and knew I needed an evening alone.

I didn't call Liza. I went outside to sit in the dark with a glass of brandy and remember everything I could about Claire. They weren't really sad thoughts, more like how lucky I was to have known her. I was looking forward to the trip with Liza but knew it should be Claire beside me.

The next morning I finished all of the arrangements for the caretaker at Marilee's house. I decided to wait until the next morning to turn off the pool heater hoping Liza and I could enjoy it one more time.

She came by in the late afternoon to give me a ride to Uncle Willy's shop. She brought her bags because we had planned for her to spend the night so we could start early the next morning. The solution Uncle Willy had devised was a classy nickel-plated rack mounted on the trunk. He even supplied me with rope to tie the luggage down. We parted with a handshake and a hug.

"You take care, Tim, and get back here safe."

I followed Liza home, and she did the last lock down of her house and put her car in the garage. We got to Marilee's for what was going to be my last evening in Dallas for a long time. I was anxious and excited. Liza fixed us a good dinner of lamb chops and squash. Afterwards, we eased into the pool with Bourbon and easy talk about our coming adventure. We turned in early with no lovemaking, just a kiss and deep sleep.

The next morning we rose early to prepare for the trip. I packed the trunk with things we would try not to take out on the trip and bags we would use for overnights on the new rack. The rack gave us room for four more bags than we had planned to take. Liza prepared breakfast and a big picnic basket for the road. We ate and did last minute toilettes and packed ice in a metal cooler for evening cocktails. I put the Packard under a tarp and locked the house. We went out Maple Avenue, to Inwood Road, across the Trinity, and headed West on Ft. Worth Avenue. It was nine A.M. when we started passing the big casino castles and the horse race track. Fort Worth passed quickly. The West had begun. The car was a dream on the highway even with the slightly booming exhaust.

Liza had regaled me with stories of growing up in Highland Park and going to Hockaday and East to school at Sarah Lawrence. Her father had been in cotton then real estate development. He experienced almost a total bust in the late twenties but came back big in oil by drilling in East Texas and Burkburnnet. Liza had met Frank in New York but they didn't marry for two years. She knew he had a wanderlust, but hadn't expected it take him off to the Far East. When they first moved to Dallas, she thought they would start a family, but it wasn't to be. Frank had first gone to Canada where she had joined him, but the oil field life and the winters were more than she could bear. So began for her a solitary life of waiting for Frank's rare homecomings, and then none after Java had lured him away. She had had no romantic liaisons in all that time and hadn't expected to. Being in the play, her husband's confessional letter, and our friendship had rearranged her life. She told stories about things that had happened among the cast of *Blood Wedding* that I had never heard. The old actor who had dubbed me "El Audaz" wanted to leave Dallas for New York for one last attempt at a theatre adventure, but his rather large family had decided he wouldn't be doing that. There had been a homosexual affair between two of the cast-crew members. Both partners were married women with families. It didn't last long but was a surprise to them and the cast. Fortunately, it had ended in a friendship with no bitterness. The couple playing the Bride and Leonardo had been seen one night making love backstage between scenes. Ginger had had to ask them to control their ardor during performances. Camila and Aurora had a screaming fight in Spanish one evening before a performance, but realized after a few minutes that it was a complete misunderstanding. They ended up crying in each other's arms and adding two new steps to their duet in the marriage party. A fuse had blown one night in the dressing room that took Ginger twenty minutes to get back on. Ginger got sick halfway through a performance one night and the assistant couldn't find her cue sheets. The only effects were slightly slower scene changes and mild panic. There had been a shock for the cast when Claire left, and everyone was worried about me and how I would take it. They had formed a Tim watch that ended when it was discovered I wasn't going to fall apart. Not long after that, Liza and I got together. Nobody suspected our intimacy, she thought, but wasn't sure. She kept me laughing for a hundred miles, but the changing terrain soon took over our conversation. I had thought Liza would be a good travel companion and I was right. Outside of Sweetwater, we stopped for a picnic and decided to take some side trips. I wanted to spend some time exploring the Caprock, and she wanted to see Las Vegas, New Mexico and the Montezuma Castle,

I looked over at her stretched out on the seat with her shoes off and knees up. I wondered what I was doing with such a beautiful, classy, and slightly older woman, well, only by three and a half years. The age difference certainly didn't seem to concern her. She had her window down, and her hair was blowing back over the seat. She turned to me and smiled then reached up and put her hand on the back of my neck.

"This is nice, Tim. I like how Texas changes to this wild Western look. You forget how many hills and mesas are really so close to Dallas, well, a couple hundred miles. How does your car feel? Is it very different?"

"It feels much more solid. I guess the bigger wheels and engine give it a new feeling of power. I believe we could cruise at eighty or ninety if there wasn't any traffic. I want to drive it a little longer before I try something like that. Besides, there's too much precious cargo to take any wild chances."

"My word, it's been a long time since someone considered me precious," he laughed.

"You're at the very least precious."

"Why, thank you sir. Well, I must say your car sure sounds powerful. I like it. It makes me feel like we're on a motor boat crossing a lake. Right after Frank and I got married we went over to France and toured around. He insisted that we go to the big Gran Prix race there. That's what your car really sounds like, one of those wild, powerful European racing cars."

"I think that's the effect Uncle Willy wanted for the car. He builds racing cars, and he says his next project, after Rosie's Auburn, will be a European-type sports convertible."

"He's really a special guy. It's easy to tell how much he loves you."

"It goes both ways. We've always been very close, much more than uncle and nephew, right on the edge of father and son. But I'm also very close to my father. Daniel and I have spent many good times with the both of them. Dan and I have talked a lot about how one brother chose wood to work in, the other metal. They're both great artisans in their different mediums. What they create is much more tangible and useful than what Daniel, Mom, now Jeordie with his photography, and I bring about."

"Don't you dare shortchange what you do! There's functional art that has its own beauty and art that changes peoples lives like painting and theatre."

"Do you really believe art changes people's lives? I mean I do to a certain extent or I wouldn't do it...but..."

Liza laughed, throwing her head back, "Well, it surely changed mine. No seriously, yes I do. People will remember *Blood Wedding* for a long time. And think of your writing that has come out of it. Daniel's paintings have affected me deeply. I can close my eyes and see his paintings, with his new uses of color and subject. Also, Jeordie's more candid photos of the cast made an artistic statement. He'll probably be asked to photograph many more shows and casts. His work will perhaps hang in the lobby just like Claire's drawings did."

"Support, support...I knew there was another reason I liked you besides your incredible..."

"My incredible what? Don't get too intimate here, Mister Sart."

"Well, that, too, but I was referring to your presence."

, She poked me in the side, "I'll accept that," she giggled, "Only because you have a pretty incredible...uh...presence, too."

"We spent the night in Sweetwater and the next day drove up to the Caprock and took some side roads for a little different view than we could get from the highway. We stayed the next night in Clovis, then went straight north to Las Vegas.

We both fell in love with Las Vegas because it was so different from what one expected to see in New Mexico. It's a Victorian town with old large houses and big trees. Liza told me it had been the end of the Santa Fe Rail road in 1800's, so the barons tried to make it like the East. It also had the hot springs and the castle.

We got rooms at the Plaza Hotel on the old town square, then drove north on Montezuma road. When we came around a bend, the castle appeared like something from Austria. It was huge, with a commanding turret on the south side. It had been closed and out of use for years but was still an amazing sight. We pulled up to the hot springs across a creek from the castle. There were about ten different springs, each having a different temperature, from very hot to just warm. We decided to join the people already in the water and got our bathing suits out of the luggage in the trunk and changed in the car. We chose a medium-hot spring and luxuriated for an hour in the relaxing water. After awhile, a couple from Colorado joined us. They were on their way to New Orleans. They were also staying at the Plaza, so we arranged to have dinner together at the dinning room.

The husband was a mining engineer, and the wife was a nature photographer who had spent the earlier part of the day photographing the castle. They were delightful company, and the evening was filled with good conversation. We ended it in the bar with many good laughs and talk about the arts. As it turned out, they were theatre buffs and were fascinated by my up coming adventures. *Blood Wedding* dominated the talk because they had read earlier Lorca poem collections but had not heard of my play. Liza proved to be a fine raconteur on the play but embarrassed me by talking about my brilliance as a director.

We both got in the overly large tub that night talking about how much fun the trip had been so far. We were almost too tired to make love, but when she cuddled next to me. We made slow, sweet love and fell into a restful sleep.

We had breakfast the next morning with our Colorado friends, then checked out of the hotel and drove around Las Vegas admiring the houses. On one street, we were surprised by a beautiful modern house that was almost Bauhaus in design. We didn't see one adobe house in the whole town. We headed west to Santa Fe after a couple of hours.

Liza's house in Santa Fe was impressive, larger, and more elegant than I expected. It was in the New Mexico stucco style with a big terrace off the large bedroom upstairs furnishing a great view of the mountains in the distance and the town square three blocks away. There was a garden in back that had been well kept up by a caretaker family who lived in quarters behind the garage. The kitchen had been stocked for Liza's arrival, so she cooked a dinner of arroz con pollo, after which we retired to the upstairs terrace to look at the stars. I had never seen the sky from such a high altitude and clear atmosphere before. It was an awesome visual experience for me.

Liza laughed at my amazement. "It's kind of a shock when you see it for the first time, isn't it?"

"It sure is. You think you've seen the night sky until this happens. I didn't know there were this many stars. It goes from horizon to horizon. Starlight takes on new meaning."

I gazed up trying to remember all the constellations I had learned as a Boy Scout, but there was so much sky that I couldn't find a place to start except for the obvious stars. I decided to get a star chart while I was out here.

The next morning, we set out to explore Santa Fe. We walked the two blocks to the Loretto Chapel and then to the square. There was Indian art everywhere and two very good art galleries. We wandered through the silver and antique shops and had lunch at the La Fonda Hotel, where I was introduced to New Mexican style food. Then we sat on the terrace of an upstairs bar watching the Santa Fe life below us. People from all over the country were sitting around the square as we headed back to Liza's house. We spent a leisurely evening with dinner and conversation on the terrace. In the morning, the humming birds were swarming around a feeder Liza had set up before breakfast on the backyard patio. We used the afternoon driving around the town and in to the country. The high desert was beautiful as it eased up to the mountains and forests of pine. The smell of piñon burning was overwhelmingly sweet and intoxicating as it wafted from cooking fires in the scattered adobe houses as we drove the back roads. Later Liza guided us to a restaurant on the Taos Road up on a bluff overlooking the highway. It was my second encounter with New Mexican style food, and I loved it. In fact, I now preferred the stacked enchiladas to the rolled ones back home. The red sauce was much spicier, and the cheese had a sharper pleasant taste. I even liked the beer more; it was from a German family brewery in Albuquerque.

We ended the evening by going to a small bar a block off the square. In a corner an accomplished guitarist was set up to play for the evening patrons. Liza suggested I try the gourmet Tequila the bar offered, and had a bottle brought to the table. It was dark brown and a cross between brandy and fine whiskey but with the tequila taste. It was every bit as smooth as the Spanish brandy Marilee had introduced me to. We drank half the bottle and took the remainder with us for a nightcap. It seemed to affect us like an aphrodisiac, for we indulged in exhausting lovemaking before falling asleep. We awoke the next morning still feeling the effects of the massive amount of Tequila we had consumed the night before. We laughed about it, snuggled, and kissed ourselves into making love, realizing only afterwards that we hadn't taken precautions. Liza was worried at first, then decided c'est la vie. She had tried to get pregnant the years before with Frank, so her reaction was if not then, why now. I took it a bit more seriously but figured it was too late to do anything. We drank two pots of very strong coffee sitting in bed talking about my leaving that afternoon or the next morning. She decided it would be the next morning.

"Since that's settled, how would you like to have some really good Huevos Rancheros for breakfast?"

"Do we have to get up to do it? This may be a good day to stay in bed."

"We don't have to get up completely, that is dress for the day. Would robes and undies be alright with you?"

"Only if you'll take a shower with me first."

"I will do, sir. Right this very minute."

We giggled and rushed to the bathroom. Everything we did together was fun. Claire and I had never had the chance to relax into our relationship. I knew we could have, but the time we were together was so intense that every minute was precious. Liza and I had now spent much more time together than Claire and I had, but it was different because there was no future other than enjoying each other's company and affection with Liza. There were no deep discussions about our love, yet we knew we loved, but not with a tying commitment of love vows. Neither of us knew whether we would ever again be with the people who truly held our hearts. I believe we both knew our being lovers was a release from her feelings of being betrayed and mine of being rejected, but it wouldn't have happened if we hadn't been extraordinarily attracted to each other.

Our showers were always much more than just getting clean. We enjoyed the physical contact, and took turns standing behind each other and scrubbing. It was always a sensual experience; I rubbed her breasts and lower areas and she my chest and...well, needless to say it was arousing. Our being the same height and the way she was built always led to our making love facing each other, wrapping our arms around the other's necks and slowly enjoying.

When we were toweling off, Liza commented, "Tim, until we became close, I didn't know or imagine people could make love like this. Frank is so tall, it would never work, but you and I are perfectly matched for it."

"Liza, it's certainly new for me too."

"Do you think we make love too much? It had been so long for me that I've felt almost innocent and it's been a revelation, or perhaps more a reawakening."

"Uh...no, I think it's been amazing how much we enjoy it, but it has seemed very natural to me. Is it bothering you?"

"No, Tim, not at all," she protested, "it's great and gets better all the time, so much so that I wish you weren't leaving in the morning."

"Well, I'm not going far, just up the road. After Marilee and Daniel have left you can come up. Oh, Hell, you can come up before they leave. I don't believe they would mind or disapprove at all. She was your friend long before Daniel and I knew her. I think they would be quite pleased about us, especially since Marilee knows about your situation with Frank. And they are experts at being discreet."

"Tim, I didn't come out here just to get my house going again, I didn't want to be away from you. I had been lonely too damn long to go right back to it. You did suspect, didn't you?"

"Of course, I hoped that was a part of it. I didn't want to leave you, either. Having you with me on the trip was great, and it wouldn't have been anywhere near as much fun alone. I would never have thought of going to Las Vegas. I didn't even know it existed. And the last two days have been very nice indeed. Now I know something about Santa Fe...and the shower we just took was, I hope, a preamble for the afternoon, and the evening, and the morning. And as a matter of fact I'm very much against this "undies" thing you mentioned."

Liza threw her head back in one of her great laughs then hugged me tightly, and finished with a kiss.

"Well, if you insist, Mr. Sart. Sometimes you're so demanding that I can't help giving in, but I do want to wear undies to cook in. After that, I suppose I could go along with your wishes. I do hope this means you like the way I look...uh...I mean without clothes."

"I would like the way you look if you were wearing a gunny sack."

"I would rather not test that idea, if you don't mind."

"Perfectly fine, I was just engaging in a pinch of hyperbole. Liza, you're a gorgeous woman anytime."

"Even in the morning?"

"Especially in the morning. Did you mention Huevos rancheros earlier?"

"Gee whizzie bing-bang, I had almost forgotten."

We sat outside, in our robes, on the patio and ate this breakfast that I now believed I could have every morning. Liza also cooked up some great sausage called chorizo. Afterwards, she brought out some English cigarettes that tasted like no other in my limited smoking experience. They were almost too good, not enough to start the habit, but they were a treat. We cleaned up the kitchen and went back upstairs. Liza opened all the windows to get a good breeze and we sat up on the bed and talked, laughed, and occasionally kissed. We faced each other and began to touch and explore in a new way. I caressed her breasts and leaned close to kiss and suck her nipples as she aroused me. I reached in between her legs as she put her legs up over mine.

"Tim, touch me inside, yes there. Oh, my God, that's so nice."

I leaned back to reach the nightstand to get some protection.

"Be in me a little bit before you put that on, please," she urged.

I pulled her up on me and entered her slowly. She wrapped her arms around me and whimpered as she moved down on me. I had a sudden strong desire to be more intimate with her, to taste her. I rolled us over and kissed my way down. I kissed, sucked and put my finger in her as she a she reached a sweet giggling climax. I rubbed my face on her tummy as I kissed my way up to her breasts and face. She wrapped her legs around me, pulling me in to her. She was having little climaxes when I realized I hadn't put on the prophylactic. Just as I started to climax, I pulled out. Liza reached down and stroked me as I ejaculated on her tummy.

"Damn, Liza, that feels so good, but what a delightful mess."

"My goodness, Tim, it's so warm, and...uh...so much. Can I put you in my mouth a little bit, please?"

There was no need to answer. I straddled her and she tilted up to take me in. I felt like I was having another climax it was so good. As I began to soften, I moved down beside her. We lay together, tummy to tummy, and dozed off.

I woke up three hours later and heard Liza in the shower. I lay back thinking of the past few days and felt a great need to get back to work on my directing book. I didn't regret the time with Liza, but it had been a distraction, albeit a pleasant one. I knew also I didn't want it to get any more serious with her because no matter how it was with us, she was still married and probably would remain so. I hoped her stated desire to be with me didn't become an obsession to relieve the loneliness she felt. Of course, I was lonely for Claire, but I could deal with it. I had to. I didn't feel the betrayal Liza did, just a kind of rejection by Claire that was really a quirk of fate not of her making. Perhaps this distraction with a wonderful woman had been good for me beyond the obvious pleasure of it. I felt recharged for the next level of commitment to my writing. I wasn't terribly guilty about us having an adulterous affair because her husband was admittedly doing the same thing far away. There was no fear of him coming to get me some day. The sexual passion Liza and I felt for each other was exciting and extremely satisfying, but it wasn't the emotional union I had experienced with Claire, and I didn't know if it could ever be. But Claire was gone and I wanted a letter from her, a phone call, or the ability to slowly forget about the possibility of a reunion.

Liza came out of the shower nude and magnificent. She smiled and winked at me. The sight of her rekindled my desire, and my recent thoughts disappeared as she came to sit beside me on the bed. She ran her fingers through my hair and leaned down to kiss me.

She giggled and said, "I woke an hour after we started dozing to go to the bathroom and we were stuck together. It was a funny feeling, but nice in a way. I didn't have any trouble going back to sleep, though I did look at you for a while. You're quite a striking man, Tim. I would have awakened you for the shower, but I didn't know if I could have handled another one of our rather active bathing experiences."

"That's alright. I don't know if I could have either, but the sight of you does inspire the thought."

"How about if I get dressed and go down to make us a late afternoon drink? I advise you to take a quick shower before the scent of you overwhelms me and causes a great need to snuggle. I'll be strong and resist. Uh...well...what would you like to drink?"

"Definitely not Tequila. That was as powerful as that stuff we smoked. Don't think I'm regretting the results, because they were extremely nice but too frantic. Both times, I felt like we should have been screaming at the top of my lungs with passion."

"I hadn't thought of that, but you're right. I certainly had the urge to scream... uh...in a good way. Now up with you, and when you come downstairs, I'll put a drink of what in your hand?"

"Bourbon and soda, please ma'am."

"Excellent. I have some very good seven year old eighty proof."

"Ah, mi mas favorito."

When I got out of the shower, I didn't have to go downstairs; Liza had brought a tray with the drink fixings, and set things up on the balcony. We didn't talk for awhile, just sat and enjoyed the view. The bourbon was very good and very relaxing. Liza had put on a light blue sleeveless sundress. Her hair was still a little wet and gathered in back. I noticed as it dried it slowly started to curl. After a few minutes, she reached back to unclip her hair and shook it out and ran her fingers through it. It was like watching a flower unfold. She hadn't put on a bra so with every movement her breasts moved freely.

She caught me looking at her, "Oh, you noticed, Tim, I didn't do it on purpose, just in a hurry."

"I don't believe that for a moment, and forgive me for staring."

"You may be partly right, and your stares are welcome. A woman likes to be admired by a man she cares about. Another subject: where would you like to eat tonight? I can fix something here or we can go to a place that I know on the edge of town."

"Let's go out. You made that great breakfast this morning."

We had another drink and prepared for the evening. The restaurant was a charming European-style place with an extensive menu. Liza had a chicken molé, and I had lamb. Over brandy, we discussed the past weeks and our relationship.

"Tim, the past weeks have been the best I've had in years, but I don't want you to fear that I'll become some sort of hanging on, obsessed woman. Yes, I do feel an enormous amount of love for you, but I know you have serious work to do. Of course, I want to see more of you. How could I not? Remember love limbo? We're both in it, with no resolution in sight. Even if it was resolved in our favor, I don't know if you would want to be permanently with a slightly older woman."

"I think they've been pretty good weeks, too. I certainly didn't expect all of this to happen to us, or better said, for us. And quite honestly I wouldn't let you become an obsessed woman. If it did happen, I would say stop, it's killing us, and if I had thought that, it would be underestimating you. I don't do that with you. Yes, I do remember love limbo; I live with it every day, as do you. Nothing is going to stop my work, but I do need to get away from it some time, and why not with you? Slightly older? What? Three or four years? That's about the same difference as between Daniel and Marilee."

"I don't know why I even brought this up. I'm married to Frank and want to stay that way, I think. Love limbo! Wow! It sure sounds trivial when we talk seriously. We care for each other and we're also in love with other people, I would never have guessed it was possible. We know we wouldn't be together right this minute if Frank and Claire were close."

"Of course, we wouldn't, Liza. But they're not here and may never be. Listen, you're great company and a whole lot more. As you said, why would I not want to be with you? Enough said, huh?"

"Yes, enough said. I guess since this our last evening together for awhile, I needed to let some things out, or at least, know how you feel about us."

"I understand. No matter what happens, we have a lot of time to see how things turn out. I don't expect our rather healthy passion to cool off, either. One thing that makes a big difference is that we were close friends before we became intimate, and I believe we're even closer friends now. Don't you think?

"Yes, Tim, and boy, I hope our healthy passion doesn't cool off. Which reminds me, let's go to the house and have a Bourbon on the terrace downstairs."

"Okie-dokie, which reminds me, I'm glad we took that nap this afternoon."

We spent a sweet and gently loving long evening in a happy goodbye, knowing we would see each other soon. The next morning, I called Marilee to tell her I was on my way. She and Daniel were excited about my arrival. When I told Marilee where I was calling from she insisted I tell Liza to come up before they left. Liza fixed something for breakfast called migas and a small steak. We sat on the patio and talked about when she could come up. She thought she could make it in a week but needed to do something about a car."

"I have some friends here who could loan me one, but I think I'll buy one."

"Buy one? I could come..."

"Tim, please, I am a fairly well-to-do Highland Park lady. I have some money of my own, and every month there's a rather substantial deposit from the oil company Frank works for. Don't worry about me on that account and I'll get something right for New Mexico."

"Alright, but if you decide not to, let me know. And thank goodness for you Highland Park ladies," I said, raising my coffee cup in salute.

We stood up, and I gathered my bag. At my car, Liza took me in her arms, holding me tight, and cried softly.

"Thank you, Tim. You've made me whole again. You're one of the good ones. I'll see you in a week or so. I'll call."

"Okay. Let me know what the car situation is."

I kissed her and was gone. In a way, it was good to be alone again. I headed north on the road beside the Rio Grande River. It was a beautiful winding drive that went rise and fell beside the mountains. My car was a dream on the hills; I could pass other cars with a roar of speed. As I got close to Taos, I saw the old church on the right that I thought was in a village called Ranchos. I was tempted to stop but knew I was going to be around long enough to come back and explore the whole area. I pulled into the town square, stopped and referred to my directions. Marilee's house was in Arroyo Seco to the north and east of town. I got out to stretch my legs and to look around. The plaza was small and quaint compared to Santa Fe, and Indians were in evidence everywhere. There were trading-post-type stores, small restaurants, and bars. Several stores seemed to sell tourist items, but they had beautiful rugs hanging in the windows. Some Indians and jewelry craftsmen had their wares out on blankets under an overhanging institutional looking building. I wanted to walk around but decided to get to Marilee's as quickly as possible. I followed the map and found her house within an hour. The property was larger than I had thought it would be. There was a large gate with a sign that said "La Finca." The house was a dark red, had three stories, and a large turquoise front door. I drove into the driveway, and Marilee and Daniel both came out to greet me. Marilee hugged me, and Daniel shook my hand with a big pat on the back. We unloaded the car and carried all of it to my bedroom downstairs.

"Don't unpack now, Timmy, I've fixed us lunch. I finished about ten minutes before you drove up."

"That sounds great, Marilee. Damn, it's good to see you two."

"You too, brother. How was the drive up?"

"It was easy and beautiful."

"Is that your old car with a super Uncle Willy touch to it?"

"Yep, and it's great. It feels like it's twice as powerful, and it has the new-type brakes."

"It sounds it, too. We heard you coming from afar." Marilee teased.

Daniel showed me the way out to the patio off the kitchen. The backyard was more like a view of Eden, with at least an acre of wild growing plants, a high cliff that led off to a meadow and a small lake. There were large oak trees and pine groves and two hummingbird lures hanging from the patio roof cover. Seemingly hundreds of birds were feeding on them. Marilee brought the food as Daniel and I set the table. After the tasty light lunch, we sat around and tried to cover everything that had happened since we were together. I told them how well the show had gone and the surprise bonus I had gotten closing night. They asked what was going on with Claire in California, even though Marilee had gotten a couple of letters from her in answer to her own letters. She was really asking for my reaction to the matchmaker situation. I tried to be as honest as possible without going into a long diatribe about feeling rejected. Then the inevitable question about Liza came up.

"Well, there's really not much to say except that she's a super lady and we have enjoyed each other's company for several weeks."

"That 'not much to say' sure says a lot. Would you like for her to come up?" Daniel asked.

"Yes, I would, if you don't mind."

Marilee asked, "What has happened with her husband, I kind of got the idea that things were bad."

"I'm not sure she would want me to tell, but since you've been friends for years, I guess it's alright. Uh...Frank wrote her a letter she's convinced he wrote when he was drunk, in which he confessed he had not been faithful; no details. That's it."

"Damn, Timmy, after she had been waiting for two years or so, probably faithfully, for him to come home. I knew about his signing up for another year."

"Yes, with that and Claire's matchmaker situation, it changed our relationship rather quickly. But there was a strong mutual attraction before."

"Yes, brother, that was rather obvious when she joined us that evening in Dallas."

"Timmy, has this changed any of your feelings for Claire?"

"Absolutely not, and Liza is still, with reservations, in love with Frank."

"Ah, the lonely quotient for two close friends is a powerful thing, brother. Well, Liza is a terrific lady and one of the great beauties of the Western world."

"No doubt about both of those things, Daniel."

"Timmy, I must say, this has been quite a spring for you; *Blood Wedding*, Gwen, Claire, and now, Liza. My goodness, what will the summer bring?"

"I would like for it to bring Claire, but there's not much hope for that."

Oh, I almost forgot. There's a package here for you from Claire. I'll get it."

When Marilee left, I asked Daniel how his painting was going.

"I have five new canvases, and I like all of them. Marilee thinks they're better than the last ones I did in Dallas. We'll go see them after you get unpacked and situated."

Marilee came back with a largish box. I opened it to find a pair of boots, jodhpurs with straps across the front instead of the wrap-around type. I had never seen such beautiful boots. They were a dark rich brown with gold buckles. A thick letter was sticking out of one of the boots. I immediately left the table and retreated to my room, almost in tears. I tried on the boots and they fit perfectly. The letter started off with a confession that she had looked in a couple pairs of my shoes for the size. She then told of her undying love for me and no matter what the situation was there, she missed me more every day. She hoped her parents would eventually relent and give in to her resistance to an arranged marriage. There was no relationship with the chosen suitor, just an occasional chaperoned meeting which, of course, he didn't like but which she insisted on. She was not attracted to him in any way and was sure it was strictly a financial opportunity for him. For the first time, Claire wrote of her deep physical desire for me. The letter was the longest she had written so far. It offered only a vague hope of our getting back together, but it was there, with time being the crucial element. She also made it clear that I must go on living as a free man without any fear of resentment from her. There was no doubt of my love for her, but I shouldn't wait in loneliness for the possibility of our reunion. She hoped I liked the boots and would think of her when I wore them. The letter was exactly what I needed, and it brought her closer to me than any of her previous letters had.

Strangely enough, I felt no guilt for what had happened between Liza and me. It made me realize even more that I loved two women, but in very different ways. I reread the letter and sensed there was something she wasn't telling me that troubled her deeply. In my next letter to her, I would try to get her to tell me what it was because I knew it wasn't just a vague suspicion.

"Well, Claire is, isn't she, Timmy?"

"Yes, Claire 'is', but she's there. Her letter is an incredible testament to our love. She loves her job, but not the chosen suitor. Damn, what a ridiculous situation. There's also something else, I don't know what. I don't think it has to do with the matchmaker problem or her life there."

"I haven't heard from her for a couple of weeks, but that's about right. I, too, felt she was holding something back. I get a letter every three weeks and it was the last one that made me feel that way. Perhaps in time, I hope she will reveal what it is. Does this affect your relationship with Liza?"

"No. Marilee, it doesn't. Claire even said I should not let our love keep me from those kinds of things, so I'm not."

"Good, Timmy, you can't become a bitter celibate. I believe Claire wants you to enjoy life, even if it's without her."

Daniel had gone out to his studio in back when I had gone to my room.

"Great lunch, almost sister; I'm going out to see Daniel's latest."

"I think you'll like them as much as I do. He actually does get better with each new series, and I wasn't sure that was possible after that last group of pieces."

"You know, love and happiness may have something to do with it."

"Could be, but enormous talent is the dominant force."

I nodded in agreement and joined Daniel. The new works were powerful, colorful, and a new blend of figurative and non-realistic.

"Your paintings are getting to be more like dreams, Daniel, except more colorful. They seem to be moving as I look at them. There's no doubt you need to show in New York soon. Have you got enough yet to take?"

"Almost, perhaps five or six more. Before we leave here, I want to do another portrait of Marilee in a different mode. I'm thinking of color planes in a background that blend into a semi-realistic vision of her."

"Oh...um...I believe I need to see it; your words sound good...but."

Daniel laughed, "But we're brothers, can't you see into my mind?"

"Wait a minute," I said as I closed my eyes and brought my hand to my forehead," As I close my eyes it's starting to come into focus...yes...yes...hell no, I can't see into your head, but it sounds, yes I can hear it, it's like those funny radio sounds when you're searching for a station."

"Stop, brother! I get the idea. I need to paint it. I've been painting since early morning. It's time for a break and to celebrate your arrival. What say?"

"That sounds good, I would like that before I start work by tomorrow. This last week has not been very productive-pleasant, but not productive. I promised to finish the book before I go down to Albuquerque to do *Yerma*."

"No place beats Taos for the artistic spirit."

We found Marilee working in the garden off the patio.

"I believe I've found my artistic nature in this garden. What do you think, Timmy?"

"A virtual garden of Eden, Marilee. I meant to say something before, but I didn't know you were responsible for it."

"It's been good to pull away from the business for awhile. I talk to my managers every day, but thank goodness, it's not like in Dallas. They're doing fine, and so am I; no crises yet and none on the horizon."

"Mi amor, the afternoon has been taken off in celebration of Tim's arrival."

"Yes, let's do that, my Sart men. I'll wash my hands, Daniel, you do the honors."

"Of course, Tim, what is your pleasure?"

"I don't care. What were you thinking of?"

"How about Martinis?"

"Fine, as long as it's not Tequila. Liza and I had a serious Tequila evening night before last. It will be a long while before I do that again. Anyway it requires a passionate companion."

Daniel laughed, "I know what you mean. Marilee and I tried the shot, lime, and salt approach a couple of weeks ago. We made a lot of noise later in the evening and the next morning. I lost a whole day of painting, but we did a great deal of smiling and giggling."

We sat around the table for another hour, remembering our last weeks in Dallas together in their back yard. The one thing they missed was the pool but nothing else except family. Dad had told me to tell them he was saving one of his folding chairs for them; his design and a model had reached the finals in the New York contest. The $250 prize was great, but the $1,000 would have been better, he said. Rosie had sent her love and her wish that Daniel and Marilee would be home for the birth. She and Uncle Willy had gone over to check on the pool and had tried out his warm water system. They liked it. Daniel and Marilee hadn't heard that Dick and Camila were both accepted to Harvard. I hadn't realized how much I had missed Marilee and Daniel and our talks about art, the family, how much love there was in the family, and friends.

After our second drink, Marilee said we should go out for dinner at an inn just off the plaza that had the only real dining room in town. I agreed, if I could take a nap first. Daniel liked the idea of a nap, and Marilee said she would join him after she planted two more plants she had bought that morning.

The nap turned out to be good thing because the whiskey had relaxed me so much I fell on the bed and into a most needed rest from the drive, and the lunch. I didn't dream at all, which was rare; usually Claire and Liza danced in my head. I woke up after three hours of good rest. I rolled over and read Claire's letter again trying to read between the lines. It was all there plain and simple. She loved me, she was only mildly happy, most of that had to do with her job. There was something else in her writing that was a different kind of sadness, but I couldn't quite figure it out. I took out the pictures of her Jeordie had taken, and looked at the one where she was facing me with that look of total giving. It was astounding how Jeordie had found that shot from behind me. Her mouth was slightly open almost inviting me to kiss her. I tried to remember the moment, but couldn't. It was either at my parent's house or in the lobby of the theatre; Jeordie had blurred the background so I couldn't identify where it was. I went through the other photos and thought about calling Jeordie to thank him for concentrating so much on Claire. I wondered if Claire might have suspected that when she gave him the Leica, he would record our falling in love. I laid out the shots in what I thought was a progression of time, and the change in her was startling. She seemed to soften, and her smiled changed. The last one was of us in the lobby holding hands and looking at each other before we left to go to the hotel. Would I ever see her again, I wondered.

We piled into the Chrysler and headed into town. I was wearing my new boots and thought it would be good to get used to them. They fit like gloves, with a softness that was an assurance of their high quality. Claire had done it again. The drive immediately impressed on me how small Taos was, and I liked it. The air was fresh with a kind of green scent. People were sitting around the plaza, and the craftsmen still had their wares out on blankets. I saw several pieces I would like to have bought for both Claire and Liza. Flowers were planted everywhere, in pots in the windows, in the square, and on the roofs of the stores and other buildings. I knew Taos was a dusty little town, but it didn't seem so with all the flowers around the plaza. We passed a small bar that Marilee pointed out as a favorite of theirs. As we walked out of the square, we turned toward the little Inn on the street that was also on the state road that we had come in on. As we entered the inn, Daniel and Marilee were greeted by the staff as regulars. We were shown through the dining room to the patio in back. It was getting close to dark, so lanterns and candles were lighted all around us on the patio. The other patrons were of a world very different from Dallas. They appeared as if they had found a sanctuary away from the other parts of the country, which was, of course, why I was here too. The meal was excellent, as were the wine and drinks. When we walked back to the car the square was quiet, almost deserted except for the music coming from the bar we had passed earlier. At the house, we had a nightcap on the patio, with easy conversation about the evening and the walk. I felt the softening atmosphere of the environment begin to inspire me for the weeks ahead.

The next morning, I slept late and had breakfast alone. Daniel was in his small studio in back, and Marilee was working in the garden. I joined her outside for a cup of coffee and watched her putter about in one of her flowerbeds. We talked for a few minutes, then I went into my room to set up my little desk with typewriter and paper. My window was open with a view of the backyard and Daniel's studio. I wrote for six hours, with only a short break for a snack with Marilee and Daniel. We spent our evening together, and this became our custom for the weeks before they left for New York. The next weekend, Liza came up on Saturday in a new Ford station wagon, and we spent two days touring around Taos. We went to the Pueblo, which was like going back in time seeing the Indians living as they had for several hundred years. The church in Ranchos was a second destination and an affirmation of the old culture in Northern New Mexico. We sat beside the Rio Grande and went skinny-dipping in the hot springs with Daniel and Marilee. Liza and I spent our two evenings in sweet passionate lovemaking with little talk of past or future.

The weekdays were concentrated work time for Daniel and me. He turned out one fine painting after another, and all of them took him to new levels of enhancing his newfound style of vibrant colors and unrealistic figures. My writing was also finding a style of how I wanted to describe my directing process with new ideas happening every week that I wished I had thought of during *Blood Wedding*. Marilee spent an hour every day on the phone with her business managers in Texas and Oklahoma. Her Far Eastern operations she handled by mail. She appeared to be happier than I had ever seen her. Occasionally, they talked about their coming marriage with an innocent anticipation. They didn't expect big changes in their lives, just more confirmation of their love. At times I envied their happiness, but mostly I enjoyed the way they shared it with me as a brother and sister.

Four weeks after arriving, Liza joined us again for a weekend camping trip up to the Twining Valley. We cooked on the campfire, hiked into the mountains, and shared brandy under the stars. Liza and I found we could make very quiet love under the blankets lying side by side. After five weeks, Daniel and Marilee packed up his paintings in a trailer attached to the back of the station wagon. They were driving back to Dallas and then taking a train to New York. Our parting was bittersweet because I didn't know when I would see them again. Marilee insisted on leaving a substantial amount of money in the bank for me; I protested, but she said it was an investment in my future.

Two days later, I moved into the bedroom upstairs knowing Taos would be my home for a long time and that I would return here from Albuquerque and Santa Fe. I was now getting close to finishing my directing book, so I set aside two days every week to study Yerma. I was also falling in love with this new project and looking forward to starting it.

Chapter 17
Los Misterios de Las Mujeres

Three weeks before I was to leave for Albuquerque, Liza called me to invite me to Santa Fe. I agreed and left on Friday afternoon. We went out for the evening and came home to drinks outside. Liza seemed distracted but not distant, as if there was something she needed to tell me. I asked, but she replied that she just excited about my being there with her and had anticipated it all week. In bed that night, Liza was more passionate than I had ever seen her. We made love several times, and she insisted I not use a prophylactic because she wanted to feel me inside her. I was hesitant but the whiskey overwhelmed my common sense. In the morning when I awoke, she was holding me and stroked me to an erection, then climbed on top of me and eased down with me inside her. She leaned down and kissed me, rubbing her breasts on my chest. Just before my climax, she rolled over and wrapped her legs around me to pull me deeper into her. I stayed with her until she climaxed, pulling me so tightly to her I could barely breathe. She whimpered, shook, and kept saying, "Oh, Tim, so good, so good, stay inside me."

As we lay in each other's arms afterwards, she said, "Tim, I've missed loving you so much. When you drove up I wanted to take you right to bed."

"My word, Liza! I'm glad you didn't or we never would have eaten, but then I probably would have let you lead me to the bedroom."

She giggled and snuggled next to me. We dozed a little more. Late in the morning, Liza took me with her to the shower where we soaped each other and made love standing up. There was a desperation in her lovemaking that hadn't been there before.

We rinsed off just as the hot water ran out. I felt like crawling back to the bed but made it on foot and collapsed, spread out and exhausted. Liza sat beside me, with her beautiful breasts bare, her nipples red from my attention earlier. She took my head to her breasts.

"Liza, I can't make love again now. Lie back and let me hold you."

"You're right, I don't think I could either." She laughed and turned toward me, "Would you, my powerful man, like some coffee?"

"Yes, I would, incredible lady, more than, well almost, anything, in the world."

"I will attend to that almost anything later." She looked at me for a minute with a focus I hadn't seen before. "Tim, at this moment, you are very important to me. Do you understand?"

"I'm not sure. How so?"

"I...uh...I'm not able to really explain it. You just are."

With that, she put on a robe and went down to make the coffee. When she came up with the pot and cups, we got into a discussion about my writing. I told her the new ideas that had come up in the process of trying to describe my work and about the problems I was attempting to solve. The one I was having the most difficulty with was warm-ups. She remembered how Aurora had led them with some simple movements as they recited the sonnets. I wouldn't always have an Aurora, so what was the answer? She asked if I could lead the warm-ups with some sort of physical thing.

"I could, but I'm not a dancer. Wait! Are there any good bookstores here in Santa Fe? Possibly one that leans more towards the esoteric, or has arts and exercise books?"

"Yes, I've seen one just north of the plaza. It's small but it has interesting things in the window. Several times I've thought about going in to snoop around. Do you want to try it?"

"Yes, I don't know what I'm looking for, but I'm ready to look in all kinds of different directions. After we eat, let's go."

"Sounds good to me. Do you want to go out for lunch or have, say, sandwiches here?"

"Either or. Your choice."

"Well...let's have sandwiches here and spend the afternoon and evening out."

We had another cup of coffee. I shaved and dressed then sat on the bed and watched Liza dress and put on her limited makeup. Occasionally she would turn to me and smile and send a kiss across the room.

She had made a meatloaf earlier in the week remembering I had mentioned how much I liked my mother's, so we had meatloaf sandwiches for lunch. Liza had put a Santa Fe touch on hers. After eating, we drove to the Plaza in my car, parked a block north, and walked to the bookstore.

I found about twenty books I wanted to buy, but it was awhile before I discovered what I was looking for. In a small collection of oriental volumes a book named <u>Tai Chi</u> caught my eye. It was bound sewn together in the Oriental fashion, with thread and thick paper covers. The script was limited but was filled with simple drawings of movements that appeared to be smooth and flowing; but the most interesting thing about it was the four way flip drawings of the process. You could flip the pages and stick drawings would move. They were on the top and bottom. You could turn the book over and go back the other way. The movements were listed in a 1, 2, 3, and 4 fashion. After reading and flipping for thirty minutes I knew I may have found the answer; it would take some study and practice, but I felt it would enhance a cast's concentration even more than what Aurora had done. I bought it and a couple more books on theatre, one of which was a rare <u>Brecht in Rehearsal</u>. I mentioned to the proprietor that I had worked Carl Franklin's bookstore in Dallas, and it turned out he knew my boss very well through correspondence. I told him what I was doing in New Mexico. He said to send him a copy of my book if it was published. He gave me his card, and Liza and I were off to spend the rest of the afternoon and evening in Santa Fe. We visited art galleries and curio shops, finally eating dinner at the La Fonda.

Back at Liza's house, we sat on the patio and drank some very good Spanish brandy she had purchased the week before. It wasn't Villa-Lobos but was close enough. After our first brandy, Liza took my hand, led me upstairs to the bedroom, and proceeded to undress me. She lighted several candles, turned off the lights, and undressed herself in the dim light. There was a glow about her that I had not seen before, almost as if she had turned on her aura, but I quickly realized it was the light gold of her skin in the flickering candles. Sitting down beside me on the bed she stroked my chest and leaned down to kiss me moving her breasts back and forth across me. She reached down to hold and arouse me.

"Love me slowly, Tim, please. Oh, my God, that's so good."

She arched her back and moved in a circular motion. She was making little girl sounds in a voice that was new to me.

"That's why I chose you, Tim. Oh my God...I hope it..."

"You hope it what, Liza?"

"I...uh...hope it happens like this again. Don't you?"

I didn't answer her. I wasn't sure I could give an answer that she wanted to hear. I kissed her in response and licked the sweat from her eyes.

I didn't know if I fell asleep on top of her or not, but I awakened feeling rested but sore all through my lower back and loins. Liza was still sleeping. I put on a robe and went downstairs to make coffee. I had one cup standing outside on the patio trying to figure out the night before. It wasn't real love, but an almost frighteningly desperate coupling. It was an exciting rage of passion, but... Why did she insist on not using any protection? I knew she cared for me, but the intensity wasn't something I wanted to experience often. I remembered the gentleness of my love with Claire and missed her deeply. I couldn't imagine that sort of rage happening between us, nor would I have ever wanted it to happen. But Claire was gone, and here I was with this powerfully passionate woman. I knew I would never understand many of the mysteries that are so much a part of women.

I took a pot of the coffee and cups upstairs. Liza was still sleeping, nude, spread out on the bed. All of her was exposed, and even with my previous thoughts, she was an arousing presence. I sat down beside her and she opened her eyes.

She smiled. "I had a little dream that you were still inside me. Coffee? Good man, Tim, I'm glad you didn't wait for me to make it."

"I can do more than direct plays, and you do look especially beautiful this morning," I laughed, "All of you."

I poured her a cup but she didn't move for several more minutes. She slowly sat up and took the cup.

"Strong. Good, I needed it to be. Thank you, sir."

We sat in silence for awhile, savoring the coffee.

"When are you going to drive back?"

"I guess early afternoon, if I can walk to my car."

She threw her head back in that full laughter of hers.

We finished the coffee and Liza took her shower without me as I lay back and tried to doze a bit more with little success. I eventually got downstairs for breakfast. Our conversation centered around the previous evenings sensual encounter which didn't help me to understand it any better except that she was thankful for my giving her a gift of fulfillment. I smiled. I felt pretty fulfilled myself. Or perhaps sated was a better word for what I felt. She asked me to stay another night as if to promise more of the same intensity. I begged off, saying I needed to get back to work early Monday. When she walked me out to my car, she hugged me in what seemed like a goodbye. She began to cry and thanked me through the sobs. I promised to call her.

On the drive back up to Taos, I had a thousand thoughts about the weekend and Liza. I wondered if it was the last time I would see her for awhile, or even ever. I wasn't sure how I felt about it. If we did see more of each other, I hoped our encounters would be less desperate. I didn't know why there seemed to be such desperation in her lovemaking. She had always been extremely passionate, but this was different, a new extreme for me that was almost scary. Being with Liza was like having a lengthy encounter with a movie star who needed as much satisfactions as she could get before heading off on another project. This didn't mean it was an unpleasant, just highly concentrated. But she was such a delightful companion that I knew I would gladly spend more time with her. I was as lonely as she was, but I was lonely for Claire, and I wasn't sure Liza was lonely for her husband. Claire seemed more than ever the perfect woman for me. Knowing Gwen and Liza had made me sure of that. Both were two of the finest women in the Western Hemisphere, but Claire was and is the perfect, albeit seemingly unattainable, woman for me. Thinking about her wasn't depressing, but instilled in me a resolve. I hoped there was a letter from her waiting for me.

There was no letter; I didn't want to start work until Monday so I just read for pleasure. When dusk came, I mixed a Bourbon and soda and went up on the upstairs balcony and watched the sun go down. It was actually good to be alone and think about what I had to do in the coming week. *Yerma* needed much more study; it was in its way even more complicated than *Blood Wedding* and almost as passionate, but more about the desperation for passion.

Desperation for passion. Oh my God! Isn't that what I had thought about Liza's intense lovemaking? No, not passion, although that was there, but not love as in being in love, the kind that Claire and I felt for each other. Well, perhaps it was a partial emotional memory I could use as a director. I wished then that I hadn't had thoughts about Liza, but I decided that when I saw Liza again, I would try to get her to explain, if possible, what had brought about such intensity. When making love with Liza, my thoughts about her as a woman were different from any I had felt before. I seemed to need to perform to whatever her expectations or needs were, and try not to disappoint her. It was disturbing and a bit mysterious, as if I was being used. Hopefully it was just an anomaly that had taken hold of her, I didn't think the reason was a strong attraction to me, but the way she had been talking in a sort of mysterious code; 'choosing me' and all that, opened up the possibility that she was using me. Liza made me feel innocent in the ways of physical love, and I wasn't sure I wanted to lose that. But in my experiences with Claire there was both an innocence and completeness.

After the sun went down, I fixed some dinner, drove into town to the Plaza, and had a drink at the small bar Marilee and Daniel had introduced me to. In bed that night, I set out Jeordie's photos of Claire. She entered my dreams as I eased into sleep. At coffee the next morning I started reading the book on tai-chi. The text was limited, but from it I realized there was more to tai-chi than exercise and movement. After I studied the drawings and then the flip pages, I stood and walked to the small lawn part of the back yard and began to try the movements. I went back several times to the book and slowly was able to do some simple exercises. I not only liked it as a potential warm-up but felt it was a good way to start the day. After a couple of hours I fixed breakfast and looked at the book more to figure out how to connect the movements. I wanted more, so I called Mr. Franklin at the bookstore in Dallas. He said he would contact a friend in San Francisco to try to find more books for me. And if that didn't work he would call New York, but he was sure he could get me several books by the next week. We talked about my writing and the life in Taos. He wished me luck and said to call him any time I needed something. A good voice from the recent past.

I spent the rest of the day writing and afterwards going over *Yerma*.

On the afternoon of the next day, the mailman brought me a letter and a package from Claire. I opened the package first to find two framed watercolors from her, they were drawn from her memories of Dallas. One was of Marilee's backyard looking out on Turtle Creek with two people in a boat, kissing. I immediately remembered it as our first kiss. The other was of me up on stage looking at someone in the audience. They were breathtakingly beautiful and brought out all of the emotions that raged through me when the powerful images of her danced in my head. The letter was a recounting of her train trip to Los Angeles, almost moment by moment. She had only mentioned it briefly in her past letters. She was very clear in her expression of how difficult the separation from me was and how bleak her future looked to her then. The writing was deeply personal and more intimate than she had written before. She described a physical withdrawal from my touch that caused her to cry and shiver almost uncontrollably. She hid these, what she called little seizures, by pulling a blanket around her. I knew exactly what she means because for our last weeks together we were always touching, holding hands, kissing, loving, our arms around each other. For the first weeks of separation I could feel her touch even though she wasn't there. I didn't have seizures but short periods of trance like blankness. She said they eased as she started her life in Los Angeles, but returned several times a week. The letter was long, with descriptions of the scenery from the train and how lonely it was to see it without me. She ended with some information about her job and how it was developing, and closed with hope I liked the paintings. She drew a tiny colored calligraphy of I love you. I sensed there was something she hadn't said.

I wrote all the rest of the afternoon on my directing book, and in the evening I wrote Claire a long letter telling her I had the same feelings of withdrawal from her touch and that it still occurred. And I assured her I had been beside her on the trip west. It was at first hard to describe how much I loved the paintings without going over all of the emotions they brought back. The Turtle Creek scene was like us looking at us, and I hoped she shared the same thoughts of how we had started our love on that late afternoon and the teasing from Marilee about being smitten. I praised the portrait she did of me on stage that truly captured the look of love I was giving her in the audience. I tried to explain that I sensed she wasn't telling me something.

Every morning I did more tai-chi exercises and began to feel the difference they made in my concentration and physical feeling. My writing continued through the week. Each day I got better at self-editing and could see the end in sight. On Saturday afternoon, I called Liza to say I couldn't make it down to Santa Fe, but there was no answer at her house. I tried later in the day, with the same result. Sunday was the same. It was probably better that she wasn't available because I didn't believe I could take another lovemaking marathon.

Slowly, I got to know some people in the community and was invited out to dinner several times. Everyone seemed to have an artistic reason for being in Taos, even if it was to recharge in this sanctuary. Except for the loneliness, I knew it would be hard to leave, but I was ready to get back to directing. I tried steadily to reach Liza, but she had disappeared. Four weeks later, I got a letter from her.

Liza had gone back to Dallas to prepare for a trip to Hawaii to see her husband. He had written saying he would meet her there for a couple of weeks. She was already on her way to Los Angeles to catch a Clipper or cruise liner and would try to write me when she got back. I doubted I would hear from her.

Mr. Franklin had come through on the tai-chi books. I got two from San Francisco and three from New York. By the time I had finished my book and was getting ready to leave for Albuquerque, I was becoming expert enough to lead exercises for every rehearsal. During my last week in Taos, I got a long letter from Marilee and Daniel that included a really fancy brochure on Daniel's coming gallery opening. They surprised me with the news that they had gotten married at the City Hall in New York. I was deeply sorry I hadn't been there for the wedding and his opening. Marilee did say she had sent Claire one of the brochures and the news of their wedding.

After a pleasant drive down, I met Dr. John Miller at his university office in Albuquerque. He showed me the campus theatre and the facilities around them. I was introduced to the rest of the faculty who had stayed for the summer. I immediately liked the technical director and the scene designer. My stage manager was a senior student who had just come back from the East doing an internship at a summer theatre in Connecticut. The theatre plant was not that different from The Civic in Dallas, except that it had more wing space, larger dressing rooms, and a big scene shop behind the stage.

My living quarters turned out to be better than I had hoped. It was a nice small apartment behind the house of an English Professor who was in England for the summer. That first evening I had dinner at Dr. Miller's house. His wife was a striking teacher of history. She had specialized in the history of Spain so there was a lot of discussion about Lorca.

The next day was spent at the theatre working with the designers. The costume designer was an Hispanic woman, named Carmen Durango, who looked like a Mexican movie star. She could have been thirty or fifty years old. Her beginning drawings for the play were very good. We talked about advancing the colors with more differentiation between the men using hats and boots. Because they were shepherds, I wanted to see sheepskins over their shoulders. Carmen seemed to like everything I suggested which I felt was a good start.

The designers and I went out to dinner together for some excellent New Mexico-style cuisine. That evening in the theatre, we had a general cast call for the University and community actors, it was going to be, thank goodness, an open call not limited to the school population. The meeting was really an introduction for me where I could talk about the play and describe my directing process including the warm-ups. I talked for an hour and a half with an hour of questions afterwards. Many of them questioned the process I was describing. They were all a little surprised about my using the whole evening for auditions, moving them in and out of a semi-run-through and scene repetition. They were all used to reading and leaving. I assured them the play could be cast in two nights with callbacks on the second. To end the evening, I had drinks with Carmen and John Miller at a great bar two blocks from the campus. Where there was music and dancing. I found out Carmen was a widow whose husband had been killed in Spain in the beginning of the Civil War. I told her about my friend Dick and Camila. John's wife, Jane, joined us bringing a friend who evidently was a companion for me. Anjelica Burana-Lobos was a raven-haired young Hispanic woman who worked in the archeological department as a researcher. She had a doctorate from the University of Arizona and specialized in studying ancient Indian sites, primarily the Anasazi ruins. She had an outdoorsy look and was extremely attractive-copper skin, black eyes, and a trim figure. We had no trouble talking and going through the getting-to-know-you routine. Her first questions were about why a young Anglo director from Dallas had chosen to direct a classic modern Spanish play. It wasn't antagonistic just curiosity. I told of my success with another Lorca play and my mild fluency in Spanish. That satisfied her and we went on to the book I was writing, which Jane Miller had told her about. I explained it was no more than a project now, even though it was finished from my side and now had to be approved and go through editing by the University Press. The evening didn't go very late, and Anjelica gave me a ride back to my apartment. She offered to show me around Albuquerque, and I accepted.

Before going to sleep, I wondered about Anjelica, thinking I couldn't let anything distract me from this important task of making *Yerma* an even stronger production than *Blood Wedding*. Well, perhaps she wasn't interested in distracting or even seeing me again, and it had been just a polite gesture on her part to offer a tour of the town. I looked at the picture of Claire beside my bed and went to sleep.

The next two nights' auditions went very well. Rehearsals started three days later. Most of the cast had spent time familiarizing themselves with the script, but almost all of them voiced doubts about learning their lines before they were blocked. I assured them it was possible because I had used this method before. One actor asked how long my rehearsal period had been when I had used this process before.

"Almost six weeks." I told them.

One University actor questioned it working in the four weeks we had to put up *Yerma*.

"With lot of concentration and good rehearsals, I believe it can be done with very strong results," I said, trying to reassure them.

Hoping to quash any more doubts, I handed out copies of the sonnets I wanted them to memorize for warm-ups and demonstrated examples of the Tai-Chi we would do together while reciting the sonnets. They first reacted with laughter, and then seemed almost resentful that I was asking them to memorize more than their lines. I calmed them down and asked the stage manager to set up a crescent of chairs for a read-through. As we read through the play, I attempted to describe how we improvised with the script. The evening ended with a great deal of grumbling and no questions.

Later, at my apartment, I reread the script, but was discouraged by the reaction of the cast. I wondered if it could be done in four weeks after hearing their doubts, but I was committed to it.

The next morning I had a meeting with John Miller to discuss the cast's reaction to the way I wanted to direct the play. He had already heard about it, but he had confidence in what I wanted to do. I mentioned the four-week rehearsal period as one of their main concerns.

"Tim, I also was worried about that, but felt it could be handled with your leadership."

"It's going to take more than my leadership; they're going to need to want to try something new and experimental."

"Yes, I certainly agree with you on that, but this cast may not be as sophisticated as the one you worked with in Dallas. Don't give up on it."

"I wasn't even contemplating giving up, I just wanted to discuss it with you, I guess as my mentor here at the University."

I left to spend most of the day working in the theatre shop, then back to my apartment for more script study.

That evening, only two of the cast had tried to memorize the sonnets, and all of them quit half way through trying to follow me in a tai-chi warm-up. I summoned all the confidence I could and tried a simple walk-through of the first scenes. They didn't understand my side directing, so they would stop, no matter how many times I urged them to continue. The concept of general directions being spoken almost constantly was so new to them they couldn't grasp it. They insisted on stopping to listen to my words and ask questions. I knew I was attempting to concentrate the process because of the time restrictions, but it obviously wasn't working. After a break, I spent more time in a simple lecture using the ideas I had expressed in my writings. It was received with little enthusiasm. We attempted more scene work, but it was even less successful than the first part of the rehearsal. We ended the evening in a sort of stalemate.

In my past experiences, especially in beginning work, I had left rehearsals a bit scared but never as discouraged about one like this. I decided to go to the bar John and Carmen had introduced me to several nights ago. There was a large University crowd, but I found a stool at the bar. Luckily, there was no one there from the cast. I worked my way through two Bourbons and pondered about the last two evenings. I ended the evening at my apartment with a glass of brandy, wishing Claire were with me for encouragement. I spent the next day going over my writings to see if I could simplify my description of the way I directed *Blood Wedding*. I wrote several pages of notes, hoping they would convince the cast it would work. When I arrived at the theatre early for rehearsal the stage manager met me in the lobby to tell me the cast was having a meeting with John Miller and for me to wait for him in his office. Dr. Miller arrived after I waited very anxiously for an hour.

He sat behind his desk. After a few minutes of silence, he said, "Tim, the cast had no idea they were stepping into what they considered an extremely experimental rehearsal process to be done in a short period for a complicated play. I know you tried to explain your approach during auditions, but they don't believe they can adapt to it in this short amount of time."

"And, what does this mean? I hope it doesn't imply we should cancel the production."

"No, it doesn't. Tim, how many plays have you directed?"

"Uh...I guess about twenty-five, not all of them full length shows. Some were touring pieces, or specialty things like Commedia dell' Arte. Probably twenty full-length ones."

"And only one of those was done using your new method, right?"

"Yes."

"I assume most of them were successful."

"Yes. Luckily I haven't had a real failure. Not all were raging successes, but all were well received."

"I explained to them that you were a successful director from a very good theatre and had directed many plays in a way they could work with. They want early blocking and extensive scene work and wouldn't mind run-throughs of the work at the end of the week."

"Well, this is a major disappointment, but..."

"Tim, I want you to know I believe in your work, and that what I saw in Dallas was extraordinary. Also, I'm not giving up on doing a production here using your ideas. This cast does like you personally and wants to continue if you will go back to the usual way of directing

"John, I like this play and this cast very much. They look great and all had good auditions. Of course, I'll do it, if that's the way you want it done."

"It's not the way I want it done, and I know it may seem like blackmail, but don't think of it like that, please. Don't consider it a setback, just an artistic adjustment.

"How does this affect my status here at the University?"

"In no way what-so-ever."

"Well, that's a relief. I have a serious day of work tomorrow."

"I know, several weeks crammed into one day, well, perhaps not that bad knowing how well you know the play. I had a strong feeling you would agree, so the cast is waiting in the theatre."

The cast was sitting in the crescent formation and obviously anxious for my decision. I took my chair in the center, smiled at them and said, "Well, let's get to work."

They already had their scripts in hand, pencils ready. Evidently, Dr. Miller had convinced them I would step right into a more conventional approach. I proceeded to describe a timetable and concept as I had many times before. There was a completely different atmosphere at the end of rehearsal. My last words were to ask them to carry their scripts and a pencil throughout the rest of the week's rehearsals. I wanted all of their blocking written down, but also said to have a good eraser ready for any changes. I promised I would have the play completely blocked for tomorrow's meeting. Before leaving the theatre, I asked my stage manager, who was in much better spirits than he had been earlier, if he could find me a chalkboard for the next rehearsal. He said it wouldn't be a problem and shook my hand.

John Miller was waiting for me in the lobby.

"That seemed to be a happy cast. They thanked me for changing your mind."

"It was not much of an adaption, I just reverted back to what I've used many times before. I have lost two days of rehearsal, though, so tomorrow will be quite busy. I promised to have the entire play blocked."

"I have a feeling you'll be using more of your new method without the cast even realizing it."

"Probably without me even realizing it."

"Do you feel good about all of the technical aspects?"

"Very much so. Your designers are terrific; that's one part of the production that is ahead of schedule."

"Tim, Jane and I want to take you out to dinner Saturday night."

"That sounds good. What's the occasion?"

"Well, I may have some good news about your book. I recommended it to the University press and the editor told me today they liked it very much and would let me know something by the end of the week."

"That's great; I certainly didn't expect a reaction this soon."

"You may have a second career as a writer, Tim."

"I'm not sure I have a first career."

"Yes you do. Oh, do you mind if we invite Angelica? You rather charmed her."

"Not in the least. She rather charmed me too."

"Good, come at seven for drinks. Do you think you can find your way?"

"Of course, I'll see you then, if not before."

I spent the rest of the evening building a prompt book from a drawing tablet I had bought on a whim in Taos. I cut the centers out of the pages and pasted in the pages of the script. It gave me plenty of room to write and draw in blocking patterns for each page to the sides. After finishing, I had a glass of brandy and thought about the coming Saturday, my book, and Angelica. I didn't know what I did to charm her, but she had entered my thoughts several times since meeting her. A slight distraction with a new friend could be a good thing after my past weeks of being alone, though I didn't expect any sort of relationship to develop because she seemed much too serious about her work for that to happen.

I went to sleep with Claire's last letter in my hands.

The next day was spent in blocking the entire play, a labor that had taken me weeks in the past. The work with *Blood Wedding* was more valuable than I had thought it would be, I just improvised in my mind and applied it to paper. After my previous work on *Yerma,* it was a true secondary visualization.

That evening I used the chalkboard the stage manager had found to describe and draw the movement for each character in every scene. We finished up with a walk-through of the first scene and I asked them to try to learn their lines for that scene. By Friday night, we had completed the blocking for the whole play. I requested an early Saturday afternoon run-through, which went very well. The cast was showing real excitement for the production, to my great relief.

I left the theatre at five and headed back to the apartment. It was cool enough to wear my boots and light suede jacket, I wanted to look a bit spiffy for the evening; perhaps this Anjelica lady was already slight distraction in my mind.

I was the first to arrive at John's house. Jane greeted me with a surprising hug and took me to their back porch, where John was setting up a bar for the drinks.

"Welcome, Tim. What's your pleasure?"

"Bourbon and soda, if possible."

"I don't have a soda bottle, but will good branch water do?"

"Indeed it will."

"Bourbon is my drink, too, Jane prefers gin with tonic. How was your day at the theatre?"

"Very productive. We had a good run-through, and the designers and I settled on the colors for both scenery and costumes. They have the advantage of being able to work all day as opposed to what I'm used to in community theatre."

"Don't downplay the professional qualities of what you did with your show there. It was as good as any I've seen anywhere."

"Thank you. I noticed your art as I came through. It's a great collection of western paintings. My mother and brother are both painters. As a matter of fact, Daniel has a show opening this week in New York."

"I saw that in the *Blood Wedding* program notes. We lean towards the Indian painters here in New Mexico. We've been here for twenty-five years now and fell in love long ago with the regional subjects. We'll be going up to Santa Fe for the Indian market later this month to look for some more art; Jane has gotten into native blankets, the older the better."

As John handed me a drink, Anjelica walked in. I had almost forgotten how eye-catching she was. She was wearing classy New Mexico garb in earth tones-a long skirt with a white peasant blouse. She looked almost like a character in *Blood Wedding*. Her hair was braided in two long pigtails down her back. She offered her hand, smiling.

"Good evening, Tim, or do you prefer Timothy? I think I do."

"Which ever you prefer, but it's good to hear Timothy."

"Then Timothy it is. How have your weeks here been so far?"

"Every moment a joy."

She laughed, enjoying the word-play. When she laughed, she looked straight in my eyes as if she was on the same wavelength as I humor wise.

"I've had to completely change my approach to directing the play, but it's going fairly well now."

"That's good to hear. I wish I could say the same. I've been out on a dig near the four corners with no great results."

Jane smiled at our quick banter, "Will you join me in a Gin, Anjelica?"

"I don't know, yet. What are you having, Timothy"

"Bourbon and water. Mighty fine."

"I haven't had any of that Kentucky juice in awhile, so make mine Bourbon also, please, Jane."

"That Ford of yours is quite a machine, Timothy. I'll bet you've gotten a lot of looks, Albuquerque is a real car town. There are a couple of shops here that do similar work, but I've never seen a paint job like that, and the lowered top is great. What else is different about it?"

"A whole bunch of stuff. Bigger engine, hydraulic brakes, new seats, bigger radiator, and a special exhaust system. You must like cars."

"I do, very much, but right now I'm doing with my Chevy Suburban. It's good for all the rough travel I do. I may try very hard to talk you into letting me drive that 'whammo' of yours."

"Whammo? Hey, that's a good name for it. I haven't driven it to its full potential yet, but it is strong in the mountains. And as for your driving it, you'll have get in it first. Which could be anytime."

The Millers were enjoying what was going on between Anjelica and me. So was I, and surprised.

We talked about art and theatre for an hour and left for a wonderful dinner. We returned to the Millers' for brandy and liqueur. As the evening was ending, Anjelica asked me if I was free tomorrow for a tour of Albuquerque. I said I was, and she said she would come to my apartment at ten the next morning so we could have breakfast at a favorite place of hers. The pleasant evening and the alcohol eased me into sleep.

I was up a little after nine the morning and was ready just as Anjelica knocked at my door. I asked her in for a cup of coffee before we left. She immediately noticed Claire's watercolors and Daniel's oils I had hung on the walls as soon as I had arrived. She also noticed the pictures of Claire, which I explained as someone from the past, but not forgotten. She accepted that, and we discussed the past evening and the plans for the day. She asked if we could take my car and if maybe she could drive it later. I agreed and we were off.

"Wow! What a great sound! Don't hold back. I want to hear it with more RPM."

I stayed in each gear longer and pulled back in third. She laughed and clapped her hands with excitement. She guided me to the restaurant. There was a variation on eggs Benedict and huevos rancheros with a red sauce. It turned out to be the best breakfast of my New Mexico experience so far. She asked if she could drive during the tour, which I quickly agreed to. There was no doubt Anjelica understood how to drive sporty cars. She took it just to the edge of legal. I think we saw everything there was to see, but she assured me we were just beginning because there was much more in the surrounding areas. As the day headed into dusk, she asked if I would join her at her house for dinner. I nodded with a smile, and we stopped at a grocery store for the fixins'. We agreed on steak and three kinds of squash and the most luscious looking bread I'd ever seen.

Anjelica's house was a small dark yellow adobe-stucco in the older part of town. It was delightful with artifacts and Indian Art everywhere in her living room. The collection was amazing. The office and den were stacked with more art and had maps covering the walls. When she showed me her kitchen, I noticed a bottle of my favorite Spanish brandy, Villa-Lobos Gran Especial.

"My word, you have Villa-Lobos!"

"I'm surprised you know of it. A branch of my family in Spain makes it. They send me a case every year. Very few people I know have ever heard of it."

"What a wonderful coincidence. I was introduced to it just this past spring, and I love it. I have a bottle at the apartment. My soon to be sister-in-law, Marilee, will love this story."

"I'll mix you a drink I invented using it."

She half-filled an Old Fashion glass with the brandy over ice, then added currant liqueur, and topped it with soda from a spritzer bottle. It became my favorite drink after good Bourbon.

"Let's go out side and sit for awhile before I start dinner," she suggested.

She had a small patio and a luxurious garden that was on the edge of being wildly overgrown.

"I've been traveling so much lately that it's gotten out of hand back here."

"It reminds me of my sister-in-law's garden in Taos. I like it. The over manicured look is not my sort of garden."

"Well, you're in the right place then," she laughed.

We spent an hour telling each other about our lives. I discovered we were the same age. She had graduated early and then gone right for her master's and Ph.D. New Mexico had hired her right after she had gotten her doctorate, and she had been working in the field for two years. Her family was from the southern part of the state, where they had a very large, successful ranching business raising cattle and farming. Her family had wanted her to go east for school, but schools there didn't have the Southwestern Archeological studies; besides this is where her heart was. She was surprised I hadn't gone to college but was impressed by my theatre experience in the last nine years. All of my family being in the arts was not a surprise to her. She had noticed my familiarity with and interest in the Millers' collection. I joined her in the kitchen and did what I could to help. During the excellent dinner, she revealed she wasn't attached or dating anyone because of her constant field work, and that she hadn't found anyone interesting enough to make the time for. Her family was insistent, or had been, that she date only Hispanic men, but she had let them know she would never limit her friendships to a racial qualification. They weren't alienated but now expressed only mild disapproval of her choices in men, most of whom had been Anglo. After dinner, we had a snifter of Villa-Lobos, as I finally stood to leave, she came to me for a soft hug and a promise we would get together again in the next weeks.

We walked out to my car, and she stroked the roof line and fenders, "I really like your Whammo Ford, Timothy, but then it seems to fit you. You're kind of a whammo, too."

"Is that good, being a whammo?"

"It most certainly is, Timothy. I'm leaving tomorrow to go back out, would you like to get together again when I return?"

"You beat me to the request, Anjelica, but I'll say it. Would you like for us to see each other again?"

"I don't know, I'm a little leery of Texans, she teased, "especially artsy ones." She laughed and reached up to kiss me. Not a passionate one, but an unqualified yes.

I got a bit lost on the way home, but that was probably because of the sweet kiss. I hoped Anjelica would return to town soon.

One week before opening, she returned. She knocked on my door after rehearsal. I had just stepped out of the shower, so I had had only time to put on my robe.

"Hi, Timothy. I know it's late, but I got in early this afternoon and my nap lasted longer than I had planned. I went by the theatre and they said you had just left, so I got up my nerve and came by..." she said nervously and quickly.

"Well, hello, Anjelica. That's alright. We ended sooner than expected. We got a lot of work done. They were all exhausted by the run-through, so I..."

"I know a nice bar that stays open fairly late, so would you like to go out for a drink."

"That sounds good. Come in and let me get dressed."

"Do you want me to wait here?"

"No, no, come on in. We're both grown-ups."

She sat down in my small living room, in the dark. I turned on the one lamp and went into the bedroom, put on my dungarees, a short-sleeved cotton jersey, my boots, and my barn coat.

"This is a most pleasant surprise, I don't think I could have slept anyway. How was your expedition?"

She smiled. "My expedition was better than the last one at the same digs. I found some nice things-two good pots and some bones. How have your rehearsals been going?"

"Very well, I think it will be a good show."

We walked outside, and I suggested we go in my Ford.

"I would much prefer that. My truck is almost a chore in the city, and I love your car, as you know. You drive, and I'll give directions."

The bar was a classy upscale Hispanic place that was almost dark except for the candles set on the tables. We chose one in the back, and the owner came over greeting Anjelica by name. She introduced me in Spanish, and I responded in kind. He took our orders and asked if we wanted something light to eat. She ordered us a plate of toasted tortillas with chicken and a mixed red tomato sauce.

"Well, Timothy, you do speak Spanish."

"Not as well as I would like to, but I can get along."

"It sounds as if..."

"I've thought of you and wondered how it was going out there."

"And I've thought of you, which is new for me. I rarely think of anyone when I'm working."

We talked for two hours over several drinks and then drove back to my place. I pulled up next to her big Chevy. I turned off the engine and we sat in the dark. After a few minutes of silence, I reached my arm around to the back of her head. She was wearing her hair down. I ran my hand through her hair, and she turned to me. I leaned to her and she towards me. She was nervous and stiff as I kissed her. I kissed her face and eyes and she put her arm around me and kissed me. We slowly learned to kiss each other. I put my other arm around her and she moved closer, not nervous, or stiff now. She moved and lay back in the seat.

"That was sweet, Timothy. I didn't know if anything like that would happen."

"I certainly didn't either, but then I didn't expect to see you at all. But yes, it was very sweet."

"Please kiss me again, Timothy."

I did, and moved close to her. She reached around and pulled me closer. After a long, gently passionate kiss, she whispered my name several times in my ear. Claire was the only woman who had ever done that before.

She sat up, "I should be getting home. When do you finish your play?"

"We open next Friday and run for three weeks. Then, after a week's break, we move the show to Santa Fe for two weeks."

"During that week off, if it is off, would you like to go camping with me? I know a place way up in the mountains that is really beautiful, and there are some hot springs. It's very secluded and there are some old trails leading up to the snow line. Does that interest you at all?"

"You bet it does! I could be off for five days if we leave Sunday and I could get to Santa Fe on Friday before the Saturday opening. I'll check with John Miller, but I'm sure it will be fine. Do I need anything special for this adventure?"

"Just some hiking boots. I've got two good sleeping bags and everything else."

"Will you be here for my opening? It would be great if you could be because it will be an exciting but lonely night if you're not."

"Next weekend? I think so. May I join you at the theatre?"

"Of course."

"I don't see how it could be lonely with all the people swarming around you."

"That will only happen if the production is very good, and I think it will be. But at that point I will have lost all objectivity. But it's always a real let-down because my job will be finished."

"Timothy, this a new thing for me, that is, wanting to spend time with someone. I'm so used to being alone but not lonely, but not lately. I don't want to impose myself on you,...I..."

"Are you kidding? If I had had the chance I would have tried to impose myself on you-at the very least, try to see you more. I've been alone for several months, or almost alone, some family and an old friend, but for the last weeks no one. Did you just hear me saying I want you to come to the opening and be with me? I expected to be alone for a long time, you are an exciting, beautiful, and interesting lady, so how could I not be happy about meeting you?"

"Dios mio, that's reassuring to hear."

"Claro que si, siento lo mismo, Anjelica."

"Well, I'll join you at the theatre Friday night. I'll be in the lab all week and working late. Come over one night after rehearsal, any night."

"I will."

I walked to her truck, where she gave me a light goodbye kiss.

The rehearsals the last week were strenuous and productive. I did go over to Anjelica's lab one night. We went out for a late drink and to her house for some Villa-Lobos. We stayed up almost all night talking, with occasional slightly passionate kisses. We were in no hurry to rush things.

The tech and dress rehearsals all went exceptionally well. On late Saturday morning, we had the last rehearsal. I went through all of my notes, working scenes that I thought could be stronger. We finished on stage and I spent an hour with the stage manager and the people running the lights and sound. I sure did miss Eddy, who would have added so much. I went back to the apartment for a shower and a short nap. I had not gotten a letter from Claire for several weeks. What was happening with her? Thank goodness Anjelica was taking away some of the burn from my missing her.

I got to the theatre an hour early and every thing was fine and ready to go. In the lobby, John Miller and I greeted the audience. Ten minutes before curtain, Anjelica arrived. John was happily surprised to see us greet with a kiss and hug. We sat in the back and watched a true success. The audience stood for an ovation to greet the cast on their curtain call. I couldn't believe it had come together after such a complete change in approach, but I was extremely relieved and thrilled. Anjelica and I went to the Millers for a cast party. John pulled me aside to ask if I wanted to take up his offer of studying at the University with a fellowship guaranteed. He said it would be a fast process to a diploma. And he asked if I wanted to direct in the early winter. I asked if I could do a workshop on improvisational directing instead, and he tentatively agreed, saying it could possibly be done with me as a guest artist.

After the cast party, Anjelica invited me to her house. We kind of collapsed into each other's arms on her couch. We mostly kissed and talked softly. Anjelica started breathing in low pants.

"Timothy, I can't...breathe," she said pulling back, "but this is very nice, you holding me. I've never kissed this much. It's always been a couple of kiss and then right to the chase."

"Anjelica," I said taking her face in my hands and gently kissing her.

"You evidently have discovered a softness in me I didn't know existed. Everybody thinks I'm so tough and rugged. Well, I did, too, until you kissed me that first time. When we first met, I was a bit put off by your overtly confident personality, but then I saw your smile, and I melted a bit. And then you taught me what a kiss could be like. A theatre man. Wow! That's something new. I'm so used to outdoor guys who are proud of their rugged ways. Softness towards women is not usually one of their characteristics. I don't mean they don't like women. Maybe they're not sure gentleness goes with strength. Does that sound right?"

"Uh...I don't have much experience with rugged-outdoorsy guys, so I can't..."

Anjelica laughed and punched me softly, "Yes...a silly question. Maybe I've just met the wrong rugged guys. And you know what, I don't know if I'm especially attracted to outdoors types. They're just the ones I'm around all the time. Well, archeological types who are out in the field for months sometimes."

"I guess people mostly have a strange opinion of folks in the theatre, and they're partly right, I've known some rather strange ones in my work. But for the most part, they're the strongest people I know. It's a ridiculously demanding process. Most characters are strong men, and it takes strong men to play them. I was an athlete before I took up theatre, and I had some of those same opinions, but I found it to be the way to express my artistic drive. Being from a family that is totally dominated by the arts is sometimes like a curse; it's almost as if I had no choice. All of my life, the arts were the primary drive, but I didn't paint or draw, design, or sculpt, so I was drawn into the high collaboration of theatre. The loneliness of the studio didn't attract me at all, although my writing has certainly headed me somewhat in that direction."

"Did you ever act?"

"Yes, in high school, but I felt a stronger affinity for directing very early on."

"I found my interest in archaeology in high school, too. And since I'm a New Mexico girl, this part of the world interested me the most. I don't really want to go to Egypt or the Gobi Desert because there's so much to study here...well, perhaps South America someday."

"I guess like I want to go to New York someday, but I'm not in a hurry."

"It's funny with all the talk we've done that we didn't get into this before. It was probably all that wonderful kissing that did it."

"If I kiss you again, will you give me one more snifter of Villa-Lobos before I go?"

"Do you want the brandy first? I like the taste of brandy on a man's lips," she said in a dramatic tone.

"How about a pre-brandy kiss first, then a brandy one a bit later?"

"Well, let me think...uh...OK." She came into my arms smiling with a new giggle.

I did get that brandy kiss later. There was a shyness between us that seemed to be right. We were still new to each other.

I went asleep that night thinking about the camping trip, hoping it would happen. Claire looked at me from the photograph, telling me she loved me, but from afar.

There was a great deal of excitement on the campus about the production. I was asked to lecture at a summer workshop of drama teachers who had seen the play. I worked with the editor of the University publishing department to finalize a galley draft. They added more performances during the week, and John Miller asked me to be there as much as possible, which turned out to be a good experience because he used it as a recruiting program. I got to talk to a lot of young people who were thinking of coming to the University to study drama. Some of them asked if I would be teaching any classes, John stepped into one of these questions sessions to say he hoped I would agree to teach some beginning classes. He turned to me with a questioning look. I nodded a yes, though a feeling of inadequacy ran through me. Teaching at a University! Boy, Dad and Mom will love that.

Anjelica and I went out to eat one night during the run, but she was so tired from work that it was an early evening. She said she would pick me up for the camping trip the next Sunday at ten in the morning.

She came in for coffee before we started. I wanted to see if she approved of the hiking boots I had gotten. She did, saying they were the best. She looked like someone out of National Geographic, except she was more beautiful than anyone I had seen in those pages. Her hair was in the double braids, and she wore no make-up, which she didn't need anyway. As we headed out of Albuquerque, I for a camera. I had only been on the main roads with some exceptions on the outskirts of Taos and up to Twinning Canyon. It was much more wide open, not like West Texas, more like Western movies with mesas and snow-capped mountains in the distance. She described the terrain and all of its history and archaeological information. Her mood was the happiest and most at ease I had seen in her so far. She even gave me a starting-the-trip kiss, which she said was for good luck. A good tradition to start. We passed through some interesting little hamlets on the way, some Hispanic, some Indian, and some Anglo. I could feel myself falling more in love with New Mexico. The only thing I missed about Texas was my family and the Civic a little bit. I knew that New Mexico could possibly be a second home, and I wasn't sure which town I liked the best.

"Do you know Taos well?" I asked.

"Yes, I think in a way it's my favorite town in the state. I don't get the chance to go up there as often as I would like."

"I have a house just outside of town in Arroyo Seco there, or the use of the house that belongs to my sister-in-law. Would you like to go up there sometime?"

"I think I would. Yes, I would like that," she nodded and smiled.

The roads got rougher as we rose higher. I knew now why she had the truck. The last was no more than a trail. We had ascended high enough to be in pine and aspen forests. Our last approach was a natural cut between trees. It didn't look like anyone had been through here in years. We pulled into a clearing with a creek running that was more like a small river. On one side, trees led up the mountain side; on another, there was a rocky abutment with levels like balconies, and from each level steam was rising. Anjelica brought out our tent first, more like an open lean-to, and we quickly raised it. I was sent gathering rocks to set up a campfire as Anjelica unloaded the rest of our gear. I began to feel helpless at this point, and I think she noticed, so she took my arm and guided me to the edge of the trees and put a hatchet and small saw in my hands. She brought limbs for me to cut and chop. In an hour, we had a respectable amount of firewood. By that time, we were both hungry so Anjelica got the fire going and I watched closely enough to be help in the future. We feasted on steaks and squash we had brought in her ice cooler. After eating, we walked the short distance to the stream and lay down in the grass to rest before the hike. I was looking forward to it. We laughed and kissed a bit, and she teased me about feeling helpless. In the late afternoon we headed up the side of the trail. In an hour, we were at the snow line and sat for awhile to admire the incredible view. We could see the high plains through the mountains in the distance and the higher peaks up the line of rising peaks. We drank some water from a snowmelt and headed back down to our camp. On arriving Anjelica suggested we go up the short way to the hot springs. We both changed into bathing outfits, took towels, and walked the fifty yards to the rock balconies. There were three hot pools; one was obviously too hot, so we settled on the third one down. The water coming from the upper pools formed a little waterfall mixing with a cold spring that filled the pool we had chosen. We eased in and lay back against the rock sides. The pool was about fifteen feet across and deep enough in the middle to swim across. It was the most relaxing hot bath I had ever taken. I told Anjelica about the heated pool at Marilee's in Dallas, and how I had thought it was warm but not like this one. Because it overflowed, we could use soap, which she had brought in a little bag. We soaped and swam under to the other side, where there was a little shelf we could sit on and be up to our necks in the water. Anjelica went over to the waterfall and washed her hair. Watching her was a new vision of a woman. Her black hair shined in the late afternoon sun, and as she swam back to me, it streamed out behind her. She settled in beside me, turning to smile.

"It would be nice to bathe like this every day. Do you like it, Timothy?"

"Very much, except that I would be so relaxed I don't think I could do anything afterwards."

"Yes, that's true, but you could do it just before you went to bed. We could do that while we're here and bring lanterns."

"What about in the morning? Over the years I've gotten used to my almost cold showers."

"I have an answer for that, too. I'll show you later."

The sun went down as we talked. I think I babbled a bit about how beautiful it was up on the trail. She promised to show me even more spectacular vistas in other parts of the state. In the dark, I pulled her to me and into my arms. She put her arms around my neck, and she kissed me with a startling abandon and a rising of passion.

"Hold me, Timothy. Close."

I put my arm around her lower back, pulling her to me. I put my tongue in her mouth and she moaned softly. I reached down to her tight little bottom and she quivered slightly. I knew she must be aware of my arousal. She moved around with her back to me, but to the side enough so I could continue to kiss her. I was very glad she was wearing a two-piece suit as I ran my hand across her soft but muscular tummy. My other hand caressed her shoulder. She took my hand and moved it to her breasts. I pulled the top of her suit up to expose her breasts. When I rubbed her nipples, she kissed me harder.

"I'm so small, Timothy. My little titties, I mean."

"You are not, and you're beautiful to touch. Don't you ever think you have to be large there to be attractive sensually."

"As long as it pleases you to touch me...oh...it sure pleases me."

I moved my hand down her tummy and started lower."

"May I?"

"Yes, do."

I touched her and slowly began to rub through her bathing suit. She kissed my face and my neck.

"Touch me slow, Timothy. This is kind of new for me...I've never been treated this gently before."

"I want to go slowly with you. It's better for me, too."

I pulled her up out of the water a bit so I could kiss her breasts. I started sucking her nipples. They grew out as I went from one to the other.

She touched her nipple, "They've never been like that before. I didn't know they would grow out that much, they have stuck out but not...Timothy...Timothy, let's get out of the water and go back to our tent. Do you want to?"

"Yes, I think this hot water is working against us."

Anjelica had set up a lantern by the tent so we could find our way back after dark.

"Are you hungry?" Anjelica asked with a tone that I took to mean she wasn't in any hurry to eat either.

We opened up our sleeping bags, spread them out then undressed in the dark, climbed in, and snuggled in the cold night air. Feeling her close to me shivering was exciting.

"Timothy, if we make love, will you be especially gentle with me? I've almost had sex before but it was always before I was ready...physically."

"How so?"

"The men I've known, not more than three, were always in such a hurry, they could never really be inside me. The last man rushed so much he hurt me. I never saw him again, and I've been celibate ever since, more than a year. I didn't expect...well, here we are, Timothy."

"Yes, if we make love, I'll be gentle, and it's your decision whether we do or not."

Her answer was to make sweet little sounds and kiss me. She squirmed closer, well aware of my hardness.

"Timothy, I've never had an orgasm, I don't even know if I can or would know it if I did."

I touched her, and she wasn't wet. I messaged her slowly and she spread her legs more. I kissed her and moved down to her breasts again. Her nipples raised up again. Her breasts were small but soft and high. My gentle rubbing was beginning to affect her, and she opened up more so I was able to touch her more intimately. She was not wet, yet but a little moist. She was nowhere near ready for me to put my finger inside her. But the whole scent of her was growing. It was intoxicating, and different from that of any woman I had known. The only thing I equate it to was roses, a thousand of them. With this reaction, I couldn't not taste her if she permitted it. I began to kiss down her slim, tautness. As I reached her soft, almost hairless mons, she touched my head.

"Timothy, are you sure you want to kiss me there? No one ever has...I'm... oh!...Yes if you want to."

I opened her up with my tongue and kissed her little partly hidden bud of clitoris. As I licked and sucked softly, she began to move and make little moaning noises. She started to get wetter, and in a minute was wet enough that I could put my finger in her, but only the tip. She was so small and tight; no wonder attempted intercourse had hurt her in the past."

"That doesn't hurt, Timothy. It feels good. Please be slow."

There was such a salty sweetness in her taste that I wanted more of her wetness, and it was happening as I began to move the tip of my finger in and out of her. She began to move her hips as I kissed her and licked.

Suddenly she started shaking all over as she moved, "Oh, Timothy, something is happening! Don't stop kissing me, be more in me." But I couldn't. "Oh my, yes, si ya vengo, yo creo. Oh, Timothy, it's..."

She pulled my head away from her, "Oh, too much, Timothy. Come up and kiss me."

I rubbed my face on her tummy as I moved up to kiss her. She held me tightly, still shaking and breathing heavily. As I kissed her, she reached and took me in her hand.

"I believe I'm ready for you to be inside me, do you think I am?"

"I don't know. If you want me to."

"I do, so much. Can we be very careful?"

I reached into my bag next to our sleeping bags hoping I hadn't taken out the prophylactics I had taken to Liza's. I found one, opened it, and put it on. She pulled me over between her legs. I tried to enter her but couldn't.

"Oh, Timothy, what is wrong?"

"You're just very small."

She reached down to guide me.

"I didn't know I was that little. Is that why it hurt me before?"

"Probably so."

"Is it going to happen?"

She guided me, and I was able to enter her just with the tip of me.

"Yes, Timothy. Don't push hard. Am I wet enough?"

"You're fine, Anjelica. How does that feel inside you?"

"So very good. Move just a little bit."

She tried to open up more for me, but I was only able to go in another inch or so. It was a wonderful feeling to be that intimate with her, knowing it was new for her to enjoy making love. I lowered myself down to her and kissed her, moving slowly and gently.

"Anjelica, here, let's turn over with you on top so you can ease down on me."

We changed positions without me leaving her. She tried to take me deeper into her, but she was just too small. But it was evidently very good for her as she was moving and taking as much of as she could. I rubbed her breasts and reached down to touch her. As I gently caressed her, she began to climax again. Her reaction was to laugh and giggle, then bend down and kiss me, holding my hand to her. There was enough of me out of her that she could stroke me. It was a new sensation to be in her and have her hold and squeeze me at the same time. As I started to climax, I tried to go deeper but could only go in a little more. My reaction was to laugh also and pull her to me. She collapsed in my arms still laughing softly. We rolled over and held each other still making soft happy sounds. She cooed and I laughed.

"Timothy, do you believe we will be able to make love completely...I mean with you in me all the way?"

"I hope so, but that was very nice the way it was. Well, it was for me."

"Me, too, but I feel like a little girl in a way. Is that silly?"

"No because you are, in a way, I mean physically down there, but believe me that's the only little girl part about you, and that will change."

"What do you mean that will change?"

"Uh...well, every time we make love, I think it will be more so."

"Goodness, I hope so. Are you hungry?"

"Ravenous."

"Let's stoke the fire; I'll make us some chopped beef and potatoes. How does that sound?"

"I'll get the fire going, and you get the food."

We cooked and sat by the fire on the ground. In the firelight, when she turned and smiled at me, I remembered a picture in a travel magazine I had seen at Marilee's house in Dallas. It was of beautiful women in Bombay, India. Anjelica looked like an East Indian princess, with her gleaming white teeth, glossy black hair, and finely chiseled features, but without the make-up. A startling vision across the fire. I slept that night with her head on my shoulder. When I woke in the morning, she was gone. She left a note on her pillow, "Gone Fishing." I put on some shorts and walked down to the stream and I could see her about a hundred yards downstream fly-fishing. I knew she wouldn't be back for awhile so I did my tai chi exercises. After that, I went to the stream, took off my shorts, and waded in. The water was very close to ice cold. In the deepest part, I went under and scrubbed myself with my hands. I came out, shaking myself dry like a dog. As I finished dressing, Anjelica walked up with four large trout.

"If you'll get the fire going, I'll clean these and we'll have the best mountain breakfast there is. But first, come here to me for a minute."

She laid down her pole and put an arm around me. "Good morning, Timothy. Did you sleep well?"

"Like a baby. Did you?"

"Like a little girl," she laughed and kissed me.

We ate the best breakfast there is and got ready for another hike, but his time down the stream into the next little valley. We found a spectacular clear pond a mile or so from camp. We rested, dangling our feet in the water. She brought out a couple of apples from her back satchel.

"Would you like to go swimming, Timothy?"

"I hope it's not as cold as the stream, but yes."

"It shouldn't be as cold because it's still and in the sun."

We stripped down and waded in and it got deep rather quickly. There was rock cliff that overhung the pool. I swam under to see how deep the water was under it. It was deep enough and clear of any rocks that stuck up. Up along side the cliff there were natural steps leading up to the top.

"What are you doing, Timothy?" She called from the middle of the pond.

"I'll show you." I called out.

The cliff that over hung the pool was about fifteen feet high, just a little higher than a three-meter diving board. I went to the edge and looked down. It was clear all the way to the bottom. I took a few steps back then hopped to the edge and took off over the pool, and achieved a fairly good one-and-a-half flip with a full twist, cutting into the water almost vertical. When I came up, Anjelica swam over to me.

"That was terrific, Timothy."

"Thank you, ma'am, but it doesn't quite equal your fishing skills."

"It was pretty good. Did you do that in competition?"

"No, just for fun, I was never really that good, what you just saw was my best dive. I want to try one more thing. It's not that precise but I've wanted to do it for a while."

I climbed back up and did more of a run to the edge to get more height. At the highest part of my leap, I did a pike and turned halfway back and dove straight in. Anjelica was clapping her hands and smiling when I came to the surface.

"What was that?"

"Several months ago, I saw a Tarzan movie where the actor swung out over a river on a vine and did that move in the air. It was fun to do it, though I wish I had a vine."

"You are my Tarzan."

We paddled in the water and put our arms around each other to kiss.

"That would make you my Jane, and you surely fit the bill, super-girl."

We swam to the edge of the pond, got out, dressed, and headed back to camp, holding hands. It was late afternoon when we got back. We ate a sandwich snack and sat by the stream and talked.

"How do you see your future, Anjelica?" Do you think you'll stay in New Mexico?"

"I think so. There's so much to do and search for here, it's actually endless."

"Marriage? Children?"

"No, neither one. I don't think it would be fair to a husband or child with me gone so much out into the field. I didn't believe I would ever meet anyone who would interest me enough for that, and then you came along."

"Yes, I came along. I have no idea where my life is going to take me. I have, as you know, the opportunity to study at the University and a good position waiting for me in Dallas when I finish here. But you've made me think there might not be a finish to here. No matter what happens, I want to see you as much as possible."

"Timothy, when I came home from that last dig, it was the first time I was eager to get back, and it was that I wanted to see you...and now...well." She looked at me for a moment, lowered her head, and said, "Things have gotten real special, haven't they, Timothy?"

"Yes they have," and I pulled her into my arms.

"Do you want to go up to the hot springs?"

I nodded, and we got up to go, this time taking a lantern and two blankets. We relaxed, bathed in the hot spring, and loved some. Anjelica was becoming more uninhibited in her affections towards me. That evening, our lovemaking was more successful. And became more so each evening. Our next-to-last night at the camp, I was able to slowly fully enter her, a revelation for both of us.

"Timothy, I can feel you all the way. Yes, it's my first time to really make love. Touch me again to help me have...."

"Anjelica, arch your back and I'll pull you to me."

She did, almost like a contortionist. She was getting wetter as we moved together, making it easier.

"Oh, it's working...you're rubbing me on the right place...yes,...yes...that's it. Pull me closer, oh, Timothy, kiss me, suck on my nipples, please."

I couldn't reach down to her breasts, so I kissed her and caressed her nipples with my hand. We were learning how to move with each other now that we were really making love. She was so tight that if she hadn't been able to get so wet, I don't know if I could have moved at all. We were both rising to climax. She twisted her slim strong legs in mine to pull me into her.

She started laughing and kissing me, issuing a long coo as I blurted out, "Oh, my word, Anjelica, hold me. Yes, your are so good, so good. It feels so good. MY God, girl...so good!"

I held myself up away from her on my arms to look at her in the moonlight. Her eyes were closed and she was smiling. I started to pull out and away from her.

"No, Timothy, don't." She started moving again under me and arching her back again. I moved slowly with her and she quickly climaxed. We rested for a minute and she once again began moving. It was so arousing that this time, I came with her. We were both breathing heavily and I felt like I was going to black out from the sweet exertion. She let me slowly lie down beside her.

"You were so patient with me, I thought the first night you would think, well, she's just too small to ever make love, but you didn't. You know, it wouldn't have happened if I didn't care so much for you, and trusted you to be gentle with me. I got a little scared that first night that even though you helped me have my first real climax, that it would be just that and not what happened tonight."

"I knew it would take some time if you trusted me and if you wanted me."

"I didn't know that I wanted you that much, I just didn't know, I wanted to please you so much that I didn't want to give up trying. I had begun to think that something was wrong with me and that I never would be able to. Do you mind me caring for you that much, Timothy?"

"No I don't mind, I'm thrilled by it because I feel the same way about you."

"Even though I don't want to ever get married or have children?"

"Do you think you will always feel that way?"

"Well, not as strongly as I used to. You've put me in a spin about those thoughts. But I know not for a long time. As I said, it wouldn't be fair."

"I understand completely, I think I feel the same way. Whatever time we can spend together will be a joy. Who knows how long I'll be in New Mexico? I do love it but this is not the center of the theatre world. Remember I said I may not finish here, but that's not being realistic for the long run. Coming back as much as possible is realistic."

"Well, what is going on right now is pretty good, Timothy. Don't you think?"

"Yes, I certainly do, and I want us to enjoy each other's company when we can in our very different very busy lives."

"I'm all for that, Mr. Sart. As a matter of fact I'm not going to be as busy for the next few weeks, I'll be in the lab a bunch and out on short digs, but not another big one for awhile. I have applied for a major expedition in the late fall, but I may not even get that."

"Would it be a good one if it happens?"

"Yes, a big career opportunity-South America for a few months, and it's something I've hoped for."

"I remember you mentioned South America. Well, I would miss you, but I hope it happens for you."

"I thought you would say that. After we had been together a few times I didn't think you would be the possessive type, and I liked that. But that was before this little trip, and you still aren't. I think you could be protective but not possessive."

"My daddy always told me the best way to ruin a good thing is to be possessive and jealous. I failed at that a couple of times but I was younger then. And you're damn right I can be protective."

She snuggled in closer, kissed me, and pulled a blanket over us, "Hold me a little bit before we decide to eat our treat. Before we had gone to the hot springs, Anjelica had put a small pot roast with potatoes and onions over the coals in a clay pot. It was ready and delicious. We built up the fire and lay out on a blanket, covered up, and looked at the stars. We talked about our future careers and laughed about the silly dives I had done to impress her. We finally snuggled into one sleeping bag and made love again. It was sweet, slow, and gently complete.

Our last day was more of the same and even nicer than the day before. We had trout in the morning after my tai-chi and our cold freshener in the stream. We hiked back to the swimming pond and ended up eating, then going to the hot springs. We slept snuggled together and woke up early for the drive back.

Chapter 18
Santa Fe y Yerma, y una Sorpresa Estraña

Before I left for Santa Fe, I asked Anjelica to join me at the La Fonda during one of the weeks I would be there with the play with the plan of driving up to Taos. She agreed. We had an evening and full afternoon of rehearsal before opening at their community center theatre. It was a big success and became something not to be missed. I actually enjoyed my first two weeks alone in Santa Fe and the luxury of staying at the La Fonda. The University paid for my room, but I paid the difference to upgrade to a small suite. I entertained the cast in my room, roamed the town, and worked on the rewrites of my book, which I completed in the second week. Dr. John Miller and Jane joined me on the weekends. One night we were eating at the hotel restaurant, and I saw Carolyn Caruthers, from the cast of *Blood Wedding*, across the room with a table of people, one of whom I recognized as her husband. I asked John and Jane if they would mind if I went over to see some old friends. We had finished eating so they agreed to meet me in the bar in awhile. Carolyn jumped up when she saw me.

"Tim! What are you doing here?"

"Carolyn, hello, I'm doing a show here."

"A play? Where?"

"At the community center theatre. It's another Lorca piece, *Yerma*."

"We're going to be here a few days. We must see it. Tim, you remember my husband, James?"

"Of course." He stood up to shake hands.

Tim, we're still talking about *Blood Wedding*. If you've got a show playing here, we're going to see it. Tim, these are the Hugheses, Jim and Sally, old friends of ours from Dallas." Jim Hughes stood up.

"We saw your play in Dallas, and it was great. As a matter of fact, we saw it twice."

"I'll arrange comps for all of you for tomorrow night."

James replied quickly, "No comps. We'll support anything you do. Are you coming back to run the Civic?"

"Yes, I think so, but I've got some things to do out here first. If I do come back, I wouldn't really be running the theatre."

"Well, that's what the patrons hope will happen. You see to the artistic side, and Barney sees to the business."

Carolyn stepped in. "I went to the last board meeting and the consensus was to offer you the title of artistic director. How does that sound?"

"Pretty good. Carolyn have you talked to any of the cast members?"

"Often. We've become kind of a club. There have been several cast parties. You really started something."

"Did Liza come back to Dallas? I gave her a ride out here to Santa Fe on my way up to Taos."

"Oh, you don't know then?"

"Know what?"

"Jimmy, do you mind if I have a talk with Tim over at the bar."

"No sweetheart, not at all. If he hasn't heard the Liza story, he needs to."

We walked into the bar, and I introduced Carolyn to the Millers and told them I was going to have a conversation with her at the bar.

We took the most isolated bar stools we could find and I ordered a drink.

"Tim, Liza moved to San Francisco."

"My word, that's a big change! What happened? She sent me a note saying she was going to Hawaii to meet her husband."

"She did go to Hawaii."

"And?"

"Since you two were good friends, I'll tell you the story, but it's not for public consumption. Ok?"

"Sure."

"Her husband, Frank, wasn't in Hawaii, and hadn't planned to be."

"Well, why did she go."

"It was a ruse, a cover up."

"What do you mean? A cover up? For what?"

"She was pregnant, and if anyone asked, she could tell them that she got pregnant when she and Frank were together in Hawaii."

"Pregnant? Are you sure?"

"Yes, I'm positive. I went with her."

"You went with her?"

"She didn't want to go alone, and Jimmy had to go to New York for several weeks so I joined her."

"Pregnant? Did she say who the father was?"

"No, and she wouldn't, except that it was someone she had known in Santa Fe. She said she had chosen him."

"She said those exact words?"

"Yes. She said the man didn't need to take on that responsibility and she didn't want him to. Tim, she had always wanted a child and knew she would never have one with Frank, and she didn't want a divorce. This was to be her secret forever."

"My God. I'm...well, taken aback. On the way out here, I asked her why she and Frank had never had children, and she said they had tried for years but it never happened."

"That's not true. Frank didn't want children, evidently not with her, and did everything he could to prevent it."

"What do you mean, 'evidently not with her'?"

"When Liza married Frank, she knew he was a rake, but she thought she could tame him, or make him happy. One of Jimmy's friends had worked for the same company as Frank in Java. When he came back, he told us the truth about Frank. He had a child by a native girl, a girl, not a woman, and had met a Dutch woman in Batavia, and had a child by her also. Frank had quit the company and moved in with the Dutch woman. The last he heard was that Frank was moving to Holland with the woman."

"Does Liza plan to stay in San Francisco?"

"She has cut all of her ties with Dallas, and her house is up for sale. Her sister lives in San Francisco and was happy to have her move there. She was recently divorced and lives in a big house there with her children. Liza has her own money and wants to start a new life with her child. Frank will be listed as the father."

"Uh...that's quite a story."

"Did you see much of her while she was here?"

I thought for a moment, "Uh...no, she did come up one weekend while Marilee and Daniel were still here. We planned to get together...but...well, I got her note about going to Hawaii to meet Frank." No matter how I felt about this revelation, I wouldn't add to any speculation to Liza's activities here. Her secret, and mine.

"Yes, it's quite a story, but I hope for her sake a forgotten one. No one really knows about Frank and his activities over there except for us and Jimmy's friend and we have no intention of going any further with it. I only told you, Tim, because...well, you were close friends and I don't think she would mind you knowing what happened to her. When I last saw her, she was extremely happy. She had gotten her wish and by someone she had chosen. End of story."

Carolyn went back to her table. I sat in a quiet state of shock. I saw underneath everything that had gone on between Liza and me. I had no doubt she was having my child, one that I would never see. She had used me to enhance her life, but I felt no anger toward her because she had actually chosen me to be the father of her child hoping I would never know.

I joined John and Jane, explaining that we had talked about what was going on in Dallas and that it was good to hear stories from home. We talked about the success of *Yerma* for a few minutes, but I was too stunned by the news of Liza to add much to the conversation. After they went to their room, I stayed at the bar to be alone and have at least another drink. I knew there would be no easy sleeping tonight.

Liza's activities that last weekend were now clear; she was trying to get pregnant. I didn't know why what was so obvious now was such a mystery then. She was surely right about my not being able to tackle the responsibility of a child by her or anyone except for Claire, but I supposed I would have. A child by Anjelica would change a career she was totally devoted to, and I suspected it could destroy our relationship. It made me very glad that the love Anjelica and I felt for each other was not demanding, and she was right about my being protective of her. I had certainly been right when I told Anjelica that Liza wasn't around anymore.

The last weekend of the production in Santa Fe Anjelica came up to stay with me at the La Fonda and she followed me to Taos on Monday. She loved Marilee's house, and it became our home for a week. She took me to places I would never

299

have seen without her, the edge of the sacred Indian lands up near the lake, and ruins north east of Taos. Our lovemaking became an even sweeter and gave her a glow of happiness. She laughed more easily and more often and she became very uninhibited about me seeing her in the light when we made love. She also began to dress more in a feminine manner. That started just before we left Santa Fe when she found a dress shop that specialized in very attractive Southwestern styles, and she continued to shop in Taos. She had an amazing collection of turquoise and silver jewelry that she had never worn. She had just collected it as artifacts, but now felt womanly enough to wear it. She changed from the striking archaeologist in pants and epaulet shirts to a stylish New Mexican beauty. We talked for hours and read together in the late mornings. She read the galley proof of my book, now named <u>Shaping the Play</u>, and was impressed by how interesting she found it. I told her about the directing experience of *Blood Wedding,* and how it had started my New Mexico adventure. Claire's drawings attracted her attention because they were of the play. I told her a limited version of Claire and me and she reacted with sorrow that I had lost her. We drank Villa-Lobos on the balcony, and she introduced me to piñon-flavored coffee.

On our next-to-last evening together, we discussed the future. We knew we would be lucky if we could spend two or three weeks a year like this if our relationship grew. There was no doubt we felt love, but we had to accept the extraordinary differences in our careers. I knew I would return to Dallas eventually and there was no place for her there, no matter how much our love grew, but we were happy with what we had and would enjoy it when we could.

Anjelica drove back to Albuquerque on Monday morning. On Tuesday, I received a letter and package from Claire. The package contained a Rolliflex camera. Her explanation was that it was to record the beauty of New Mexico in a larger format. I had written her so many pages about how astonishing the state was. The incredible gifts she kept sending were an expensive way for her to express that she was thinking of me. In one of my letters to her, I said she didn't have to send me anything. She replied she could and she would. Her letter was sad, and I got the impression she was having an even more difficult time with the matchmaker's choice, though I had to read between the lines to discover it. Her strongest statement was she felt it was affecting her health, but she revealed not much more than that except her continuing pleas that her parents revoke the promise went unheeded. The work at the museum was interesting, but because of her lack of seniority, it had become rather routine. She was drawing as much as she could, and it all centered around us in Dallas, and if a good one came out of it, I could have it. She went beyond the colorful calligraphy in the last letter to actually illustrating her thoughts with little drawings of us and her memories of Dallas. The most touching part was that she wanted me to be happy and not to hold back my potential to love someone else. The letter ended with her promise to love me always no matter what happened. With her signature, she had drawn an eye with a teardrop just below. It was so sad I was sure there was something she wasn't telling me.

I spent the afternoon in thought about the last six months. I had known four very different women in a very short time, all endearing in different ways; Gwen as the friend and teacher; Liza as the mature, desperate lover; Claire as perfection, and now Anjelica as the strong adventurer with a loving, gentle side. I remembered several years ago a rather egotistical actor telling me all women were the same, I had thought that was stupid then, and now I knew how wrong he was. Although none of these women were to be my life partners, knowing them has probably changed my life in more ways that I could begin to understand. They had helped me to realize I adored women and their difference from men; certainly sexually, but also their sensitivity to feelings I had difficulty expressing, and a different way of looking at problems. Each had given me a change of perception, a different outlook on existence, and each had helped me to think more clearly about sharing the experience of living. I didn't believe I was especially selfish or boringly macho before them, but I was sure a lot better person, partner, and even a better artist, because of them. I can't remember having an argument or strong disagreement with any one of them...well, with Liza on unprotected sex, which had its own answer. Gwen had given me a sexual freedom and an understanding of patience in lovemaking, and I had shared that with Anjelica. Claire was in my mind, but so was Anjelica now. I think I believed because I would never have or find another Claire, what Anjelica and I had was the best thing that could have happened. There was really no doubt that in the future, we would go our separate ways. I knew she loved me and we would love each other more in time. This was possibly the kind of love she wanted, knowing she couldn't give herself completely to me, but she knew I was there to come home to as long as our time lasted.

I was beginning to come to grips with a strong change in me. I didn't want to be alone; I wanted a life companion, a woman to share with. I had thought several months ago that I was destined to be alone; but that was before Claire and Anjelica. The parents of both of these two fine women would probably never approve of me. It would be almost cruel to marry Anjelica, and it was now next to impossible to marry Claire, yet I still felt there was a chance for Claire and me to come together. Our life apart had sadly been very different; Clare living sadly with the potential of a forced marriage and my encounters with two new women. I felt that if I hadn't met Liza and Anjelica, I would have become bitter with the unending frustration over losing Claire. I in many ways, wish I had not encountered Liza because I felt used by her, but before her, I knew I had been headed toward a deep depression and a debilitating loneliness. I suppose I used her, too. The thought of Anjelica just being my New Mexico girl friend didn't seem to be the answer for a happy life. The difficulty of yearning for one woman and being happy with another was becoming an emotionally strange life encounter. It was discouraging to think that my letters to Claire were not helping Claire in her situation except to ensure her of my enduring love. I could not conceive of the idea that I would try to release her and not think of me or us. I knew I could release Anjelica and she would be able to deal with it. I knew I must tell Anjelica about Claire. I believed she was aware of her because of Claire's paintings and photographs being so prominent in Taos and Albuquerque. Twice in my dreams, the drawing Claire had done of the eye with a tear appeared as a passing image with a powerful message. Yes, she was going through something I didn't know about.

I spent the rest of the afternoon studying the information on the fantastic new camera. It was fairly complicated and different from Jeordie's Leica, but I had it figured out in several hours. I did my tai-chi, then went to the Plaza to buy some rolls of film and have dinner. I spent the evening writing a long letter to Claire. I wrote about the success of *Yerma* and an edited description of the camping trip. I didn't name Anjelica or our situation-there was no need to add to Claires' sadness no matter what she said about me finding love. I told Claire know how much I missed her and wished she could be with me, and I wanted to know how she felt about me studying at the University or going back to Dallas to work at the theatre. I mentioned the conversation with Carolyn and her husband and what they said about the artistic director position. Her advice had always been so solid, and she never hesitated to give a different viewpoint. In asking for her thoughts, I knew I faced a coming choice and I had doubts about both of them. The educational opportunity was good, and I could continue with Anjelica in our limited relationship, or go home to a possibly challenging job. I mentioned my verbal commitment to John Miller, and that I knew if I reneged, there was no coming back. I believe Claire knew from afar that I would probably choose New Mexico, but I wasn't totally confidant in the decision. I admitted I missed my family and the familiarity of Dallas and that most of all I missed her. I ended with the open statement of how my proposal to her in the hotel on our last day was still my wish and would continue to be. In a P.S., I said she could call me if she ever felt the need, here in Taos or as soon as I got a phone in Albuquerque.

Anjelica called me the following Sunday to ask when I was coming back. She was leaving for a dig but would be back in two weeks and hoped to see me. I had made several calls home, and even to New York, to ask what the family thought of the University offer, and they all said I should try it. With Anjelica's call, that was enough, I made my decision and left to set up residency in Albuquerque. I packed up and left on Tuesday. I found a very nice apartment close to the University, and moved out of the borrowed one.

I contacted John to make an appointment for a conference. He was happy about my decision and even offered me a job in the department. I would be called a studio assistant, and it would entail running the two theatres and working with box office staff. My experience in Dallas had prompted his offer and he said the whole business side of the department needed an overhaul. I accepted, with the agreement that I got the weekends off and started to work the next day. I also started to furnish my new dwelling but decided to wait for Anjelica and get her help for buying major things because I admired what she had done with her place. I hung paintings and *Blood Wedding* drawings on the walls of the empty living room. For the first time, I had a real garage for my car.

One of the interesting things about Albuquerque was that it was a modified car town, and many times people wanted to talk about it and ask who did the work on it. One day while at a grocery store, I found a note on my windshield. It was an invitation to exhibit the car at a show the coming weekend. There was a phone number attached, so I made the call and said I would. I couldn't wait to write Uncle Willy about this recognition of his work. On Friday morning, Anjelica called me. I had posted the new number on her door, and she asked if I wanted to spend the weekend at her house. I quickly agreed but said I was exhibiting at a car show on Sunday, and asked her to join me. She laughed, saying it sounded like fun, especially since she was also a car fan and loved my car. When I arrived at her house, she pulled me through the door to greet me with a hug and a kiss.

"Hi, Timothy. Wow! I don't believe I've ever welcomed anyone like that before. It's good to see you."

"It's really good to see you, too." She looked super, dressed in her new approach to style. I took both of her hands and stood back to take her in. She was wearing a turquoise peasant blouse with coral beads sewn into the neckband and at ends of the puffy sleeves, and a semi-pleated shorter than usual black skirt with a mountain outline in grey tones. It was a spectacular outfit. Even more unusual, she wore light makeup.

"You're embarrassing me, silly man. It's just me. You look pretty good, too."

"Yes, thank goodness, it's just you. How was the dig?"

"A good one, I want to hear about you. You've decided to be at the University, haven't you?"

"Yes, I'm going to give it a try."

"Well, I'm certainly glad, Dallas is a bit inconvenient," she replied with a laugh and another hug.

"Let's have a drink and sit on the patio. I want to know everything."

I tried to describe the studio assistant job and the changes I would try to make.

"I've been working on a mailing list of past and potential supporters of the department and redoing the ticket office. I took a concept to the art department for a season ticket brochure, which should go out in a month. I also got John to agree that I get weekends off except when there's a production up. He's really bending over backwards to make it good for me here."

"It sounds like it. Are you going to direct a play soon?"

"I don't think so. I want to pull back from directing for a few months"

"I don't blame you. From what you've told me, it has been nonstop work for a long time."

"Support, support...don't stop."

She smiled and leaned over for a kiss, "You asked about my dig. We've discovered a new burial ground at an Anasazi site. It really is exciting and could take years to fully excavate. I don't think there's any doubt I'll get a major publishing effort out of it. And it's about time. The university isn't a publish-or-die school, but I need to get something of high caliber in the journals."

"I understand completely. My book, if things go well, should be able to get me directing jobs."

"You're ahead of me. The closest I've come to writing a book was my dissertation...well, it was a book, but not of the published sort."

"You read mine. Could I read yours?"

"You might find it rather esoteric, but sure. Tell me when you're ready to eat; I've made a leg of lamb."

"Let's wait a bit longer and have another Bourbon. It sure is good to see you, Anjelica."

"Siento lo mismo, Senor Sart. I've missed you, I mean really missed you."

"And I you. You dressed up for an evening at home?"

"I wanted to look special for you."

"You surely did that. Special is sort of a limiting word for how you look."

"Thank you, Timothy. You've made me want to look special. I like the way I feel about choosing my clothes now. You've changed me for the better, I think. I never thought of trying to look good for someone before...well, except at least clean," she laughed.

I laughed, realizing I had tried to dress in a more spiffy fashion for her. "I also feel the change you made in me. But I don't want you to change too much."

We stopped talking about each other and discussed our trip; we hoped we make another, perhaps in the winter. I commented on what good snuggling that would be. We finally ate the terrific lamb and had Villa-Lobos on the patio and eventually couldn't resist being close. Our lovemaking seemed to be better and better with our getting to know the most intimate things between us.

Later that night, as we lay side by side she said, "Timothy, I think I will grow to love you as much as I do my work. I don't want that to sound as if I don't love you now, because you know I do, but you also know how much my work means to me and probably always will. I guess what I'm trying to say is that I never thought I would find a man who could mean as much to me as you do. When I work, I'm totally consumed by it, but at night you enter my mind as no one ever has. I don't mean just sexually... that of course...but I just think of you and how good it is when I'm with you."

"I feel the same way about my work, which has changed in the past weeks and in a way is even more consuming than before; and, naturally you are in my mind at night also when we're apart, which is most of the time. Sometimes I wish you weren't away so much, but then perhaps it's better that way. Each time we come together, we're both a little different, and, I believe, closer for it. Our different work demands that we both learn, constantly, think, and grow. It brings something new to what we already have."

We eased into sleep. The next morning, we greeted the morning very sweetly.

We went into town and I started taking pictures with the Rollie. I explained it had been sent as a gift from a friend and she asked nothing else. The camera had come with a portrait lens attachment, so I took several shots of her. We ate in town and headed out into the countryside so I could get some good pictures of the mountains in the distance. Back in town, we dropped by the Millers' and ended up going out with them for dinner. When the women left the table for a few minutes, John commented on the change in Anjelica.

"Tim, I can see her change in dress, but there's also a look of real happiness I've not seen before, and we've known her for three years. Whatever is happening between you two has sure been good for her."

"Well, we're having a good time, and I think we've both changed because of it."

"I see that in you too. There was a kind of sadness about you that's not there as much now."

"Perhaps you're right. There are things that don't have anything to do with Anjelica."

"Tim, is it about the lady who did the paintings?"

"Yes, but it's a very difficult situation. I don't have any intention of hurting Anjelica, I think she would understand and accept if the other situation changed, which is highly unlikely. She is a strongly independent person."

"You do know how important her work is to her, don't you?"

"Oh yes, we have discussed that in great detail. There's no real danger of us making any unreasonable demands on each other. She's also aware that someday I'll be going back to Dallas, not soon, but someday. But for now, it's very good between us."

"Yes, she is one strong young lady, but it's this new softness about her that I approve of greatly, and I'm sure Jane does, too."

Later that evening, I told Anjelica about the conversation.

She laughed and said, "Jane said something very similar to me. I took it as a compliment."

We had set up candles in her bedroom and poured snifters of brandy. As we undressed each other slowly, I stood back to admire her.

"I need a sip of our brandy."

I handed her a snifter from the bed table. She drank it down in one gulp.

Later, she said it was wonderful lovemaking, and we fell asleep cuddled and close, her head on my shoulder.

We got up early the next morning and prepared the car for the show. We washed, polished, and rubbed every surface clean, especially the wheels. When we arrived, they gave us an assigned parking place on the exhibition row. The Uncle Willy special was a real hit, and Anjelica and I took turns standing by the car while the other walked around to see the other cars. I could only answer about half of the questions I was asked, but it was great fun. We joined some of the other car folks for a beer afterwards and got home at dusk to eat and spend the evening together.

After eating, we were sitting on the couch when Angelica turned to me and said, "Tell me about the lady who did the drawings, Timothy."

She hadn't asked in a jealous manner, but just to know more about my recent past.

I told her almost everything. She was shocked when I revealed the reason why Claire had left.

She leaned over and put her head on my shoulder, "Timothy, that's so sad. I know you planned to go home tonight, but I would like for you to stay with me. One of the women who loves you wants to hold you."

I did stay, and she did hold me.

Chapter 19
Destino Malo

The next morning Angelica told me she was going on a long dig back to the Anazazi site. I suddenly had an urge to leave Albuquerque and go back to Taos. I went to John Miller's office to see if it would be alright with him if I left the University until the spring semester started. I explained I wanted to write more and perhaps go back to Dallas for Christmas. He was disappointed about the department losing me because my work on the season ticket campaign had been so successful. I assured him I would be back.

I packed and left the next morning. The drive past Taos to Arroyo Seco was the most beautiful I had seen it yet, fall was showing in the trees. The colors were spectacular. I had phoned the caretakers I was coming so the house was ready for my arrival. I unpacked, then went into town to stock up on groceries and writing supplies. The next two nights were lonely but I did start writing for about four or five hours during the day. Forcing the discipline was not hard, but I wasn't sure the work was as good as it needed to be. Perhaps I was written out, with no new ideas on directing.

On the third day, I wrote a long letter to Claire. I tried as softly as possible to ask about her health and family situation. I tried to express how much she needed to be candid with me. After finishing the letter, I reread it, tore it up, and started again. At eight o'clock, I stopped the third rewrite, fixed some dinner, and took a short walk up the path to the pond.

When I got back to the house, the phone was ringing. It was Claire, barely able to talk through her intense sobbing. When she calmed down, she was able to tell me things had gotten worse in her conflict with her father. The man the matchmaker found had become very aggressive sexually with her after a Hollywood party for a film he had helped produce. Claire said he was all but staggering drunk. Her father said it was probably a misunderstanding on her part, but that he would talk to him.

She quoted him as saying he is a good Jewish boy who would make her a fine husband.

"Timmy, I told him I don't know what kind of Jew he is, but he's not a good boy, and I won't marry him. My father slapped me, telling me to pull myself together and go back to my job at the museum."

"My, God, Claire, you can't live in that kind of situation."

"I don't know what to do, Timmy. I am scared. My father has always been so gentle. He has changed so much since moving to America. Ever since I told him weeks ago I didn't want to marry this man he's gotten more and more furious with me."

"Can you leave and come to me here?"

"You know I want to, but I'm frightened of his reaction. He would do everything in his power to stop me. He doesn't know about us, of course, and if I did tell him, I don't believe my mother could even protect me from him. He has already told me once that I could be sent to a hospital for awhile until I came to my senses about this marriage."

"Claire, I will come and get you, which may be the only solution. There is no doubt about our love for each other, and perhaps your parents would eventually accept us."

"I think my mother would, but I know my father never would."

"He wouldn't have a choice when we get married."

"Do you truly love me that much, Timmy? Without any doubts?"

"Yes, I do love you that much, my dearest heart."

Oh! Timmy, I've got to go! My father just drove up. I love you."

And she was gone. I mixed a stiff bourbon and soda and went out to sit on the patio in the dark. Claire seemed on the edge of a nervous breakdown. I felt unable to comfort or help her from afar, especially on the telephone or even in letters. I needed to talk to someone, even Angelica. I then had an idea. Marilee and Daniel had returned to Dallas two weeks ago, so I tried them there.

Even though it was very late there, they hadn't gone to bed yet. Daniel answered the phone.

"Well, hello there brother, what are doing callin' us so late? Is something wrong?

"Yes, I got a very troubling call from Claire, and felt the need to talk to Marilee."

"She's right here. Are you in Albuquerque?"

"No, I'm in Taos. I needed to get away from the University, It's good but still a new life to me. Also, I wanted to be alone."

"I thought you had had enough of living alone."

"I thought so to, but..."

"Is something wrong, Tim? You sound bad, brother."

"Yes, but..."

Dan called away from the phone, "Marilee, Tim is on the phone and wants to talk with you. She's coming. I hope she can help. I've never heard you this upset. Here she is."

"Timmy, what's wrong? Are you alright?"

"Hello, Marilee, and no, I'm not alright. I talked to Claire this evening, and something is very wrong out there. She was so upset, she could barely talk. It seems the thing with her father has gotten worse. She sounds on the edge of a breakdown. I think she has been sick and hasn't been going to her job at the museum?"

"No, I didn't know. I haven't talked to her in quite a while, but she did write me a couple of weeks ago and I could tell she was having a hard time out there. Is it about the man the matchmaker found?"

"Yes. Her father even hit her when she said she wouldn't marry him, but I suspect there's more to it."

"Listen, Tim, I'll call her in the morning and get back to you tomorrow. Are you in Albuquerque?"

    "No, I'm in Taos."

    "Good. You'll hear from me tomorrow, for sure."

    "Thank you, Marilee."

    "Do you want to talk to Daniel again?"

    "No. I don't have anything more to say right now."

    "Good night, Timmy, and try not to get too down about this."

    "I'll try. Good bye."

Chapter 20
El Viaje Segundo

It was a difficult night after my talk with Marilee. I got very little sleep. The next morning I did not leave the house in anticipation of a call from Marilee. She finally called just before noon.

"Tim, I called Claire, and you were right. I am very worried about her state. She feels as if she's in a hopeless situation. She even said she wished she never had left you in Dallas."

"So do I."

"I asked her if there was any way she could leave and her only answer was to cry and say she didn't know how, but I'm not sure she's strong enough to do that on her own, anyway."

"I don't think so, either. I offered to go get her, but I think she's too frightened of her father and of an encounter between us. My God, Marilee, I feel so helpless and mad about what she's going through."

"I know you are, and so am I. Tim, do you truthfully feel your love for her is strong enough to help her through this and be with her, marry her?"

"Yes, without any doubts."

"Is there another woman in your life?"

"Yes, a very fine woman, who I could never marry. She knows about Claire and how much I love her."

"Would there be any complications?"

"No, if they ever met, I think they would become friends."

"I talked to her mother, too, and she's as worried about Claire as much as we are. I'm not sure, but I think she knows about you two. Claire may have confessed-no that's not right. She does not need to confess anything. There was nothing wrong about your falling in love. It is a beautiful thing for you both; it's just very complicated."

"At the very least complicated. Do you think I should just go out there and try to bring her back?"

"I don't think you should do that now. Perhaps the situation will calm down and she can come to you, or...hell, I don't know. Maybe I could go out there and get her. Her father would be angry, but I don't think he would get violent with me."

"Whatever happens, I must be the one responsible for getting her."

"Tim, I'm also responsible. Remember I introduced you."

"Yes, well, you may be able help somewhere along the line, but not going to get her. If that's a possibility, I'll do it."

"I'll try to accept that. I understand how you feel, especially the helplessness, but who knows right now what's going to happen? I'll attempt to talk to her again tomorrow, and I'll stay in touch."

Thank you, Marilee. How are you and Daniel doing?"

"Fine, we're glad to be back in Dallas, Daniel didn't want to spend the winter in New York. He misses Taos, and so do I."

"You can solve that by coming back here, and I wish it could be soon."

"Daniel and I are going to discuss it this evening."

"Good, please let me know if you have any news tomorrow."

"I will, Timmy. Be strong."

"Don't worry about me. It's Claire who needs to be in our thoughts."

"And she is. Goodbye, dear Timmy."

"I miss you both very much. Give my love to Daniel Goodbye.

I spent two days in a limbo of confusion, wishing Claire or Marilee would call. I did not dare leave the house and stayed close to the telephone.

On the morning of the third day, Claire called.

Her first words were, "Timmy, will you come get me?"

"Oh, my dearest Claire, of course I will. How will we arrange it? I mean, where will I come to, your house or somewhere else? Will your father be a problem?"

"He has gone to Canada to solve some sort of oil well problem. He will be gone at least a week. His last words were that I needed to go to a hospital for awhile. What I need is to be with you."

"Yes, you do, sweetheart, and I with you. Don't you have any doubts about my love."

"I don't Timmy. I have changed, but I'm still not very strong. I hope you still find me attractive."

"That's the least of any worries you may have."

"My mother knows about us and has been surprisingly supportive. She doesn't really approve, but she accepts my being in love with you. She is deeply concerned about my father's reaction, but I will be gone. I don't know if he'll ever accept us, but I don't care anymore about what he thinks."

"Tell me your plan."

"My mother wants you to come to the house so she can meet you, but it may be hard for you to find. How long will it take you to get here?"

"If I leave early in the morning and drive straight through, I think I could get there by the next afternoon."

"That's Wednesday. The museum is open late. I think it will easier for you to find it and it's close to downtown with signs pointing the way. I'll go there at noon and wait for you; afterwards we can go to my house and get my bags. I won't bring much with me."

"That shouldn't be problem. Uncle Willy made a luggage rack for the back of the car so you can bring several bags."

"Oh, Timmy! There is something I need to tell you, but it can wait now. Please be careful on the drive, I want you to get here safely. Is your car alright?"

"The car is fine. You won't recognize it."

"Timmy, I love you."

"And I love you, Claire."

"Goodbye. Au revoir."

As I hung up the telephone, I realized I was breathless and had to sit down. My world and life had changed in a matter of minutes and I had to plan quickly for the longest journey in my life. I jumped up and called Marilee and Daniel.

Marilee answered on the second ring.

"Timmy, I was hoping that was you. I talked to Claire this morning. She told me she was going to ask you to come get her. I told her I thought it was the right thing to do. You have talked to her, haven't you?" She asked anxiously.

"Yes, I'm leaving early in the morning."

"Daniel and I have talked, and we want to come to Taos as soon as we can. If everything goes well we can be there in four or five days. Daniel and I both think Claire will need me as a friend. I guess I should ask if you mind if we do come so quickly, we don't want to intrude on the time you and Claire have together."

"I want you to come. I know Claire will need you. You've been very much a part of this."

"Good. Timmy, please be careful. Here, Daniel wants to talk to you."

"Hello, brother. I agree with Marilee that this is the right thing to do, though we all hoped it could have been less dramatic."

"Yes, me, too, but I'm just glad it's happening"

"Is your Uncle Willy special up to it?"

"He said I could drive it to China and back with no problem, so California and back should be easy."

"Well, we miss both of you, so it will be good to get back to Taos. Please be careful. If you get too tired, stop and take a nap."

"I think I'll be too excited to get tired. I'll see you soon. Thanks for the support, brother."

I spent the afternoon packing and getting the car ready. I got the oil changed and checked everything on it. After a very restful night's sleep, I left Taos just after dawn.

The drive was beautiful and easy. I pulled over just beyond the California border and slept for an hour. Along the way, I regretted I had been unable to make contact with Anjelica to let her know what had happened. I knew she would be sad and disappointed but accepting. Nevertheless, I couldn't dwell on that. I could only think of being with the woman I loved as much as life itself. I also knew she needed me very much. I had never given up, but I hadn't thought we would be able to be together so soon. My hours of driving were spent in reminiscence-the vision of Claire across the room at the country club, our work together on *Blood Wedding*, waking up with her on our last weekend, and our tearful goodbye at the train station. I did not think of the future, just the immediate present and getting to her safely.

I arrived in Los Angeles and found my way to the museum just after three. I parked and went into the lobby. I saw her sitting on a bench. She lifted her head and saw me, jumped up, and ran to me and into my arms.

"Oh, Timmy, you're really here."

I was holding a different young woman in my arms. Her face was much thinner, as was her body, and she was pale without the rosiness I remembered, but no less beautiful, perhaps even more so.

She started crying and holding me tight, "I never thought I would see you again."

"I was afraid of that too, sweetheart."

We stood there for what seemed like a long time, not saying anything else. The other people in the lobby were staring and smiling. We must have looked like something out of a tearjerker movie.

"Let's go, Timmy. My mother is waiting and I want us to leave as soon as possible."

When we got to my car, she was surprised, "Timmy, is this the same car?"

"Yes, but with much work by Uncle Willy."

"I like it. It looks more like you."

Her mother was waiting on the front steps of their rather magnificent house. She was a striking woman with almost the same coloring as Claire. Claire took me by the hand and introduced me. I apologized for looking so ragged. She was reticent but appeared to almost accept me. She insisted I come in and freshen up. The only thing she said was to take good care of her daughter. I promised I would. We gathered up Claire's bags and packed them in and on the car and were on our way in less than an hour. I regretted not being able to get some rest, and also that I hadn't met Claire's brother.

Almost immediately, Claire sighed, put her head on my shoulder, and went to sleep. It was as if a great weight had been lifted from her.

It took awhile to get out of Los Angeles, and I began to fade from the lack of sleep. I found a roadside hotel in San Bernardino and woke Claire up, registered, unloaded the car, and went to a restaurant across the street. We both ate voraciously and didn't talk much, but looked at each other, smiling. At the hotel, we both showered and fell into each other's arms. She had put on the nightgown she had worn at the Adolphus our last night together in Dallas.

With her head on my chest Claire began to cry, "Timmy, there is something I must tell you."

"Tell me, baby."

"Two months after I got to Los Angeles, I realized I was pregnant."

"What?! Claire, why didn't you call me?! I would have come to get you then. Oh my God, sweetheart...what?

"I was so scared, and my father was getting very insistent about...well. I couldn't eat or sleep and was getting weaker every day. I started losing weight and having a hard time at my job...I mean just being there, even though it was a good place. One day at work, I started bleeding and a friend at work took me to the hospital. Timmy, I had a miscarriage...I lost our baby."

"Oh, Claire, dear God. I should never have let you leave Dallas."

"I thought I had to leave, you know that. If I had known about the baby, I wouldn't have, but it must have happened during our last weekend. There was no way to have known."

"Are you alright now? I mean can you...?"

"Can I have another baby? The doctors said I should be fine, in time."

"Did your parents know what happened?"

"My mother did because she came to the hospital. Luckily my father was so busy and in and out of town. She was shocked and furious, even threatening to tell my father, but she quickly changed her mind, knowing that would be more of a disaster than it already was. In the days that followed, I told her about us. She tried to convince me it was over now between you and me and that I must give in to my father's wishes. There was constant tension in the house and I just couldn't get well. I was so lonely for you. When my father started getting violent, she began to change her mind. She also accepted the depth and sincerity of our love."

"We're together now. You're going to be fine. Claire, will you marry me, very soon?"

"Of course I will, Timmy."

"We'll do it in New Mexico. Oh, Marilee and Daniel are coming to Taos in a few days. They can be a part of our wedding."

"That's wonderful. It will be so good to see them. Marilee helped me through my fear of asking you to come get me; I think I was afraid you wouldn't come.

"I tried to assure you in all of my letters that my love for you was solid and true. You should never have doubted me. If you had told me you were pregnant, I would have been there for you, no matter how difficult the family situation was, but that's all in the past. We're together now."

"Oh, Timmy, I'll be the finest wife for you."

She snuggled into my arms and we both fell asleep.

Chapter 21
La Vida ha Cambiada

I slept for eight hours. Claire was still sleeping peacefully. I let her sleep for another hour. She awakened with a start, sat up, and saw me reading beside her.

"I didn't know where I was for a minute."

"You slept for nine hours; I didn't dare wake you up. I knew how much you needed the rest."

"I haven't slept that long since I was in Dallas. Did you sleep well?"

"Yes, I did. It was very sweet waking up to see you beside me."

Claire cooed and eased into my arms.

"Did what I told you last night upset you? I had to tell you."

"Of course, it upset me, but only because of what you had to go through. It's sad, but we have all our lives ahead of us."

"Yes, we do. Uh?...I'm a little hazy from all that sleep, but did you ask me to marry you last night?"

"I certainly did, for the second time, only this time you said yes."

"I didn't say no the first time as I remember. I was hoping it wasn't a dream. How soon do we need to start traveling again?"

"Well...we're not in any hurry now, but we have a long way to go."

"I want to take another shower, really just to wake me up. Is that alright?"

"How about me joining you?"

"Oo...that sounds good, Timmy. Give me a few minutes and I'll call you in."

"A sus ordenes, mi amorcita," I bowed.

"You know, I think I need to teach you French, mon amour. I'm a bit shy about you seeing me; my figure has changed so much. You may think I'm too, is it 'skinny'?"

"You may be thinner, but you're far from skinny."

She laughed, reached over for a quick kiss, and literally pranced into the bathroom. I smiled thinking how good it was to hear Claire's familiar laugh. In fifteen minutes, I heard the shower and then her call.

"Ti-mo-thee!"

When I stepped into the shower, I saw a new and even more beautiful Claire. Yes, she was thinner, but had not lost the fullness of her figure. She seemed to have matured into a trimly svelte young woman.

"I guess I've lost my baby-fat."

"You look great, Claire."

"My breasts haven't gotten much smaller, but my bottom..."

"Is even rounder...and cuter."

We proceeded to soap each other.

"I want you to touch me, Timmy, but be very gentle."

The shower was long and sweetly passionate. When I was toweling off her back, she started giggling, then turned to kiss me, and then pulled back and said, looking into my eyes...

"Timmy, I hope we can be good lovers again soon, but I want us to be careful. It would not be good for me to get pregnant for awhile."

"Of course, I'll be careful. You let me know when you think you're ready. Remember, we were not careful only once before, I think."

"Yes, I know. Perhaps that means I can have babies with you easily. In my mind I'm ready because I want you so much, but I'm not sure the rest of me is ready."

"Claire, dearest, it's good just being with you. We have lots of time to be lovers again, and it will be even better than before."

"Better? My goodness! If my memory is right, we were pretty special before."

"It filled my dreams, both asleep and awake."

"Me, too."

"How are you feeling, Claire? Do you feel stronger? You're already getting your color back from the paleness I noticed when I first saw you at the museum."

"I do feel stronger, perhaps because I slept so well last night. Oh, Timmy, the last months have been terrible, and it wasn't all about us. The idea of having to marry someone I didn't love, and then finding out I was pregnant...everything just fell apart. I knew if I stayed in Los Angeles, everyone would know. I was so scared and unable to do anything. The only good thing, other than having our child in me, was when that man noticed my condition, he would reject me. But my father would have...well, I don't know what he would have done, but it would have been bad. I probably should have called Marilee. Several times, I thought you may reject me."

"Now, that is ridiculous, sweetheart. I would have been thrilled. Knowing Marilee, she probably would have come out here to get you herself."

"I'm still frightened of what my father may do when he gets back to Los Angeles."

"Claire, you're with me now, for good."

"I know, thank goodness. Timmy, can we get something to eat? I'm starving, and it's a good feeling. I haven't wanted to eat in weeks."

We went to the same restaurant as we had gone to the night before, then packed up the car, and started our long drive back to New Mexico. Claire snuggled up with the pillows her mother had given her and went to sleep. She woke when we crossed over into Arizona and began marveling at the sights.

"When I was on the train, I was too sad to really be interested in looking out the window. This part of the country is beautiful and open. I've never really seen desert before. Some parts of Spain are similar, but not this big. Where are we going to spend the night?"

"I think we can make it to Flagstaff."

"That's a funny name. Is it pretty there?"

"Everything is pretty and very dramatic all the way back to Taos."

We talked about almost everything that had happened to us since we were last together. I told her how well *Blood Wedding* had gone and that everyone wanted one of her paintings. She told me about her job at the museum and the newness of Los Angeles. She did like the beach but thought it was too cold for swimming, much preferring Marilee's pool. She missed my family and the friends from the theatre. I tried to compare the three towns I knew in New Mexico and to tell her about seeing the castle in Las Vegas. She wanted to see everything and meet John and Jane Miller in Albuquerque. We made several good stops to rest, had lunch in Blythe. Claire slept most the way to Flagstaff, though she tried not to. We got into Flagstaff late but found a real hotel that had a restaurant that was still open. We slept in each other's arms until the middle of the next morning. At breakfast, I had an idea."

"Sweetheart, since we're not in any real hurry, would you like to go on a side trip?"

"Oh, Timmy, I would love it."

"Let's go up to the Grand Canyon, I've never seen it and have always wanted to."

"There were pictures of it in the books I read about the West. They didn't appear to show it as I imagined it to be. Is it far? Not that it matters, because you are right about not being in a hurry now. The farther away from Los Angeles we get, the safer I feel. This is beginning to feel more like a vacation than an escape."

"I felt the same way when we woke up this morning. Almost all the way here, I imagined we were being chased. Several times, I realized I was driving too fast for such precious cargo."

Claire threw her head back laughing out loud for the first time on the trip, "Timmy, are you referring to me as 'cargo'?"

"Yes, I am, very valuable cargo, very precious cargo."

"Well, I'll accept that definition."

We started north to the canyon, both feeling refreshed and very happy to be together. The drive up brought a constant string of delightful squeals from Claire.

"This is even more beautiful than I imagined. Is New Mexico this nice?"

"Very much so, but different."

"America does seem to go on forever and changes all the time."

"This is the longest trip I've taken, and I think you're right. You know, Claire, on the way out to get you, I didn't think about the trip coming back. My only thought was to get there. This is so good and exciting being with you that I wish we could keep on going and see everything, but I'm afraid we would run out of money before long."

"No, we wouldn't."

"Dear heart, we're not going to use any of your father's money."

"I've never used, well, not for a long time, any of his money. I've known I would have to tell you about the money as soon as you said you would come get me.

So...my uncle, his brother, was a very successful engineer and inventor with many, many patents. When he died several years ago, he left me a sizable monthly stipend. I will inherit the rest of the estate when I'm twenty-five. I never used much of it, and I brought some of it with me, plus a letter of credit."

"Uh...I don't believe I want to know how much until after we're married. Is that alright with you?"

"Of course, I never thought it would make a difference to us, I just didn't want to talk about it, especially before when I thought I was leaving you forever. But, Timmy, deep down I had hope that we would be together again. It just seemed so wrong for us to be apart."

"I always had hope, too, but I was so discouraged when you told me the matchmaker had found someone. At times, it was like a fantasy, my hope, that is. Many times I wished I had had the power to keep you from leaving, the power of persuasion, I mean. My God, it was terrible when you got on that train."

"It was for me, too, All the way to Los Angeles I wished I had had the strength not to leave. I believed I could convince my parents to set me free from the matchmaking and then tell them about us, but...well...here we are, Timmy, I'm so happy now and I hope you are."

"Claire, let's get this straight, I love you and will love you more day by day. Yes, I'm happy...well...more than happy. Do you remember talking about your fate when we were at the hotel in Dallas?"

"Yes, but that fate has been dissolved, gracias adios."

"Indeed, gracias adios. It is our fate to be together. I believe it was our fate not long after we met, even though we didn't know it at the time."

"Maybe we did know it."

"Could be. Claire, I think I should tell you about some things that happened while we were apart, I guess sort of a confession."

"Timmy, you don't have to confess anything to me. I set you free. I thought you were lost to me. I didn't want you to be a celibate dreaming of us being together again. Don't worry, I'll never be jealous or upset about anything that happened."

I had nothing to say, I looked at her and smiled. She leaned over and kissed me on the cheek.

"Anyway, you're my man now."

"That I am. Now and forever."

The scenery got so dramatic that we stopped talking. In another hour, we pulled up to the first lookout at the Canyon. It must be a shock for everyone who sees it for the first time. Nothing prepares you for the grandeur of it. We stopped at every viewing station until we finally got to the big lodge. We unloaded our bags, locked them in the car, and went in to the restaurant. We decided during the meal that we would try to get a room. There was a big crowd, but they did have a very expensive suite available. I looked at Claire.

"Maybe we can find something cheaper down the road."

"Ti-mo-thee Sart, have you forgotten our discussion on the road?"

She opened her shoulder bag, pulled out a large zippered case, and handed me several hundred-dollar bills.

"If possible, can we stay for two nights?"

I asked, and it was possible. A porter was sent to carry all the bags up to our suite. It was western rustic but very classy, with a big bathroom and a balcony looking out to the canyon. We both showered, dressed, and went downstairs for our first drink together on the trip. We found a small table with a window looking out on to the lodge courtyard. Even in the late afternoon light, it was a beautiful vista of the far side of the Canyon, gathering the red rays of the sun on the rock faces. I ordered a Bourbon and Claire a Martini.

"This is a special place, Timmy, I had no idea it would be as dramatic and beautiful. It was a wonderful idea to come here. There's a peace about it that I think we needed."

"We sure needed that. The last two days have been sort of frenzied. I'm still shaking a bit, even with the rest last night," I said.

"Me too. I think I'm still scared a little bit of what may happen."

"What could happen now, except us being together, getting married, and starting a new life?"

"All of that is not what I'm frightened about. It's what may happen in California."

"What can your father do now...now that you've left? Claire, we are old enough to make our own decisions."

"I know that, but it doesn't mean he will accept it. I am afraid of what he may do about my mother and the support she gave us. I just hope he's not violent toward her."

"Do you believe he would take out his anger on her?"

"I hope not, but he's changed so much since moving here. I don't know what's caused it, perhaps the situation in Europe and having to leave France and his not being happy in England. I know he didn't want to move to America, but this evidently is where the work is for him."

"Well, all we can hope for is that, even if slowly, he accepts our being in love and getting married. No matter what comes about, you know I'm going to protect you, and there's no way he could take you back there, I promise you that. You are my lady, now. We waited long enough for this and it's not going to be taken away."

"Yes, we have waited long enough. I know you will protect me...and us. I'll try not to think about it. We don't need any more problems. It's almost hard for me to believe we're really together, I don't mean like it's a dream, but I had all but given up."

"I don't believe I ever gave up completely. At times I thought it would be better if I did. But I couldn't. I always believed in what we had, our falling in love, was too important, that somehow..."

Our drinks arrived before I could finish. Claire, lifted her glass, and looked at me smiling, "My fine Timmy, here's to our 'somehow'."

"I love you, my Claire."

We had one more round of drinks and went outside for a walk, hand in hand. I think we both realized there were subjects we didn't need to talk about any more because they were resolved. No more yearning for each other's presence, no more fear of loss and disapproval. We sat at the edge of the Canyon and watched the rest of the afternoon pass. Before dark, we went back to the lodge and ate in the dining room. I remembered I had packed a bottle of Villa-Lobos brandy, hoping we would have a peaceful evening on the way back to drink it. We sat on our balcony and enjoyed it.

When we entered our room, Claire came into my arms.

"Hold me, Timmy. I want to feel you all up and down me." We kissed with a passion we had experienced months ago. I pulled back and began to undress her, as she did me.

"I want to make love with you, my Claire. Can we?"

"Yes, I don't think I can wait any longer. Do you have...?"

"Yes."

"Give me a few moments."

I went quickly to my bag that had my shaving gear, found what I needed, got under the covers, and sat up waiting for her. When she came out, she paused and looked at me shyly. I froze the image of her in my mind. I was startled once again by the changes in her. The new slimness gave her a maturity that only enhanced her beauty. Her thinner face accented her eyes and mouth. I wondered at my good fortune at having such a woman as Claire. Yes, intelligent, witty and funny, but what a beauty.

"Timmy, my goodness, what an expression!"

"Come here, baby."

She slipped under the covers and folded into my arms. We kissed and writhed in a rising rush of desire. I kissed her breasts and touched the soft and wet lips between her legs as she opened up for me."

"Let's go slow, Timmy. I want to savor every moment before we make love."

I tasted her sweet essence and she whimpered to a shivering orgasm.

"Now, Timmy, be inside me, slowly."

We made love until we both were panting with sensual exhaustion.

She whispered in my ear, "I don't think we need to worry about being good lovers again."

"I was never worried, sweetheart."

She sighed and fell asleep, her head on my chest. As I stared into the darkness, I felt tears of happiness going down my cheeks. I kissed the top of her head and drifted off.

We spent our next day talking about a thousand things. We laughed and got used to being together in our new freedom. Before, in Dallas, there was always that cloud of the coming separation, but not now. I told her about the University in Albuquerque and the problems with directing *Yerma,* and how much I had missed her help. She described her new fondness for painting and drawing that had been awakened in Dallas. My family was a major interest for her, that is how were my parents, Uncle Willy, Rosie and their coming baby, and Jeordie's photography? I let her know how pleased they all would be about us. We decided to get married in New Mexico as soon as we could after Marilee and Daniel got there. Claire wanted to go to Dallas some time soon after the wedding. A two-week honeymoon at the Finca in Taos would be enough time before the trip home. We toured the lookouts to the Canyon we hadn't visited the day before and spent the evening with a gathering sweetness between us.

We drove into Santa Fe late the next afternoon, booked a room at the La Fonda, and planned to get our marriage license in the morning before driving up to the Finca. Claire was charmed immediately by Santa Fe. She insisted on touring the Plaza and side streets, finding several shops she wanted to investigate in the morning. The evening introduced Claire to New Mexico-style food.

"Timmy, one of the first things I want to do in Taos is set up a good French kitchen and then learn to cook in this style. I think I prefer it to the Mexican food we had in Dallas. You've never experienced my cooking. I'm very good."

"As I remember, you made some great sandwiches."

"Please, Timmy, sandwiches are a small part of my culinary skills. Marilee and I collaborated on some fine meals."

"Let's see, an art historian, painter, and now, great cook; is there anything else?"

"Hmm...well, I can sew and make clothes." She laughed, "All of those skills are expected of a good French girl."

"My dearest, you are, at the very least, a good French girl."

"Thank you, my good Texas man."

The night in our room was sweet and restful. In the morning, Claire gathered her various papers, British and French passports, along with her U.S. resident visa. I hoped all I needed was my driver's license and birth certificate, which I had brought on a whim, not knowing what I would face on the trip. We breezed through getting our license except for a few moment of confusion over Claire's many papers. We had thirty days to get married anywhere in New Mexico. We spent the late morning and early afternoon shopping. Claire insisted on getting a beginning New Mexico wardrobe. Watching her getting excited about almost everything was great after her first couple days of anxiety and exhaustion. She thrilled with each purchase and pulled me from shop to shop. I was starting to wonder where we going to put everything in my overloaded coupe. Luckily, I found some extra rope in the trunk.

A light was falling on our drive up to Taos. It gave the trip an unexpected lyrical quality. Claire was wide-eyed and smiling all the way up through Taos and out to the Finca.

Claire broke her silence as we drove in the gate, "Oh my, I thought it would be nice, but this is idyllic. It's like a painting from the old west."

Before we unloaded the car, Claire took a tour of the house. "Where is our bedroom?"

"Upstairs to the left."

After unloading and unpacking, we took a walk down to the pond. When Claire saw the chicken house, she began to plan and tell me all of the amazing things she could do with chicken. Back in the house, she asked about the rifles racked over the fireplace.

"Are they real guns?"

"Yes, one is for varmints, the other for deer in season."

"Varmints? What are they?"

"Pesky animals, like coyotes and foxes, that occasionally come after the chickens."

"Have you shot the guns?"

"No, not yet."

"Good, and I hope you don't have to."

Getting used to living together was easy. We shopped in Taos for groceries and kitchen equipment, even though I had thought it was a good kitchen before, but Claire had other ideas.

On our fourth day at the Finca, Marilee and Daniel arrived. It was a happy family reunion. Marilee and Claire spent two hours on a walk, hand in hand. Their time together gave Daniel and me a chance to catch up. New York had been very good for him as an artist. They had even considered getting a place out at the Hamptons, but He decided he would rather paint in Taos or Dallas. I told Daniel about Anjelica and my feelings for her, but that she knew I was committed to Claire if we could get together. A big question when the women get back from their walk was whether Claire should call California, but Marilee advised against doing it until after we were married.

Two days later, we all went into town and arranged for the wedding that afternoon by the resident judge, who happened to be a good friend of Marilee's. We lunched at La Fonda and then walked back for the ceremony.

Claire cried, and my knees shook.

Our honeymoon was a happy period of days with Daniel and Marilee and intimate nights as a new married couple.

Chapter 22
Encuentro

A week and a half after our wedding, I was working at my desk in our bedroom, Claire was downstairs working in the kitchen, preparing a fabulous meal for the celebration Marilee had planned for the evening with her Taos friends. She came up to join me, coming up behind me and putting her arms around me.

"Hello there, husband."

"Hi, baby. How's it going down there?"

"I think all will be pleased. I'm trying the chile rellenos you like, but I believe mine will be an improvement. I'm putting a French touch to it with pecans and two types of meat."

"Hmmm. When are Marilee and Daniel getting back from town?"

"I don't think they'll be too long. Daniel needed some wood for frames and Marilee some vegetables from the market for tonight."

"Come lie down with me for a bit, Timmy."

I stood up and stretched, "I could use that, maybe even a short nap, which is new for me. Before I never could nap, but now with you..."

"Does that mean I'm a good influence?"

"In every way."

I sat up on the bed. Claire leaned into my arms, "I think I'm about ready to call California. I should have done it before now, but I just hadn't gotten my nerve up yet."

I thought I heard a car drive up. Thinking it was Marilee and Daniel, I paid no attention. Suddenly, after a few minutes I heard someone running up the stairs, the other bedroom door was slammed. I sat up as a man stormed into the room."

"Who...?"

"Papa, what are you...?"

"Your father?"

"Yes, I'm her father. I've come to take her home with me."

"No, you can't Papa. We are married."

"Yes, Mister Levant. She's my wife now, and she's not leaving. Please try to..."

"Yes, she is leaving with me; I'll do everything in my power to get it annulled. You have no choice. Claire, gather your things."

"I'm not leaving, Papa."

"You will, even if I have to..."

He started speaking to Claire in French. She began crying. "Non...non."

He reached into his pants pocket and pulled out a pistol. Claire started screaming, "Non...non, Papa, don't do this. We are in love, and have been for..."

"Yes, your mother told me. This man seduced you, and only wants your money..."

"He didn't know about my money."

"I do not believe that. Do what I say, now!"

"She's not leaving with you. She is my wife."

He pointed the pistol at me, "Young man, if I have to kill you, I will. The old laws will forgive me."

"Papa, the old laws don't..."

"Timothy?!" A call came from downstairs.

Claire screamed for help. I heard someone running up the stairs. Anjelica rushed into the room.

"Anjelica, what are you...?"

I drove up to see...What's happening? Who is...?"

"Is this another of your...?"

I stood up, "Mr. Levant, leave us alone. Yes, this is a friend. Please go..."

He pointed the gun at me and fired twice. His first shot missed and the second glazed my arm.

Anjelica screamed," No!" and rushed at him.

He turned the gun on her and shot her in the chest. Anjelica screamed and fell to the floor, bleeding badly. Claire was now screaming at her father to stop. More noises outside and rushing up the stairs. Daniel burst into the room holding his deer rifle. Levant fired at Daniel, hitting him in the shoulder. Daniel fired and Levant was thrown back against the wall and fell to the floor.

Marilee ran in, "Oh, dear lord, Daniel."

She bent over Daniel, "Daniel, are you...?"

"I think, I'm alright, but...call an ambulance and the police.

Claire went to her father, "Papa, why...did you come, why...?"

Daniel's shot had killed him instantly.

I held my arm and tried to raise Anjelica to a sitting position. She was coughing up blood."

She looked at me, "Timothy, is this Claire?"

"Yes."

"Good, The other woman who loves you." These were her final words as she died in my arms.

I then lifted Claire up and led her out of the room. Daniel was able to walk with Marilee's help. The police and ambulance arrived soon.

It was crowded in the back of the ambulance with both Claire and Marilee comforting Daniel and me.

The death of Claire's father was a terrifying shock for her, but eased by her concern for me. I was bandaged but Daniels's wound required more care. He had to get some stitches, pain medicine, and an arm sling. The bullet had gone right through the flesh high in his left shoulder, which luckily wouldn't affect his ability to paint. By the time we got back to the Finca, the medical examiner and coroner had removed the bodies of

Mr. Levant and Anjelica. On the way back, I told Claire about Anjelica. Her reaction was sadness. She had heard what Anjelica said before she died.

"What a beautiful young woman she was, I wish I had had the opportunity to meet her."

"She would have felt the same way."

Marilee called Claire's mother in Los Angeles. Mrs. Lavant had been terribly afraid of what might happen when he left in such a state of anger with a gun. He had reacted violently when she had tried to stop him. Marilee immediately talked to her about moving to Dallas because she was now family. Claire had a long tearful conversation with her. Claire was in shock for a couple of days, but came out of it fine though she was terribly sad about the horror of the event and the loss of her father in such a terrible way. Marilee told me Levant was able to find the 'Finca' by asking people in town. A memorial for Anjelica was held, which I attended, at the University. While in Albuquerque, I met with Dr. Miller. I tried to explain how the terrible event had happened in Taos and that Anjelica was an innocent in the shooting. I told him Claire and I were going back to Dallas for a couple of weeks, and he insisted that we stop in Albuquerque on the way to Dallas so he could meet Claire. I knew he also wanted the opportunity to try to talk her into coming to Albuquerque.

One week later Marilee, Daniel, Claire and I were sitting in the Finca living room in front of the fireplace on a cold evening. We had just received the good news that Uncle Willy and Rosie had had a redheaded little girl. Marilee had served Villa-Lobos all around. Claire was snuggled in my arms when she suddenly sat up.

"Timmy, I remembered a dream I had this week; it had been troubling me for two days. I think it scared me so much I refused to remember it. I dreamed we were the characters in *Blood Wedding*, and what happened here became a part of the play, with all kinds of gruesome things happening. It's still not very clear."

Marilee reacted quickly. "Perhaps it would be better if it never is."

I pulled Claire back into my arms. "Sweetheart, don't try to bring it back."

"No Timmy, Marilee, it isn't that. My thought on remembering part of the dream was that I'm glad it wasn't prophetic, the play that is..."

Dan leaned toward us, "What do you mean, prophetic?"

"In *Blood Wedding,* the bride and the husband both died."

Dallas Blood

About the Author

Christopher P. Nichols was born in 1938, the year that <u>Dallas Blood</u> takes place. He is a fourth generation Dallasite. His father, a well-known painter, told him many times that his family was Dallas blood. Almost all of his educational training has been in Texas, first in the Dallas and Richardson public schools, then The University of North Texas for a Batchelor of Arts in Speech and Drama and a teaching certificate. His graduate work was at Southern Methodist University where he received a Masters of Fine Arts in Professional Stage Direction and later studied in England in an advanced theatre studies program.

In the sixties, he taught in Bogotà Colombia and the Dallas Independent School District. There, he taught Speech, Theatre, English, and Spanish. In 1972, he joined the staff at SMU's professional Theatre training program. After graduating in 1974, he founded The New Arts Theatre Company, a professional regional theatre. During those years, he directed 30 plays and administered the running of the theatre company. In 1979, he won the National Theatre Critics award for one of the best eight plays produced outside of New York, *War Stories* by Dennis Trout. In 1984, he left New Arts and directed six more plays as a professional freelancer. He returned to Dallas and DeSoto Public Schools to teach Theatre. In the 90's, he ran the theatre programs at Grayson College and El Centro College. His last years of teaching theatre were at North Dallas High School. He retired from teaching in 2006.

During the last fifteen years, Mr. Nichols has written ten plays, four of them are published by The Dramatic Publishing Company and are produced all around the country. In 1993, he won the Lee Korph play writing award for the the best play written in the U.S. that year for *Lamia*, also a published piece.

All of Mr. Nichols adult life, photography has been an interest. He specialized in theatrical photography, keeping a record of every production he directed or produced. He has made two sixteen millimeter documentaries, one of a rock pop festival in 1969 and a film for the Department of Education named *Chile and Its People*.

Mr. Nichols family started going to Northern New Mexico, where the last third of the novel Dallas Blood takes place, in 1948 and he has been returning every year since. His brother, David has lived in Taos New Mexico for thirty years.

Now, Mr. Nichols lives and writes in Dallas with his wife, Libby, and his son, Perry Brooks who is a talented painter.